REGRETTABLY, I AM ABOUT TO CAUSE TROUBLE

Copyright © 2022 Amie McNee

Published by Amie McNee

www.amiemcnee.com

The moral right of the author has been asserted.

For quantity sales or media enquiries, please contact the publisher at the website address above.

Cataloguing-in-Publication entry is available from the National Library of Australia.

ISBN: 978-0-6451905-3-3 (paperback)

978-0-6451905-4-0 (ebook)

978-0-6451905-5-7 (audiobook)

Editing – Kate O'Donnell

Cover design – Lena Yang

Publishing Consultant – Linda Diggle

All rights reserved. No part of this book may be reproduced or used in any manner without written permission of the copyright owner, except for the use of quotations in a book review.

This book is a work of fiction. Names, characters, places, and incidents either are products of the author's imagination or are used fictitiously. Any resemblance to actual persons, living or dead, events, or locales is entirely coincidental.

REGRETTABLY, I AM ABOUT TO CAUSE TROUBLE

AMIE MCNEE

CHAPTER ONE

I tried to cover myself. I held the sheet so it fell in front of my naked lower half, but it really was no use.

"Put it down, Magdalen!" my mother snapped.

"It's Maude ..." I mumbled.

"Modesty went out of the window when your skirt was taken off!" She snatched the cloth out of my hand and I was made to stand entirely unclothed in the middle of my chamber. Had my hair been down, it would at least have covered my chest, but I never let my hair down: it was wild, curly, unsightly. I crossed my arms over my chest then reluctantly drew my eyes to the women fussing around my nether region. Was I allowed no dignity?

"This isn't working." My mother sat back on her thick red skirts. I saw a drop of sweat roll down her brow. I felt her anger.

"My lady." Agnes, my mother's lady's maid, took her to a chair. "You really shouldn't be doing this, not in your condition." Only a few months until full term, my mother had her seventh child cooking away under her gold-embroidered bodice. No doubt it would prove to be her sixth boy. God smiled upon her. I looked down at the progress they had made between my legs. God certainly did not smile upon me.

My wedding was in five days. To Lord Edward Beckett. A very handsome man. With very nice blue eyes, broad shoulders, and a shockingly large estate. He was my delight. And soon I would be his, and I would please him with lots and lots of baby boys, just like my mother. My family was famous for producing strong, healthy men. I looked forward to carrying on this Godly tradition. We just needed to get over this nonsense.

It had been labelled a lot of things by many different physicians. A large scar. A growth. A mark of death. A mark of lustfulness. A mark from a bad birth. A witch's mark. It was speculated that perhaps my mother had seen something that frightened her during her pregnancy, cursing me with this blemish. Or perhaps she had touched her belly too roughly during an eclipse of the sun — but she doesn't remember doing that. Nor does anyone remember an eclipse. A very bold wiseman even suggested my mother had had relations with a Moor. I doubted that one: my mother was a devoted, goodly wife. Personally, I had not decided on what it was. I only knew how I felt about it. I hated it. It looked like someone had rubbed mud up the inside of my thigh, thick, dark mud, with hairs in it. They had rubbed it up the inside of my thigh and all around my lower belly, even under my private hairs.

We were trying to cover my mark up with a paste. And if it worked, we would cover it every single time Edward was to lie with me. It was an uncomfortable process, and I could feel the paste dripping down the inside of my leg like I had pissed myself.

"You're so pale everywhere else, Magdalen. Why has the Devil afflicted you in such a way?" Why couldn't you be a boy?

That's what she was thinking. I could see it in her furrowed brow.

"I don't know, Mother." I was a Godly woman. I was still a virgin. I prayed each night. I went to mass. I knew for certain I would be a good wife. I was everything a woman should be. It was true, I didn't have blonde hair like my mother or the Virgin Mother. But I had lots of other virtues exactly like my mother Mary and the Mother Mary.

"Magdalen gets her pale facial complexion from you, my lady," simpered Agnes. My mother could bathe in her lady's maid's flattery. "How do you make yourself look so beautiful and white?"

"I'm hardly as pale as I used to be," cooed my mother. Agnes slapped another layer of the paste on the upper part of my inner thigh. "My colour comes naturally, but I know several ladies at court who go to great lengths to reach this true, Godly paleness." She gestured to her skin.

"Do tell, my lady."

Zounds. Let this be over.

"Well, I know for a fact that the Queen herself, her sister, Lady Boleyn, and the insufferable Lady Agard all swallow gravel and ashes to spoil their stomachs, just so they can achieve that real ghostliness in the cheeks. I've never had to do such a thing, of course. God blessed me."

"It's familial, obviously. Your family is blessed." Agnes self-consciously patted her splotchy cheeks. My mother turned to me, and her smile faded.

"You can hardly tell that Magdalen is pale with all her freckles. It's a waste."

My cat, Jimmy, twisted his way between my legs, eager to lick at the droplets of beeswax, cow's milk and hog's lard that was dropping onto the floor.

"Ooo!" said Agnes. "Feeding time!"

"Quiet!" I snapped, scooping him up. I'd had enough. "Mother, it's no use. He will see my affliction no matter what we do." I pushed past the maid, flung Jimmy onto my bed and grabbed my sheet. Mother sighed bitterly. I was such a waste of her time. She had six, soon seven boys to worry about and fuss over. I was a burden. I could see it in her eyes. I nearly always knew what my mother was thinking, as if there were a ghostly unbroken umbilical cord between us. I could tell her mood just by listening to her footfalls. I knew how angry she was by the height of her eyebrows.

"Show me one more time." She sighed. Extremely reluctantly, I pulled back the cloth and rotated my leg outwards. The dark skin of my affliction was impossible to hide.

"It doesn't matter if you can cover this." I gestured to the part of the mark that crept up my inner leg. "You cannot cover that." I crudely pointed to my purse. "You'll cake the hair in white gunk! He'll think I have a disease! He'll wonder at what whorehouse I work."

"Oh, Magdalen! You distress me and your unborn brother." She got up, balancing herself against the wooden panelling. "Clean her up. Clothe her. We will have to think of something else."

She left the room. I envisaged good word being sent to her of what a devoted and dutiful wife I was. Of the babies I was birthing as Lady Beckett. I would have more boys than she. That would show her. All of England will know me as the wife that birthed eight boys.

I got dressed immediately, back into my billowing dark red gown and tight cream bodice. I insisted Agnes top up my face powder and rouge my lips. Just cover me up. I shushed her every time she began to speak and I did not feel guilty about it.

"Do you want me to clean your leg, Magdalen?"

"It's Lady Magdalen, you obnoxious woman." I tugged my skirts from her weedy little grasp. "Leave." She thought herself better than me. She thought my mark meant I was less than a servant. She took a long moment to appraise me, but then she left. No one had any respect for me in this house but at least she did as I said.

I sat on my bed; I could feel the mattress vibrating with Jimmy's deep purr. Reluctantly, I navigated my hand up my thick skirts and began picking off the paste. I hoped none of it had actually gone up me. I caught my own gaze in the glass and saw my thick, dark eyebrows squint in apprehension. Ew. I flicked a bit of congealed beeswax at the cat. He opened one eye. I peeled another piece off, flicked it at his whiskers again. A paw flung out from under his black body and caught it. We entertained one another until I was clean again.

I walked down towards the drawing rooms, running my hand against the walls, enjoying the feeling of the cold stone being interrupted by intervals of soft, threaded tapestries. Mother would reprimand me for touching them, but I was Lady Beckett, pregnant with eight boys, so Mother could fuck herself. I descended the stairs slowly. Taking each corner gracefully, as I would when I was presented at the wedding. Servants bustled past me, working triple time to prepare for my nuptials. I ignored their curtseying and greetings of "Lady Magdalen".

I tried to focus my gaze on one point, even as I turned. Lady Beckett. I glanced towards the east wing corridor. I had always felt sorry for those rooms. Shirburn Castle was too big for a family always at Court. I was pleased that it would soon be packed to the brim with actual courtiers; the great oak wardrobes were at this very moment being aired for the gowns and bodices embroidered with pearls and jewels. And there would be jewels glittering everywhere and — I took a deep breath. Could I smell swan?

I took my seat in the drawing room, by the window. We had guests already. My brothers' wives, of course. My nephews. A few of the wives' parents and siblings were somewhere else in the castle, lording it over our servants, no doubt. But it was just my immediate family in this drawing room. I felt the pompous energy even as I entered. Six personalities scrambling on top of one another, desperate to be the loudest, desperate to be heard. Every single one of my brothers had strong opinions and a loud mouth. None of them had been blessed with an ounce of humility. Not one.

My mother sat in her chair by the empty fireplace, rocking back and forward, holding her belly, smiling at her loud, unpleasant offspring. No one acknowledged my entry.

They were discussing the increase in prices of wool.

"Lady Mother." John, the third oldest. Long beard. Beady eyes. He came and bent by her. "We mustn't argue about these things in front of you. Especially when you are so far along." I watched him as he whispered a prayer under his breath and laid a hand on my mother's stomach. She stroked his hair fondly. "And we mustn't bother Magdalen with these things. Big political and economic matters are not for your ears — they are messy and complicated."

He was trying to get me to talk back.

"There's nothing complicated about half the town going cold this winter."

It worked. All six of them were expert Maude antagonisers.

"If business is strong, everyone benefits. If we do well, the people do well." Stanley — third youngest, seriously deluded.

"Our gold trickles down, Maude. You wouldn't understand. Wealth works in complicated ways. Besides, you shall not be complaining when this high wool price fetches you new dresses." That was Oswyn, and he wasn't exactly wrong about the dresses.

My father entered. He had a detestable way of entering a room when he was at home. (I doubt he swanned around like that at Court — or maybe he did. I don't know. I'd never been to Court. Not yet.) He used both hands to open the doors, always with enough force so that the wood banged against the stone. The servants were eternally cleaning up the crumbles of wall and splinters of door he left in his wake. His facial expression was stern as he stood still in the frame of the doorway but it softened upon seeing his wife and the shape of his unborn boy. He took the other seat by the unlit hearth and beckoned for wine.

"How are you feeling tonight? Are you prepared for the feast?" My father took a large swig of wine and some of the droplets hung from his brown wiry beard.

"I am fine, my lord," replied my mother fondly, still rubbing her tummy. Maybe that's why I got my mark, from too much tummy rubbing. She should be careful.

"And you, daughter? Are you prepared?"

Seven pairs of men's eyes turned to me. I could see Harry glaring at me from behind a book he was "reading" and young Thomas was licking his lips as he peered at me. For God's sake, I'm pretty sure I saw my mother's stomach jolt, as if the unborn boy turned to look at me too.

"I have no doubt Lord Beckett will be pleased with me, Father," I managed. I could almost hear their unspoken thoughts. They washed over me in a cold wave of suspicion and shame. All seven heads turned to my mother. It was eerie to watch. All moving as one.

"Our final challenge is yet to be overcome," she said, her voice constricted.

I looked into my lap as they all exclaimed.

"Take her to someone!"

"This will not do!"

"It could ruin everything."

I said nothing. It was not my place to say anything. My woman's problem was a man's issue.

"If only you had bigger breasts, he might not be so focused on down there." That comment rung out louder than the rest. I looked up to stare at Thomas. He was thirteen years old. No one reprimanded him. My own boys will never talk to me like that. I will be their mother and their matriarch. Their own corporeal Mother Mary.

Jimmy tucked himself under my skirts and wrapped his tail around my ankles. I tried to think only of his softness, how he could wrap himself around my shape.

"We will think of something," my mother whispered.

"Damnit!" My father banged his fist on the small table in front of him. There was a clattering and a splashing as goblets and wine tumbled. Servants sprang to action. "You better think of a bloody good idea by tomorrow eve! This could ruin everything."

"It might not," I said.

"What?" he snapped. I wished I had put more paint on my face and I should have known to wear my pearled headpiece today. I was naked without it.

"I could explain to my husband that it is a malady of the skin, nothing to be concerned about. That it has been with me since birth. Perhaps a blessing from Christ. I have read that saints are often blessed with a mark of Godliness. I know that —"

"Do not speak of what you don't know!" Father waved away the servants buzzing around him, clearing up his mess.

"I do know. You are speaking about me." But no one listened. Every brother had decided it was time to have his voice heard, and I got lost under the racket. I stared out of the open window and watched a bumblebee disappearing in and out of the flutes of the hollyhocks, but I could feel my family's anger and disgust in my bones. I reached for a poem in my mind that would most suit this horrid day and found an appropriately dramatic and sombre one by the King's own poet, Wyatt. I recited it in my head, drowning out the noise of my kin.

And I, alas, by chance am thus assign'd
Daily to mourn, till death do it relent.
But since that thus it is by destiny,
What can I more but have a woeful heart;
My pen in plaint, my voice in careful cry,
My mind in woe, my body full of smart;
And I myself, myself always to hate,
Till dreadful death do ease my doleful state.

CHAPTER TWO

My wedding gown had been chosen by my eldest brother, who had brought it back from France. He was friends with my betrothed and assured me it would please him greatly. It was a French design, obviously, with the cuffs of my sleeves turned back to display a lining decorated with pearls. I wore the matching French hood, which had a creamy band and gold lining. It covered enough of my hair. The gown itself was black, which I found disappointing, though I hadn't said anything.

"Are you nervous?" asked my mother as we prepared to leave my room to join my nuptial feast. We had just applied a light layer of the paste to my mark and would thicken it later. We had not made any discernible improvements to the concoction, but we intended to make sure that my husband be heavily plied with the finest of wines, in the hopes of keeping him distracted.

"I have been nervous for three weeks straight," I mumbled. It had been the banns that had made the nerves so consistent. Every bloody Sunday having to endure the Father asking the congregation if anyone knew of any reason why this marriage should not occur. Every bloody Sunday I envisioned someone standing up. Pointing a long accusatory finger. *Witch!* they would yell.

"Well, no one said anything in the banns, did they?" said my mother. She had a knack for knowing what was on my mind, as I did with her. "Now we just have to get through tonight, let him plant his seed in your belly and you will be safe."

She dusted off her hands. Like she was dusting off me.

"I'm sorry, Mother." My mark had burdened her just as much as it had tormented me. Maybe more so.

"Just get today over with." I could hear the strain in her voice. If my whole family was one person, my father would be the head, of course, my mother the stomach, my brothers the hands and feet, and I would be my mark. Crawling up the side of my family's person. Shaming each of them. Causing each of them unease.

I took a deep breath and inhaled the smell of the feast coming up from the kitchen, and the perfume from the banisters, adorned with flowers. I turned into the hallway to see the revellers in the entrance hall beneath me. They cheered as they saw me, and the cheers got louder as I descended towards them.

"Graceful, Magdalen. Slow your steps." Mother could speak without opening her mouth.

I slowed down. I let myself sink into this moment. My moment. These cheers were for me. I smiled. This was my day. Maude was getting her powers.

Shirburn Castle was on a lot of land. We walked through the very green fields and the sheep, some black-faced, some white-faced, all looking up as we proceeded through. My family, the

Shaftsberrys, had sheep. Lots of them. And they made Papa and the boys very rich. I did not fully understand where my husband's money came from — no one had cared to explain it properly. I assumed it was old money, which I thought sounded better than sheep.

Everyone around me was singing dirty songs, and trumpets played and my family danced and clapped despite the fact that every single one of them had his or her mind on my inner thighs. I stayed composed and walked slowly through the fields. My mother always by my side.

The old Church of St Peter's lay at a crossroads ahead, its tall tower rising over the thick copse of trees that surrounded the base of the old stone building. The church's bells soothed my soul. Ringing in my new life. My rebirth.

Edward would be in there. In that building. Waiting for me. He would be my freedom. I didn't want to be the wrong stitch in the pristine tapestry that was my family. I wanted a fresh start. We walked into the shade of the church's trees. The important people walked into the church first, then the servants and the village people filed in at the back; they all wished me well as I passed.

I waited with my father and mother. I pushed down my curls. I wished Jimmy had been allowed to be here.

"It's time," my father said roughly, leading me forwards.

I don't remember being declared husband and wife. But I remember Edward's vows. He had said them evenly, without eye contact. I also remember when I said, "I promise to be bonny and buxom in bed and in board," because people laughed, and I wondered whether it was because I was anything but buxom. I remember feeling hot in the church. I remember worrying about sweating too much. I remember the sound of my dress against the stone as I stepped slowly and deliberately down the aisle. I remember trying to walk without my thighs touching one another. But I don't remember the part when we became husband and wife. I don't remember the moment when I was relieved of my family. When I was detached from them and re-attached to this man. There was too much noise. There were too many people. I knew too many of their names but didn't know their faces. And how, how could I think about what was happening right now, when the nighttime would inevitably come and my legs split open and my curse revealed? And even if the best were to happen, even if he did not object, then he had to ... you know. Enter me. Like the way that piece of white gunk had got stuck up there, but presumably way worse. That was what I was thinking about as I became Lady Beckett. Beeswax up my purse. That's what this concoction had been: whisked egg white and beeswax. It did not feel good. But it covered the mark, more or less.

It was tradition to walk from the church back to the feast, but I don't remember much of that either. Just my stupid, wide steps, like a cow, or a lame sheep, trying not to rub off the mixture.

I felt better after a cup or two of wine. The table-clothes were pristine white and I sat in the centre of the long top table, in the big chair, which had armrests. Sitting next to my husband. Lord Edward Beckett. I was number one at this feast. *Nombre Uno, Numero Un. Numerus Unos.* I was a little drunk. I suppose my husband was actually number one, in retrospect. But I was number two at the very least. *Numerus Duos.* Not too shabby. And after tonight, I would have a little boy in my belly. I would be bearer of the *heir*. Then I would be number one. I would be the vessel. I would be able to speak on what I wanted. Do what I pleased. Carrier of the next of the Beckett line. My first child would be named after his father, of course. Then we would have a Henry. After His Highness. I think we should name number three after my father, but I would have to consult Edward about that, because he might want the third to be named after his grandfather. But it didn't matter really; either number three or four would be the namesake of my family line. I let my hand lazily rest on the arm of the chair. As my mother would do.

"My lord husband?"

He turned to me. Cheeks flushed from drink. His eyebrow raised. "Yes?"

"How do you find the wine?" He had been drinking it copiously, thank Christ.

Someone called for him down the table, and he turned away from me and didn't answer. He had a lot of friends. And they were all very loud. I felt a shiver of annoyance mixed with shame. I looked out at the Great Hall and hoped no one had witnessed the exchange. Everyone was busy with their own food, and no doubt enjoying the very pleasing wine. It was a blur of colours and sounds. Clinking of cups with laughs and music. I entertained myself watching the musicians for a while and I smiled at the important people on the lesser tables.

I sat up a little straighter. My huge skirts plumed out around me, as if I were sitting in a bath of black damask, but instead of sitting in water with lavender petals and flecks of rosemary, I had been sprinkled with rubies and pearls.

"Edward?" I tried again, basking in all my glory.

I don't think he heard me. He was telling a story to his kin. It was about relations with France. They were being rude about the Dauphin Francis, something about him having a tiny member. I suppose it wasn't a conversation for me to intervene in, despite the fact I personally had heard a lot about the unfortunate French heir, including confirmation that his tackle was indeed — petite.

"And the lies he tells his Court! All his land is awash with fraudulent news about our kingdom and our strength! Our king must show his power! Otherwise they will walk all over us!"

There was a chorus of "ayes" from my husband's kin.

"If this kingdom gets any softer, it is simply going to cease to exist," my husband declared. That was very well received, with lots of patting on the back.

I wondered if he had the guts to say that to His Majesty in person.

"Edward?" I tried again. He was porcelain white. His skin, so English, so untouched by the sun. Perhaps his only knowledge of trees, grass and light were their portrayals in tapestry, or maybe a quick glance out of the window at Court. He had green eyes, and they suited his golden tunic. His dark hair flopped in front of his face, and I thought I might be bold enough to whisk it away. I reached my hand up, but a cold draught got to it first; I was no longer needed. I let my arm fall limp into my lap. Finally, he turned to me.

"How do you find the wine?"

He leant into my side. Shivers ran down my spine at the feeling of his breath on my ear. "I wish it were all over now, so we could be tupping right this minute." He was whispering, but it was a loud whisper. His kinsman heard and laughed. I wondered if the quip was more for them than me. Still, I smiled at him and let him kiss my lips. My husband. My husband Lord Beckett kissed me. Me. Maude. Lady Beckett. In a few days we would move to our property, with my own staff and grounds, and I would be with child. What did it matter if he didn't answer my question about the wine, when we were on our way to making a dozen tiny little Becketts, birthed from my loins? I bit my lip at the thought of my loins. I wondered if my affliction would be passed down to my baby boys. It would probably be passed down to a girl, if I had one accidentally. Like my mother.

As these things go, the tradition is that my female kin would take me to the wedding chamber, and the lord's kin would escort him to his. At a normal girl's wedding, the bride would be undressed by her mother, sisters and cousins. And the man would be undressed by his men. This was not to be the case for me. I was to be undressed by my mother. My mother and the toadspotted Agnes. I needed to be slathered up.

"We are to retire!" Edward had a big voice for someone so slight in body. I jumped as the Great Hall erupted in cheers and jeers. Edward indicated I should stand. My legs felt heavy. I hoped I was smiling. I looked out at the rowdy horseshoe of important courtiers. I could feel each of my brothers' eyes on me. Stern. Threatening. The crowd began shouting: they wanted their final kiss.

"Make this good," Edward grunted. The last kiss of the night. The raunchiest kiss.

I looked up into his green eyes and he pulled me forwards in a sudden jolt. It was violent and intrusive. He whirled the tongue around and around like he was trying to whisk butter in my mouth. This couldn't be visually pleasing, but by the sound of the crowd, they were enjoying it.

After what seemed like an entire farming season, his tongue withdrew. Before I could even wipe the saliva from my cheeks, his kinsmen had picked Edward up and were whisking him away. I scanned the room for my mother. She stood, holding her belly, and, with the eyes of envious women upon it, she beckoned me to be with her. We left the Great Hall.

CHAPTER THREE

My mother slathered the inside of my naked leg.

"Don't tense up," Mother hissed, blowing on my lower belly to make the cream dry. "Just let him do what he wants, and if you're like me you will have a baby boy within you as soon as he's done. Focus on that."

"Yes, Mama." I imagined what I looked like. Spreadeagle on the petal-strewn bed, my curls unbound, my mother in between my loins. The Devil's version of birth, with the mother protruding from inside of my legs, and the babe the one in labour. I started to shake.

"Don't shake! You'll sweat!" Something caught at the bottom of my throat. No. I did not want to cry. "That's done. It's dry. Get under the bedclothing, but leave your breasts out."

My mother tucked me in as if I were a child, then she gestured to Agnes, who physically cupped my breasts and plopped them over the fold in the eiderdown. I gritted my teeth. Mother looked at me. "Actually, no." She shook her head. "Cover her breasts." My eyes stung with the effort of not crying. "Don't sulk." She was rubbing her belly. "This only needs to be done once. As soon as he's tupped you he won't be able to annul the marriage. He'll have to put up with your affliction after that."

"I feel like I'm tricking him," I muttered. "I don't know that this feels Godly."

"You'll feel Godly as soon as you birth him a boy, darling." My mother cocked her head to one side and then she left, her pet Agnes in tow.

I tried to stay completely still. I could feel the crusty layers between my thighs. Maybe I should lie split leg. I pried them open. I took a sneak peek under the thick red blanket. Nothing had fallen off.

I shut my eyes. *Holy Father. I promise that after this one sin of deception I will please both you and my husband, that I will be a good wife and fertile mother. Please, Lord, may this marriage be consummated under your good grace. Please, God —*

"Wife?" I heard a sound and the door opening and closing. I opened my eyes. It was just Edward. He had left his kin behind the door. My husband was entirely naked. I had seen a man naked before. I had grown up in a house of six boys, after all. But I had never seen a fully grown man this naked. He was laughing, reacting to the banging on the door and the snickering through the wood. The laughing made his thingy jiggle up and down, and it didn't appeal to me. He was walking towards the posset. The drink that was meant to invigorate him and calm me down. The banging persisted. I still hadn't said a word. He downed his drink and smacked his lips together. I tried to smile. This is what I was made for. I am to be a goodly wife.

I had expected him to bring me a goblet. He had not. I had been depending on that. Every single muscle was taut with fear, but he was approaching me empty-handed. I needed the posset. Was I smiling?

"Magdalen," he said.

"You may call me Maude if you like," I suggested.

"The boys want some evidence of our consummation."

He wasn't very good at listening.

"Evidence?" There was a frog in my throat.

He sat on the corner of my bed. "Yes."

"What sort?" I whispered, hopefully seductively. He wiggled his dark eyebrows. "You could give them my shift?" I suggested, gesturing to my long white undergarment that lay on top of the trunk at the end of the bed.

"I want you to moan."

I recoiled. "What?"

"Moan."

"Out loud?"

"What do you think, Magdalen?" He had got up onto the bed, on all fours. It was not ... not flattering.

"How do I ... do that?"

"Just try."

"Lord Beckett, are you sure you don't want to just do it? Put a son in my belly as soon as possible?"

His face wavered. He was displeased at my attempt to wiggle out of his embarrassing command, but he liked the mention of his son. He recovered, moving towards me like a dog on all fours. "Keen, are you?" He was straddling me over the covers. I could smell his breath, see the light hairs that carpeted his chin. "Yell out my name. Then we make my son."

I tried to swallow but my mouth was dry. I wanted to get out and get myself some of that drink, soothe my throat and soul. But I couldn't: I would disturb the paste. I needed him to do his business first. I needed to close this marriage before he found out. I was just going to have to yell out his name. There was a banging at the door.

"COME ON, EDWARD, STICK IT IN HER."

Tears were threatening again.

He glared at me. Astride me.

I took a breath in. "Edward!" I yelled out.

He laughed in my face. A little bit of spit landed on my nose. I left it there. I didn't want to move. "It sounds like you're calling for help. Here, let me help you." He grabbed hold of my breast as though it would throw me into fits of sexual ecstasy. "Again," he instructed, giving it an uncomfortable squeeze.

I yelled out for a second time, "Edward!"

There were giggles and shrieks and the battering of the door. He laughed again, overjoyed at his kinsman's approval.

"Edward, Edward, Edward!" they began to chant from outside the door.

It was becoming obvious that he enjoyed the sound of his kinsman. Was it usual for men's pricks to get hard because their friends called their names? His eyes glazed over as the banging on the door and the chants got louder and louder, until he ripped back my covers. It took all my might not to snap my legs back together. I grabbed hold of his face with my hands, trying to keep his attention away from my leg and groin. It worked. Instead of inspecting what he was about to do, he just fell on top of me and lay on my body. He shoved and bruised my already blackened in-betweens, thrusting against my inner thigh. I thought I felt a bit of the beeswax fall off. Finally, after many attempts at entry, he succeeded. I gasped at the strong sensation and the men outside erupted in shouts and joy. I heard the door bang open. My eyes went to them. A dozen men poured through the door, thrusting their arms into the air, bouncing up and down. I got intermittent glimpses of three of my own Goddamn brothers as Edward thrust in and out of my vision. One doesn't expect to make eye contact with one's brother when losing one's virginity, but life is full of dreadful surprises.

"Peace, gentlemen, peace!" My eldest brother Harry had had enough. "Let us go and get some of our own fun!" He wouldn't want them to be there too long lest they see what Edward couldn't. I heard the moans of disappointment as the men were ushered out of the door. Edward was sweating, laughing, shoving himself into me. I tried to relax. It was done now. I had done my family proud. He was mine. Why would God make this process so uncomfortable? But before I could really harass the Lord of Heaven and Earth, I thanked him because the whole ordeal had stopped and Edward peeled himself off me and lay looking up at the roof of our bed. Panting.

Was I now — a woman?

He lay there breathing for at least a minute. I didn't dare move. I tried to assess the situation. I could feel blood, or seed or something. Or was it the beeswax? Was it both? I needed the covers over me, but I didn't know if I could sit up and pull them.

Suddenly, Edward rolled over.

"By the new year we shall have a son," he declared and at the very mention of his offspring he became overcome with exhaustion and drink. He put a hand over my belly (God willing, the home of his heir), and he fell asleep. I dared not move. I watched him for over an hour, wondering if I could remove his hand from around my middle. I was cold. I needed to check the sheets. I needed to re-plaster my thighs, and I needed wine to mask the dull throbbing pain between them. I needed my own bed. But he was fully draped over me. Eventually, I must've fallen asleep. I woke with the light. His hand still over my belly. Was he dead?

I touched my husband's head lightly.

I felt him stir. Shift. Then stretch. He looked at me, blinked. Then sat up, holding his head. He would have a bad hangover. He was making small moaning sounds as he rubbed his eyes. I hoped his headache would not be my fault.

He yawned. "Time for the morning inspection."

"My lord?"

"I need to check if you bled," he said abruptly, turning himself over to look at me in the eye.

"I see, my lord."

"Get up."

"I'm actually ..." I began. "I'm still in pain."

That's when I saw it. My tummy knotted. He had white smudges all over his own private hairs. Oh God. Oh God. He was pale, but his hair wasn't fucking white. Eventually he was going to notice that. I tried not to look at it.

I felt his mood change before his face changed, before he said anything. "Are you not a virgin, Magdalen?" I couldn't believe he would say such a thing. I tried to defend myself but only a low grunt came out. "Move!" I rolled off the bed, with a bed-cloth covering me. I made my eyes look at the mattress. Blood. Thank God. But also ...

"What in God's name is this?" Big chunks of white beeswax had stuck to the sheets. He prodded it with his finger. Could I pass this off as some sort of womanly thing? We don't just bleed when you take our virginities ... we beeswax?

I hadn't said a word.

"And what's this?" Okay. Jig was up. He started violently brushing out the bits of it stuck in his Goddamn hair.

"Have you got the clap? Are you a bloody whore?" He was backing towards the door.

It was time to take over.

"Edward, sit down."

"What?" He was looking at his hands as though they had just caught fire. I felt his emotions as if they were my own. He was terrified. I tied up the sheet around me with a knot, and walked over to him, taking him by the hand and putting him down on a stool. "I will explain."

He was shaking. He looked like a boy, his tiny pale body concave as he stared at his white-stained white hands. "What in God's name is your explanation?"

I winced. He might look like a boy but he sounded like my father. I took a deep breath.

"I have a mark on the inside of my thigh."

His lip curled. Disgust.

I moved over to the basin and dabbed a cloth into water. Indelicately, I removed my makeshift gown and slowly, without looking at him, rubbed the white paste away. I revealed to him my black mark.

"Some say the mark is a sign from God that I would be a goodly wife. I am inclined to believe it is a sign of fertility. It has been with me since birth. I hid it from you, for fear it would hinder our Godly union."

Now, surely, he would relax. A Godly symbol of my fruitful loins. Please. Don't you want to believe that? It sounds so good. He beckoned me to come closer to him.

"Let me see it," he croaked.

I moved closer. His face was drawn back into himself; he had many a chin.

"It is on my loins as a sign of fertility," I repeated.

He reached his hand out to the inside of my thigh. He touched my mark, almost curiously. I felt tears fall I hadn't realised were welling. To have someone so gently touch the bane of my life. The blackness of my whole existence. I could have wailed.

"It is on your loins ..." he whispered, repeating my words.

"A black mark on your loins."

Jimmy appeared. How he managed to find his way into the marriage suite, I did not know. I presumed the Devil had let him in, because my black fucking cat chose at that very moment to wrap his body around my legs.

Edward looked at Jimmy, then he looked at my leg, then he looked me right in the eye. Like he was learning to add simple numbers together. I could see the calculation form in his head. I felt his fear move to anger.

"No," I whispered.

"Witch!" He shoved me in the stomach. I fell backwards onto the floor. My bottom smacked hard against the stone.

"No!"

"It suckles at your teat! It is an imp!"

"NO!" Jimmy jumped at my sudden outburst. And I instinctively went to comfort him, grabbing him and holding him close to my chest.

Edward moved lightning fast. From the corner of my eye I could see him tearing the bloodstained sheet we had lain upon. He threw it into the fire. He was lucky it didn't smother the flames, but, the Devil on his side, it lit up in red-hot fire. Probably the beeswax. Heat flooded the room, as if I were in Hell before I had passed.

He was still as he watched it burn. I knew what he was thinking. We had witnesses. He couldn't deny our union. Now I loved those boys for barging in, for seeing me. But still, what would my mother do? What should I do? I was immobilised on the floor, clutching my cat.

As soon as he was satisfied the sheet was going to perish, he began dressing.

"If you put a curse on my prick, I will know it was you, and you will burn," he whispered, his hand on the door lock.

"I can't. I wouldn't know how. I'm not —"

"SHE WILL NOT LIE WITH ME!" His voice reverberated off the stone, no amount of tapestries on the wall could swallow his lie. "SHE WILL NOT LIE WITH ME." I couldn't tell if it was an echo or if he had yelled again. I curled myself into a ball. I heard the calls of his kinsmen from down below. He went to them. I heard feet on floorboards, and the occasional loud shout of horror or accusation or shock or fear. Of me. No longer woman. *Witch.*

No one came for me for a long, long time. Jimmy was asleep at my breast, his purrs measuring the long lengths of time that went by.

He would want an annulment. That's why he burnt the sheets. I wondered whether he would want to denounce me as witch.

Eventually my mother and her lady's maid entered. I was still on the floor.

"Dress her." I could hear the anger in my mother's voice. Agnes lifted me up. I did not let go of Jimmy.

"I can't get your dresses on if you don't let go of the cat," Agnes snapped.

I shook my head.

"Let go of the Godforsaken cat, Magdalen, or I'll join the rest of England in believing you a witch." My mother snatched my baby boy from my hands. "Did you lie with him?"

"Aye! Harry saw! So did a dozen others!"

"Thank God for my boys," she whispered. "If you're truly my daughter, you will be with child. Your husband has left to stay at the inn in Watlington with his family. He will seek an annulment. I doubt he will bring charges of witchcraft against you: it is not fashionable to do so. A letter will be sent reminding him that you could be with child and that your union was witnessed. We will wait to see if you get your monthly course. If you do, I will make further arrangements."

It took me a while to realise Agnes had dressed me in my nightclothes.

"You must not leave your room," my mother instructed.

I looked up at her, finally making eye contact. This would never have happened to her. Only to me.

CHAPTER FOUR

Being isolated in your room for days on end allows too much time for thinking. And plotting. And scheming. And planning retribution. I'd never felt more witchy.

Agnes was giving me snippets of information every time she brought me food or came to bathe me. My husband was still in town, apparently causing havoc each night with his men. Waiting for his wife to bleed.

I was listening intently to my body, every shift, gurgle and minor pain was either a baby or my monthly bleeding, depending on how I was feeling. My father and my brothers would have met to discuss what to do with me if I bled. At night, when I was asleep in my bed, I wished I would bleed, because I didn't want to spend my nights with that man. But in the days, when the sun was out, it was another story. If he couldn't get an annulment, he might go the way of the King and get a divorce. Me, my father's daughter, a divorced woman. After one night of marriage. I hated myself. I could see the conversations they would have about me. All of them. Thomas especially. Dirty little prick. Father would call me the blight on their family. I suppose he already did that, but he would do it more. All the work my family had done crawling their way betwixt the Tudor house's buttocks would be destroyed, by me. The elf-skinned witch in a family of courtiers.

Day seven. Torrential rain. No bleeding. No one had seen me except Agnes. She had surpassed Thomas in my list of hated people. She had obtained the top spot.

"Why won't you get up to greet me?" I had been lying on my bed, looking at the beams in the roof for well over an hour. I didn't respond. Agnes put down a plate of something bad smelling. "It is cabbage!" she said, seeing my nose wrinkle. I continued to ignore her. "Do you have any news?" she asked me for the third time today. I said nothing. "How were you born of your dear mother?" she exclaimed, banging my door shut. If my body hadn't been so heavy, I would've thrown something in her direction, but it felt as if someone had tied me to the bed.

I continued to stare at the beams. There were thirteen that ran diagonally across the room and then two that ran the other way.

I felt a tugging on my mattress. I flipped myself onto my tummy and looked under my mattress. It was Jimmy, of course, digging his claws into the mattress and pulling on the hay. It looked cosy under the bed so I decided to join him. I took a blanket under there, then I lit my shortest candle to give the space a safe but sultry glow. I lay on my back, listening to the heavy rain and watching as my cat pulled the hay from my mattress. It was satisfying, and destructive. I wish I could be angry at my baby boy, but I couldn't. He was my one true friend. I thumbed a piece of straw and watched as his cat eyes caught the candlelight and became glazed with the terrifyingly wonderful glow. I wondered if he really was my imp. If so, did that make me a witch? I guess when you added up my mark, my cat and my penchant for writing poems and playing with words, it didn't look good. But I wasn't made for witchyness: I was made for womanhood, wifeliness and baby boys. I was trying so hard to do what I was meant to do, but no amount of compliance or obedience was working.

It was day nine. Red sky at night, shepherd's delight. Red sky in the morning. Shepherd's warning. The sky was a brilliant red. The storm never came, but I bled.

I had always hated my bleed, but I hated this bleed the most. I think. Or maybe I was grateful for it. I withheld the information from my mother. I needed time to think, without everyone else intervening. I lay under my bed, staring into space. How funny it is that the very thing that is shared with other women takes my womanhood from me and turns me into a witch.

Perhaps I was not my mother's daughter at all. Was it possible there had been some sort of hiccough? A switching of babes? A wet nurse with a marred child swapped her cursed babe with the lord's?

I began making a list of possible next moves. These were my options:

Actually curse his prick. Make it constantly floppy. Cons: I don't know how to curse pricks, and if I figure it out he will probably know it was me.

Purchase poison and become a young widow, with all his estates and property. Cons: don't want to be hanged or go to the Tower.

Fake pregnancy. Con: tricky to do. Could eat a lot to get a rotund belly. But eventually I would be found out.

Entreat the advice of real witches. Con: ...

I was plaiting the straw as I thought.

I knew there were wise women in Watlington. They were

well known. Respected. Once I had heard about an elixir they had sold to the notoriously crazy Widow Thatcher. Supposedly it had made some man mad with lust for her. The servants had talked about it for weeks. My whole body shivered. The witches in town would know what to do. They would have some potion, or spell, or some potent words at least, surely. I had torn my piece of straw into thin shreds. Was this madness? I didn't know.

Darkness.

A big cloak.

The courage to drop about a foot into the air.

I had two of the three. I looked down into the black garden bed that lay beneath my window. Just do it, Maude.

I squeezed myself through the small gap that my delicate diamond-paned window afforded. I hung from the stone sill by my fingertips. Drop, Maude. Drop. I landed. Smiled. Then tripped over a protruding root with a thud and a small whimper. I looked back up at Shirburn from the dirt. It was not a fashionable home, but it was intimidating. I imagined the kings of the past would like it: sturdy, all sandstone, thick walled and unmistakably a castle. No one seemed to be stirring. No candlelight at the windows. I just had to hope the town was quiet too. I half regretted not bringing my own candle, but I had been right to be cautious: the walk to town would take thirty minutes and I would stick out like a sore thumb with a light bobbing along the lane. My tummy looped at the thought of being seen by someone on my way. I wished again I were a witch. I could conjure a protection spell to prevent myself being attacked or having my money stolen. I set off, fantasising about what my mother would do if she knew what I was up to. It half scared me, half delighted me.

The path was straight and not complicated, but trees in the breeze looked like highwaymen. Wandering sheep in the dark looked like crouching brigands. The sound of my own quick feet on the dirt road sounded exactly like someone else's feet on the dirt road. Thirty minutes was an eternity, but eventually I saw the light of an inn on the outskirts of town.

I had grown up a walk away from this town, but I had rarely been in to Watlington. I had been once with my mother when I was young, and I remembered little of it. And another time when I was ten years old, when I had begged my older brother to cure a bad case of boredom. But really, I had no need for public spaces. What was I to do in them?

The high street was nearly empty. I saw a few beggars and strays lingering in doorways but I gave them a wide berth. There were a lot of inns, five or six on one street — candlelight flickered from within and there was the comforting sound of people laughing and talking filtering out of the windows. I wondered which house my husband was staying in. I walked quickly along the cobbled road, peering up at the emporium signs, trying to read their names. I could hear them swinging in the night air, but it was too dark to make out the words. Feeling panicked, I took a right-hand turn down another lane lined with shoppes. I started peering into the windows. A bakery. Someone's bedchamber. Too dark to see. A butcher. No idea. No.

I stopped outside one of the older stone houses. It was unlike the rest of the newer, half-timbered buildings. It had a crooked window and a slanting door. I could see shelves filled with small bottles and tinctures being reflected in the moonlight, and there was candlelight flickering from somewhere further within the shoppe. This was my best bet. I knocked. I looked back up the road towards the street with all the inns. I hadn't thought this far ahead. What if they would not see me so late at night? No one was answering. I knocked one more time; if no one answered I would go home. The light flickered — someone had picked up the candlestick and was moving within.

A dark figure came to the door. Be brave, Maude.

"Hallo?" It was a woman, curvy and kind-looking by the light of her candle. Her head was cocked in the same slant as the door.

"I'm sorry to disturb you so late, goodwoman. I am in desperate need, but I do not want to be seen."

She stared at my lips, not my eyes. It was unnerving. "You do not want to be seen?" she repeated.

I nodded.

"Come in."

I entered.

I'd never met a real witch. I stared at her face as she sat behind a wooden counter. She was fair-haired, round-faced, with rosy cheeks. I looked far more like a traditional witch than she did. She indicated I was to sit on the other side of the counter upon a stool. It felt like a normal apothecary, nothing specifically witchy about it, apart from the fact I was there in the dark.

"How can I assist you?" She used hand gestures when she spoke. Almost one gesture to each word.

I looked around the dark room. Shoppes just shouldn't be visited in the nighttime. Any money exchanged at night seemed wrong, illicit. This is wrong, I reminded myself. "I need advice. Or perhaps a potion. Or a spell ..." I jumped as I felt her hand on my arm.

"I am deaf, child," she said kindly. "Speak to my face, so I might read your lips."

"I'm sorry," I said, blushing in the darkness.

"You need not fret. Simply repeat what you said."

"I need you to make a man love me," I said, slowly this time. The more I said it, the more stupid I felt.

"Tell me more."

"A visitor, Hildy?" Another woman entered the room. This woman looked far more terrifying. Fine features. A stern face. She put an elegant, long-fingered hand on Hildy's shoulder.

"This is Zita," the first witch explained.

"And you are Lady Magdalen," Zita said, unsmiling. I recoiled. How could she know me? This had been a mistake. I needed to leave.

"No," I said, getting off the stool and backing up. "How do you know who I am?"

"We are the wisewomen," she said. "We know all there is to know around here."

"Do you know everything?" I asked, almost hopeful that they might know of my situation so that I did not have to explain it.

"We know your husband's staying at the Old Swan," said Zita. "Do you want a potion to stir up his loins?"

I flinched. Not really. "I cannot speak with you now you know who I am. It is too risky. You could tell my parents, my husband, you could sell it as gossip to local busybodies."

"Don't be a fool. It would be bad business to start selling gossip." Zita sounded insulted.

"Why?"

"Because every single day we receive dozens of people in our home, telling us the most abhorrent, disgusting, personal and downright damning truths about themselves. It would not do well to have a reputation for leaking stories."

Hildy was approaching me with the candle. I backed away from her. She lifted her hand high, putting the candle flame to a sign that was hung above the door.

CONFIDENTIAL WISEWOMEN

"We don't tell secrets," she explained.

"My secret's really big, though."

"Everyone thinks their secret is the biggest, but our services have been called for at the King's Court, and His Highness most assuredly has bigger secrets than Magdalen does." Zita had a pointed tone. I got the feeling she wasn't taken by me.

"Maude," I said instinctively.

"Maude." She corrected herself and held out a hand to indicate I was to move into the next room.

It was even darker in there, but the two of them went about lighting a plethora of candles. The ceiling was rendered invisible by hundreds of hanging dried flowers and herbs, as if I were looking at a forest upside down. It smelt beautiful — like a woodland after a storm. We sat at a large round table in the middle of the small room. Sitting in the centre of the table was a large glass ball. I winced. It was so inauspicious.

"Don't be frightened of things you don't understand," Zita said sternly.

Hildy passed me a hot chalice of something steaming. "For your nerves." The drink was pepperminty. "Now, tell us. What is your problem?"

"Are you really invited to Court?" I asked, curiosity getting the better of me.

"Don't evade the question," Zita snapped. She reminded me of my mother.

I took a shaky breath. "My husband wishes to get rid of me through no fault of my own and I must protect myself."

Zita relayed what I had said to Hildy with hand gestures, whisking them wildly in the air. Hildy nodded. Understanding. My heart was beating so fast I worried all the beats would blur together into one long, neverending note.

"Why does he want to be rid of you?" asked Hildy gently.

"Why do you need to know?" I whimpered, at risk of a full tearful breakdown. This was all too much. "Can't you just give me a spell, or a potion?"

"We need to make sure what we give you is applicable to your circumstance. Let me help you: is he wanting to be rid of you because you were found not to be a virgin?" I shook my head. "Because you were found to be infertile?"

"God forbid it! No!"

"Try to help us, Maude," Hildy said cooingly.

"Because he didn't like how a part of me looked," I managed. Hildy tutted. Zita appraised me, as though taking a guess as to what part of me he might not like. She would never guess.

"Maybe he's keen on the boys," Hildy suggested.

"No!" I protested. "No ... he ... he enjoyed my womanly form well enough."

"Ahh. So you have lain together," Zita said.

I hated this conversation. "Yes."

"Just the once?"

"Aye."

"Did he not find pleasure in it?"

"He thinks I'm a witch!" It exploded out of me. I couldn't tolerate another guess.

Hildy tutted. "I'm not sure we've got a tincture for that."

"What?" My breath caught in my throat. I had thought they would be able to fix anything.

"We don't have anything for that," repeated Zita.

"Nothing?" A cacophony of self-loathing thoughts overwhelmed me.

"Men rarely recant accusations such as that."

I felt lightheaded. "Then what shall I do?"

"Did anyone witness the union?"

My nose wrinkled as I remembered. "Many did."

"Then he will have a hard time annulling it."

"Jesus swiving Christ." I lay my head on the table; it smelt like lavender.

I felt a soothing hand on my back. I hadn't had any one touch me so affectionately in a long time. I let my tears salt the wood beneath my cheeks. "What am I to do?"

"You'll have to face the storm, Maude. It is not common to out someone as a witch nowadays. I think it more likely he will ask for a divorce." Zita was getting ready to leave the room.

I could not stem my tears. My body began to shake from the force of my sobs.

"It's not so bad. If divorce is good enough for the King, I'm sure you can withstand it." Zita wanted me gone; I could hear it in her voice.

"Don't you have some sort of lusty tincture? That riles the men and makes them mad with lust?" I tried.

"Of course. But how will that help you?"

"I could get pregnant! Give him a son!"

"Maude," Hildy said softly.

"Just give it to me," I demanded, wiping snot from my nose.

Hildy left the table, returning with a glass vial. "You could use these." It was filled with small flakes of something white. "It's shredded mushroom. They are strong. Put them in his drink."

I bit my lip. "What will happen?"

"He will be driven half mad for lust with you."

I hiccoughed. "How long will the effects last?"

"Perhaps a few hours."

"Do you have anything stronger?"

"These are as strong as you're going to get." Zita clasped her long fingers together.

I sighed. "What type of mushrooms are they?"

"Curious, are you? Interested in the practice, Maude?" asked Zita.

"I only ask to make sure you're not poisoning him!" I said defensively.

"Don't trust us?"

"Zounds! No matter! How much are they?"

Zita opened her mouth to speak, but Hildy cut in front of her. "Nothing, pet. Go fix your mess."

"What?"

"Go," she said. "Tread carefully. Get them in him quickly. Before he does something stupid."

My breathing was out of control. "Should I do it now?" I asked, panicked.

"I would think so."

"I am bleeding. He won't want to lie with me today!"

"He will not notice, or care."

"Will I conceive?"

"Possibly," said Hildy, handing me something. "Eat this. It's a fertility charm."

"Eat it?" I looked at the piece of parchment with a scrabble of Latin on it.

Zita impatiently shoved it into my mouth. I chewed, tasting the ink.

"Swallow," she said.

I gulped, feeling it getting stuck halfway down my throat. "How do I do this? I don't know in which inn he abides! Even if I did, he would not let me into his rooms! He thinks I will curse his cock!" Zita translated this for Hildy, with a truly obscene final hand gesture.

"Annie will help her," Hildy said confidently.

"Who is Annie?"

"They call her the Tawny Moor. Her name is Annie Cobbie, and you'll find her at Mrs Bankes's house."

My mouth fell open. “Isn’t that the whorehouse?”

“Annie has been spending some time with your husband.”

I was shocked. Of course, I shouldn’t have been shocked, but I was. “How do you know?”

“We see with our witches’ eye.” Hildy wiggled her eyebrows. I think she was fucking with me.

“Don’t think badly of Annie: she is a good woman.” Zita began leading me to the door. “Tell her we have sent you and I would think between the two of you, you could orchestrate something.”

“I don’t want to go to the whorehouse.”

“Don’t be snooty,” Zita snapped.

I put the mushrooms in my cloak pocket and let my finger rub over the smooth glass.

“If things go the way of the dog, Maude, come back to us.” Hildy smiled at me warmly. I looked at Zita, but she was staring at the floor.

CHAPTER FIVE

It was only when I was out in the cold in the middle of the main street that I realised I knew not where the whorehouse was. I looked up and down for a sign of disturbance. A sign of ... whoredom. But the town was empty. I had always thought of Watlington as a bustling hub of activity. It was eerie being in the streets with no carriages, no people. There were no stalls, no peasants spruiking cherries and apricots. Just darkened doors and empty streets with upturned cobbles. I decided to turn left, towards what seemed to be the seamier end of town. I took an educated guess and turned down Cock's Lane. There was movement and candlelight flickering down the other end.

There was no sign saying *Whorehouse* but the women within with their breasts out felt like sign enough. I drew my hood closer to my face and walked through the door I had opened as quietly as I might, careful not to touch anything with my bare skin.

It was like a tavern. With a bar and lots of chairs. A big fireplace. And music. It felt a bit like Court.

But ... the breasts. They were everywhere. I peered around the busy room looking for Annie, the Tawny Moor.

I moved further in. Squeezing in between fully erect men dancing around with no shame. Oh God. What if one of them touched me?

I found myself in the far corner of the room. I put my back to the wall and took a steadying breath, telling myself, The next time you will be in a room like this, you will be in Court, with a rounded belly and a lorded husband, and all would be right with the world, and never ever again would you have to witness inebriated men straddling working girls. Good God. I wished I could look at my feet, but I had to continue searching. I really didn't want to see a man with his codpiece unattached. What was this Godlessness? These women were wild, with no restraints, nothing contained them, not even their clothes.

"Darling girl."

I froze, my whole body taut.

"Are you looking for a lady tonight?" The woman was heavily rouged, with bright blue eyes. She looked friendly enough, despite her large breasts also not being contained in her bodice. She didn't even look surprised at my presence. Did women often frequent brothels?

"I'm looking for Annie, the Tawny Moor." Her eyes squinted a little. "I have money," I added.

She nodded. "You looking for her services?"

"In a way."

"I think she's just finishing up with someone, love. I'll let her know you're waiting."

I wondered if she was finishing up with my husband. I couldn't quite summon the strength to feel jealous. It had not been a nice experience.

I saw Annie immediately. Her skin was dark and she had long braided hair. She was speaking to an older woman, perhaps the owner of the brothel, but she must've felt my gaze upon the back of her head because she turned to me. My heart thumped. I thumbed the mushrooms in my cloak pocket.

"What can I do for you, my lady?" She had a Spanish accent.

"May we speak privately?"

"Of course." She gave me a broad, genuine smile. I tried to return the gesture and waited for her to lead the way, but she didn't move. She was still wearing her large, stunning grin.

"Where shall we go?" I pressed.

"We can go to my rooms." She stroked my arm. Her hands were so soft. We didn't move. "You going to make me be unladylike, my lady?"

"Excuse me?"

"It's not nice to make a lady talk about money out loud."

"I have the money." I showed her my purse. She studied it carefully, as though determining its weight. Decidedly pleased, she nodded and led the way.

The room she took me to was nice enough. It had a large bed and a tapestry hung in between two windows, but it smelt horrific. I actually gagged as she shut the door and the smell seeped into my nostrils. She didn't say anything. She just stared at me.

I took off my hood. Then quickly put it back, worried the smell of piss and vomit and God-knows-what might soak into my curls.

"Would you like to lie on the bed?" she asked, sitting on the mattress herself.

Just speak, Maude, you don't have another option. I swallowed. "My name is Lady Magdalen Beckett and my husband visits you."

Her face changed drastically. She moved quickly past me to re-open the door she had so seductively just shut.

"I'm afraid you are mistaken, my lady. I've never met your husband before."

Shakily, I walked over and put my hand on the door. Pushing it closed. I heard her take a deep breath, like she was about to scream.

"I want your help," I said quickly. She paused, lungs full of air. "Zita and Hildy sent me."

She let the air out slowly. Blowing it in my face. It smelt sweet, like apples.

"Why would the wisewomen send you to me?" She crossed her arms.

"Because my husband is about to annul our marriage."

"It is not because of me! He's not in love with me or anything of that sort!" She was intent on defending herself. "He couldn't be with a girl like me, I'm a Moor." She was playing with her hair. "And a whore!" she added as an afterthought.

I shook my head. "He thinks I'm a witch." She cocked her head and looked me up and down. "I want to pay you to give him this." I got out the diced-up mushrooms. "Do you think it possible? You just need to put them in his drink."

"So you are a witch?" She was sporting a sideways grin.

"I bought these from the witches. I am not personally a witch. I am a lady, with a good family name, and a fertile belly. I don't deserve his accusations."

"Well, obviously you've deserved them somehow." My face must've looked so pitiful, so sad, that she actually came forth to embrace me. "Forgive me, peach." She wrapped her arms around me and held me tight, seeming to suck the tension out of me. I felt myself fold into her arms. "I suppose once we get labelled something, we become it one way or another," she murmured, releasing me. I wiped my eyes of my tears.

"Will you do it?" My voice broke.

"You know he is paying me good money every single night? If your mushrooms work, then I'll be losing a client."

"He is waiting to hear news as to whether I am with child. If you do not help me with the mushrooms then I will tell him tomorrow I am not pregnant and he will leave." She tapped her foot, thinking. "Will you do it?" I repeated.

"Yes, my lady, I'll do it."

I exhaled. "When will you next expect him?" I asked, preparing myself to leave.

She cocked her head to one side. "He's here."

"What?"

"Ye didn't see him? He's at the bar with his kinsmen; he likes to drink himself under the table before he fucks."

"Christ."

"So do you want to do it tonight?" she asked after a while.

I nodded.

"Why don't you sit in here?" She had walked over to a large trunk that stood at the end of the whore's bed. She opened it and started pulling out dresses and sheets and what looked like a horsewhip. She shoved them under the bed. "I'll knock on the door when I bring your husband in. You shut the lid, and then I'll give him your drink."

I looked at the trunk. "How will I know when to come out?"

She bit her full lips. "I'll leave the room after I've given him the drink. You'll hear the door shut." I nodded slowly. "You sure you want the man to be your husband, love?" She touched my arm. "He isn't good in bed, and I be knowing when it comes to people's souls and he's let the Devil sit in his for far too long."

My whole body convulsed in shivers. "How do you know?"

"I be knowing."

"That's not an answer."

She led me over to the trunk. I stepped into it. "Women have to trust their feelings. Sometimes, we just know things."

I had been sitting in the trunk for a half an hour. I had taken off my head cap and was wearing it like a mask around my face, so I breathed in the scent of cotton, not the scent of the excretions. Perhaps Annie hadn't managed to convince him to tup. I stood. It would be morning soon and I couldn't walk back home in the daytime ... I needed to leave. What an absurd night. I took one step out of the trunk and there was a knock on the door. Good God.

I squatted myself down and let the lid fall on top of me as gently as possible. Perhaps I would be sick in there and then I could swim in actual vomit, an upgrade from simply bathing in the odour.

"Lemmmmma touch your soft skin, Annie the tawny bore." I heard him knock into something.

"You can touch whatever you want, my lord." I heard the heavy sinking of bodies on to the bed. Was she going to do as I asked? Had she tricked me? "You just gotta be drinking this drink. Gives your friend a little bit of help." I heard him giggle like a young boy.

"Is not as easy when you drunk a whole barrel."

"This will help him out. Why don't you drink this?"

"It has bits in it!" He sounded like a child. "You know I don't like bits!"

"If you want to have any fun tonight, you need to drink the bits." I heard a guttural spluttering sound.

"Good boy. Now I'm going to fetch you a little surprise."

"What sort of surprise?" His voice had changed; it was harsh.

"Trust me." Her accent was smooth, convincing. "You won't be disappointed."

The door shut. I heard the sound of goblet on bench. I waited a few moments. The witches hadn't told me how long it might take for the potion to take its effect.

How had it come to this? I pushed open the lid.

I stood, standing in the trunk at the end of a whore's bed, staring at my naked, drunk and now, God willing, bewitched husband. My tears fell, inexorable. This was not the life I had envisioned.

My husband had not been surprised by the emergence of his wife from the trunk at the end of the whore's bed. He merely blinked as though something had got in his eye. He blinked again.

"Magdalen?" he said eventually.

"Maude," I whispered.

"You know your father told me you had light brown hair," he said conversationally. "Bloody liar." The mushrooms mustn't be working. "I can see now your hair is very dark indeed. But I like the way it curls," he added, nodding to himself.

I stepped out of the box, tripped on the lip, and hit the floor with a loud thud.

He came to me, taking me by the elbow and bringing me to the bed. He sat me down and began playing with my hair. It was working. His eyes were glazed, not just from alcohol but from something else ... from magic, I supposed. I let my hand go up to his cheek and he melted into my fingers, pleasured at my touch. This was how our wedding night should have been.

"Magdalen," he whispered. Poor enchanted boy. He began tracing my face shape with his fingers. "Your skin is nearly as soft as Annie the Tawny Moor's, and she has the softest skin in all the land."

"Thank you," I whispered. I was sweating but also shivering.

"I don't care if you're a witch." He was kissing my fingers.

"I'm not."

"I don't care."

"No ... no. I'm not." I took my finger out of his mouth and he looked like a baby who had been told to stop sucking. He grabbed for my hand again.

"Let me have you."

"I am bleeding," I told him. Feeling myself blush.

"I don't care. Let me have you. We must be one. We are one."

He was grabbing at me; the elixir seemed to have entirely possessed him now. His eyes were more manic and he looked at each piece of me with obsession and desire. He was overcome by a mind that was not his own. "I'll do anything to have you."

How long did they say this would last? An evening? Was I going to have to keep giving him the mushrooms? With every meal? For our entire married life? I stood and let him undress me. I guess it wouldn't be too hard to give it to the kitchen staff and have them put it in his mead. He was constantly muttering praise about each of my parts. My skin, my skin was so soft. My hair, so ringletty. He had never seen such perfect hands. Or more supple breasts.

But just one mistake, one slip-up, one day when he didn't want mead, then he would see me for who I was. He might imprison me. Murder me. Divorce me like the King. When my skirts fell in a pool around me, he caught sight of my mark.

"This." He bent down between my legs. I let out an audible

sob, but he was so transfixed upon my mark that he did not notice. I shook with fear and sadness and shame. "It looks like a river … a winding river that goes all the way up the inside here" – his fingers tickled my inner thigh as he tracked the shape up my leg – "and then pools out here, in a lake." His hand brushed through my private hairs. "It is magic," he said in awe.

Time stood still. I looked at him, hand on my lower belly, caressing the thing that had destroyed my life, that repulsed him and ruined my week-long marriage. He didn't move. Like God had given me extra time to assess the situation, and he was frozen in a moment.

This was all I ever wanted.

But it was not real.

It was forced, by the means of which I was accused. If I lay with him, he would regret it. His tenderness for the rivers that ran over my body was not real. It might as well have been the witches themselves who knelt before me. Because it was their doing. Not Edward Beckett's.

If I lay with him, it would be some sort of perverted rape. He did not deserve me. He did not want me.

"I cannot do this," I whispered down to him. My small words triggered time. Seconds trickled by once again.

He looked up at me like a dog, begging from the dinner table.

"What, wife?"

"You do not want me. I am a marred woman."

"I want all of you. I want you to bear my children. I want to parade you around Court. I want you tonight and all the nights after this." He got distracted momentarily by the clothes tucked under the bed, he reached for them, intensely interested in the fabrics. Smelling them, fingering them.

He was not in his right mind. After this had worn off he

would want anything but to see me again. I began redressing myself. His attention came back to me.

"Magdalen! Magdalen! Don't leave me! Let me gaze upon you a moment more! Please!"

Why was it so hard for people to call me Maude? I walked away, pulled the door open and saw Annie, leaning against the corridor wall. She cocked her head.

"He hates me," I told her. Edward had followed me to the door and now fell at my feet, still naked, muttering my name repeatedly.

"It does not look to be the case."

"He will hate me in the morning."

"They all hate me in the morning." She was watching the man-child mildly as he clawed at my legs, half sobbing, half laughing, begging me not to go.

"Why do you do it then?" I asked.

"Because it pays for my dresses."

I tried to shuffle myself away from Edward, but he was attached like a limpet.

"Will he pay for your dresses?" Annie asked, now petting the distressed Edward on the head.

"I suppose he would have."

"I'm her husband!" giggled the fully grown naked man on the floor. "I will buy you anything, and you will be the most beautiful women in all of Court and even the King will be envious."

"Ahhhhhh," cooed Annie. "He will pay for a lot of dresses."

"He is bewitched."

"He is an arsehole," Annie confirmed, with a nod. I wanted her to tell me what to do. "A bewitched arsehole," she mused, her soft accent rolling over the words. "That is two reasons to walk away right now."

It was all I needed. I gave her a firm nod, and she bent down and physically detached my husband from my dresses.

"Magdalen!" he bellowed down the hall, and I ran fast, tripping over my half-done-up dresses, and then I ran home, the whole way home. A lord's daughter, dresses undone, reeking of the whorehouse, running in the early-morning light.

CHAPTER SIX

I didn't sleep. I just waited on my bed until I heard people getting up, then I made my way downstairs.

"I have bled."

My oldest brother, Edmund, dropped a piece of bread on the floor.

My father stood up from his chair as if he had sat on something prickly.

Thomas made a gagging noise.

I didn't have time to register the others' reactions, but I felt them all — furious.

"Are you sure?"

I stared at my third oldest brother, Paul. "Do you want to personally check?"

There was an uproar. Several more brothers were on their feet, people were arguing now. Several were yelling at me directly.

"Will he definitely call for an annulment?" my father asked above the rest.

Charles, a friend of the Beckett family, piped up. "I have no doubt."

"On the grounds they did not lie together?" my father asked. I beckoned a servant to bring me wine and food.

"Yes. He will claim it was not consummated."

"And presumably that she is a bewitcher?" added John, his long nose crumpling at the word. I lay back into the wooden winged chair and put my dirty feet up onto a stool. I watched as my future whirled around me, spat out of different men's mouths. I didn't care. Decide for me. Fix it. I was too tired.

"Was it consummated? I'm confused," asked someone, I couldn't tell their voices apart anymore.

"Yes, it was consummated," I said, staring at the ceiling.

"Are you lying?" demanded my least favourite, Thomas.

"You watched, you pig!"

"I didn't see the specifics."

"Oh my God."

"We could get a physician to prove she is no longer a virgin?" suggested one of the twins. That sounded unpleasant and mortifying.

"This isn't worth the fuss. Leave the Beckett family be. Let him annul the marriage, and we will tell him we won't put up a fight if he doesn't defame our family."

Murmuring of agreements.

The second twin spoke up. "Hear, hear. It's not worth saving this marriage. We have good enough connections with the Becketts through my own marriage."

"What shall we do with her now?"

Silence.

I did not need to be a part of this conversation. I turned to my mother. Her eyes were shut.

"I'll be in my room," I told her. Nobody acknowledged I had spoken. My feet were filthy. I should've gone to my chamber as I promised. I should've bathed and got changed, but I hadn't the energy to get back up the stairs. I sat down, ignoring the servants' stares, and leant my head against the door to the Great Hall. I could hear my family's anger, their fear, reverberating through the oak.

One of my brothers was pacing up and down the hall, probably Edmund. He was husband to Edward's sister. This was awkward for him.

I wondered if Edward would tell anyone what had happened last night. I wondered if he would even remember it. Either way, I was unsure he could harm me more than he already had. I would be sent off somewhere now. Maybe married to a farmer. Or perhaps a nunnery, or maybe I could go to a distant relative in the country and be their child's carer. Whatever would happen, I did not have long left in this house.

Nun, nanny, nimwit. Whatever I was to become, I would never show my mark to anyone else ever again. I would hide it under layers and layers of dress and I would continue life as a perfectly normal, albeit disgraced, woman.

I fell asleep, head dropping suddenly into my own lacking bosom. I did not fight it.

The door banged open into my back, shifting me across the floor and nearly flattening me against the stone wall. I made a small noise, but my father didn't realise I was there. My brothers tailed after him, still shouting opinions in his wake.

There were so many of them. How come not one was on my side? How come none of them wanted to make sure I was well?

I felt my mother's presence in the door frame.

"You are blessed, child." My mother had seen me. She noticed everything. Though, admittedly, she had missed how incredibly un-blessed I am.

"What have they decided?" I asked, still pressed between door and wall.

"Well ..." She stared in the direction of her recently departed boys. "You were very nearly sent to a nunnery." My heart turned over. "But that is Catholic, and disgraceful." I breathed a slow sigh of relief. "I believe they want to send you far away. To a farm. With a boy who requires no dowry."

"To be married again? I cannot, Mama!"

"Go to your room, Maude."

I stood and stared at her. She had used my name.

"Go."

I needed to find the smallest space possible. My den under my bed was too big. I needed to sit in my clothes trunk and shut the lid and stay there forever. My coffin.

I am so disgraceful. I am so disgusting. I opened the trunk, filled with neatly folded underclothes and some of my older dresses. It smelt a lot better than the one at the brothel. I started pulling at the cloth, wrenching the pieces out of the trunk. I was crying out loud. I could hear myself, wailing like a banshee. Christ, I was a weak child. I could see my tears, creamy from my face powder, marking the dresses. Shoes were at the bottom. I grabbed a pair and threw them into the unlit hearth. I wondered how long until someone came to tell me to be quiet.

Finally, an empty trunk. I got in and curled up and then, careful not to trap my fingers, let the lid close over me. Darkness wound its way around me like a blanket. I exhaled. My tears stopped. I would stay there forever. When I was younger I had been afraid of a monster that lived in the trunk at the end of my bed, but it was just me. I had ended up being the thing I feared.

I rolled over onto my side, my shoulder brushing my coffin

lid. I was not sure whether my eyes were open or closed, but I felt myself drifting to sleep.

The heavens opened. I had been asleep long enough to have woken up panicked at least half a dozen times. But now, light poured into my grave.

"What?" I managed. Blinking repeatedly.

"You're not dead yet." My eyes focused and I saw the flickering of candle, eclipsed by my mother's great belly. I sat up. My joints ached. "It is decided, Magdalen. The men want you married off to some lumpish hedgepig on a farm about ten miles south."

"Why marry me again?"

"This one won't care about your affliction." I gaped at her. "Fine: he'll care. But he won't divorce you for it."

"Edward hasn't even decided what he's going to do yet!"

"He's going to divorce you or annul the marriage; either way, you need a new husband."

"I will not go."

"You have no choice."

"*I will not go.*" Was I condemned to live in a loop of time where all that happened was men staring at my body, revolted and afraid?

"We tried to cover the mark with powder, Maude. You are what you are."

"No." She left the room. "NO!"

Jimmy meowed loudly in my defence.

I wouldn't. It wasn't a question in my mind. I wouldn't be shipped off to a life in the muck, with the dirt and the peasants. We hadn't heard from Edward yet, so we didn't know what he would do. But I wouldn't set foot in some poor man's house. A week earlier I was to be on my way to fucking Shropshire House, with a hoard of servants and all the dresses I've ever wanted. I was going to Court.

CHAPTER SEVEN

It was three days since they had decided my fate. I had conjured up dozens of plans in my mind. Few were executable, though one ambitious plan was to get Edward actually executed. My father's plans on the other hand had moved quickly, and consequently, I was standing at the front of Shirburn in a virginal blue dress, about to be packed onto my carriage and sent down south to marry my lumpish hedgepig. My body was shaking. I wondered if I'd rather die. I hadn't seen or heard from any of my brothers or my father. I may never see them again in all my life and they didn't give a sliver of a fuck.

My mother was looking at me. I wondered if she would kiss or embrace me in farewell. She did not. I could read her emotions easily, but I was never able to determine whether she loved me or not. "You shouldn't be wearing all those jewels, Magdalen. Give them to Agnes."

"I will be allowed some inch of dignity, Mother." I knew I looked ridiculous. I was wearing everything I could possibly fit upon my person: multiple necklaces, my biggest pearl earrings, my most lavish dress, Jimmy tucked under one arm. I wanted to remind myself of who I was. A lord and lady's daughter. I was meant for Court. Not for farmers.

Mother sighed. "Your father will be displeased." But she made no gesture to snatch my jewels. "I will write to you with any developments."

I looked at her. I was glad I hadn't inherited those thin lips, but I would do anything to stay with her and her perpetual bad mood.

"You are making a mistake," I reminded her.

"I will write," she said again.

I turned to the carriage. I made eye contact with John the groom, who nodded sheepishly.

"I expect I will be back very soon," I said to no one in particular. No one in particular replied. I got in the carriage. The wheels began to turn and I felt the ground slip out from beneath me. I sat down. My tummy was turning over and over and over also. With each turn of the wheel, I went around. It was nauseating. I wondered if I would be sick. I sat focused on the floor of the carriage for some time, trying to stem both my tears and the bile rising in my throat. The dirt road turned to cobbles. We were heading into town. There was a heavy lurch and my eyes widened in a panic. I was going to be sick.

"John!"

"My lady!"

"Pull over! Be quick!" The horses slowed and without waiting for John to open my door, I jumped out and sprayed my last supper all over the side of the road. A bit of chewed bread sat delicately on the petals of the wild carrot.

"Shall I fetch help, my lady?" John asked, giving me some distance.

I took a raggedy breath. "I've heard that the wild carrot flower has been renamed — they call it Queen Anne's Lace. They've named it after her." I wiped my mouth and looked up.

"I just vomited on the Queen's own flora." I tried to laugh, but it turned into a sob. I could not go through with this. I looked down the road we were destined to travel.

"John." Time to attempt one of my last-resort machinations.

"Yes, my lady."

I exhaled. In my bust, I had put coins. It would've been more than half a year's wage for John.

"If I give you thirty shillings, will you drop me off in town and pretend to have taken me to the farm?"

He stared at me, shocked. Unembarrassed, I put my hand down my dresses and reached for the purse of money. I had taken it from Thomas's coffers, but not even that could make me smile. I handed it to him.

"What if they ask me what happened?"

"Tell them you dropped me off. When they find out I'm not there, they'll just think I ran away after you left me."

He winced, but his eyes were fixed on the heavy purse in his hands.

After a long, long moment, he gave a small nod. "Where shall I drop you?"

"The apothecary," I said, hardly getting the words out.

I climbed back into the carriage for my short ride. Sometimes you just have to take things into your own hands. I knew what I was really destined for. Glory. Court. If I was shipped off to a farm, I'd be forgotten. I couldn't let it happen.

I looked out of the window, focusing intently on not throwing up again. In what felt like mere minutes we were stopped outside the apothecary.

I waited until John opened my door. He looked anxious, but he helped me down the carriage steps with a steady hand.

"I am indebted to you, John."

"What am I to do now?"

"Go use the treasure I gave you to eat and drink. Get a room and stay the night in the next town over." He was still looking upset. "Go, get my trunk down, and then leave."

It would've been around eight at night, not yet dark. I needed to get inside quick. I knocked on the door. Fucking hell. Lady Maude Beckett, seeking refuge in the witches' den.

Zita answered.

She looked me up and down. "We don't do refunds."

"I need help. I need to take you up on your offer."

"I offered you nothing."

"Hildy said that I might come here if I was in trouble."

"You do not look in trouble." She glanced at the obnoxiously sized ruby around my neck.

"You may have my pearl earrings if you let me stay."

"Stay?"

"I just need a place to stay for a little while. I'm in *trouble*," I repeated, damn tears coming to my eyes again.

Hildy poked her head around Zita's middle.

"Is that Maude? Come in, poppet. Come in!"

John followed us in with my trunk and laid it down.

"You may go, John."

"Good luck, miss." Miss? I almost chastised him, but I held my tongue. There were greater issues afoot.

"I need a refuge for a little while. I can pay you."

"Of course."

"No." Zita was shaking her head.

The two witches looked at one another. Zita began using her hands to speak to Hildy. Angry sharp gestures and then one final long finger pointing at me.

Hildy was a sweet, harmless-looking lady. I worried about her ability to fight for me.

"She stays." Hildy spoke clearly. Perhaps I need not doubt her.

"No, Hildy." More hand gestures. "No more strays." I looked down at Jimmy bundled up in my arms. This cat was pristinely bred! Hadn't been on the streets in his life. His supper consisted of meat and bread, for God's sake. I was about to defend him when Hildy spoke.

"She is not a stray." T'was I that they called the stray. Rude. "This is foreseen in the stars and the tea leaves."

I shuddered. I was foreseen? Zita had gone quiet at this. Hildy took hold of her hand. I wondered what their relation was. Sisters, perhaps. They were close.

Hildy rubbed Zita's hand gently, looking up at her with the most pitiful, sweet look. I watched Zita's tight lips quiver.

"I will not have it any other way." Hildy turned to me. "You may take refuge here, Maude."

I let out a long exhale. "I just need to hide for a few days, while I decide what to do."

Zita finally took her gaze off Hildy's face and turned to me. "You will not pay us with your Godforsaken jewels," she said. "We will give you board and some food, but stay up there and out of sight."

"We need someone to help us around the shoppe. You can work for us," Hildy said sweetly.

"No," Zita said.

Hildy's face melted back into that soft, pleading visage. "T'was written we would find a helping hand. I see it in my tea leaves each day. You have seen it in the stars. Maude is she. I am sure of it." Zita pinched the bridge of her nose. "Besides, my love — much as I adore you, your opinion matters not. This is my apothecary." Zita may have the temperament of the matriarch, but it seemed Hildy was in charge.

"You can have this ruby. It is worth the wage of three helping girls for an entire year." They would be a fool to refuse it.

"If you need sanctuary, you can help us in the shoppe," Hildy said again.

"I can't. I am not a witch." My pulse had ramped all the way back up: this was my punishment for disobeying my parents. This was the Devil's chosen path for me. He had led me straight to the witches' den, to become what I feared I truly was.

"Then you can leave." Zita moved to open the door.

I looked pleadingly at Hildy.

"What happened at the whorehouse, poppet?"

"I couldn't go through with it. It was false." She nodded empathetically. "He'll be getting a divorce, or an annulment, soon I expect."

"And what did your family want to do with you? They didn't send you here?" Zita asked.

"No. I came here on my own volition. They wanted me married to a farm boy."

"You couldn't abide that?"

"He'll think I am a witch too!"

"Why?"

"Probably because you're making me work as one at an apothecary!" I said loudly. Zita squinted at me. "My parents." I swallowed. "They will see the error of their ways soon. Farmers are below my station."

"You sound like your mother."

"Do you know my mother?"

"Of course I don't. But I know what all noble women are like. I see you. You are selfish, and blind to the real world."

Well, fuck. I put Jimmy down. He moved slowly to Zita, wrapping his tail around her ankle. Traitor. I didn't know what to say. I had nowhere else to go.

"We'll give you a room, food and protection, Maude; we just need a little help at the counter," Hildy said.

"As you wish." I breathed. "Thank you," I managed.

"We can discuss particulars in the morning." The two wisewomen led me through a door behind the counter. It was a small kitchen with a large fire and a cauldron. "Take your things to the second floor." Hildy indicated the small staircase to the left. "There is a spare room." I looked at my heavy trunk. I would not be able to take it up there by myself.

"Try," said Zita, reading my mind like the demon, witch, horrid woman she was.

I grabbed the handles at both ends and lifted. Christ. I had to stop five times on the short staircase. Zita followed me, watching without words. The room they had spare was clearly for storage. It was filled with trunks, bottles and plants, but there was a mattress in the corner.

"This used to be my mother's room," said Hildy, bustling in through the door with a cup of something steaming. She passed me the mug. "Ginger and honey." She smiled. "Do you want a candle?"

I shook my head. "I'm fine." I wasn't fine. I did want a candle. Who would want to spend their first night in a witches' coven without light? She went searching in a trunk and found a blanket, and placed it on the dusty mattress. "Do you need anything else?"

"I'm fine," I said again. I looked to Zita. Her long and elegant body was framed ominously in the doorway. They couldn't be sisters. If they were, never had I seen two more different-looking siblings in my life.

"Well, good even, poppet." They left.

The only light in the room came from a half-clouded moon. I hit my head violently on a low roof beam and spilt half my hot water all over my hands and the floor. I hated myself for not having accepted the candle. Gingerly, I navigated my way. There was only one point in the room where I could stand up straight: right in the centre of the chamber. "Jimmy?" I whimpered. I could hear his light padded feet wandering around somewhere, but I couldn't see him. I bent down and moved to the corner of the room, where I sat on the filthy mattress. I put the blanket over my knees. I wouldn't be able to get out of this dress without help. I had expected there to be help. It smelt funny in there. "Jimmy?" I called again, hoping he noticed the pain in my voice. He brushed past my leg. I exhaled and scooped him up, sitting him in my lap. His soft touch released something in me, and no amount of pride could stifle my wails. Who cared what the witches thought anyway?

After a while the sobs softened down to a steady but less aggressive flow of tears. I laid myself sideways and trapped my poor cat in an iron grip. He didn't seem to mind. Agreeable fellow.

The house creaked. I could hear things happening outside and the roof seemed to compress and release as if it were breathing. I thought I could hear someone coming up the stairs. I pulled the blanket up higher.

"Maude?" It was lucky Hildy had such a recognisable voice or I would've screamed.

"What?" I shouted, and the door creaked open.

"I think you do need this." She was holding light, but it was not a candle. It was a red orb.

I shook my head frantically. I didn't need demon work in my room.

"It's nothing Devilish," she said, reading my mind like a demon. "The candle is within a glass sphere, and like the windows of a church it gives off a soothing warm light. It will calm your troubled soul and let you sleep." She placed it at the foot of my bed. The red light bounced softly off the wooden floorboards. She clambered her way over to me and sat down on the edge of my bed. I whimpered in fear, but the sound fell on her deaf ears. She placed a hand on my head and I felt my body uncurl. She must have cast a spell, but as my body unravelled, I did not care. This spell was a good spell. She patted me, just like I patted Jimmy. She stroked my hair, and I stared at the soft light flickering off the walls and then I wasn't staring anymore.

I woke, and I had to remember.

Jimmy was nestled in the huge folds of my skirt.

I lay there for a long time.

Jimmy did too.

I had no one but myself.

And Jimmy.

I wondered if I cut my entire leg off, would I be more marriable? I wondered if I could still have baby boys if I had one leg.

But it wasn't just my leg. It was all over my tummy too. I couldn't live without a tummy, let alone have babies.

My breathing was laboured from having to sleep in a corset. I tried to fill my lungs with air. I couldn't. But I would be fine. I didn't need to take a full breath. I stared at Jimmy, who was playing lazily with a thread come loose from my skirt.

With some effort, I sat myself up and stooped over to look out of the window. I watched as people walked by and entered the apothecary. They were a varied bunch of customers, of all ages, men and women. Some offputtingly poor-looking, some more respectable. After I had seen a dozen patrons enter and exit below, my tummy rumbled so loudly it gave me an actual fright. Jimmy and I ventured downstairs into the kitchen-cum-Great Hall.

Zita was sitting at a small table in front of the hearth. She was stirring a pot on the fire with one hand, and she gazed at me intently as I entered. "There're food scraps in the garden." She pointed to the back door. Holy shit: I was to be treated like a stray dog. "For Jimmy," she added. "There's bread here for you." She gestured in front of her. I tore myself a large chunk and slathered it with thick yellow cream. She kept stirring and staring. It was unnerving. I opened the back door in search of Jimmy's scraps.

My mood shifted for the first time in days. I felt a lightness in my chest and a small smile tug at my cheeks. A kitchen garden was sprawled out before me in undulating thickets of different plots and plants. The witches were keen gardeners. I scooped Jimmy up under my arm and we followed the small pathways in between the raised garden beds of tall bean stalks and cabbage and carrots. Big bumblebees accompanied us on our tour. I smelt and tasted herbs I'd never seen before. These women just got to do whatever they wanted to do — they got to tend their garden and dirty their nails in the earth. I felt a strange surge of envy within me. I chewed on some mint. The sun shone. And for a moment, it didn't matter that I was in a witches' garden; I was just happy to be outside in the sun.

There was a splash as someone poured out their chamber pot. It broke the mood. I looked up at the back of the houses; we were in a long line of timbered buildings, the black criss-crossing beams stretching all the way up the street, interrupted by the small stone apothecary wedged between the neat modern homes. The woman who had thrown the chamber pot of piss was watching me. I was holding a black cat, in the witches' garden. At any moment I could cast a spell or disappear altogether. I was almost tempted to stretch my hands in the air and yell some sort of gobbledygook. I refrained. I found the bowl of scraps by the back door and re-entered their not-so Great Hall, plopping Jimmy and his food on the stone floor.

"How did you sleep?" Zita asked.

"Fine." I took another hunk of bread.

"Is sleeping in a corset and fine jewels a courtly beauty regime?"

I winced and took another large bite. "Where's Hildy?" I asked, not really interested.

"She's with a patron. She'll be here in a minute and we may talk about how this will work."

"We won't need to discuss anything, I don't think."

"Why is that?"

"Because I will be leaving soon."

"And where are you going?"

"Back to my family, I would think."

Zita nodded. She didn't look disbelieving, but she wasn't convinced either.

"I was born a Shaftsberry, and I still hold my status. I still have my mother's potency for child bearing. This has been an unfortunate week, but I have thought it over and they need time to reconsider, to brush off the drama. They will call me home soon enough."

She nodded again. "That might be true, Maude."

"It is."

"Very well. But whilst you stay in our apothecary, you work for us."

Hildy walked in. Her face was covered in blood.

I took several steps back. "God save you!" I gasped. She went to the bucket of water in the kitchen garden and splashed her face. She left the door open, and a warm breeze came through.

Zita signed to her as she came back in, speaking at the

same time. “Maude wants to know why you have blood on your face.”

Hildy smiled. “A vigorous leeching,” she explained. “Sometimes when you try and remove them, they get very sucky.” She made a noise with her mouth that was incredibly unpleasant and then she giggled. She was undeniably sweet. She sat next to Zita and placed a hand on her knee.

“We were thinking you could sit at the front of the shoppe, Maude? Help people with simple requests for herbs and ointments?”

“No.” I shook my head. This wasn’t debatable. “I would be recognised.”

“I doubt it,” said Zita. “Yours is not a well-known face. If we get you some more modest clothing and perhaps let your hair down, you won’t look anything like a lord’s daughter.”

“No.” I clutched at my skirts.

“Maude?” Hildy’s high-pitched voice stilled the small room. “Maude, would you like to tell us why everyone thinks you are a witch?”

Unexpected tears started flowing from my cursed eyes. Bewitched tears. She made me cry. Hildy made me cry. And they were unstoppable. She stood and came to me, and she put a hand on the small of my back and guided me into a seat.

“No,” I said eventually. I wondered if either of them had a mark like mine.

The witches glanced at one another.

“I’m going to explain the day-to-day workings here, Maude. All you have to do is listen.” Hildy was stroking my arm gently. “We are an apothecary. People come here for lavender to sleep, rose oil for skin ailments. Basic cures for basic ailments. People come here to see me for my expertise in the humours and the corporeal body. People come to see Zita for her astrological knowledge.” Hildy was smiling at Zita, pride emanating from her soft blue eyes. "Zita of the stars," she added. "People also come for charms and problems with poltergeists and what-not. Neither of us are experts in that field but we do what we can."

I shuddered but didn't try to stop Hildy's soft petting.

"Hildy uses the room with the hanging garden, and I use the smaller room next to hers for my practices," Zita added. "Do you have questions?"

I had quite a lot of questions.

"Do you call yourself witches?"

"Witches, white witches, wisewomen, healers, charmers, astrologers, apothecaries," Zita said, taking the pot off the fire. "But yes."

"If you're witches, why don't you fix Hildy's hearing?" There was a silence. I blushed. That had not been an appropriate question.

"We have tried to fix Hildy's hearing. We have done everything we thought sensible. And when nothing worked, we sought other people's sensible. When that gave us nothing, we resorted to the insensible. We blew trumpets in her ears, we have poured oil and honey, vinegar and garlic juices down there. One wizard attempted to drip a mixture of eel fat and human blood into her ears."

"No!" I gasped.

"I lost my hearing for a reason, Maude," Hildy said, smiling. She took my hands and put them over her ears. "Without my hearing I see more clearly." I didn't know what she meant, but I didn't ask her to elaborate.

"Next question?" Zita asked.

This question was one I'd been thinking about for a while, but I was nervous about asking it.

"Do you ... do you lie with demons?"

Zita signed the question for Hildy, finishing with a

horrible, horned, manic impression of a demon's face. Hildy laughed. I almost joined her in her mirth, her laugh tinkled so prettily around the not-so Great Hall, joining the streams of sunlight that came through the window.

"No, no, no, there is no Devil here; only learned women. We do not lie with demons," Hildy explained, still laughing. "I lie with Zita."

I looked between the two of them, back and forwards.

"How?" I asked eventually.

The shoppe door banged open and the bell rang out manically. "WITCHES!"

CHAPTER EIGHT

A very stout woman with wild greying hair and mad eyes was stomping her foot on the ground in the middle of the shoppe. I peered at her from the slit in the doorway.

"This bloody charm didn't ratting work!" She was stomping on the charm. I could see it now. A small piece of parchment.

"Madam Muggleton," said Zita firmly. "What's wrong?"

"I went to the wizard." She said the last word with such vitriol it sounded like a curse.

The witches nodded sympathetically. Hildy beckoned me forwards, indicating that I could take a seat on a tall stool behind the counter. I shook my head furiously.

"What did he give you?" Zita asked. Madam Muggleton reluctantly stopped stamping, revealing the now tattered piece of paper.

"He said it was a charm. He said it'd be better in four nights' time."

"How long has it been?" asked Zita, trying to decipher what was written on the paper.

"Seven long nights! And I've seen each night all the way

through. I can't sleep, I can't work. It feels like the Devil's made camp in the back of my Godforsaken mouth."

"It's a toothache," Hildy confirmed.

"Do you know what the charm reads, Madam Muggleton?" Zita asked, looking at the piece of parchment with a raised brow.

"I can't bloody read." She was holding her cheek; the woman looked in a horrible amount of pain.

"Did he tell you what it said?"

"He just said it was magic words. They look like magic words, don't they?"

"Can you make this out, Maude?" Zita opened the door to the not-so Great Hall and pulled me out into the apothecary, where Madam Muggleton looked shocked to see me. I stood up tall and took the piece of paper from Zita, flattening it out on the gnarled wooden counter.

It was Latin.

There were only three words, though they were all smudged with a bootprint. *Disce Legere Porce.*

I looked to Zita, then to Hildy. I gave the tiniest shake of my head. I didn't want to say it out loud.

"Let's get you some ointment and relieve that pain, Madam Muggleton, then we might need get in contact with the surgeon." Hildy took her into her room with the forested roof. She shut the door.

"What does it say?" Zita asked, looking down her nose at me. "My eyesight is failing me."

"It says, *Learn to Read, Pig.*"

Zita let out a small hissing noise. "I swear one day I will curse his horse and ask my father to personally haunt him."

I crossed myself unconsciously. "Why would the wizard do this?" I asked, watching Zita burn the charm with a thick-wicked candle.

"Reggie is a toadspotted weed, who calls himself a wizard, but he is nothing of the sort. Only women are magic, Maude. Men are just coming along for the ride."

"I didn't know that."

She let the ashes float to the floor. "Reggie claiming he has divine power is like saying he's given birth to children. And even if somehow he produced a child, you would know he's stolen the poor thing from a distressed mother, who's probably crying into her pillows a mile down the road." She dusted off her hands. "Reggie was a priest. He used to visit us, had problems with his prick. Then one day, after his congregation dwindled to too few, he decided he could dispense magic himself. Now he spends his days writing insults on parchment and selling them to people who can't read."

"UnGodly."

"Indeed. He is far more a Devil than all the demons I've personally met."

I recoiled; why did she keep saying horrid things like this?

The door to the shoppe opened. "Ah, Goodman White! Just in time." A very, very elderly man, with a back so bent he looked like he was about to ram someone head first, craned his neck upwards to look at Zita.

"The planets have got a lot of explaining to do!" he barked, waddling off to Zita's room. He slammed the door shut with surprising strength. I looked to Zita.

"I swear to Christ that man has his own personal planetary system where nothing is ever well aligned," Zita muttered. She turned to me abruptly. "All the oils and ointments are labelled. I run an organised ship." She pointed to a large scroll of parchment to my left. "This is Hildy's scroll; it details the remedies you can dispense."

I unravelled it.

Moist nose — The hot oil. Expels all moistness.

Aching in head — Sage lavender potion. Five drops in hot water.

Aching in stomach — Chamomile and ginger. Three drops in hot water.

The list went on, matching each of the glass bottles that were stoppered and stacked around the front room.

"If you have any questions, ask Hildy."

My tummy was turning. "What?"

"All you have to do is sit here, and if you're confused, just talk to Hildy or me."

"No. I won't do it." I stood up from the stool, swallowing. "I'm a lord's daughter. It is not good for my prospects to sit here, especially not when I've been accused of being like you!"

She held up her hand. My back straightened as if a bolt of lightning had been struck down it.

"Keep your eye out for miscreants stealing tinctures. We've had a group of young men coming in to steal the hardening mixtures."

"I won't! I will be in my rooms."

"Room," she corrected. That lumpish, rump-fed harpy! "It's not hard. Just sit here, and make sure the Randy Gang don't come in."

"Zita!"

She followed the old man into her room.

I sat down on the floor behind the thick wooden counter, where no one could see me.

This was ridiculous. I was wearing damask, for Christ's sake. Though there was an unfortunate chance I was indeed a witch, I certainly wasn't a shoppe girl. I wouldn't. I got up and went into the not-so Great Hall and ate more bread, staring out of the small paned window into the rapidly declining day. The sun was clouded over. I couldn't see a single bumblebee. I watched Jimmy lash out at the far inferior fly.

I needed parchment — I needed to write to Mother. I wondered when they would receive word I had not been delivered.

The door tingled. I felt a wave of nausea. I sat still, listening. I could hear quick steps against the stone. Christ. I got up and went back into the shoppe. Sure enough, two boys, perhaps fifteen years of age, were searching the shelves in a very deviant way.

"Oi!" I snapped. They jumped. "Get out!"

"Who are you?" said the one with missing teeth.

"Who do I look like?" I demanded, swooping my skirts about dramatically. "Leave!" I grabbed a broom with craggy snapped sticks from where it rested near the counter and began waving it, hitting their bottoms and sweeping them out of the door. They ran straight into another patron. Oh God. This customer was about my age. A farm girl, judging by the cowshit on her smock. She stared at me for a good long moment. I tried to read her expression. She was confused. Did she know who I was?

"Good morrow; is Hildy in?"

"She is with a patron. What seems to be the problem?" My damn voice shook.

"Can you help me, my lady?" She knew who I was, or perhaps she was just playing it safe, what with all the fucking pearls encrusted into my dress. I think my lips were quivering.

"What seems to be the problem?" I asked again.

"Got a runny nose." She shrugged. "Mother sent me. Said she wouldn't have me sniffing around her no more."

She needed hot oil. The one that expels the moistness. I flipped over the parchment and checked the list to confirm my suspicions. Correct. I went to look on the shelves.

"You need to take this."

"How much?"

"A few drops in hot water will dry it up." Sounded like it could be right.

"Thank you ..." She seemed to be searching for a way to address me. "I'm sorry, my lady. I don't know who you are, so I'm not sure how to address you."

I let out a slow breath. "You can just call me Maude."

"Oh." She was taken aback. "It was just your dresses. They're ..." Her eyes widened as she ran her eyes over the jewelled dress. "You look so beautiful."

I smiled. I had not been expecting this exchange. "Thank you, goodwoman. But I'm just your humble apothecary." I thumbed my ruby pendant. She was still perplexed but we exchanged coin and she left.

My first sale.

"All well, Maude?" Hildy escorted Madam Muggleton out of the shoppe.

"I just sold a vial of the hot oil." I picked up Jimmy and kissed his little head, smelling his fur.

"Indeed! Were her humours wet?"

My cat wiggled out of my grip and fell onto the floor, with my heart. Had I done something wrong?

"I don't know. She had a runny nose," I said defensively.

"Then it was a perfect diagnosis." Thank Christ.

"How much did you tell her to take?"

I clenched my jaw. "A few drops in hot water."

"How intuitive. That is exactly right."

"I know it was," I muttered under my breath, exhaling with relief.

"I was going to get myself some minty tea. Would you like a brew?"

"Is it magic?"

"Only as magic as mint is."

Was mint magic? "Very well," I said hesitantly.

She brought back a mug with the leaves and steaming water. "Zita's expecting a Thomas Spotter at some point, he's getting a palm reading. Will you send him through?"

I nodded, and she left.

It had been quiet for some time. I had fetched my needlework. I had decided I would become an expert at needlework in my time here, so it wouldn't be time wasted. I would use my time in this coven apothecary to become the courtier. The erudite Lady Maude. My hands were bleeding from where I had pricked myself, and the flowers I was embroidering looked like spiders, but I was practising. Practising for Court.

I saw a man approaching the door.

"Good afternoon, sir."

"Is that you, Lady Magdalen?"

Cock and balls. Thomas Spotter. Father Thomas! I really hadn't expected the priest of my parish to be visiting the witches for a palm reading.

"What in God's name are you doing here? Where is your husband?"

I had frozen. I didn't know what to do.

Why hadn't Zita fucking told me the fucking priest who fucking married me was going to fucking turn up for a fucking palm reading?

"My humours are wet," I whispered.

"Does your father know you're here? Do your brothers?"

"Well, why are you here, Father?" I asked defensively.

"I have a meeting with the wise woman Zita." He clasped his hands together. "To discuss her practices," he added lamely.

"Indeed."

I walked around the counter and knocked on the door. "Zita!" I bellowed.

Her door snapped open.

"Father Thomas is here!" I spat. She looked at me, confused. "A fun coincidence. We know each other! He sees my father weekly." I glared at her. "Fix this," I hissed under my breath.

"Just this way, Father Spotter," she said kindly, as if she hadn't heard me at all.

I snatched the ink pot and quill from the counter and sat on the floor behind it. This had been such a Godforsakenly ridiculous idea. I was in so much trouble.

I tore off a corner of the remedies list and wrote a line of poetry that had been floating around my head. *They Flee from me that sometime did me seek.*

"What're you doing?" I jumped out of my skin, spilling the pot of ink. I quickly righted it and looked up at Zita. I felt powerless, sitting cross-legged on the floor.

"Where is Father Spotter?" I demanded, keenly aware of the dark ink running across the floorboards.

"Who's down there?" The father's face appeared over the counter. "Good afternoon, miss!" he said joyfully. "Are you a new recruit?"

I looked to Zita, who gave me a tight smile. "She's our new apothecary, Father Spotter," she explained.

I sat very still. Confused, almost afraid.

"Well, I expect I'll see you again very soon, new apothecary!" His voice was very loud. Much louder than it had been before his reading. "Good day!" The doorbell jingled merrily as he left.

"Have you written on our inventory list?"

"Did you fiddle with the father's mind?"

"Did you blunt my quill with your fanciful, depressing line of poetry?"

"Did you bewitch a Man of God's senses?"

"Did you spill my ink, worth a half-shilling, onto my floors?"

"Did you erase the father's memory?" I stood. Speaking louder.

"You confess first," she demanded.

I took a deep breath. "Yes, I wrote an elegant, enjoyable line of poetry on the corner of your inventory list, blunting your quill and spilling your half-shilling of ink onto your apothecary floors." I crossed my arms. "Your turn."

"Yes, I fiddled with the father's mind. I put him into a little trance. No, he has no idea who you are, and I didn't erase his memory, I just muddled it a bit."

"Fine."

"Fine."

"What shall I do about the ink?"

"There's a cloth in the bucket outside and a stall for quills and new pots on Market Street."

"Fine."

"Fine."

We glared at each other.

CHAPTER NINE

Morning four at the apothecary. It was daybreak. I picked at the crumbling stone wall by my bed, irritated. I could hardly breathe. I was getting consistent pain in my ribs now, from the reed ribbing of my kirtle digging into my lungs. I also didn't smell like roses. I was used to smelling like roses. That, or lavender. I would put it in my baths and the scent would linger on my skin. Four days in heavy dresses in the hot final days of summer had done something about that. I had tried to get out of my dresses, but I had chosen to wear one that laced at the back. I really hated myself for that. Today, I was going to have to ask Hildy to help me out. She would only need to help me with the kirtle. Which meant nothing needed to be ... revealed. Still it made me sick with nerves.

I crept downstairs. I wanted to get Hildy on her own. No doubt Zita would have something abhorrent to say about it. I was hoping to catch her as she went about the garden collecting herbs for her tinctures. Sure enough, there she was, bustling around in the early morning sun. She was humming to herself; I wondered why she did that, when she couldn't hear her own song.

"Hildy!" I whispered, moving into the garden. Her eyes were focused on the herbs. I didn't want to frighten her, but I was unsure of how to get her attention. I waved my hands. Nothing.

"In situations like these, you have to approach her slowly and touch her gently on the arm."

Zita was in the doorway watching Hildy. Her bright blue eyes seemed almost kind, but then they snapped back to me. "But you will not disturb her. This is a sacred time for Hildy. This is part of her divine practice." She moved towards me. "You're filthy, Maude." She span me around and begun tugging at the string of my kirtle.

"I don't need your help!" I tried to shoo her away, but she held me still.

"I need help. I cannot be around you for another day with that smell. You will take a bath this morning too." I really did want a bath. I wondered if Hildy would give me lavender from her garden.

"Is it somewhere private?" I asked.

"It's just there." She pointed to a tub resting against the back wall of the apothecary.

"Why?" I asked, mortified.

"We heat the water over the fire in there," she gestured towards the kitchen, "and then we bathe in the garden. It's nice in the summer," she assured me. "In winter it is a little so-so. Put your hands over your head." I did as I was told and felt a great deal of relief having the heavy thing removed.

"I cannot bathe outside."

"Why not?"

"It is unGodly! People will see my nakedness!"

"No one is interested in your nakedness, Maude."

I wished that were true with my whole Maude heart. I put my arms around my tummy. I was completely covered, but I could feel a breeze around my midriff. I hardly liked the wind to touch my tarnished skin, let alone have the whole of Watlington see my mark.

"You don't understand." I tugged my kirtle out of her grasp and went inside.

I sat at the bottom of the stairs and stared at the flagstones. I should be with my husband, with my new household, in my new dresses. I should be telling my servants to fill my bath, to bring me the soaps and the perfumes, to brush my hair and prepare my jewels. Instead, I was a runaway, sitting in a witches' cave, in my underclothes, staring at the floor.

Fuck it. I would just make myself some sort of rose-smelling perfume and rub it all over my body. I didn't need a bath.

I looked up. Both witches were in the kitchen. "I need help." The words tasted sour in my mouth.

"I'm sure you can fill your own bath."

"I'm not talking about that, Zita. I need parchment, to write a letter to my parents. I won't trouble you much longer. I must contact them and tell them they need to take me back."

"Parchment?" Hildy confirmed with a hand signal. I nodded. "I have a small piece you can use."

"I also need some plain clothes to wear for the next few days."

"We have that too."

"I will give you payment in one of my earrings."

"We don't want your earrings, Maude," said Zita. "We want you to bathe."

"I won't bathe outside!"

Most high Lord and Lady Shaftsberry,
Hitherto I have not wished to let you know of my affairs here, but it will be obvious to you that I have run away, and was not delivered to Mr John Smyth safely. John the Groom is not to be blamed, as he did not know of my schemes. I am unharmed, but each day my troubles increase. You must find an alternate path for me, or else I will never reveal my hidden place and I may even cause you some trouble. You do not want people knowing about this unseemly situation.
You will send word of my annulment or divorce, and your plans to retrieve me by sending word to the Watlington town bellman, and I will seek him out and retrieve the message.
For my part, I pardon you of everything, and I wish to devoutly pray to God that He will pardon you also.
Lady Maude Shaftsberry

I hadn't actually pardoned them of anything, but I thought it would be good if I looked forgiving. That would be Godly. I also did not know of the farmer's name, but I supposed his name was probably John, and it seemed likely he had a poor and boring family name like Smyth. If I was wrong, they would know who I spoke of. I had given it to Hildy to find a messenger not an hour earlier, and I was already anxious to go and find the town cryer to see if there had been a response. But Hildy wasn't even home yet. I sat behind the counter, too nervous to sew. I played with the hem of my new apron. I was wearing Zita's clothes. They were light and didn't restrict me. I wouldn't tell her, of course, but it was comfortable. She had made me pour a floral oil all over myself before I was allowed to wear them, muttering something mean about my noble stench. I wasn't upset about it. I might not have actually been clean — but I smelt divine.

. . .

Two hours later, Hildy still wasn't home. I was passing time by flicking bits of straw off the counter for Jimmy to catch. Jimmy's presence really gave this place a sense of witchy authenticity. They should be thankful I came to stay.

The door opened. Finally.

"Hildy!"

She smiled at me. "Is Zita with a client?"

"Yes! Did you get the letter sent?"

"You must speak slower for me, Maude."

"Surely you know what I am asking," I said slowly, annoyed.

She smiled. "A traveller coming through town said he will deliver it. He didn't know who I was, so I don't think it will be traced back."

I breathed a huge sigh of relief. "Thank you, Hildy."

She touched her chin. "This is how you can thank me with your hands."

I copied the gesture. She winked at me. I smiled. It felt good taking action and sending the letter. I wasn't a pawn to be played off; I was Maude, maker of my own destiny.

Day nine in the apothecary. I came out of my room, Jimmy under my arm, my pearl earrings tangled in my hair reminding me of who I was. I had slept well, despite the fact I had no bed curtains and my mattress was a few inches away from the floor. I was surprised my eyes hadn't been eaten out by rats; I supposed Jimmy was to thank for that, my ward. *Your imp,* said Edward, who lived in my mind. I leant against the railing of the stairs and stretched. Surely Hildy would have got the morning bread by now. I was starving. If I had become

Lady Beckett, I would have made breaking of the fast formal. In the Great Hall. With lots of food. Not just bread, butter and a bit of sage.

I fancied a cup of that mint tisane, but I'd never had to put the pot on the fire before. I didn't want to get my white nightgown dirty, and I was afraid of burning or, God forbid, blackening my hands. My tummy grumbled uncomfortably. I had gone to see the town cryer every day since I had sent the letter. Yesterday I had only to appear across the square and he had shaken his head. I was expecting action. I thought I was a liability, something to worry about. They surely didn't want their only daughter wandering the streets at night. I could be killed! But I had not heard a peep. Mother would have read it, of course. She was only a half hour's walk away — she could've sent a hundred letters in the time that had gone by. Unless the traveller had got confused and taken it to someone else; how I hated that traveller!

No one was in the kitchen. I went to check the apothecary. It wouldn't be open yet, but I had heard them clinking away with the bottles and the herbs hours before dawn. Did the witches never sleep? I pressed my ears against each of their locked offices: no noise from within. I actually stomped my foot. Hunger did not bring out the best in me.

I sat on the small window seat, tucking my knees to my chest, staring out at the street, absent-mindedly watching people go by, hidden in the shadows.

When they came home, I was going to say to them, "Isn't there a spell to make bread at home?" Or perhaps, "Wouldn't flying be quicker?" I practised the jeering look that would accompany my witty attack. My tummy grumbled louder than ever.

There they were. Hand in hand. Pottering down Sheeps Street. Goddamn it, they were dawdling. I saw my bread under

Hildy's arm. I stood up and patted my curls down, pulling my cap tightly around my head. My hair had got bushier since arriving at the witches' den. It was wilder and harder to tame. I needed someone to brush and oil it.

The door clicked open and their shop bell rang. The noise sent a shiver down my spine.

"Good morning, Maude!" Zita smiled joyfully. Hildy made a half circle wave I recognised as her good morning symbol.

I returned it unthinkingly, then, remembering my anger, I opened my mouth, ready to spit my prepared poison.

"I see you've met the fairy," Zita said before I could speak. I looked at her, confused. She gestured behind me.

I turned around.

A very, very tall, very black man was sitting behind the counter.

"Jesus Christ!" I blasphemed, leaping away and behind the witches.

"Maude, this is the fairy. Hildy and I captured him this morning. Fairy, this is Maude." Zita said something to Hildy with her hands. The sign for fairy appeared to be the linking of thumbs and the twiddling of fingers.

"Have you been there the whole time?" I was clutching my chest, still hiding behind Hildy. I was in my nightclothes. My hair was only just under my cap. This was bloody indecent. The man nodded. "How did I not see you?"

"Because he's a fairy," Zita explained.

The big black fairy just stared at me with his bright eyes. Had he been watching me all morning?

"What do you mean he's a fairy?" I asked, preparing myself for some witchy bullshit.

"Sign as best as you can, so Hildy knows what you're saying, Maude."

I sighed, moved out from behind Hildy and made an

angry, questioning gesture with my hands and then pointed at the big black man in our house.

"We caught him," Hildy explained. "We put out a fairy trap last night. The usual fairy trap: bread, milk, custard. We laid it at the woods' end, and we found him in the early hours, eating it."

"And that makes him a fairy?" I tried to sign my sentence but Hildy didn't understand.

Zita answered. "Yes. We laid a fairy trap and we caught a fairy."

"He doesn't look like a fairy." I made a cross sign with my arms, pointed to my eyes and then joined thumbs and twiddled my fingers.

"All fairies look different. What matters is that we caught him, and now he will help us around the house. Like all good sprites."

"In return for custard," interrupted the fairy. His voice was deep, calm. He seemed mildly amused.

"Yes. You reach our top shelves, and we give you custard." Zita smiled.

"What's your name?" I asked cautiously.

"Something devious and curious, no doubt?" Zita predicted.

"My name is Rufus."

"Oh, very devious." Hildy muttered. Had she even understood what he said? Or was she just playing with me?

"Are you a fairy, Rufus?" I asked.

He glanced at the witches. He was far too big to be this shy. His head touched the ceiling — he had to bend himself down to stand.

His silence spoke for itself.

"I thought not."

Zita tutted. "You can deny your true nature all you want, fairy: we know the truth."

Honestly, it was like living with children.

"Where do you come from?" I asked. He could be a rapist or a Catholic, for all anyone knew.

"The Fairy Queen," Hildy answered for him.

This would get us nowhere.

"Can you go cut the bread, Hildy? I am starving and have been waiting to eat for hours and hours. Isn't there a spell to make bread from home?" I raised an eyebrow. Excellent delivery, Maude.

"Yes, but only witches can eat it," Zita hissed, taking Hildy by the hand and going out the back, leaving me with the big scary fairy.

"Rufus, where did you come from?" I asked again, covering my stomach; this was a very flimsy gown. He looked reluctant. "Did you eat the fairy bait?"

He held his chin high and then brought it down in a firm nod. "Yes."

I waited to see if he would say anything more. He didn't.

"Are you someone's servant?" I asked. No reply. "Have you run away?"

"I'm here now." His voice was deep. Reassuring and sonorous. "I will help the wisewomen. I'll get things off top shelves. Do fairy things."

"But you're not a fairy."

He shrugged again, lifting those big shoulders up and down. "Are you a witch?" he asked.

"Certainly not!" I snapped.

He chuckled softly. "Do you know a lot of Hildy's hand language?" he asked.

"I know a bit."

He moved from behind the counter. I took several steps back, but he wasn't interested in me, he was looking at the bottles of potions and remedies. "I will teach you the signs if you are to stay." He smiled and took a bottle of lavender oil and smelt it. "She can read your lips if you speak clearly. The gestures just make it a bit clearer." Perhaps Rufus would go out early to get me bread for when I wake. Maybe he would make me porridge.

"This is such a nice smell!" he remarked, surprised, re-stoppering the lavender oil. He would be my servant and my student.

"You should learn how to ask if Hildy needs help," I said clearly, imitating the voice of my old tutor.

He put down the vial and turned to me, paying attention.

"To say 'I' or 'me' you touch your chest." I demonstrated. "'Help' is like this." I gestured passing something to him with my hand. He repeated it easily. "Do both signs with a questioning face, she'll get what you mean." I hadn't exactly missed my younger brothers, but I had missed my older sister voice. I had missed bossing people around. Rufus nodded and went to investigate the not-so Great Hall. As he disappeared the doorbell jingled.

"We're not open!" I yelped, hastily following him into the back. I needed to get some fucking clothes on.

I sat at the tiny kitchen table; the back door was open onto the garden and the fields beyond. A cow grazed nearby, as though to eavesdrop on me. But I wasn't saying anything. I just tore at my bread and butter. Not even any sage today.

"You eat like a wolf," Rufus noted, sitting opposite me.

Slowly I looked up. His eyebrows were raised, probably anticipating a verbal beating from the look on my face.

"Zita!" I yelled. Rufus jumped. I got up, chewing viciously. I found her in the front of the shoppe.

"Maude?"

She was stewing something in the fireplace behind the counter.

"What role does this fairy play in this house? Is he beneath me?"

She stood up slowly. The pot bubbled dangerously, not quite unlike my temperament.

"What role does he play ...? That is a good question, Maude."

I squinted at her.

She put her hands on her very slight waist and looked beyond me. "From what I can tell, he's a guardian spirit. That's why he's used to this domestic home and why he will be useful around the apothecary. But I could be wrong. If he is a trooper sprite, we will know soon enough: he'll have stolen our drink and bewitched us all to dance. Have you felt the sudden, unprovoked urge to do the volta, Maude?" I made a dismissive noise but she ignored me. "If you're asking me whether he is beneath you, in a courtly manner, in a Shirburn Castle manner, if you are asking me whether he is less than you, because he is magical and dark of skin, then — no." She looked down her long, pointed nose. "I dub you of equal status. There is no difference between witches and fairies. We will treat one another equally."

"I am a lord's daughter, and that man is a vagabond." I had whispered it.

Zita stared at me, her lip curled.

"I think you should take that back," said Hildy, exiting her room. She had not even been in the apothecary when I had spoken, so how had she heard?

"How did you know what I said?" I snapped accusatorially.

"She saw the prejudice pouring out of your eyeballs." Zita's own eyes were dark, flickering with firelight. Hildy made a humph noise in agreement.

Spotted, toaded witches.

CHAPTER TEN

Each day that passed without hearing from my family worsened my mood. Which, to be fair, hadn't been great to begin with. It was a Sunday afternoon. The witches were busy. A bad bout of sniffly noses had taken over the village, and both Zita and Hildy were dispensing an array of different cures, raking in a small fortune for consultations, charms, potions and blessings. It was a wonder to watch them jingling with coin, brazenly asking for money. At first I winced when they'd tell patrons the prices, but the more acquainted I became with the process, the more fascinating it became. I liked to witness the exchange of the coin: it gave me tingles. Almost as though I were watching something Godly.

Today, they were letting me count the coin. I sat in the back and made Rufus sit out the front. I thumbed the coins over in my hands, making notes of the amount, and then placing them carefully into a pouch. Despite the witches' accusations that I was prejudiced and arrogant, I knew the ways of the world. I might not be wearing my full gowns, but I let Rufus see the way I held myself, and I hoped he was intelligent enough to know what I was. Peasants didn't hold themselves the way I did. I had made him sweep the apothecary floors multiple times today. I had watched him from afar and I had felt like the lady of the house for a solid few hours. I re-counted the coins, just in case. It was the same amount. I played with the riches for a little bit longer and then I had to admit that sitting in the not-so Great Hall all by myself was boring and the perfect environment for my sour musings to multiply.

I sneaked back out to be with Rufus. I told him he was to stand behind the counter, while I, a Lady, would sit and do embroidery, like I was in Court.

I was stitching my seventh rose. I hated roses. How could the ladies at Court do this day after day after day? I suppose they had good gossip to discuss, royal affairs to speculate over.

I looked up at Rufus, wondering if he had any ability to make good conversation. I pricked myself with my needle.

"Fuck!" I yelped. Rufus looked over at me, one eyebrow raised. Amused. "Stitching is boring!" I smacked down the stupid, strange-looking flowers. The thorns were almost as big as the petals. It looked all wrong of proportion. "These look like shit!"

Rufus looked over at my work. "They are shit." He nodded. "The thorns are too big."

I glared at him. The nerve.

Hildy glided out of her rooms. "I need lavender oil."

I turned to Rufus. "Get Hildy lavender oil," I commanded. "The one you like the smell of."

He nodded and went to peruse the bottles.

"Did I hear you say you're bored?"

I squinted at her.

"You're deaf!" I protested loudly. She grinned cheekily. "Are you deaf?" I looked to Rufus, but he was frowning in concentration at the dozens of small vials, not listening.

"I only say it because you're slumped over like someone has stabbed you in the back, and you've stitched seven roses, and each of them looks like shit."

"I think you can hear perfectly well."

"Pardon?"

I stared at her, mouth open, not sure whether to laugh or swear.

Hildy wriggled her eyebrows playfully. "Thank you, Fairy Rufus." She took the lavender oil. "Exactly the right bottle."

Rufus had a smile it was impossible not to mirror. It was infectious. I wondered how old he might be. Older than me, definitely. But it was hard to tell.

Hildy said goodbye to her heavily pregnant patient. Everyone always looked content when they left the shoppe and no one ever resisted parting with their coin when they paid.

Hildy sat with us for a while and began teaching Rufus a few more signs.

"Is it usual for Zita to be with someone for so long?" I asked both verbally and with a few gestures. It had been awfully quiet in there.

"Astrology is complicated and timely. She has all the stars to explain, it takes time to —"

She stopped.

"What?" I asked. She was looking out of the window. A very short man was approaching the shop. At speed. In courtly clothes. Sporting a bad attitude. The door banged open.

"WITCHES!" The man was weedy and very ugly. But his temper alarmed me more than his pockmarked face.

Brave Hildy very calmly opened the door to her room. "Come in, my lord." The man stormed past her. She followed him without looking at us.

I looked up at Rufus. "Can fairies protect witches from harm?" I asked him.

"I certainly can." We sat listening to his yelling.

"It amuses me greatly that she cannot hear his yells," Rufus noted, grinning. I smirked. "Who is he?" he asked.

"Hildy called him 'lord', but I do not recognise him. He does not run in my father's circles."

"I don't recognise him either," he said.

Obviously, I thought.

"You are high born?" Rufus asked.

"Very high," I said, smoothing down my skirts. I couldn't help myself.

"Why are you here then?"

Blessedly I was not required to answer that question: Hildy had poked her head out of the door.

Rufus stood to attention, ready for fairy action.

"Naught to worry about." She smiled, hardly flustered. "Maude, please enter my room for a moment."

I was taken aback. "Me?"

She nodded.

"Call if you need a fairy," Rufus said seriously.

I entered Hildy's room. When I was in the shoppefront I could pretend I worked in an actual apothecary, but there was no doubting where I was when I went into Hildy's healing rooms. This was a Godforsaken witch's cave. Candlelight flickered on the hanging dried flowers. The trinkets that lined the shelves sparkled and glinted magically. She was burning dried lavender, and it smelt ... warming but overpowering. The table was littered with sparkling rocks. The biggest one, at the centre, had a hundred purple jewelled teeth jutting out of the stone. But what really gave it away was the hunched man pacing up and down the room, waggling what appeared to be a severed finger.

"Are you the charmer?" he snapped at me.

"Excuse me, my lord?"

"This healer witch said you're the resident charmer."

Hildy's eyes bore into me, begging me to say yes.

"Aye," I mumbled.

"Well, it's not working!" He thrust the blackened, severed finger in my face.

"How do you mean?" I asked, revolted.

"I mean it's just a severed finger now! I have been asking it for Lady Armstrong's affections, and I have been getting nowhere. She won't even look at me! It's broken! The finger's broken."

"Aye, it certainly is broken," I whispered.

I turned to Hildy, with an expression that hopefully read, What the honest fuck? Why am I here? Why has that man got a severed finger in his hand?

"Charmer Maude." Oh no. No. No. No. "This is Lord Astell, and the thing he holds in his hand is a relic of St Peter, once of great power, and it has now ... waned. I have called you in, as master of charms and spiritual practices."

"That's the finger of St Peter in Chains?" I asked incredulously.

"Yes," said the lord loudly. "Can you fix it?" He smacked it down on the table.

"Who gave you the finger of the Prince of the Apostles, the Father of the Church, Christ's Dear Friend?" I pressed, guessing the answer.

"The wizard on Stonor Green. Reggie."

"I see."

Hildy nodded, giving me a sideways glance.

I sat down at the table, thinking this over.

"Did you ask Reggie to fix this powerful relic?"

"He said he got it from you!"

I looked at Hildy. Had she understood that? I tried to sign it to her.

"I think the person we really need to take issue with is St Peter," she said lightly.

"Oh, for the Lord's sake, will you fix it?" Astell barked at me.

I swallowed. "Why can't Hildy fix it?"

"Because she is the healer. You are the charmer." Oh Lord. I gathered myself.

"I might suggest that St Peter, though powerful, has no interest in intervening in the matters of the heart?" I tried. I saw Hildy watching my lips. She gave me an almost imperceptible nod of the head.

"Well, that isn't what Reggie said! He said —"

I held up my hand before he released the full tirade.

"It's not your fault." I picked up a semi-translucent piece of stone and let my thumb slide over its smooth surface, thinking frantically. "You see, St Peter is renowned as a celibate man. It was inappropriate for Reggie to give you his finger when your matters are far from the Apostle's purview."

Hildy's eyes stayed focused on my lips, trying to interpret what I was saying. Her eyes were now wide, surprised perhaps. I imagined I also looked surprised; I had no idea how I was coming up with this codswallop.

"Exactly, my lord," added Hildy gently. "That's what I've been saying. You need a proper charm direct from we white witches — not something the wizard has incorrectly —"

"Silence! Let the charmer speak." Astell was looking at me intently. "What do I need?" he asked me. He needed an attitude adjustment.

"Sir, when you approached your desired lady, what happened? What went wrong?"

He took a few huffy breaths. "Well, I must admit, I haven't

yet approached her. Not properly. She's very beautiful, you see."

"I do see." He was calming down.

"May I see the box of charms, Hildy?"

She passed me a small trunk of trinkets.

What a lot of junk. I found a plain-looking shirt toggle and held it between my fingers as if it were consecrated bread.

"This is what you need," I said loudly. "This is an amulet of attraction and power!" He gaped, mouth open like a dead fish, staring at the toggle. "You must keep it on your person and you will be filled with confidence and sexual power!" I heard him let out an impressed breath through his teeth.

"You will approach Lady Armstrong and tell her how it feels when you look on her, and that you hope she will open her heart to you. She will respond as you desire her to." I put the toggle in his open palm; he flinched as though afraid of its power.

"Praise God," he muttered.

"Is that all, Hildy?" I asked, desperate to be away.

"That is all, Maude," she said gently.

"Bless you, charmer. I can feel the power you have imbued it with."

What. An. Imbecile.

I left.

Rufus had been listening at the door.

I walked straight out the back into the kitchen and sat down at the table. My arms hung limply by my side.

"So you are a charmer!"

"Am not!"

He sat down opposite me. There was a silence. I wondered if the witches had a plan to slowly coax me into their practices. To fulfil the prophecy that my husband had made. Like it was a curse he put upon me. I put my hands between my legs and felt the raised skin under my skirts. I heard the sound of the shop door closing.

Hildy came in. “Forgive me, Maude.”

“You’re trying to make me a witch!”

She squinted at me. I had spoken too quickly. I felt a hot flush of anger reach my cheeks. “YOU.” I pointed at her. “MAKING ME.” I pointed at myself. “A WITCH.” I snatched at the broom in the corner of the room and pretended to ride it.

Her lips twitched with amusement. She had better not laugh.

“Forgive me.” She took the broom from my hand and propped it back up against the wall. She escorted me back to my chair and put a ladle of whatever was brewing over the fire in a chalice and handed it to me. “He wouldn’t listen to me. He wanted to speak to a professional ‘charmer’. I treat his family for physical ailments, thus he thinks I am only a healer. I thought on my feet.”

“I won’t do it again,” I said, sipping at the gingery tea.

“You exceeded expectations.”

“I am not a charmer,” I said into the tea, blowing steam into my eyes.

“You read him.”

“I played him,” I corrected her.

“Same thing.”

“Anyone could have done it.”

“Untrue.”

“Aye, it is untrue,” echoed Rufus.

“You weren’t even there, Rufus!”

“I listened at the door.”

“Fairies have excellent hearing.” Hildy smiled.

My eyes should fatigue from the amount of rolling around they were doing.

“A man listened to you,” Hildy whispered.

I put down my cup. “I have not heard of the Astell family. Is he of high status?” I asked.

“King Henry wouldn’t know him by name. But I would suspect he has been to Court from time to time.” That was quite high status, and he was a man, and he had listened to me. Maybe that’s why my whole body was tingling with tiny needle pricks.

I shook my head. No. I felt angry. The witches did not give me a voice. They took it away.

“Do not try to trick me,” I said under my breath.

Hildy put her hand on my back, and a wash of irritability rushed over me. Of course, she couldn’t fucking hear.

“Can you say it again?”

I turned to her and moved close to her face. “Do not trick me.” She looked sad. “You do not give me a voice. You take it away. The courtier listened to me because he thinks I am a witch, not because he thought I was worth respect.”

“Can we only be respected if we are married to horrible men?”

I stared at her. I didn’t know what to say. Her face was so infuriatingly friendly. Not a hairy mole or craggy witch line touched her porcelain skin.

I turned and went upstairs. I was angry and sad and irritable and I wanted to hit things. I wanted to be looked after, and I wanted no one to be near me. I wanted to be tucked into bed, and I wanted to punch whoever dared tuck me into bed. I hated how these witch clothes were so comfortable and easy to put on. I hated how they allowed me to actually breathe and move with ease. It was like my body had found its way home. But of all the things that were making me mad, I hated how much I had liked being listened to.

I slammed my door.

I missed my lady’s maid brushing my hair in the morning.

I missed my mother wandering around the house swaying left and right with the weight of her belly. I missed my future. I missed the experiences I'd never even had. Having a round tummy of my own. Being known as mother of boys. Having a household to manage. Becoming part of Queen Anne's Court. The intrigue and politics. I was picking at a loose thread in my mattress on the floor. I had not touched my trunk. If I unpacked, I would be giving up. There was no point unpacking when I'd just have to repack and go back home again. I should go to see the town cryer again, but I was beginning to annoy him. I let my hair fall in front of my eyes, a curtain from the world. No one could see me cry in here, with these thick curls protecting me. Jimmy reached up and pawed one of my ringlets. I took him by his middle and pulled the thin blanket over my head and we sat together in my tent. I was at the Field of Cloth of Gold, King Henry's famous meeting with the French king, where there were fields of dazzling gold silk tents, like the one I was in now. Where everyone who was anyone was dressed in their finery, drinking from fountains of wine, with music and dazzling jewels wherever you looked. I took that ragged three-toned breath that happens after you cry. The evening light shone through my window and then filtered softly through the sheet. My tent sparkled.

CHAPTER ELEVEN

Zita had woken me up early to teach me more signs that I could use with Hildy. My first instinct was to be angry. I served her a glare I would typically reserve for the likes of Agnes or Thomas. But then she said we were to take the lessons in her astrology room, and I had wanted to see her room for some time. She shushed me unnecessarily as I tiptoed noiselessly down the stairs and then she opened the door to her hidden world. It took a few moments for my eyes to adjust to the candlelight. There were no herbs hanging from the beams in here, but I was not disappointed.

She had painted the stars.

Hundreds of them floated atop dark blue walls. Lines connected them all, one to the other, spiralling across the ceiling and walls. Some were large, some just tiny golden dots, others had rings, and some had tails. It was as though God had scooped me up and placed me in the heavens.

Zita let me take in the spectacle. I dragged my eyes away from the painted heavens and examined the other things that filled the room. The candlelight was flickering off spindly gold instruments stacked upon shelves. Most of the contraptions moved, rotating in some non-existent breeze.

"Did you paint this?" I asked, gesturing to the walls and ceiling.

"I did," she said sternly, sitting behind a large writing desk, which was also stacked with instruments. I sat down opposite her.

"Let's begin."

My bad mood returned. "Why doesn't Rufus have to learn the signs?"

"He's a fairy, so he already knows a lot."

"He is not a fairy."

She didn't reply. She just looked at me, her eyes squinted, as though contemplating something. My tummy knotted.

"And why are you teaching me? You're not the one who is deaf." She was protective of Hildy. Quick to do things for her. Always asking after her. Bothering the room with pestering questions about her wellbeing. Persistently translating my words into sign. I even had a feeling this lesson was before dawn so Hildy didn't have to know we took the trouble. It could be perceived as endearing, but this morning, an hour before sunrise in the summer, it was not endearing, it was unGodly.

"I am teaching you our hand language because Hildy is my wife."

Speaking of unGodly.

"Pardon?"

"She's my wife."

My ears wrung. "Ordained by a priest?" I asked, incredulously.

"No, Maude. Ordained by Satan."

I fell off my chair. I don't know how anybody falls off a

chair when sitting completely still upon solid land, but I achieved it.

"I'm joking, Maude." She whispered from over her table. "It was a jest." I didn't move from the floor. Zita got up to look at me. "Our marriage is ordained neither by God nor Satan. It's a self-declared union."

"I've just ..." I said, looking up at the Zita, framed by the stars. "I've never heard of such a thing."

"Hildy told you we lie together on your first day here."

"I thought you meant you shared a bed. Like ... you're sisters or something?" Zita just looked at me, as though her mind could not comprehend my stupidity. "Is it because you're a witch?" I asked.

She contemplated that. "I don't believe so. Maybe though. Let us begin our lesson, Maude. Sit back on your seat."

It was dull. I would've been more inclined to remember the movements if my tummy had been full of bread, butter and warm milk and I wasn't mulling over their un-Christly union.

She was demonstrating the signs for different types of food when I stopped her.

"Do you kiss each other?" I asked.

"Ask me with your hands." I frowned but did my best, blowing her a reluctant kiss at the end.

"Maude. This isn't an arranged union, forced in the name of heirs and honours. This was in our stars." A strange warm air filtered across the room. "It was foretold. It is a love story." The stern woman with the constantly frowning eyebrows was fiddling with her quill. Her eyes cast down. Her pale sharp cheeks blushed. She was smiling softly. The picture of vulnerability. Hildy had cracked her heart right open. I could've cried just to witness it. I stared at my lap and collected myself. After a while I spoke.

"So you sleep in the same bed?"

"Yes," she said clearly. The first glimpse of sun was sneaking through the window, lighting up the lowest hanging stars with soft sunlight. "Hildy says you assisted with a situation yesterday." I was armed for this. We were not going to discuss it. I crossed my arms, pursed my lips and looked at her through my eyebrows. I said nothing. "Hildy can be quite vulnerable and I am pleased you were there to help her." Still I said nothing. She cocked her head at me. "Take off your armour, Maude. You'll get tired lugging it around day after day."

"I won't be here day after day," I reminded her.

"We can only hope." Cow.

"Do you know why I am here?" I demanded.

"Your husband thinks you ugly."

I cringed. "It is more than that!"

"He doesn't like your ugly temperament?"

"I have an affliction!" I said loudly.

She was quiet for a moment. "Is it an affliction like my affliction?" I wondered for a moment if she also had a mark. "Because all of my diagnosed 'afflictions' have given me great joy, Maude."

She was talking about her love of Hildy. "No! It's nothing like that!"

"There is no need to be so defensive." There was an awkward silence. She put a long finger on one of her whirling gold instruments. She pushed the contraption gently and small gold planets began moving around and around in a circle. We both watched it, bewitched. I wonder if she knew something I didn't. I wondered if she had read my stars. We caught each other's gaze.

"Are you going to tell me about what happened on your wedding night?" she asked.

"No."

"Then you can leave." I hadn't been expecting that. "Leave," she said again, almost aggressively.

I was taken aback. It felt like being chastised by my mother as a child. But I did as she said.

I returned home from my daily trip to the town cryer. There was still no word from my family. I needed to send another letter; it seemed obvious to me they hadn't received the first.

Rufus was in the shoppe helping a patron. They exchanged money. I wondered if he knew how to count. I should check. He'd probably never seen so much money in his life. I knew I hadn't. I supposed only merchants really got to see money: peasants didn't have any, and nobles ... well, I didn't know where we kept our coin. But I did see many pure silver candlesticks and a lot of gold and jewels.

I held the door open for Rufus's patron. God, the witches were so lucky to have me.

"Good day, goodwoman."

I smiled.

"Goodbye, Rufus!" she replied.

I frowned, turning to him.

"Why did the witches take you in?" he asked.

I went to stand behind the counter with him. "Because I am a delight."

"You are not," he said with an apologetic smile.

"Well, it's none of your business." I picked up my stitching. "I mean, why did they take *you* in? I suppose they just collect strays off the street or something."

"No, you must be special. They must see something in you."

I shivered. I wondered if they saw me as a witch. "Well, why are you special?" I demanded.

"I am a fairy." He grinned.

The witches came in from the not-so Great Hall.

"We are going to dispense a few tinctures around town, small things!" Hildy said, smiling. I looked up at Rufus, the man was hardly a small thing.

"Don't do anything foolish while we are gone. I'm talking to you, Maude." Zita held the door open for her ... wife. It made a lot of sense, now that I thought about it. They were always holding hands.

"You know they're lovers," I whispered conspiratorially when they had gone.

"I do," said Rufus, unbothered.

"Have you seen them kiss?"

"I have. Haven't you?"

I hadn't. "Of course I have."

"They are good women."

"Zita can be a toad."

Rufus laughed. "She doesn't like your bad attitude."

I rolled my eyes. "Do people know about them? In the town?" I asked. Rufus shrugged. "I would think not. I suppose they could get into trouble."

"Hmmm." He made this noise a lot: a deep low rumble in his chest.

"You have soot all over you, Rufus, do you know?" He looked surprised and rubbed his large hands all over his face, fixing nothing.

"Got it?" he asked.

"No."

. . .

The witches returned not an hour later and they had bought me bread.

"We're pleased to see you were honest about your nature, fairy," Zita declared, carving the large loaf. "You haven't stolen our drink or danced on our tables. Though I did notice you rolled around in the ashes." Rufus wiped his face again, grinning. "We have acquired you a proper mattress to sleep on."

Rufus began to say his thanks when I interrupted. "Where?" I demanded.

"We'll put him in the opposite corner of your room, Maude," said Zita.

"I'm a lady!"

"Then go home," Zita said, almost politely. I shut my mouth. "And, of course, we will provide you with cream for your every meal." She had a straight face, but there was a twinkle in her eye. Was she fucking with him?

"I would be very happy with bread," Rufus replied.

"Nonsense." She poured the poor man a bowl of cream.

We sat in silence, this strange new family, eating our food, drinking our tea, and Rufus, like a cat, licking up his cream. The shoppe door banged open, and all of us, barring Hildy, jumped.

There was silence. Could it have been a strong breeze?

"Go see, Maude," Zita said expectantly.

"I'm not a servant!" I crossed my legs and arms.

"What is happening?" Hildy asked.

"The door banged," Rufus explained. He used hand gestures. "I will go."

"Nay. I'll go." Hildy got up.

Zita rounded on me in a fierce hushed whisper. "You need to be the one receiving guests, Maude. Hildy needs help!"

We all got up to see who it was.

It was a man in livery. He had unrolled a long piece of parchment, filled with words. Everyone had tensed. The witches threw a glance to one another. Zita put a reassuring hand to Hildy's back. I clutched hold of Rufus's wrist, fearing for myself. Then I noticed he was tense too. Eyes wide. Slowly, the two of us backed out of the room. I quietly shut the kitchen door, and we turned to each other.

"Is he looking for me? Maybe my family found me!" I knew Rufus couldn't possibly know the answers, but I stared at him, desperate for him to respond. He was shaking his head, repeatedly.

"He looks for me! I am discovered!"

Hildy poked her head around the door. "Nothing to fret about, little sinners. We are not in trouble." Her tone was light, but she still looked a little flustered. "He will recognise no one."

My breathing was shaky.

"Come."

Rufus shook his head.

"Both of you. Come," Hildy said again.

I looked up at Rufus. What had he done? Where had he come from? Discovered by who?

The door to Hildy's room was open and the official-looking man was sitting down with Zita at the table cluttered with crystals.

Rufus and I stood by the door. It reminded me of how I used to wait before being presented to my father and brothers.

"We cannot do these ones." Zita pointed a very long fingernail to an item on the parchment. "They're too far away and we have a lot of business at the shoppe. We will be away too long. But we can deal with the ghost house." She pointed to another long section of writing. "And I think Maude should come along." Hildy nodded in agreement.

"You have another woman of power in your midst," simmered the man, looking at me.

Woman of power? "Perhaps," said Zita sternly. "She hasn't decided yet."

"And what of your Moor?"

I felt Rufus stiffen.

"He is a sprite," Zita explained. The messenger's eyes squinted. "A domesticated one; fear not."

"Hmmmm," he said quietly. "Be careful, wisewomen: you know how that kind can be."

"Fairies are troublesome but we will rein him in," said Hildy loudly.

I could feel a sort of energy bouncing off Rufus's body. I looked up at him. His eyes were lowered, his whole head bent, as though in prayer. I squeezed his hand. He squeezed mine back.

"We can also look at this one here, as it is local," Zita said with a tone of finality. "Does that please you?"

"Certainly. We thank you."

The man stood. The witches bowed. So did Rufus. I followed suit. The man looked at Rufus suspiciously and edged his way around him to get to the door.

Zita showed him out, then returned.

"Who was he?" I snapped. I felt anger, though I didn't know why.

"He's just a Justice of the Peace."

"Are we in trouble?"

"Nay. Nothing to fear."

Rufus sat down, his large back hunched over. He reached out to touch the purple-toothed rock. Hildy watched him fondly and passed him the crystal to inspect further.

"Every so often there is a need for us to serve the kingdom."

"You mean ... you mean, the King has asked for your help?" I was aghast.

"I don't know if Henry is himself dispensing orders, but the orders come from on high."

"What must we do?"

"Mostly they are small local matters, but if not dealt with swiftly and by professionals, they can come to trouble."

She had transcribed information onto her own piece of parchment.

"Firstly, we have a spirit." My whole body erupted in goosebumps. "He has taken up residence in Lord and Lady Sotherby's home, about an hour from here. We will need to deal with that swiftly. Ghosts are Catholic, and it will not reflect well on the Sotherby family."

Rufus and I exchanged looks.

"Secondly, we have the festival of St Mary's happening at the church in Wolvercote."

"I think you could help us out here, Maude." I made a face. "There's a statue of the Mother Mary there. It is blessed with the ability where, upon being offered breadcrumbs, she will deal with and rectify troublesome husbands."

"What?" Hildy handed me a large piece of rosy stone, as if to distract me from this absurd turn of events. I took it, despite myself.

"It's a shrine that, upon being offered a sacrifice, in this case, crumbs of bread, she will deal with troublesome husbands."

"So let her deal with them! What's this got to do with me?"

"We assist Mother Mary in her endeavours."

"How?" Zita opened a trunk behind her desk. I stared at her small behind as she rummaged. My heart jumped when she turned around.

"These are yours to borrow." Two thick pamphlets. Not

bound properly. But the closest thing I'd seen to a book in a long while. My whole body began to vibrate with excitement.

"You were taught to read?" Zita asked.

"Of course."

"These are yours to study if you wish."

My brothers and father had books sent to them regularly. We had the largest collection of bound manuscripts in the area. I knew that because my father told everybody who came near him, but I had never had free access to them.

"What're they about?" I asked, though I didn't really care.

"Take them. Read them. They will prepare you for our duties." Zita held out the papers. I didn't move. I wanted them. But I didn't want them. Why did the witches make witchcraft look so appealing? Called upon by the King, books to read, men who listened to you, comfortable dresses.

Rufus took the papers for me and pressed them into me. The parchment was thick and I could see extravagant lettering sprawling across the pages. I held it to my chest.

CHAPTER TWELVE

I got my bleed again. That meant I had been there from one full moon to the next. I had sent another two letters to Shirburn. Still no reply. There was a war within me, causing erratic and strange behaviour. Most of the time I refused to help anyone. I would not witch. I said the phrase repeatedly, whenever I was asked to do anything remotely related to their craft. Yet I spent my days sat down on the floor behind the counter, in my "court", reading my witchly texts. Ordering the poor fairy to fetch me warm drinks and bread and butter and honey. He even brought me flowers to decorate my floor court. I had fashioned my throne out of a blanket and my reading desk out of a small stool. I would whisper the text out loud as though I was reading to the ladies of Court. If the ladies of Court were witches who chanted spells, of course.

The first book was a handbook of charms and magic remedies.

I was reading a spell to soothe monthly cramps.

> To help the Crampe.
> Take a piece of Parchemint as much
> as will goe about your legg in the
> gartering place; write thereon theis
> folowing words Gut + Gut +
> Egul + Getaul + and weare it
> next your bare leg. It will help.

I would need to try out this charm in private. I wondered if my mark would stop the spell from entering me.

"Have you read anything that would help us with this ghost?" Rufus asked from above. We were to leave for the haunted house later that day. I bit my lip. I had seen a page that had looked potentially useful, but it had scared me so much I had skipped it, reading a "Cure For Toothache" instead. He looked down at me in my court. I smoothed down my skirt. Whilst it was nice to move so freely without layers and layers of material, my mark was just that tiny bit closer to the world.

"No," I decided upon.

He frowned. "Makes me fucking nervous," he said, the profanity surprising me.

"Me too," I confessed.

Reluctantly, I thumbed through the pages until I found what I was looking for.

> To Speak with Spirits.
> Call their names Orimoth, Belmoth Lymocke
> and Say thus. I conjure you by the names
> of the Angels + Sator and Azamor that
> yee intend to me in this Aore,
> and send unto me a Spirit that
> does fulfil my comanding and desire
> and that can also understand my words
> for one or 2 yeares or as long as I will.

Who, in God's name, wanted to have contact with a spirit for one or two years? No. I shut the manuscript. This was the Devil's work. It was like I could feel the presence of the fallen angel around me. This was not the work of God. I snatched at my lavender bundle within my skirt pocket and lit it on fire, letting the soft fumes cleanse my tiny court. Why was I being tempted like this? What kind of test was this? Or was it not a test at all? But a calling? Was my mark drawing me to these texts, to this life, because it was the only life I could lead? I threw the manuscript under the counter. I stood up. I crossed myself.

I decided to write yet another letter, this time directly to my mother. I splattered it with exaggerations and some downright lies. It was mere hours before we were to leave for a house occupied by a ghostly spirit. I needed rescuing.

Mother.

Regrettably, I am about to cause trouble. I am going to publicly declare myself a witch, seeing as you have left it as my only option. I will let everyone know that I am yours, and will carry our family name and put it out the front of my witch's practice. It would be wise if you would send word to me before I lie with demons and the whole of England believes that your daughter is magic. (I am still of the opinion that I am not.)

Is there any news of my annulment? Any news at all would be appreciated. How are my brothers? How are Thomas's lessons coming along?

Maude.

PS I am currently sleeping in the same room as a very large Moor that came off the streets.

Of course, Rufus was the most gentle roommate and hardly even snored, but I didn't need to add that detail.

"Are you ready, Maude?" Zita had come down the stairs carrying a trunk. I shook my head.

"We aren't to go for hours." I stared up at the witches. Hildy had several sacks of Lord-knows-what slung over her shoulder, and both were dressed in their travelling cloaks with lavender bundles sticking out of the pockets.

"Rain is coming. We should leave now."

I shook my head. "I have a letter to send!"

"You will have to send it upon our return."

"I won't come. I don't want to be a part of your demon work."

"Then don't come and pack up your things and leave our home," Zita commanded.

"What's upsetting you, Maude?" Hildy signed.

"I have ... bad cramps," I said stupidly.

"You are bleeding?" Zita asked. I checked to see if Rufus was in earshot, but I think he was in our room.

"Aye."

"You bleed on the full moon." Zita sounded impressed. "You must come with us: a woman's bleed makes her potent and powerful."

"Nay. It makes us weak. We bleed and we have not even been wounded." I had heard a brother say that before.

"And yet we never die," Hildy said matter-of-factly. I frowned. "You can stay back if you want. Will you be well here, all alone?"

"Rufus is coming with us then?"

"Would you like him to come?" Hildy replied with an annoyingly sly smile creeping up one side of her mouth.

"Having a spirit when we are facing a spirit might be a good idea!" I said defensively, my voice shrill.

"He's coming, don't worry." On cue, Rufus appeared down the stairs with a small sack of his belongings. "Gather your things, we are leaving." Zita spoke with a tone of finality.

My tummy flipped.

We stood outside the locked-up shoppe. Hildy was writing a curse to leave upon the door to scare away thieves and wrongdoers. I had a cape over my head and my curls were out in force. No one would recognise me as Lady Maude. The coat I was wearing was lent to me by Hildy, and it had a large internal pocket where I had put Jimmy. I had been waiting for the scratches and chaos, but he was placated enough. I enjoyed the feeling of his purrs vibrating against my chest.

"Rufus!" I whispered across at him. I felt we all needed to

be quiet when out in public: we were not meant to be seen. Witches and fairies.

He looked over at me, and I flashed him a look at my hidden cat. He cracked a big smile at the sight of Jimmy's ears poking out past the fabric.

"Jimmy!" he whispered back, pleased.

"Jimmy!" I confirmed. I smiled at him. I bent my head to kiss my cat's little black muzzle. As I did so, I heard my husband's voice in my mind. He suckles at your teat. What if Jimmy started trying to feed from me? He was sitting at my breast. A cold sweat broke out over my skin.

"Finished!" Hildy said, pocketing her chalk.

THOSE THAT ENTER THE WITCH'S SHOPPE
WHILST WE ARE OUT ON WITCHLY BUSINESS
WILL BE CURSED WITH ONION-EYED SORES
AND THEY WILL DEVELOP ONLY
UPON THE SINNER'S BOTTOM.
NEVER TO BE CURED.

"That cannot be a real curse," I said, looking at her, my eyes squinted in suspicion.

"You look so wild with your curls all loose," she said evasively, touching my hair.

Beneath her curse were several words in a language and letter I did not know.

"What does that part mean?" I asked, not wanting to know the answer.

Hildy shrugged. "It's Welsh. I think that part means Dog, and the second part means Cat."

"Is that part of the curse?"

"No. But the language looks ominous, no?"

"You're just as bad as Reggie!" I exclaimed, signing as

best as I could; there was no sign for the flap-mouthed Reggie, so I just pulled a stupid face and said his name loudly. She didn't have time to retaliate — a small brown carriage rounded the corner, Zita at its helm, a small mutty-looking dog sitting upon her lap, entangled in the reins.

"All aboard the ghost train!" she said loudly, in a surprisingly good mood. "Rufus, you sit with me."

"Nay. I won't," he said firmly.

"Why, sprite?" Zita's thin eyebrows were raised.

"I don't like dogs."

"Oh, of course you don't!" said Zita, as if he had told her before and only now she remembered. "Hildy will take the bitch in the carriage." She passed Hildy the placid animal. I felt Jimmy stir. Rufus gave Hildy a wide berth and stepped up to sit next to Zita.

"Why the dog?" I asked Hildy, loading the luggage under the seat.

"Bitch," she corrected. "A spayed bitch."

"Very well. Why the spade bitch?" I asked, sitting down opposite her.

"She's our ghost hunter." She placed the dog on her lap. The sound of the mutt's panting faded under the rumbling of wheel over cobbles. "As you can see by Rufus's reaction, spirits are warded off by her. She has a lot of power in her tiny little paws." She touched the soft padded feet.

"What's her name?"

"She belongs to one of our kin. She puts her on loan, for spiritual situations." She had not understood me. "I didn't answer your question?" she guessed.

"Never mind. It's fine," I assured her. I noticed my voice shake a little and I was glad she couldn't hear me. I was nervous.

"Don't worry, Maude. You'll be safe with me," she said softly.

I stared out of the window, longing to be in the gentle bustle of Watlington town and not in a carriage destined for demons. I wanted to be amongst the clusters of people in the emporiums and stalls. Invisible. Lost in the songs of the fruit girls and the harsh barks of the traders. My steps hidden under the steady sound of horses' hooves clipping the cobbles. I would rather have my slippers in the filth that lined the stones than be going where I was going.

We left town. The air cleared, quietened. The fire smoke had left the air and so had the sound. But it did not soothe me. I got out my needlework and pretended I was on my way to Court. Hampton Court. Henry's newest residence. I had heard it was something to behold. I brushed down my skirts and pushed my hair behind my ears. I should have brought ribbon to tie it back. Why had I let it free? I was patching together a chemise for Rufus. He had come to us with only the clothes on his back. My hands shook as I tried to manoeuvre the tricky seam under the arm. A drop of sweat ran down my side. My mark squished uncomfortably against my other thigh.

I felt Hildy's eyes on me.

"You're as pale as the ghost we are about to meet."

"This is always my colour," I retorted defensively.

"Stick your head out the window and let the Oxfordshire air invigorate you. The smell of manure soothes the soul."

Sceptically, I did as she said. Clutching my cat to my chest, I leant my head out into the open air. The wind whipped my hood down and my hair flew backwards. It felt good. My temperature dropped. I looked out over the bronzing forests and harvested crops. I blinked away tears. I wasn't sure if they were tears from the wind, from sadness or from fear, but I blinked them away, watering Oxfordshire's fields. I took several deep breaths. I was just beginning to feel better when I saw the Sotherby house about a mile away, its stone dark against the soft landscape.

CHAPTER THIRTEEN

The carriage crunched to a stop outside of the manor house. It was large and dark. Even a child could have told you it was inhabited by the Devil.

"Everyone out!" yelled Zita from the front. Hildy and the dog jumped down excitedly.

I remained where I was.

Rufus's head appeared in my window.

"Don't open the door, Rufus." I shook my head vigorously. Jimmy poked his head out of my cloak. Perhaps he was aware that the carriage had stopped, or perhaps he was aware of a ghostly presence. Upon seeing the house, he retreated. I wished I was in someone's pocket.

Another man's face appeared at the window behind me. I jumped and let out a small squeal. "Are you a witch?"

"Good God!" I clutched my chest.

"Are you sent by Court? You are here to rid my house of its demons?"

"Lord Sotherby?" I asked, my breath irregular from fright.

"Verily," he said curtly. He looked haggard, but important. I resigned myself to the job at hand.

"Aye, we are here to help you." I got out of the carriage. "The witches are over there." I pointed to the big grand entrance doors, but they had already gone inside. "They must've entered."

"Lord protect them."

"Come, we will find them together," I said reluctantly, giving Rufus a meaningful stare. "Don't leave my side," I hissed at him. He nodded.

Lord Sotherby gave each of us a wide berth but followed us as we approached the Devil's home on Earth.

"I will not cross the threshold," its owner muttered.

"Hildy!" I yelled into the entrance hall, my voice ringing around the room.

Rufus had apparently taken a short break from fearing the Devil in order to laugh at me. "Why would you call for Hildy?" he asked, trying to wipe the smile of his face.

I glared at him. "Zita!" I corrected myself.

"Be careful!" the lord hissed. "You might call the spirit!"

Goosebumps erupted up my arms. The dog began to bark. The lord, ghostly white himself, fell onto his knees and shielded his head with his arms.

"SAVE ME, WITCH!"

I stared at him, then looked to Rufus, who shrugged unhelpfully. I picked the lord up by the arm. "Do not fear, my lord. It is our animal. We brought her here to defeat the demon." He was shaking. "I am going to take you inside, but you will be protected by this fairy." I gestured to Rufus, who straightened up and changed his expression to look serious about his ethereal business. We guided the lord inside; he was muttering prayers and I prayed that his prayers would protect us.

"Zita!" I barked. Angry now. What the fuck did they expect us to do here? We had no actual power. Right? I checked on

Jimmy. He was content. Maybe he didn't care about demons or ghosts. I wished I didn't.

The spade bitch came tearing down the stairs, nose diving into the floor.

"There you are, Lord Sotherby!" Zita was holding a smoking bundle of leaves. Hildy was behind her, holding a candle. I signed angrily at both of them. WHERE HAVE YOU BEEN? I made sure the gestures were sharp and angry — screaming signs.

"We had to do a patrol of the perimeter. I am glad to see you were under the protection of the fae, my lord. He is handy in these precarious situations."

Rufus inclined his head in a comical manner.

Sotherby was still shaking violently.

"Have you caught her?" he whimpered.

"You feel it is a female presence?" Zita asked.

He didn't reply.

"Come, come, Lord Sotherby." Hildy tried to detach the lord from my arm. It was no easy task. "This will be over with soon. We just need you to show us where you are feeling the presence most strongly."

His gaze went up the stairs. It appeared we were in the company of a deaf witch and now a mute lord.

In the silence my fears returned.

The lord seemed slow-witted. It had dulled my demon fears for a quick moment, but as we trounced around this great big empty house, I couldn't help but feel something too. Something stirring. Like the house was taking quick, intermittent breaths, hoping not to be heard.

He led us to a drawing room. It was dark.

"Sit down, my lord." Hildy and Zita stood above him as he backed himself onto an engraved wooden chair. He was glancing towards the empty fireplace.

"What can you see?" Zita asked.

"You mean you cannot see them? The room is full of spirits." Zita translated to Hildy, and he stared at the gestures in alarm. "They're in every nook and cranny. In the ceiling, in the walls. A thousand. More. Terrible black demons with fearful faces, they mutter and terrify me. They go on and on. Visiting me from Purgatory."

Shamefully, I felt myself well up with tears. I couldn't see the faces but Hildy's fucking candle kept flickering shadows onto the walls — were they shadows? I got my sleepy cat out from my pocket and put my nose into his fur, and the smell calmed me.

"My lord," Zita began. "It is not possible for someone to be visiting you from Purgatory."

"It isn't?" He sounded almost hopeful.

"Certainly not. Purgatory is a Catholic place."

"Are you Catholic, my lord?" Hildy pressed. Both witches were bent over this poor man.

"God believe me, no! I am loyal to the King, the true head of the Church."

I wondered briefly whether this wasn't an exorcism at all, but an inquisition from the Royal Court. Two birds with one stone, I supposed.

"If you are speaking true, my lord, we do not have a visiting soul from Purgatory problem."

"Well, could it be a ghost from Hell?" he asked, this only seeming to upset him further.

"Have you tried to get in touch with someone who has died, my lord?"

"No!" he said loudly. A single tear slid down his cheek.

"It's very improper to get in touch with the dead, my lord," Zita explained.

"But if it is a spirit from Heaven or Hell, we needn't worry too much." Hildy relit a bundle of herbs with her flint. "Commonly such spirits be friends. And if you have invited them into your home, I expect you may ask them to leave."

The dog began barking. "God save me!" I yelped, unable to stop myself. Instinctively I turned into Rufus, sandwiching my poor cat between our torsos. He placed a hand on my back soothingly, but I could hear his heart beating just as fast as mine.

"Tis just a mouse," declared Zita as the dog ran out of the room chasing the small ghost rodent.

Jimmy began to stir against us both, as though he knew the word "mouse". We were unable to contain him: he wiggled free from our bodies and soundlessly ran out of the door.

"Jimmy!"

Rufus grabbed my hand, willing me not to chase the cat out into a world of ghosts. But I wouldn't let poor Jimmy be the victim of the Devil's work, and I followed the animals.

"Jimmy!" I hissed. I could hear the dog barking at the back of the house. I flung myself around dark corridors and down servants' stairs, following the sound of the ghost-hunting bitch.

The noise stopped. I stopped. It was dark. I couldn't remember what turns I had made. I was at the top of a new corridor, having taken two staircases down. Kitchens would be somewhere. Perhaps that's where the mouse lived, with the scraps and the crumbs. I swallowed, but my mouth was dry. There was a flickering light coming from a room at the end of the long, wooden-panelled hall. "Jimmy," I whispered.

The door was ajar.

I pushed into it and forced it open.

I had found her.

I had found the ghost.

Ashy white. But not translucent like I had imagined. She

had my Jimmy under her arm. She was feeding the dog something off the kitchen benches.

"Give me back my cat," I whispered.

Her head turned quickly to me. I had given her a fright. I had given the ghost a fright.

"Oh, miss, I'm so sorry!" She made a move towards me, and I took several steps back.

"Give me my cat. Put him on the floor," I said firmly. She put Jimmy on the floor and the fucking cat wandered off in the wrong direction. "You need to leave," I said firmly. "You need to go back where you came from."

"I'm sorry, miss, it's only that I'm on instructions from the mistress to come gather any leftovers, in case they go foul."

I grabbed hold of the door frame. My heart rate was slowing. "You are not a spirit?"

"No, ma'am. I'm the kitchen maid."

I nodded and let a long exhale escape my lips. "My apologies," I said, not looking at her. "You're very ... white."

"Irish, my lady." I walked into the kitchen and picked up the rogue, spleeny, worst cat in the whole of Christendom.

"Is this your dog too?" she asked, smiling as the little mutt jumped up and asked for pats.

"We're here upon request of the lord and lady. We are investigating the ghost ... demon ... situation," I explained in stunted speech. "The dog, she's meant to sniff out spirits."

"Ahhh," she said gently. "I think she sniffed out dried meat." She gave a small piece of mutton to the unrelenting, drooling beast.

"Do you know anything about the spirit?" I asked. "Does it not frighten you to come here?"

She looked at me reluctantly, her freckles standing brightly against her pale skin.

"The lord and lady lost their daughter around the time the ghost came calling, ma'am. If you know what I mean."

"You don't think it is a ghost?"

"It could be her ghost, I suppose. But it's a bit Catholic." I nodded. "If it is her spirit, she was a very gentle child. Used to run down here all the time and ask Cook for sugared almonds. She wouldn't do anything harmful."

"What happened to her?"

"Oh, it was horrible, miss." She continued filling up her hessian sacks of leftover food from the cupboard. "She tripped. Hit her head."

"In the drawing room?"

She nodded. "I think she must've fallen over something. Or perhaps she was playing. Running around. Dancing. Whatever she was doing, she hit her head on the hearth. The lord found her in a pool of blood."

"Tis no wonder he's haunted," I muttered.

"Aye. I had to help clean up." She shook her head and took several moments to compose herself. "I wouldn't take a step back into that drawing room."

"What was her name?"

"Little Beatrice. He used to call her B."

I swallowed. Surely this was the root of all this madness. A ghost of his mind's making. "Do you know what name Beatrice referred to the lord by?"

She frowned a little. "I think she just called him Papa."

"Thank you for this," I said, scooping up the dog, holding each animal under either arm. Cat and dog eyed each other suspiciously. "I'm sorry for thinking you were the ghost."

She laughed. "Tis all well, miss."

I searched the next few rooms for paper and quill and found them. I locked the door and set the animals down. Jimmy jumped on top of the writing desk, not a fan of the dog.

I was shaking but no longer from fear: from some sort of anticipation. Excitement almost.

I shut my eyes, took a deep breath and wrote the following.

Papa.

I stopped. I stared at Jimmy, who was staring at me. What would I want to say to my father if I was dead? I'd probably haunt the shit out of him, and make sure he knew my death was definitely all his fault. That did not help. Christ save me.

Resigning myself to the task at hand. Resigning myself to this journey. I reached into the pockets in my skirts and retrieved the spell I had torn from the book. It was just like poetry, I reminded myself. I could handle a bit of poetry; poetry was my thing.

"Lord protect me from the potential Evil within this ... poem," I began. "I do this only to relieve a poor man of grief." I un-crumpled the spell.

"I conjure you, Beatrice, B, daughter of Lord Sotherby,
by the names of the Angels + Sator and Azamor that
yee intend to me in this Aore,
and send unto me a Spirit that
does fulfil my comanding and desire
and that can also understand my words
for only the next minute or so,
so that I may write a letter to your father,
in your name."

I swallowed.

Nothing happened. Nothing tangible. No ghostly apparition appeared. No noise reached me from the darkness. But I picked up my quill and wrote.

I only wanted to tell you that I am safe. I am with God in Heaven. Christ has a neverending supply of sugared almonds.
I will leave you in peace.
B

I felt a warm shiver run up my back. I sat up straight in my chair. This was unGodly business. Or, I suppose, it was very Godly business. Writing letters from Heaven. I was merely transcribing what the spirit wanted to say, I told myself. I had no idea if the spell had worked, or if I was just a dirty rotten liar.

The letter itself looked very corporeal. Very of this realm. But it would have to do. Arming myself with the dog and cat, I marched back to the library.

"Where is he?" I asked. Faced with only the witches and Rufus and no lord at all.

"He's outside. The presence was too much." They were all seated. Relaxed. Not doing anything witchy at all.

"Do you have a solution?" asked Hildy. There was something in her eye. It was less of a twinkle and more like a deviant glint.

"Well, your stupid dog isn't working, is it?"

"We'll try holy water next," Hildy said, getting out a small bottle of clear liquid from an inside pocket.

"No. No holy water. Not yet. I need to speak with him." They followed me outside. He was sitting not far from the home, his back against a tree, looking up into the branches, no doubt getting wet from the slight sprinkling of rain that had begun. It was a dark, miserable day.

"My lord?"

"Is it done?" he asked, his face desperate.

I knelt down next to him. I saw his story now, swimming in his eyes.

"It is done, my lord." I saw him take a deep breath, and I wondered if he was almost sad to have his daughter leave his side. "She left you this." I handed him the letter. My breath got clogged in my body. I watched, rigid, as he read my letter. My transcribed letter, I reminded myself.

"B," he said, after a long moment. He looked at me. Eyes dry. Only the slightest frown on his face. "You found this?"

"In the library. By the hearth," I managed.

He nodded. "She didn't know how to write," he said softly. Not accusing, but a little confused none the less.

"God blesses many with gifts in Heaven," said Zita firmly.

He nodded. Completely accepting. He needed this letter, and he had been given it. He wasn't about to throw it to the wind.

There was a breeze. All of us turned into it. I felt each of our bodies move as we put our faces into the brisk, autumn air.

I took a deep breath, then returned my gaze to the lord. His body was unwinding, like a wrung cloth being hung out to dry, the creases unfolding.

"We can return home," he whispered. "I am in great debt to you. You set her free."

"She only wanted to tell you it wasn't your fault. She loves you. She didn't mean to frighten you." I spoke intuitively, without thinking. Again, he nodded. A quiver of the lips this time. "I must pass on B's message to her mother." He stood.

"God bless you, witches." He stopped and kissed my hand, then left towards the stables.

There was a silence. The rain fell through the leaves and onto my face.

"You *are* a witch," murmured Rufus.

I looked to him. “I am nothing of the sort.”

“What will happen if he still feels the presence in his house?” Zita asked sternly. Like I was in trouble.

“Do you think he will?” I asked, turning to her.

She looked at the big dark home. “What did the letter say?”

“Only that his daughter will leave him in peace.”

“What else did you say?”

“How do you know there is something else?”

“Because I know you are deviant.”

“I just wrote that Christ has an endless supply of sugared almonds.” I shrugged.

The witches looked at me for a long moment. “Yes. We are done here," Zita concluded. “This place has no haunting anymore.”

We walked, in silence, back to our carriage.

CHAPTER FOURTEEN

Rufus was sweeping the floor, setting up the shoppe to re-open after our day away. I had slept badly. If at all. I was sitting on my floor-court, head resting against the cool wall, chewing on bread and butter, not bothering to close my mouth.

"Do you believe there was really a ghost at Lord Sotherby's?" the fairy asked, sweeping around me.

"I don't know!" Bread flew out of my mouth onto the floor.

Rufus swept up the chewed residue with a blank face and then turned to Hildy, who was re-organising the shelves.

"Do you believe that it was a ghost, Hildy?"

"It is possible. Sometimes we deal with real presences. Sometimes they are crabs with candles attached to their shells."

"What?" said Rufus and I at the same time.

"St Benedictine's in Little Worlington," she explained. "Father Bannom was losing his congregation to the Father in Great Worlington. Each night he would set a dozen crabs loose in his rival's graveyard, with lit candles strapped to their shells. It worked a charm until we showed up and realised what he was doing. They had a full exorcism before we divined the truth."

"I'll be damned ... crab ghosts," Rufus muttered.

"Crab ghosts," Hildy confirmed. "But as for yesterday, well, I certainly felt something uneasy in that drawing room. What do you think?"

Neither of us answered. The whole experience had made me feel ill. I had performed a spell. And it hadn't been a light and breezy one. It wasn't a spell to stop the milk souring, it was a spell to summon a spirit. Was that bad magic? Or good magic? Or not magic at all? I shivered. If we were in France, I would be found out and burnt at the stake.

There was a knock on the door.

"Good morrow, witch," said a voice. It was the bellman. I jumped up, giving him a surprise. His old face was creased in a smile. "The day has come! I have a letter for you!"

"FINALLY!" I said incoherently, mouth full. "Thank you, sir, you can be rid of me now."

"Wouldn't want that," he said friendlily. "Been nice to see you three to four times each day every day."

"Don't exaggerate," I reprimanded him. He laughed jollily, in a way that only town cryers could do, and left the apothecary.

I paused, looking at the seal of my family. Then opened the letter.

I am confined. Come see me in my rooms today.

"They want me back!" I held my chest. "They want me back!" I literally jumped with excitement. I looked at Rufus, who was smiling. Then I turned to Hildy. "Will you help me dress in my old finery?"

She didn't answer straightaway, so I signed it for her.

"I will get Zita, and we will dress you." She left.

My heart was in my throat, but not in the fear-of-demons way, in the excited I-am-returning-to-my-true-life way.

I grabbed hold of Rufus's hands and danced around. "She must've thought of a better solution for me, Rufus!" He smiled at me and span me around. "They want me back!" I turned around and around until I reached the stairs, then hobbled dizzily up to my room.

Zita and Hildy came to my chamber a few minutes later. I had laid out my dress.

"Let's get back into this thing! Hildy, could you do my hair? I would like it tight back, and maybe we could use some oil."

Zita held up a hand, silencing me. "We will help you dress and put up your hair, Maude. But fair warning." I frowned. Do not ruin this moment, Zita. "Planetarily speaking, this is not a day of harmonious union. This is a day of fire. The stars … they are not in a favourable place."

Fuck your stars. I held my tongue and made a loud huffing noise.

"We just don't want you to get hurt," Hildy added.

"My mother wouldn't send for me if she did not have a new idea, a better solution than the one I am currently living."

"If you say so." Zita held up my bodice.

Hildy, whether through skill or spell, had flattened all my curls. Not a single one sprang loose as I walked to my home. I had left Jimmy at the apothecary, and I hadn't the strength to lug all my belongings back on my own. I would fetch them later. I would send people to fetch them later.

I didn't like walking in all my finery through town and

across the fields without a carriage, or at least an escort, but I kept to the dry paths and made eye contact with no one. No doubt people would be wondering who I was and why I was out alone, but I couldn't have turned up at Shirburn in my witch's outfit: I would have been sent straight back to where I came from.

After what seemed like an awfully long time I walked over the stone bridge that separated my family's home from the town, and Shirburn rose up above me. I had expected to feel relief, a sense of homecoming, but instead I felt nervous and out of place. She was not a welcoming building. Stony. Crenellated turrets. Small thin windows. A big fuck-off moat. It was a castle made to keep people out, not to invite anyone in. Still, it was my castle. Mine.

I did not want to see my brothers or father. Presumably they would have all dispersed after my banishment, but I couldn't risk it. I walked around the back of the castle, keeping my head down. It was very quiet, no one working in the grounds. I entered the servants' entrance to the kitchens.

"Christ protect me!" someone yelled. I jumped. Our cook, Maggie, had jumped higher.

"Sorry, Maggie! I didn't mean to frighten you. I'm here to see Mother."

She gave me a pitying look. I wondered how much the servants knew. Probably everything: Maggie was more masterful at gossip than at cooking, and she wasn't a half bad cook.

"She's confined, poppet, in her regular quarters." I nodded. "Do you want me to fetch someone to take you there?" I frowned at her.

"I think I know where I'm going," I replied incredulously.

"Of course, Magdalen." She hadn't addressed me as "my lady". My hairs were on end, my breath shallow. The excitement of getting my letter had dissipated entirely. Something was wrong. I felt tears preparing themselves to be shed.

My mother's lady's maid was standing in front of her chamber doors.

"Agnes," I said sternly, summoning all my strength.

"Magdalen." She was not surprised to see me.

"Lady Maude," I corrected, but she ignored me.

"Did you come up the servants' stairs?" She had a smirk on her face. A hot rage crashed over my body.

"Get out of my way. Let me see my mother. And you would do well to remember your lowly place in society." I pushed past the insufferable woman.

The room was, of course, extremely dark. My eyes struggled to adjust as I entered. The windows were boarded up tightly and the fire was only embers.

"Mother?" I whispered into the dark. I felt as if my heart was being worn on the outside of my body. I felt so small. So young. So vulnerable. "Mama?" I said. I moved towards the large bed, grabbing hold of the large wooden poster to support myself. Was she not well? Was that why I was summoned?

"Magdalen?" she murmured, clearly waking from a deep sleep.

"Aye. It's Maude."

"Come sit on the bed with me." I felt my tears begin to fall, a little earlier than expected. I climbed onto the warm bed and found my way next to her. My mother propped herself up, and I pushed a pillow behind her back.

"How are you, Mother?" I asked, finally seeing far enough through the gloom that I could see her face. She looked wasted. The baby must be stealing all her food.

"Where in God's name have you been, Magdalen?"

She had let me on the bed, but she had given me no

signals to touch her or embrace her. I gave her the distance.

"I couldn't be married off to a peasant, Mother. I had to protect myself."

She sighed; she seemed too tired to chastise me.

"How is the babe?" I asked.

"It feels different this time around."

"Maybe it is because you are a little older?"

"Yes." She nodded. "I feel thinly spread. My last, I think."

"Your body has done this many times, Mother; it will know what to do."

We sat in silence. I didn't want to ask her what the plan was. I didn't want to leave this moment. It was so nice, clouded in darkness, speaking soft words between mother and daughter.

The door creaked open. I was ready to rip Agnes apart. But it was not Agnes. It was my father.

I jumped off the bed.

"Magdalen." He nodded at me. I bowed, my virginal blue skirts billowing out around me.

He came to stand by my mother's side.

"How do you do today, my lady?" he asked stiffly.

"Well, my lord," said the tiny, frail thing.

"Only one more after this and you'll be on par with Lady Mary of Kent." He snorted. I saw my mother wince. There was a silence. I needed someone to say something, anything relevant to me and my life.

"You summoned me here?" I managed.

"There have been unfortunate tidings."

"My lord?"

"You've died," he said flatly. There was a beat.

"Am I a ghostly apparition?" I tried to laugh. "What do you mean?"

"Edward cannot annul the marriage." I stretched my hand

out, trying to find the wall. I needed support. "There is evidence that he did lie with you, so an annulment on the grounds of you withholding conjugal rights is not possible."

"What evidence?" I asked.

He sighed, unwilling to talk about it. "Something about the remnants of sheets in the fire, something about his kinsmen being witnesses. I know not the particulars. It is distasteful to talk about and it is not important."

"Then we must get a divorce," I whispered.

"He does not want a divorce."

"I do."

"He will either get his annulment on the grounds of maleficence or he will become a widower."

My humours turned cold.

"You do not want to be convicted of maleficence, Magdalen," my mother whispered.

"I do not want to die either," I replied.

"And yet die you must." My father strode to the door. He was done. I shut my eyes. I could see them ... my brothers, all standing behind the door — he was going to let them in, let them attack me, break me apart, tear my mark from my body with their teeth. I heard him turn the latch. I awaited my fate.

But Fate never came. The door closed again. And it was just me and my mother.

"What does he mean?" I said, eyes still closed.

"Your father will put out the notice tomorrow. Sweating sickness."

"I don't have the sweating sickness."

"You did, and it was the end of you."

"Where am I to go? What am I to do?"

My mother's eyes were cold.

"You seemed to look after yourself well enough without us before. I'm sure the farmer would still take you, but you're too good for him, aren't you?" I stared at her. "Are you too good for him now that you're dead?"

"Jesus Christ," I whispered. "What sort of a mother are you?"

"You must forge your own path now."

"No."

"Would you rather be tried as a demonic witch and be jailed — or burnt?"

"I ..." There was a buzzing sound in the air, a vibration that seemed to be entering my body. It buzzed around my legs, around my mark. I think my mother was talking to me but I couldn't hear her.

Burn the mark.

Sucks at your teat.

Burn the mark.

Sucks at your teat.

"You will need to give back your dresses, and the family jewels." That sentence rang loud and clear.

I walked towards her. Each step shot another stronger buzz up my body. "No."

"Then you can deal with the authorities, be accused of maleficence and bring shame on this entire family."

"Not if I am already dead, you can't."

I stared at her for a long while. She could not look me in the eye.

"You are a bad mother," I whispered, like the Devil was in me, or was me. "I hope your unborn babe dies, for his sake. Life would be far better in the dirt than with a mother such as you."

Her face changed. Not angry. Not even sad. Horrified perhaps.

"Leave, Magdalen."

"It's Maude," I spat. "And I curse you."

CHAPTER FIFTEEN

I left. In all my dresses, walking through my house like it was filled with viscous honey, not air. Each step took forever, despite how much I wanted to leave. I went down the main staircase, my large skirts plumed out behind me as I descended. I saw myself as if through someone else's eyes, framed by the large tapestry behind me of the men and women at Court.

"Leaving us, Magdalen?" Thomas was standing by our great doors.

Something rose within me. Uncontrollable. I was unsure I would be able to talk, but words came flowing, clear, loud and unwavering.

"Leaving forever, Thomas."

He grinned.

"I am to return to my true calling. Witchcraft and maleficence." His stupid smile wavered. It didn't really matter what I did right now. I'd be dead tomorrow. None of this mattered. I could deck the shit out of him and there would be no consequences. How badly did I want to hit his pudgy little face and upturned nose. Could I punch his nose back into a normal shape? Or should I kick him right in the dick?

I bit my lip. I'd never actually hit anyone before. A wind whisked through the open door, I felt my hair beginning to unravel and a strange calm descended over me. Maybe Zita and Hildy had sent the winds to me from town.

I took hold of his shoulder and leant into him.

"I'm going to die tomorrow, Thomas, and then I'm going to haunt you for the rest of your life. And whenever you lie with a woman, you're going to think of me, and my witch's mark, and your tiny piggish penis will never rise to the occasion. And it'll be all your fault."

His face had flushed pink; his breathing became heavy. His hot breath was getting all over my skin.

"You ... you can't do that. I've done nothing wrong."

I pushed him backwards. He tripped over his feet and fell to the floor.

"Father!" he yelled.

"Remember this moment," I whispered to myself, trying to imprint the image on my mind.

I stepped out into the autumnal night, becoming one with the whirls of golden leaves.

I did not go back to the apothecary. I went to the forests that lay above Watlington. My feet took me there — I had nothing to do with the decision.

Something in me wanted to be with the trees. I wanted trees above me, trees behind me, trees beside me, left and right.

So I'm no longer a Shaftsberry. I'm no longer a lady. Does that make me a witch? If one wasn't a lady, was one a witch? Or was I now just a peasant? A no one. A fallen woman. With no money or status. What did such people even do? Was I an actual witch, with magic, with power? I had cursed my own brother, which would be bizarre behaviour for someone who wasn't a witch. The sun was setting. It was getting dark earlier now. The trees in here were all turning: it was like a fire raged above me. It raged within me too. There was a heat in my chest, right in the centre. Like something within me wanted to escape. A demon? My breathing was getting irregular. My family had disowned me. More than that: they had murdered me. They had murdered Magdalen. Given up. Handed me over to Satan. To witchcraft. Burnt my future, my prosperity.

"You don't even want to be a lady," I said to myself, out loud. I picked up a stick and began whacking the trees as I walked. It felt good. "You hate stitching and sewing and reading the Bible out loud."

"It was my right!" I yelled in reply, snapping the twigs in half and flinging them deeper into the forest.

"Your right is fucking boring!"

"No, it isn't!"

"Yes, it is! And you never even wanted this!"

"Yes, you did." I hissed, embracing the madness that was descending over me. "You wanted all the glory of your parents. You wanted to be like them."

"Why would I want to be a cunt?" I began kicking at the fallen leaves.

"You have fallen." I didn't know who had said that. I looked around for someone else. Perhaps my mother had followed me here, or my brother. There was no one. I turned around and around and realised I had walked too far into the forest to know where I was. I began to cry, loudly, shamefully, like I had never cried before. A purging. I yelled out and screamed. Fucking God. Fuck him. Why hadn't he looked after me? Or was I not a daughter of God? Was I daughter of the Devil? Was *he* meant to look after me? How does the Devil look after his subjects? I found myself kneeling on the forest floor. In the dirt. The baby blue skirts were covered in mud. "They have no idea what they've unleashed," I whispered loudly to an old oak. She groaned in a breeze like she agreed with me.

My breath was laboured. Fuck this bodice. I began tearing at my back. Damn this dress! It was inescapable — I could take off these skirts. I tore off my thick damask gown and drove it hard into the mud. I imagined the look on Agnes's face if she could see me now. I was laughing. I took off my sleeves and chemise and did the same to those, picking up big lumps of dirt with my hand and squishing them into the white frills. I grappled again with my corset, but I couldn't undo it.

I began to run in my underskirts. Feeling the air whip against my face. I was leaving a wake of sounds in my path — laughing, crying and screaming trailed behind me, until I found the edge of the trees. I was on top of Watlington Hill. I was not actually that far from the apothecary. I could see it in the distance. If I wanted to, I could walk down the hill, skip a few stiles and get in via the back garden. But I didn't want to. I sat with my back against a large oak and looked out over the world. Maybe I needed the Church. Maybe someone would look after me there. My body was aching from the flood of emotions and feelings and tearing of skirts and hitting of trees. I leant my head back against the bark of the oak and shut my eyes.

"Maude?"

My eyes opened with a start.

"What?" I barked, disoriented.

"I'm sorry, Maude. I'm sorry!" The big beast of a fairy was consuming my view. I hadn't heard him approach.

"Rufus." I took in the scene, remembering where I was. "How did you find me?"

"This is where the witches found me." That didn't really answer my question. I frowned. My day was descending on me in flashes of memory. Rufus had brought a blanket. He placed it on my knees. I pulled it up to my chest, cold.

"I am disowned," I mumbled. "I am on my own now."

He nodded, not asking for any more explanation. The world was turning gold as the sun became a sliver of itself.

"You can be anything now," he said.

Could I? Or was I confined to being nothing now? I didn't know.

"You only had one path before. Now you have any path," he continued. "You can be Maude."

I reached my hand up to my hair and began pulling out the braids. Letting them free. "Can you undo my corset?" I asked, standing.

He nodded and began undoing them with surprising ease; if I hadn't been so consumed in misery, I might've questioned him about his possibly lustful skill.

"Can you be anything now?" I asked him. I felt his long fingers pause at my back.

"I am more than I was."

"What were you before?"

"Not Rufus," he said. I did not press him. He hadn't pressed me. The piece of material fell forwards onto the ground, and I took a full deep breath. Then I took another.

My thin undershirt would not keep me warm but I felt better now I could breathe. I relished a few deep breaths.

"Let's go home, Rufus."

"Yes, Maude."

We walked down the hill, the pieces of my dresses lying strewn behind me. I felt my hair fly out behind me in the wind, wild, wild, Maude. I arched my body backwards, feeling the freedom of being unbound; I could go wherever I wanted to now. No one would care. Even so, I would like to go back to the witches' coven.

"Zita might throw me out now that I don't have a plan. I don't want to talk to them tonight."

"You can do what you want, Maude." The fairy helped me over the apothecary garden wall.

The witches were in the back room, by the fire, sipping at a broth. They both stood as we entered.

Rufus shook his head subtly, but clearly. He stood behind me and gently pushed me up the stairs. I heard my cat following. He took me all the way up to my room.

"Do you want me to get you food?" he asked.

I didn't respond. Hildy had put fresh water on my sill. They had known I would return. They had known. I splashed my face and washed my dirty hands. Rufus returned unbidden with a bowl of the broth. I drank it on my bed and let Jimmy lick the remains. Rufus sat on his mattress on the opposite side of the room and watched me.

I wondered if I would ever see my mother again. The last thing I had said to her was that I had cursed her ... did I want to curse her? Had I actually cursed her? Had I killed her baby? My sadness turned quickly to panic.

"I think I cursed my mother," I whispered.

Rufus came to me and pushed me gently back down onto my back and he pulled the blankets up over me. "You need to sleep, I think."

Maybe I did.

"Jimmy. Jimmy!" Rufus made a beckoning noise with his lips, convincing my cat to get under the covers. His little head rested under my chin. I breathed in Jimmy's smell. Had someone let him outside? He smelt like hay. Like he had been rolling in the bales.

Rufus brought the candle in the glass near me. He was

making me my haven. The tears were unstoppable, but my breath became measured with each inhale of my little imp. Rufus sat cross-legged next to my mattress and began to hum. A low, soft vibration. Not like the buzzing I had felt and heard in my mother's confinement chambers, but a good version of whatever that was. I watched him, his eyes shut, and he swayed to the soft rhythm of his song. I wondered if he might be a fairy, after all.

I liked sleeping because I could leave my experience. But waking made it very nearly not worth it. I hated the few seconds before I remembered what had happened, because the remembering was just as painful as when it first happened. I was forced to relive it all each morning, and all the times I woke with a start in the middle of the night.

The paste on my leg. The paste on his body. My father's voice, declaring my death. My brothers ripping my witch's mark from my body. With their teeth. My mother's pale cheeks witnessing my pain and allowing it to happen. My madness in the woods. I had not come downstairs in four days. Rufus and Hildy took turns bringing me my needs, and each of them, including Zita, took turns trying to convince me to come and do some work downstairs. To distract me. They all said it would distract me. My death notice would be out by now. I wondered if they would hold a fake funeral. I was lying on my mattress, arms splayed out like I was crucified, staring at the eaves. My trunks still surrounding me. My dresses and jewels, still waiting to be returned to the grieving Shaftsberry family. How horrific to lose a daughter so young.

My legs were starting to ache from how little I had moved in the past week. How could my legs ache when I hadn't moved them at all? It didn't make sense.

"What was your room like in your old home, Maude?" Hildy was sitting with me today. She had been so quiet I had almost forgotten she was there. But there was always someone there. Rufus and Hildy were devoted.

"It didn't have a crazy deaf witch in it!" I had spoken loudly but had turned my face away from her.

"I can see you are speaking," she said softly. "Are you being rude to me?" She seemed amused.

"Why would you ask about my home?" I said slowly to her face.

"Would you like to make your own space here?"

"Zita does not want me here."

"She just needs a little convincing. Wouldn't you like to have your own room? A little hermitage, if you wish. Something that reflects Maude."

"This space reflects me just fine."

"This space reflects a vagabond's cave."

"Then I am a vagabond." I sat up. Glaring at her. All my anger funnelling towards this completely blameless witch. "A. Dead. Vagabond. And this is my coffin."

"You are not dead."

"I am."

"Fine!" Her face changed. Her lips were pursed. I had never seen her look so stern. She rose eerily upwards, as if there was a string being pulled from her head. "But your parents didn't kill you. You have killed yourself. You have entombed yourself. Do you understand?" I scowled at her. "Your parents did not kill you; you have hanged yourself with a rope of your own despair."

Her words rung around the room: perhaps she had used magic to make them echo. They repeated in my mind. I blinked.

"You don't understand."

"You think we haven't had to overcome great pains?"

"Have any of you been killed by your own family?"

"Far worse has been done to each of us. You have no idea of our stories! So caught up in your own pitiful misery! You're blind, Maude, and you hear far less than I!" Timid, softly spoken Hildy was gone in a whirl of rage.

The door slammed and I was left in the eery silence that comes after raised tempers.

Jimmy was staring at me from across the room. I knew what he was about to do. Very slowly he went down into a squat, preparing to defile my space with cat piss. Rufus's space too, I supposed. Jimmy was going to disrespect my vagabond's cave.

"Don't! Go outside if you need to go!" He paused. Cocked his head. Then slowly walked over to my bed.

"Did you even need to go?" I asked accusingly. His tale swished. "Fucking cat."

I got up. I went to the peaked, small window. I looked down onto the street and let my mind settle as I watched the stragglers waddling along the cobbles below.

The witches wanted me to stop moping. I didn't want to do what they wanted me to do. It would annoy me to please them. Someone threw a pot of piss out of the window opposite. I caught the old woman's gaze. She smiled at me. I returned the gesture. That was nice.

But I suppose by entombing myself in the witches' house I was doing exactly what my parents wanted. What I was doing now would please them. That was unthinkable.

It did seem that trying to displease everyone else meant mostly displeasing me. I was getting caught in my own venomous, vindictive crossfire.

Jimmy's tail wrapped around my leg.

"What do you want me to do, Jimmy?"

I shut my eyes and remembered the moment I leant against the old oak in the woods. What had I whispered to her? "They have no idea what they've unleashed." Unleashed. I wanted to be unleashed. On nobody's rope.

I watched as a younger woman entered the shoppe. I couldn't see her clearly from where I was standing but she was rubbing her eyes — she was crying. I heard the jingling bell ring, floating up the stairs to my ears. Curious, I cracked open my door. I could hear mumbling. It was clear she was distressed, but I couldn't make out any words. I tiptoed down the stairs into the not-so Great Hall and pressed my ear to the apothecary's back door.

She was still crying, her words all jumbled together. I pressed my ear even closer to the splintering wood. Something, something, mugwort, something, wailing. Someone pulled open the door. I fell, ear first, into the apothecary.

"Good," said Zita, steadying me. "I was coming to get you."

The unintelligible woman had retreated to the corner of the room, huddling over her knees and rocking. Her long red hair was dark with sweat.

"What's wrong with her?"

"We don't know. I can't make sense of her."

"Well, what can I do?" I asked defensively.

"Read her."

I would've protested, but her wails were getting louder. I approached her. She looked up at me with her large round eyes. Terrified. I bent down to her. She grabbed both my forearms. I felt her strong trembles in her grip. She was not just sad; she was ill.

"She is not well," I told them.

"What does she need?"

I looked into her eyes. "Are you with child?" I asked.

Her eyes grew a little wider. "Mugwort," she said again.

"Mugwort is an abortifacient, isn't it?" I asked.

"Yes. A powerful one. Is that what she's saying?" The two witches were crouched a few steps behind me.

"You want to be rid of the child?"

"Nay, nay!" she wailed.

I took a deep breath. "Help me understand."

"Reggie!" she wailed. The hairs on the back of my neck stood on end. Reggie.

"Have you lost your baby?" I asked clearly. She un-gripped my forearms and grabbed her lower belly, wailing. "What cure did you ask the wizard for?" I demanded. "What did you need from him?"

"I ..." Her nose was running into her mouth. I wiped her face with my sleeve.

"Go on."

"I was being sick! I couldn't eat. Nothing would stay in," she managed. "I needed help."

"Reggie gave you mugwort for your sickness?" Hildy confirmed, loudly.

She nodded.

"Then you lost your baby?" Zita added.

She crumpled, crawling onto her side and letting her tears seep into the apothecary floors.

"Why would she go to that man? Why wouldn't she come to us?" I asked.

Hildy had begun frantically rummaging through the bottles on the walls.

"Perhaps it was commissioned by others. The babe might've been a bastard." Zita was propping the poor woman up, but she was limp. Like a corpse.

I could hear them continue to talk. I was vaguely aware of Rufus being called to fetch the mortar and pestle.

But my body was preparing for something. I felt that buzzing again. This time, the buzzing was in my feet. Like they were preparing to flee. Or attack. Or fight. Fighting feet. I didn't flee anymore. I was unleashed. A shiver, like a spell, ran up my spine. I was changing from the inside out. My feet were ready, prepared for whatever it was they were intending. They walked me out of the door.

CHAPTER SIXTEEN

"Maude?" Rufus was calling for me. "Maude, where are you going?"

Hildy and Rufus followed me out into the street. My ears were filled with my own heartbeat.

"You're in your underclothes!" That was Zita's voice.

I didn't reply.

That motherswiving Reggie. I saw him in my mind's eye, gaunt, thin, all in black, with cheekbones like the Devil. Sharp. The Devil had sharp, evil cheekbones presumably. And so does Reggie.

I could feel people's gaze on me, wild woman in her nightgown marching up the street. I knew where he lived. I knew where he destroyed women and killed their kin. It was out the back behind the high street shoppes. In a dark, damp, death hole, no doubt. More like a cave than an apothecary, I bet.

WIZARD WORKER AND HEALER

I squinted at the sign erected outside of the thatched

cottage. It swung lazily in the breeze, and autumn leaves rustled playfully and welcomingly around the open door.

That fen-sucked flap-dragon. No wonder people were getting suckered into his evil, non-magic magic. I walked through the door, waiting to see the Devil incarnate. Lucifer in the flesh. This was just another exorcism. I had done one of those before.

The scent of lavender hit me in the face. I felt the soothing smell conflict with my rage. There he was. He had his back to me.

I stormed up to his bench and smacked my fist on the wood.

"YOU!" I bellowed. A young man turned around.

"Good morrow, goodwoman. Is something amiss?" His face was kindly, crinkled with concern. He was incredibly appealing to behold: bright blue eyes and a stylish mop of blond hair.

"Where is Reggie?" I demanded.

"I am he." I stared at him. "Are you well?" He stretched a hand over the counter to gently touch my crossed arms.

I tried to gather myself. My anger was fleeing. Fuck. It was seeping out of my skin. Stay, rage! Stay! "No. I'm not — quite — well." I tucked my curls behind my ears. No, I wanted my curls out. I took my curls out from behind my ears. I noticed him looking me up and down. I recalled I was in my nightgown. Fuck. He didn't look a thing like the Devil. "Did you give a pregnant woman mugwort?"

He stopped, ran his fingers through his hair.

"Mugwort ... mugwort. No, I don't believe I did. Are you sure I can't do anything for you?" He had the silkiest voice, Goddamn him. What was he doing, seducing his clients into taking his poison? Well, two could play that game. I took a deep breath and leant on the counter.

"She had long red hair?" I suggested.

"Oh yes! I remember. She had a sensitive issue. Not one for your ears."

"I'm standing here in my nightgown, sir. With nothing underneath. My ears are not as sensitive as you might imagine."

He took a step back to take me all in. He had a small smile on his face. "Why are you in your nightgown?"

"I like the way it feels against my skin."

"Are you trying to seduce me?" he asked, not angry about it.

"Yes," I whispered, watching the way his eyes lingered over my breasts. "I want the gossip."

He was still confused, but I think the strangeness of my appearance and my dress had cast a spell over him.

"She was harbouring a bastard," he explained.

I swallowed. Zita had been right.

"You gave her mugwort for her morning sickness?"

He chuckled. His laugh was delightful. "Oh no. I gave her mugwort to purge her of the child."

"Did she want to be purged?" I asked, trying to keep my voice steady, wanting to know his sick excuse.

He beckoned me to come in closer to him, like he wanted to tell me a secret. I gave him my ear. "I was instructed by her father. I have a very good relationship with all the lords around these parts." His breath was sweet. I turned my face towards him. He smiled. He liked this game. "You have the most brilliant eyes," he said. His eyes glanced down at my lips.

Idiot. He moved in to kiss me. I let him. I sucked his bottom lip. I heard him let out a small moan, and then I bit it. He tried to pull away, but I held on. Panicked, making a ridiculous noise like an animal caught in a trap, he pushed me in the shoulder, and I let go.

"What the fuck!" His lip was bleeding.

"You shouldn't have done what you did."

"What the *fuck*?" he said again.

"*You shouldn't have done what you did*," I said again.

"It is my Godgiven calling! The people here need me!" he said.

I felt that shiver down my spine. I moved around the counter. He backed up against the wall.

"This is woman's work."

He held his chin high, trying to maintain his power. "It was a financial agreement between two men. A lord at that."

I could feel the bees buzzing around my body. The energy rising. "You must stop practising."

He gave a short, sharp laugh. "You're a succubus," he declared.

Maybe I was.

"You must stop with your false curses, and your profane relics and your evil doings." I was close to him again; I saw a dribble of blood drip down his chin.

"Do you think me the Devil? Do you think I am the doer of Lucifer's bidding?"

"No." I shook my head. "A wizard of Lucifer's bidding would actually be able to perform magic. All you do is pretend."

"You must leave."

"I will leave when you promise to stop your fraud."

"Who are you?" he said.

"I'm Maude. I'm the charmer."

He squinted back at me. "Hildy and Zita's new witch?"

"Aye."

He took a short sharp breath, then pushed me out of the way. Moving to the door of his shoppe. "I should've known. If you do not leave right this moment, I will call the steward and have you removed and locked away as a madwoman. I promise you he will not need much convincing." He touched his lip again and winced.

I stood taller. My dress had come up around my ankles. I had never felt more powerful.

"You are indecent," he said. "I can see your breasts under your dress." If he looked closely, he would see my mark.

"You liked it a moment before," I reminded him. He opened the door. "Will you persist in your practice, Reggie? Or will you leave it to the women with the true power to wield it?"

"I'm calling the steward."

He went to exit. I blocked his path.

"I do not fear you," he said.

"Where God bids a curse, there is cause to fear cursing."

"I do not fear you," he repeated. "You have no powers."

I lifted my skirts. I didn't want to flash him my purse. I might have been mad, but I would have some dignity. I lifted the hem just high enough that he saw the beginnings of my mark on the inside of my leg. His eyes baulked at it.

"Witch," he whispered.

"Aye." I replied. "It stretches all the way up my body," I assured him. He crossed himself.

I shut my eyes, went down on my knees, and put my hands in the air. "What's your last name, Reginald?"

"Baldwyn," he whispered, then gasped and put his hand over his mouth as though I had compelled him to say it.

"Reginald Baldwyn." I did not hear footsteps. I had frozen him to one spot. "I have three curses for you."

"Three?" I heard him breathe.

"ONE!" I barked. "I wish that all the meat and drink you eat might up and down in your belly. Never to settle!"

"Codswallop," he choked.

"TWO! May nothing prosper nor go forth that Reginald

Baldwyn has taken in his hands. May his false work fall to the ground." The words were spilling out of me — had I read them before?

"I will undo these charges!"

"And finally." My calm words cut through his hysteria. "I wish that before you die you might crawl upon the ground like a toad on all fours." I had pulled that one from nowhere. I was unsure what it even meant. But it was affecting him; I felt his hot breath on my face.

I stretched my hands above my head, pushing my chest forwards and feeling all the Godliness of my body. I smiled and opened my eyes.

"You curse me because you cannot be bothered to kill me." He shook his head, his mop of blond hair falling in front of his eyes. "You are a murderer. A lazy one at that."

"Trust me, Reggie. Death will come." I rose to my feet. "But in the meantime, if I hear a whisper of you continuing your practice, I'll send the ghost I recently evicted from Lord Sotherby's place to you. I know it is looking for a new residence."

"Leave now!"

I loved how afraid he was of me. He could easily pick me up and put me out, but he wouldn't touch me.

"Gladly." I opened the door and walked out into the cool morning air. I heard Reginald slam it shut behind me. I had not been cold on my journey here, but now the air bit through my nightgown. I took a deep breath and breathed out a puff of cloud. Like a dragon.

"Are you done, Lady Maude?" I jumped. It was Rufus.

"You follow me, fairy?" I asked, momentarily affronted. Then I noticed he was carrying a cloak.

"I worried you might be cold," he said, "or murdered."

I walked to him and let him wrap me up in the thick green material.

"I am very cold but still un-murdered. Thank you, Rufus." I had been so close to being proud, to walking home cold for the sake of being independent. But I didn't have the energy. Not after that. I looked behind me. Reginald was nowhere to be seen.

"What did you do to him?" he asked, as we began the walk home.

I held in my reply as we passed an apple merchant. I could feel him goggling at us.

"The villagers are scared of me. People can tell I'm a witch now."

For some reason Rufus laughed. A cold laugh that didn't reach his eyes.

"What? What's funny? It's true, I saw it in that merchant's eyes: he can tell that I'm a witch. He knows I just laid some Godawful curse on another human being. I am an outsider."

"Maude," Rufus said sternly, "they're worried you've been stolen by a Moor. They're not scared of you, pretty, small, pale lady." I blushed. "Do you think you really cursed him?" he asked.

"I'm not sure. We'll have to see. I only hope he stops ruining people's lives." I dug myself tighter into Rufus's side. We turned onto the high street. There was no avoiding the high street. The apothecary was off it. It was a wide path, with lots of good shoppes. My mother got her dress materials and broaches from the gentleman to my left.

"He was so handsome, Rufus. It surprised me."

"The better-looking you are, the more you get away with." He smiled at me. "That's why you get away with being so rude."

"All well, young lady?" said an old woman from an upstairs window.

"Perfectly well, goodwoman!" I replied.

Rufus picked up his pace and looked straight forwards.

"We don't need blackamoors brought into our kingdom!" yelled someone behind us. I wanted to yell back, but I did not.

By the time we stood outside of the apothecary, Rufus had been yelled at nearly a dozen times. He hadn't said a word. Nor had I. I stared at the door. I didn't know whether my heart was thumping because of our walk home, or if it was because of what had just happened, or because now I was back at the witches' den. Had my actions changed me? I stared at the small wooden door, my eyes fixed on the fox-shaped knocker. Did my actions mean there was no turning back?

"You don't have to go in," Rufus said quietly from behind me. He was so patient with me. Always waiting for me. Always giving me space to bewitch men and stare at door knockers. I bit my lip and put my hand against the wood of the door. It was old, splintered.

I thought of the only home I had known before. It had big doors I wasn't strong enough to open by myself. I did not like the thought of giving into these witches. Of letting them think they might've been right about me all along. But this door was warm from the soft sun's beams. Soaking up all the heat it could get. This door welcomed anyone. Including me. Including my mark.

"I like this door," I told Rufus. He made a deep noise in his chest. In agreement, I thought. I turned to him. "Hildy told me I wasn't dead."

"Hildy was right. You are not dead."

I sighed reluctantly. "I suppose."

"Did you try to fight her on the fact?" he asked.

I nodded.

"You like to argue with the witches." It was a statement, not a question.

"They always try to tell me how to feel, what to do and what I am."

"Like Hildy telling you that you are not dead."

"Exactly."

"Why don't you tell them how you feel then? Why don't you tell them what you want to do and who you are? You tell them whether you are dead or not dead."

I lifted my chin up, surveying the fairy. I took a deep breath.

"Do you know what you want?" he asked.

I had never been asked that question. Not ever in my whole life. I did not know what it felt like to think about what I might want. I thought for a long moment. Rufus stood completely still, giving me time.

"I want to bury my trunk of clothes and never return it."

"I can help with that," he assured me.

"I want to fill our room with dried lavender and hang it from the beams like Hildy does in her rooms." His lips twitched. Hinting at a smile. But I kept my face deadly serious. "And I want to find some of those purple stones, the ones with the teeth that shine."

He nodded ceremoniously. "And what shall we call you?"

I thought about it for a moment. "You can still call me Maude. I like the name Maude. But it is no longer short for Magdalen. It's only Maude."

"Then all those things will be." We stood staring at each other for some time. "Let us go inside, Maude. It is the witches you must tell, not me."

I put my hand on the fox's nose and turned his snout, lifting the lever of the door.

"What if Zita doesn't let me stay?" I whispered.

"You won't know unless you talk with her."

The witches were in Zita's room, bent over a chart of the stars.

"Are you trying to divine what I did to Reggie?" I asked.

"What were you thinking?" snapped Zita.

"I don't know," I admitted.

"What did you do?"

I shivered to think back on it. "I cursed him" – they looked at each other – "I think." There was a long drawn-out silence. I looked at Rufus, begging him to say something. Someone say something. "He was fairer faced than I expected."

Rufus stifled a laugh. The women continued to stare at me.

"I kissed him," I confessed.

Zita sat down behind the desk. "What?"

"I kissed him," I said again, tapping my lips to aid Hildy's understanding.

"Oh I understand perfectly well what you said, my dear," she said. "Did you kiss him or did you curse him?"

"Both." I said. Zita gave a long exhale. "It was some sort of a seductive, cursing combination."

"I would've paid a lot of money to see that," Zita mumbled. I think I may have impressed her.

"He had given the woman the mugwort upon her father's instructions. He's fucked up." I was trying to validate myself. Validate what I'd done.

"He is a piece of work," Zita confirmed.

"So I kissed him and then I cursed him." I shrugged. "What more do you need to know?"

"Do you wish to stay with us, Maude?" asked Hildy.

"I hardly have anywhere else to go, do I?"

"If you wish to stay," Zita replied, "you will have to prove yourself worthy. We are not a poorhouse. There is one nearby that will take you in if you cannot tolerate our rules. You cannot use this place as you have been. You cannot make Rufus sweep the floors. You cannot look down your nose at our craft. And you cannot pretend you're at Court anymore. You can stay here as a witch, or you can leave as a peasant. You cannot go anywhere as Lady Magdalen anymore, and you must remember that."

I felt suddenly small, vulnerable and weak.

"Have you heard the death knell?" I asked, my voice constricted. "Is there word on the street of my passing?"

"Aye. Sweating sickness. Lots of talk. Poor Lord Beckett. Only a few weeks after the wedding. So sad." Zita's expression was flat. Her voice completely even.

Rufus touched the small of my back. "What were we talking about before we came in?" he asked me in a whisper.

"I want to stay," I told him.

"Tell them."

"I want to stay, and I want to fill my room with dried lavender and hang it from the beams like Hildy does in her rooms."

"Of course." Hildy nodded.

"And I will not return my trunk to the Lady Shaftsberry. I wish to bury it, keep it hidden, so that even when they send their people to pry it out of my hands, they cannot find it."

"That can be done. But there will be a period of probation." Zita spoke clearly. "We will make our final decision at harvest time. You must prove yourself worthy between now and then. Do you agree to those terms?"

"Why don't you like me?"

"Do you agree to those terms?" she asked again.

"If I must."

CHAPTER SEVENTEEN

Probation sucked.

Zita didn't let me do anything other than fetch remedies, collect things from the garden and clean. Rufus wasn't allowed to touch the broom. I had to sweep. A lot. I wasn't allowed to sit on the floor behind the counter. I had to stand and I wasn't even allowed to sew — not that I was upset about that part, but my entire courtly fantasy had been robbed. It felt like I had nothing left of my old life. We had buried my trunk of Shaftsberry heirlooms under the not-so Great Hall's floor, in case someone came a-hunting for them.

"Why do you think she is so tough on you?" Rufus had never once spoken to me at night. The witches had hung an old and deteriorating tapestry to divide our room in two. He always came to bed after me, and he made so little noise that I regularly gave merit to his actually being ethereal.

"You mean Zita?" I asked.

"Hmmm."

"I never thought about it much. Lots of people don't like me. My entire family don't like me — I've just always accepted that I am quite a dislikeable person."

He went silent again. I lay my head back down.

"I like you," he said eventually. I smiled into my blanket. "Hildy likes you; Jimmy likes you. So why doesn't Zita?"

I gave some thought to it, wrapped my blanket around my shoulders, and went to sit where I could see him. He was sat, relaxed, in bed, leaning up against the wall.

"She was abrupt with me from the very start," I explained.

"You didn't think to ask why?"

"No."

"What happened to your marriage?" he asked softly.

I wanted to tell him in that moment. Something about the dark, the intimacy of sharing a room, it made me want to give it all over.

"It's a secret." I managed, trying to smile.

"This house is full of secrets."

"It is?"

"Well, do you know anything about anyone? Do you know anything about the witches, about me?"

I knew that Zita had a very heavy footstep and made far too much noise, far too early in the morning to be polite. I knew Hildy had made up blasphemous hand gestures for when she was in a bad mood, I knew that Rufus hated sweeping, but not quite as much as I did.

"What is there to know?" I shrugged.

"Your lack of curiosity is strange."

I scowled at him. "You're strange."

"I am! But you are still not curious."

"Your business is your business," I said simply. I'd always been reprimanded for curiosity in my home. I was never allowed to ask questions or be involved. But I *was* interested in who he was. Where he came from.

"What secrets are you hiding from me, then?"

"You're not interested in my business!" he retorted. I thought I might've upset him.

"I'll tell you one of my own secrets in return." I felt my tummy turn; my mark didn't want to be revealed. I had spent my whole life manoeuvring myself, hiding myself so I never had to reveal my secret. Why would I give it up now?

"Go on." He moved to lie on his tummy, cupping his head in his hands. Why did I want to do this? But if I could ever tell anyone, surely it would be this strange, mysterious, not even quite human man named Rufus. He wasn't from Court, so he couldn't damage my reputation any more than it had already been damaged. I mean what *was* my reputation? My reputation was dead. I had a reputation for being dead.

"I have a mark on my body." There was silence. I wondered if I would be sick. "I think it might be a witch's mark."

"Is it why everything that happened, happened?" His voice was relaxed; he didn't sound revolted.

"Yes. That is why everything that happened, happened." The feeling of something rising in my chest spilled up and out of me. But it wasn't bile, or tears, or a chewed-up dinner. It was a laugh, just a short outburst of mirth. It was so strange and so sudden I felt embarrassed. I looked at him; he had his head cocked to one side, curious. I felt giddy and light.

"Is it a big mark?" he asked.

"Verily, it is huge." I was shaking, but it wasn't a tense, scared shake. It was a tired, unravelled, exhausted quivering. "It is my family's shame. It is my shame."

"Do the witches know?"

I shook my head. "I've never told anyone in my life."

"I will be the keeper of your secret."

"Are you a good keeper?"

"The best. I keep many."

I moved myself onto his side of the curtain now. "Well then, tell me one of yours. You owe me."

He drummed his long fingers over his lips, as though rifling through his many untold tales. "My secret is that I am not a fairy." I opened my mouth to complain about how utterly shit this secret was, but he kept talking. "And that I too ran away from my marriage."

"Oh." I felt deeply soothed. "What happened?"

He frowned. "She was afraid of me. She had been coerced into our union by forces greater than us both. She believed me a flesh-monger, or a thief, or a scoundrel."

"Why?"

"Why do you think, Maude?"

"Because you are a Moor?" He nodded. "She was blind!" I said, almost angry. He smiled.

"I am a Moor!"

"I know that! She was blind to who you are!"

"She was convinced I was villainous."

"Did you have nowhere else to go?"

"I knew the witches would take me in."

"How did you know they would?" I asked.

He just smiled. "Will you keep my secret safe?"

"I will keep your secret safe," I promised.

We smiled at each other.

"Good night, Rufus."

I crawled back to my bed.

I looked around for Jimmy. I made a beckoning noise with my lips.

"He's with me, Maude."

"Traitorous cat!" I heard Rufus's light footfalls; how a man so big and tall could make so little noise was beyond me. I felt his presence above me.

"Here," he whispered, handing me my baby. "He is your little sprite." Our fingers brushed.

The four of us were cleaning Hildy's room. The hanging flowers and drying herbs were enchanting, to say the least, but they caused havoc on the floor. I, of course, was sweeping.

"Could I have one of the purple sparkly rocks?" I asked, pointing at the collection of crystals on her table.

"Amethyst," Zita corrected me.

"Can I have some amethyst?" I asked.

"Do you even know what its properties are? Do you even know why you want some amethyst?" She raised her fine, blonde eyebrow at me.

"Sparkles," I murmured under my breath.

"It's used to calm the client."

"That's why I want it." My hair was frizzing with the sweat and effort of today's chores.

"You can buy one with your hard-earned coin."

"But when will I get my first client?"

"When you prove yourself."

"I got rid of the Sotherby ghost! I cursed Reggie! That's not proof of my devotion to your craft?"

"We don't know if you actually cursed him ..." They doubted me.

"Well, have we had to remedy a single one of his poor clients since I spoke with him?"

"Nay," said Hildy. "Verily, you are right there."

"And I did get rid of that ghost! And don't forget I helped that obnoxious man with his detached finger."

"Aye, but did you or did you not run away from the patron with the maladies of the face?"

"She had boils all over her face! She smelt like she bathed in her own shit!"

I looked at Rufus to back me up. "She did smell like shit," he agreed.

"See!"

"You exercise no compassion." Zita shook a bundle of lavender with more vigour than needed, and it sprinkled its fragrant purple petals on the floor. She pointed at them. "You have missed a spot."

"What issue do you have with me?" I felt hot, like I was about to do something drastic.

She stared at me, her perfectly pale face going red. Then she abruptly turned on her heel and left.

I, too, should leave this place.

I should leave and bathe in shit and get boils, and die on the streets. Rufus would look after Jimmy and no one would care.

"Come with us today on our calls around the village," Hildy said.

I didn't want to do it, but she insisted.

"Fairy, you'll be fine, won't you?" They were hurrying me out of the door. Rufus was sitting behind the front desk with Jimmy in his lap. He nodded seriously. "Thank you, goodman!" Hildy sang out loudly, taking my hand and leading me down the road after Zita.

In the first cottage we visited, in the fields at the back of the town, we met a woman called Betty. Her husband had died in the summer. She was left alone with a small babe, not yet a year old. Her home barely had four walls. I replaced a stone that had fallen out of its place, and helped Zita sweep the floors. She couldn't work the land while she looked after the baby, so her field was a desolate wasteland of twigs, sticks and unharvested hay.

She had no family.

"I need a man," Betty said, pushing a prematurely greying hair out of her dark eyes. She tried to laugh, but it ended up a coughing fit.

"Maude has a good few spells for attracting a mate," said Hildy, who was cradling the tiny baby.

I had been keeping myself busy sweeping, confronted by the poverty and unsure what to say to this woman who had nothing. From my calculations, she didn't have a chance. The baby was severely underfed, with no juicy fat rolls or chubby cheeks. Her farm was going to waste — she'd lost an entire harvest. I didn't know what on Earth a bunch of my own words could do.

You could give her hope, said the gods in my ears.

Fine. I rested the broom against the stone wall — a bit of it crumbled off onto the floor. I glanced at Zita, who was watching me closely. I didn't know if I wanted to please her or disappoint her. Focus, Maude, this isn't about Zita. It's about Betty and her babe. I made myself sit on the ground by the poor woman's feet.

"Is there a man you have your eye on, Betty?"

She looked down at me, thinking. "There is a young man two lanes away. Single. Able."

"What is his name?"

"I don't know," she whispered, ashamed.

"What does he look like?" I asked.

"He has big broad shoulders." She bit her lip. "Dark eyes ... long hair." I let my mind relax, asking the world for a poem, a spell to cast, an enchantment to give her some hope.

"You'll beguile him with your smile, Betty," I told her. "But he can't see your smile from in here."

"I have no reason to go over to his farm." She wrung her hands. "And I have baby John. I have nothing to give to anyone. Only debts and a sickly babe." There were tears in her eyes.

"Ask him for help," I said.

"I cannot."

"You must."

She whimpered a half-hearted protest. I shut my eyes, playing with a few words rolling around my mouth.

"*For weal or woe I will not flee*
To love that heart that will loveth me."

She looked at me, shocked. Good God, I was the Thomas Wyatt of witches.

"You must remember these words, and repeat them to yourself, okay? They will make you strong, and give you strength to ask for the help you need."

She nodded slowly.

I took another breath.

"*That heart my heart hath in such grace*
That of two hearts one heart will make;
That heart hath brought my heart in case
To love that heart that loveth me."

"To love that heart that loveth me," she repeated. "He will love me?" She was visibly trembling.

"Repeat the poem to yourself as much as you can. Then go ask for help. Ask him to help you clean the fields of the rotting hay."

"Would you repeat the spell to me again?"

I sat with her for some time, helping her memorise my poem. We left her with colour in her cheeks, and a small, tired smile on her face. I hoped I hadn't set her up for more disappointment.

"You've not set her up for disappointment," said Hildy, the mind-reader, stroking me on my back as we walked away from Betty's shack.

"How do you know?" I signed.

"Because we are about to visit the broad-shouldered, dark-eyed, long-haired man."

The witches were deft at this. Weaving their gossip-cum-magic through the villages, placing a thought here, a rumour there, all coming together to make a web of energy that pulled people in the right direction. We told the broad-shouldered, dark-eyed John that he had a Godgiven calling to help those in need. Like Christ himself he would use his great strength and generosity to grant grace to those who needed it. We told him that through his Christ-like endeavours he would find love. He ate it up. I couldn't believe how he ate it up. Doe-eyed. Nodding. Asking questions. Excited.

When we left, he gave us a coin. A coin! I couldn't believe it. Zita refused, but he insisted. So we thanked him and we left, richer.

Was this magic? Was this evil? What was this? Whatever it was, it had felt good. The generosity of these people made me want to weep.

We were nearly off his property when I heard fast footsteps approaching us from behind.

It was John; perhaps he realised he couldn't spare the coin.

"Wisewomen!" We all turned in time.

"I think it's only proper for me to tell you about someone who might need your help in the town. I don't want to be gossiping but ..."

"Well, since you are ordained by God to help those in need, it only makes sense," said Zita practically.

"Exactly." John nodded. "And he is one of your kind too."

Fuck. I looked at Hildy, whose face had frozen in a look of mild curiosity, but I saw her body stiffen.

"The wizard, Reggie, in town." Fuck. "He's been unwell." I

thought I was going to be very, very unwell. Perhaps all over John's shoes, in fact.

"How so?" asked Zita.

"I went to try see him only a few days past and he said he wasn't seeing anyone because he was sickly. He looked bad. Pale in the face, hardly able to stand. Said he couldn't keep any food down." John nodded at me seriously. Well Jesus fucking Christ.

"Thank you for letting us know, John." Hildy touched him gently on the forearm. "You are truly a divine conduit on this Earth." She was still weaving her magic. "The wife you take will be no doubt be grateful for your blessings."

He stood up taller.

We turned and walked in silence until we were some way down the road.

"Oh my God," I moaned; my hands were shaking. "What if I have killed him?"

"You haven't killed him," Zita said impatiently. "You probably just frightened him sick."

"Do we have to go and see him?" I looked down the country road. I didn't want to keep walking — I wanted to fold myself into one of these hedges and stay there forever.

"I think it's probably best we pop our head in," said Hildy. "Just in case."

"That was my curse," I whispered, staring at the hem of my mud-encrusted skirt. "I cursed him so that all the food he eats may never settle."

The witches looked at each other. Zita signed something I didn't quite catch.

CHAPTER EIGHTEEN

"I don't think it will be helpful for me to see him." We stood outside his cottage, and I couldn't see any movement from inside. I needed to piss, badly. We'd been on the road all day. "Do we even care if he's unwell?" I asked, jiggling up and down. "He's an old codpiece, killing wanted unborn babes and dispensing people's dead body parts as relics."

Hildy asked Zita to translate what I had said; understanding, she turned to me. Her gentle face was serious.

"Do you want his death to be on your hands?"

"No! But I don't want to piss on his floors either."

"You can hold it," said Zita, knocking. No one answered. She knocked again. The door was locked.

"Oh well! We checked!" I said, starting off down the road. I turned back to see Hildy getting something out of her basket. I couldn't see exactly what it was, but she went up to the keyhole, rattled something around, and the door was open. Couple of brigands, these two were.

"Reginald?" Zita called out. I tottered in after them. I looked around his shoppe: nothing looked out of place. Then we heard a groaning.

"I'm closed!"

"It's the wisewomen!"

There was a yelp. "GO AWAY!" He was in the room out the back.

The two witches gave no mind to his explicit instructions and pushed through the door into the back room.

He was in bed, pale and shaking, just as John had described.

"Get her out of here! It's her! She's the reason I'm in here!"

I stayed by the door. He was still pleasing-looking even in his sickness.

He was staring at me, blue eyes wet.

"What are your symptoms, Reginald?" Zita asked, sitting on his bed.

"My symptoms are written in her curse!"

"Which is?"

"I can't keep food down!"

"For how long has this been?"

"Since she visited!"

"What've you been trying to eat?"

"Whatever's been in my pantry!"

"Let me see what you've been consuming," Hildy demanded.

"Issin there." He gestured back out from where we came.

Both the witches left. "Why don't you lift the curse?" Zita whispered as she passed me.

"What?"

"Lift it."

"Is there anything to lift?"

"I don't know. But do you want him reporting to the steward that you're using magic to cause people ill?"

"He causes people ill all the time!"

"Don't die on your own sword, Maude. You don't have a

family name to protect you anymore. Nobody wants a witch wishing men sick in town. They'll get rid of you, and no one will notice or care."

They both left. I turned to the man. He was groaning and moaning and I began to suspect he liked the drama.

"I'll undo the curse," I grunted, coming nearer.

"Oh would you? Would you?"

"Aye." I wondered how I would do it. He'd know more than I would about removing curses. How embarrassing.

"I just want to eat again!" he cried, like he was in a Goddamn playhouse.

I put my hands in the air, like last time, feeling ridiculous. "I recant my curses." I paused; that didn't sound thorough enough. "May they never come to pass, and if any have begun their workings, may they be forever reversed." I put my hands down and looked at him.

He took a shaky breath and nodded. "Oh, thank God. The Devil has left!"

I rolled my eyes. "Listen. I'll have my ear out for your bullshit remedies though. And if you purge a woman of her beloved child again ..." I looked at him threateningly. He met my gaze. "I'll reverse my reversal."

He nodded feebly.

I wondered when the witches would be back; I looked at the door awkwardly.

I noticed Reggie's breathing become steadier. I wondered if this was my power, or if he had worked himself up into this mess.

"I've been dreaming of you each night," he said breathlessly. "Was that a part of the curse?"

"All your own doing," I assured him.

"Perhaps they were prophetic dreams." He looked at me.

"I've had dreams come to fruition in the past." He was begging me to ask.

"Tell me my future," I pleaded sarcastically.

"You will kill another of your kind," he said suddenly, darkly.

There was a beat, where my breath left me, and my head span. I pulled myself back to the reality of who was speaking and what he was saying.

"What?"

"That's what I kept seeing. You will kill a witch."

"Get fucked, Reggie." I tried to laugh.

"Verily, it is true! I saw it." He was nodding vigorously. "Each night. The same dream. You kill a woman, a wisewoman. A witch."

He was seeking vengeance for my curse. That was what he was doing.

"How come you do what you do when you're so very bad at it?" I asked.

"God called me here."

"How? In what manner did God call you here? Via what route?"

He looked like he might protest, but he shrugged and continued to speak. "I was meant to take over from my uncle — his parish was about a mile away. But when he died, the congregation ..." He looked distressed. "It was a Satanic, Devilish village. They defected to another church — I was left with no flock."

"So you ran your church into the ground?"

"No, the congregation were Satanic." I raised a very sceptical eyebrow. "It was not my calling. Christ had other plans for me. I really have to thank the witches for my practice. I came to get advice from them. They were useless, of course, and I realised that I had just as much to give as them, if not more."

"But you have no training in astrology, or making remedies, or anything relevant at all."

"It's not that hard — you should know that. I doubt you have any training. I didn't need education. I have a new flock and they trust me with their lives. The people prefer a man to dispense medicine and advice, you know."

"So you're a priest turned wizard?"

"So?" he said, defensively. "Zita was a high-born lady, and she gave it all up to examine the stars. The Almighty knew my powers were better used elsewhere than within the crumbling walls of that shitty little church."

"Zita was a lady?" I sat down on his bed.

"You didn't know?" He found that amusing. "I suppose most don't. I was privy to the information because my uncle knew; he knew everything about everyone when he was alive."

"To what family was she born?"

He smiled wide, seemingly entirely better. God, this town loved gossip.

"I forget the name but you would know her family. Her sister is married to Lord Shaftsberry of Shirburn."

I blinked.

"Reginald!" The witches were framed in the doorway. "Do you think your turning insides could have something to do with the maggot infestation in your poorly salted meats?" I watched as Zita harassed the young man about basic food hygiene. Zita. With her pointed nose and thin lips, even the sound of her footfall: that ominous, impending doom footfall. Exactly like my mother's.

I turned my gaze to Hildy, who was watching me closely. Reading my facial expression. She took Zita's arm gently and gestured towards me.

"What's wrong?" Zita said.

I stared back at the two of them.

"What?" she said again.

"Is this why you don't like me? A reminder of where you've fallen from?" I heard an amused giggle from Reggie, and I rounded on him. "Shut up, you fraudulent little shit. You don't know the half of it."

"Let's go home," suggested Hildy. "Reggie. Don't eat the meat: it's making you sick."

Zita and I looked at each other fiercely. I tried to see my features in her own. We were both pretty fucking stubborn, I supposed. "Let's go," Hildy said again. "Zita will explain everything once we are home." Hildy tugged at her wife's sleeve. Zita relented and walked out of the door. Hildy beckoned to me. "Come, come, not all is as it seems." A past version of myself would've refused to follow them. She would've stomped and huffed and then not returned until the wee hours of the morning, where I would have reappeared dramatically, and loudly. But my curiosity overran me. I followed them out of the door.

"I will be returning to my practice," sang Reggie from behind me.

"Stick it up your arsehole, Reginald!"

CHAPTER NINETEEN

Rufus was sitting by the fire, warming his toes with the flames. He turned to us all as we entered.

"What happened?" he asked, sensing the tension that had walked into the room.

"I will tell you what happened." I sat down next to him. I wanted to hold court. Zita had been treating me like shit this whole time — hiding this from me. This was her mistake. Her deviousness. I sat in the chair next to Rufus, pulled off my shoes and placed my feet next to his. "Zita is my fapsucking aunt!" Rufus didn't look that surprised. "Did you know?" I hit him in the shoulder. He shrugged.

"The fae folk know everything," Zita said.

I turned to her with a flounce. "Don't talk to me about the Godforsaken fairy folk. Explain yourself!"

She sat herself on the kitchen table. It was a very un-Zita thing to do. She moved the glass jars of dried fruit and made space for Hildy, who hopped up also.

"Why didn't you tell me?"

"I've been asking her the same question since you first arrived," Hildy said.

"Don't try and get on my side," I snapped at her.

"I didn't want you to know," Zita explained. "I like who I am now. It took me so long to detach myself from them. I don't like anyone knowing."

"Why not?"

"Because I do not like my family and they do not like me. It was volatile. I was thrown out. Surely you can understand, Maude. You don't go around telling people where you came from."

"But your family is my family!"

"Neither of us *has* a family."

I felt infuriated. She was being so obtuse. "Did you know who I was when I first came to the apothecary?"

She flushed. "They may not be my family but I've kept an eye on them. You only lived down the road."

"How did you end up here? In an apothecary? Is it because thou art a witch?" Did she have a mark? Did she know about my own mark?

"Our story is a long one." She took Hildy's hand.

"I am owed it."

"Tell her, Zita," Hildy whispered.

"Why?" she signed angrily.

"She is your kin!"

"I don't have any kin."

"Why don't you tell her how we met?" Hildy suggested.

"She won't like it."

"Just tell me!"

"I've been working at this apothecary since I was a girl," Hildy started.

I swivelled to look at her.

"It was my mother's practice before it was mine, and it was my grandmother's before it was my mother's."

"Did you visit her for remedies?" I asked Zita, wanting her to take over the story.

"Of course not. Your mother's family —"

"Your family. Your family," I corrected.

She cringed. "They only used the family physician, but on one particular occasion we could not."

"You were with child?" I guessed.

She gave a thin smile. "No, Maude. Your mother was with child."

"What?" I demanded. "When was this? When she was pregnant with John?" I knew she had had a difficult pregnancy with my eldest brother.

"She would've been but fifteen.'

"What?" I was struggling to understand.

"Don't be obtuse, Maude." She wiped down her skirts. "Your mother wouldn't tell me who the babe's father was, but she had told me, in perhaps our first moment of true sisterly connection, that she wanted to be rid of it, and so I took her to the witches. We told our parents we were going for a long walk, and we came straight here."

"But it was not my father's baby?"

"To my knowledge, she had not met your father yet, no."

Two thoughts were at the forefront of my mind. The first was an angry tangle of words that went: Good God, my mother? A hypocrite. Pretender. Liar. A more coherent thought lingered too: Holy shit, my mother could conceive a baby by glancing at a codpiece. But she hadn't just sneaked a peak, she'd lain with someone outside of marriage. I felt a hand on my knee. I turned to Rufus.

"Art thou well, Maude?" he asked.

"Perfectly." I nodded. "Continue."

"Hildy and Hildy's mother took great care of Mary. They

sat with her for some time after she had taken the right herbs, explained everything that would or could happen."

"Was she upset?"

"She was brave," Hildy said.

"Hildy looked after your mother gently and kindly. It was, of course, the first time I had met a wisewoman, one of my kind. I did not feel any call to the practice immediately. I was a Montague, promised to some lord's boy, whose name I can't recall."

"You can't remember the name of your betrothed?"

"Soon you will forget the name of yours."

"I'll never forget."

"You will," Zita said firmly. "My connection to Hildy was immediate, despite the circumstances. I remember catching her eye as I waited by my sister's side. I remember the butterflies in my stomach, and how I had tried to play them off as nerves for Mary."

"Did my mother recover?" I mean, of course she did, but I had to ask.

"She did. She experienced discomfort, but she was back to her usual self in no time. I, on the other hand, found excuses to return to the shoppe. I had remained obsessed with the apothecary girl since I left. I did not know what to do with the feelings. I had never heard of such a thing. I wondered if I simply really wanted to be her friend, and I wondered if perhaps she had cast a spell on me."

"No one says I haven't," Hildy said, smiling.

"I began sneaking into town. Hildy's mother taught me about the stars, about the practice. Over time, I became one of them." Zita stopped, a tone of finality in her voice.

"What happened then? You were expelled from your family?"

"Obviously."

"After only a few weeks of Zita's visits, we weren't just exchanging stories about remedies and planetary placements, we were sharing our lives with one another." Hildy explained. "When I got sick, Zita stopped going home all together. She stayed by my side." Hildy nudged Zita gently, asking her to continue.

"My parents thought I had been abducted, taken away by some vagabond, but Mary knew where I was. I was by Hildy's sickbed." She swallowed. "We thought she had the sweating sickness. We did everything we could to break the fevers. I thought she was going to die: she would drift in and out of consciousness, hardly seeing or hearing me." I looked at Hildy, who seemed much less bothered by the story of her near demise than Zita, perhaps because she couldn't hear it. "Mary came to confront me on the day Hildy's fever broke. She had awoken but her hearing had gone."

I waved at Hildy, needing her attention on my lips. "The fever took your hearing?" I asked.

"It was like I had been offered to the gods, but they'd only taken a part of me. I sometimes hear a glimmer of sound and I wonder if it is noise from Heaven, my hearing having been taken to the skies but the rest of me left on Earth."

She rested her cheek on Zita's shoulder.

"Your mother asked me to come back. She told me I was bringing shame to her name. I told her I wouldn't, so she called the steward on us," Zita said.

I felt a rush of anger at my mother. Venerator of rules she'd broken herself. "For what? Devil worship or something?" I asked.

"Nay." They were both silent. "I'm going to bed," Zita announced abruptly.

"You owe me this story!" I protested. Her bright blue eyes glistened. "Please, Zita."

"I gave you a shelter, teaching, food, whilst you paraded around my home in my sister's jewels. I owe you nothing." She marched up the stairs.

I looked to Hildy, and without me asking, she continued the story. "My mother passed not long after I awoke. A similar fever came upon her, but the gods took all of her, not just her hearing. And that sealed our fate. Zita wouldn't leave me. I told her to return home, but ..." Hildy shrugged. "Then, your mother visited again, for the final time. I was still draining eel fat from my ears when I saw them both. I remember I had my head on the side, gazing blankly out of the window as Zita tried to coax the fat out of my ear cavity. That's why I saw them first. I recognised Mary, of course, but I also knew the man next to her. He was a Justice of the Peace. His name was John Crawley, and he was a notorious pest. He was practically drooling as he stood outside the apothecary. I remember being nervous, not just because we had a Justice in our home but because I wasn't going to be able to hear anything. I remember watching his lips moving, trying to understand what he was saying. I could only assume, just as you had, Maude, that he was accusing us of maleficent witchcraft.

"But that wasn't why he was there. I remember watching Zita try to explain what had happened to me. It would've been funny if it wasn't so tragic. The miming, the looks, the moment Zita got the actual eel out and began flinging it around. I remember just standing there, the centre of this sad story. But they were not here to accuse us of maleficence."

I felt Rufus stir next to me. He went and sat where Zita had been. He held Hildy's hand gently, and she smiled at him and stroked his cheek.

"I hardly knew I was in love," Hildy continued. "So in a way, I'm grateful for Mary and her accusations. They were prophetic. We had been summoned to face charges. We were accused of something not even written in the law. Of something so foul we were tried in secret." She laughed softly to herself. "After the Justice and your mother had left, Zita explained what Mary had accused us of by writing it down on a wax tablet. Your mother had lied, told a story to get us in trouble. I remember the words Zita wrote. We are accused of vice with one another. Of course, I replied that we hadn't committed any such sin! Because we hadn't. So she kept writing; I remember her blue eyes flickering from my eyes to the wax. She was so hesitant to write it. It read: *She claims she saw us in the fields.* Of course, I had been in bed for weeks, but your dear mother was determined. She wanted to make up naughty stories about us, and I swear the smell of wax tablets still sends shivers up my legs to this day. I asked Zita what we were supposed to have been doing in these fields. She wrote: *We were unclothed.* And then she wrote: *We were kissing.* Of course she had to write it on a pallet, it would've been unwise to make it permanent on parchment, but sometimes I wish she had written it with ink so I could read it every day. I wished she had tattooed it into my skin, so it was a part of me. Instead, a few moments after she had handed me the tablet, she kissed the words into my lips." Something moved at the top of the stairs. Zita was sitting on the landing, head leaning on the railing, listening.

The fire crackled, filling up the silence.

"What happened after that?" Rufus asked.

"After the kissing?" asked Hildy cheekily.

"He means with the accusations!" I said quickly. "Don't you?"

"Not necessarily." He shrugged. Rufus was a scoundrel.

"People don't like to deal with our ... special sort of sinning. It turns out that when you're a woman who loves a woman you don't get burnt or imprisoned or anything so novel. You get forgotten."

"Nay, nay," said Zita from the top of the stairs. "Not forgotten. You get eradicated. Even our trial wasn't recorded."

"People don't want to think about it; they don't want to talk about it. The courts had physicians inspect us, they pried open our legs to make sure neither of us had a member hidden somewhere between our thighs. They looked thoroughly, very much wanting to find even a hint of a prick. But once it was decided that neither of us did, they demanded that the court records be destroyed; they didn't want our story getting out."

"Why?" I signed.

"Women run hot, Maude. If the ladyfolk in the town realised they could find pleasure with their own kind ..." She trailed off for a moment. "I think they honestly believe that all women might be put off men entirely."

I managed to laugh. "How absurd!"

"The male mind is frail, Maude. Do you know in the church records Zita shares my own last name? Zita Gold."

"They let you marry?"

"Nay, we are sisters in the eye of the Lord," she said, a tiny smile on her face. "It makes them all feel a lot better. That is why we live together. That is why we love each other. That is why we sleep next to one another. Sisters."

"You didn't worry about incest being added to your charges?" I asked.

"Never bothered us," said Zita.

CHAPTER TWENTY

The witches had gone to bed almost an hour earlier. I was still staring into the fire.

"You should go to bed," Rufus mumbled; he had been waiting with me.

"You go."

"It is harvest festival tomorrow. You need some sleep."

"Do we have duties?" I asked. "As witches?" I don't know why Rufus would know.

"We do," he said, one of the coven apparently. "You'll see." Why did he know so much?

"How many secrets are you keeping from me, Rufus?"

"A few." He stretched, stiff from a long night of sitting. "How many secrets are you hiding from me?" he asked.

"I have only one secret and I told it to you already," I said. "Everyone else has hundreds. It's immoral."

"To bed then, Moral Maude." He gave me his hand, I took it and we dragged ourselves up the stairs.

. . .

I had never been to harvest festival. It was not for people like me. For what I used to be. It was for the people, the farmers, the peasants. Nobility stayed inside. I always imagined it to be a filthy affair so I was not looking forward to it. Harvest morning had already fulfilled my very low expectations. I had been involuntarily baking since sunrise. Seed cakes. For the farmers.

"How many seed cakes do the farmers need?" I asked, wrapping the seventh cake in cloth.

"How many farmers do you think we have in this town?" Zita asked pointedly. "Because I can assure you it is more than seven." Zita had been more or less the same to me this morning. I had followed her lead and responded as rudely as I had before I knew of our relationship. But I was noticing more and more now the similarities between her and my mother.

"We'll spend the whole harvest baking!" I complained.

"It has been an abundant season, Maude. They deserve cake."

"This is the last one," Hildy said, sliding the sloppy cake mix into the baking oven.

"Now as this one bakes we must get ready."

I put the warm cakes down on the table. "Am I not ready?" I had nothing else to improve my look. I had my woollen dress and my apron and I had tied my hair back and put on my bonnet. Hildy, face splattered with flour, was looking excitedly at Zita.

"What?" I asked suspiciously. "Must I wear a pumpkin over my head? Dress as a scarecrow? What does this festival require of us?"

"We have made you a harvest dress," Zita explained.

"Why?"

"Just say thank you, Maude," Rufus reprimanded me.

"Thank you," I said quickly.

They went to fetch it. I thought of my finery hidden under the floors, how I wanted to retrieve my dresses and jewels, but it made no sense for a peasant witch to be wearing pearls and damask. It would only draw attention and questions. One day soon I should sell them; the coin would be more useful than the ruffles.

The witches came back with deep crimson material. I couldn't understand the cut from looking at it folded in Zita's long-fingered hands.

"Thank ye," I said, receiving the gift.

"It will please us both if you would wear it to the festivities today," said Zita.

"You do not like my plain clothes?"

"We just thought you might like another option," Hildy explained.

I nodded. "Thank you," I repeated.

I stood outside the shoppe in the sun. I was balancing on a wobbly cobble, waiting for them all. The dress they had made me was beautiful. Simple, with no lace. But it was hooded: a thick heavy hood that let me feel mysterious and powerful. Someone to be frightened of, for no one could see my eyes. I had let my hair out in all its curls, and even they were protected under the canopy of crimson.

"Off we go!" Zita called to the air, locking the apothecary behind us, and passing me half of the cloth-covered cakes. We caught each other's eye. She seemed lighter, less severe. Perhaps the airing of her dirty laundry had lifted her spirits.

"Morning, Mrs Lambsbroth," Zita called to a regular patron who was walking in the same direction as we took.

"Morning, Zita! Hildy!" She stopped, eyeing me and Rufus

warily. I relished in my anonymity and grinned up at Rufus from under my hood.

"You love to be looked at like we are heretics or demons?" he asked, keeping his head low as we moved onto the town's high street.

"It makes me feel powerful," I whispered. "Like they fear me."

"The thrill of being feared wears off."

I didn't know what to say to that. Even in the ever-growing crowd, no one would come near Rufus or myself. It was like there was a magic circle drawn around us that none of the villagers could enter. A space for just Rufus and me. The local smithy was walking with Zita and Hildy. I eavesdropped on their conversation about healing bad burns.

"Have you ever been to a harvest festival before, Rufus?" If he wasn't going to tell me his story outright, I'd have to get glimpses.

"I've seen them from afar, but never been to one up close." That was interesting. "Have you?"

I shook my head. "It's for the peasants."

"And the witches," he added.

We arrived in the market square where we were quickly engulfed by the masses. Rufus towered above me. I stood close to him, not wanting to get lost or have, God forbid, someone knock a seed cake to the cobbles. He gently redirected an early-morning drunk who bumped into me. I retreated into my hood. It was a fun sight: all the stalls in the marketplace were open and teeming with customers buying their harvest hauls. The four of us found a spot near the market cross; we stood on the step and watched the farmers bringing in their carts of produce. I could see them all now, entering from the other side of the square. The people began singing.

Merry, merry, merry, cheary, cheary, cheary,
Trowle the black bowl to me;
Hey derry, derry, with a poupe and a lerry,
Ile trowle it again, he trowle it again.
I craned my head backwards to see if Rufus knew the words
and my hood fell off. He was singing.
Hooky, hooky, we have shorn,
And we have bound,
And we have brought Harvest
Home to town.

The farmers were dressed as lords, albeit, to my trained eye, not very wealthy lords. Lords down on their luck. They were adorned with foil jewellery and sported hats stuffed with magpie feathers, but they were all holding themselves with the pride my father himself felt in his position. It was a wonder to witness. The crowd cheered for them and handed them bits of money and food.

Hooky hooky hooky.

The people had stopped singing and were now chanting this one single word. I could do that. I joined in, and felt my heart and soul swept up with the feeling of unity. These people were so grateful to these lordly farmers who had toiled all year to make sure we were fed.

Hildy and Zita had been separated from me and Rufus by the swelling crowd. Hildy waved at me, trying to get my attention. "Give the farmers our cakes!" she yelled over the crowd. I nodded, pulling Rufus down off the step and towards the witches.

"We need to put our hoods up!" These women loved to

fuss. They disappeared into the folds of the material. We looked like a coven. A coven laden with cakes.

Rufus walked in front of us, guiding us to the front of the crowd.

The nearest fruit-laden cart pulled to a stop in front of us. The dishevelled-looking farmer looked at us blankly, his eyes lingering on Rufus.

Hildy leant towards me. "Best to give him a bit of witchy advice with your cake."

"What?" For the love of all things holy, could they not have told me earlier?

Zita stepped forwards. I watched her, taking note of what I was supposed to do. I couldn't hear what she was saying. She handed the farmer her cake and ... then what? What was she saying? A swarm of bees had erupted from their hive and were buzzing around my guts. Rufus had resumed his position behind me. He put a hand on my shoulder. That farmer kept moving, and we waited for the next one. Hildy moved forwards. She bowed lower than Zita had. Should I bow that low? And then she gifted the man with her cake and her words.

The next carriage was coming. This farmer was extra bedraggled. Be witchy. Witch. Healer. Astrologer. What was I? A reader? A charmer? This was ridiculous. I turned to look at Rufus. He nodded at me. What're you nodding at, Rufus? Why am I so nervous? Gently, he turned me around and pushed me out into the path of the cart.

The farmer stopped. His lordly clothing was made from sewing little bits of foil onto an old cape. I smiled at him and bowed my head, presenting him my seed cakes with shaking hands.

"In gratitude," I whispered.

The farmer took them silently and gave them to his boy

sitting on top of a bunch of pumpkins in the cart. Then he turned back, expecting ... expecting something.

"You are Maude," he said before I had summoned the words.

Toadspotted fuck. He knew me, he knew I wasn't dead. "You are the charmer," he added.

I swallowed and nodded. "Can I serve you with my gift, my lord?"

His back straightened and chin rose at the reminder that today he was noble. "I am widowed," he said, then he lowered his voice. "I had to make my costume by myself." He indicated the bits of foil sewn inelegantly to his person, clearly embarrassed. My heart wrenched for him. I touched his shoulder.

"You look Hampton Court ready, my lord."

He blushed. "I've been hopeless since she passed, and the boy, he needs a mother's love."

"The seed cakes you have just given to your son," I began. "Share them with the woman who is sitting in your heart right now."

"The woman?" he said, brow furrowed.

"There is one who resides there, no?" Please, please, please have a crush.

He took a moment. "Yes. There is," he admitted. There always is.

"Go to her, with the seed cake, share it with her."

"The cake is charmed?" Verily ... the cake is charmed. I nodded, smiled, bowed and then backed away.

Fuck, am I a fraudulent, deviant scammer?

We backed into the crowds and I ripped down my hood. "You could've told me I had to give them a witchly gift!" I snapped.

"Looks like you did just fine." Hildy took my hand and we began walking out of the crowd.

"Are we going home now?" I asked.

"How many more cakes have we?"

I looked down at our hands: a fair few more.

"We go when we've given our gifts."

We walked up the high street. I was excited to return home. Rufus and I had surreptitiously saved a cake for ourselves and Zita seemed in a good mood. I wondered if she might tell me other stories about my mother. I fell in step beside her. She didn't stiffen or walk away. I needed to say something.

"I'm sorry if my presence reminds you of your pain," I tried.

"Is Rufus hiding a seed cake under his coat?"

"Aye," I confessed.

"We shall have it with butter when we get home."

I threw a relieved glance at Rufus, who was walking behind me. He wiped imaginary sweat off his forehead.

"I am sorry if at times I have treated you as though you were your mother. I see that you are different from her."

"Thank you," I said sincerely. "Have you had word from her recently?"

"The last I heard or saw of her was last Christmas, at Court."

I opened my mouth to ask questions about why in Christ's name she'd been at Court when she made a small noise of surprise. I followed the direction of her gaze. A man in livery was standing in front of the apothecary.

Both witches had turned hard on their heels and were looking at Rufus. He was frozen.

"Hookey hookey!" The man approached us. No one was speaking.

"Hookey," I replied, trying to ease the awkwardness.

"I have a summons," he said, clearly perturbed by the lack of response from the witches. "May I come in?"

Again, I waited.

"Please do!" Hildy said eventually, snapping back to her usual self and showing him in through the door.

I lingered behind.

"What's wrong?" I whispered. "Summoned where?" I was beginning to panic, but they were ignoring me, talking only to each other. Rufus looked like he was about to fucking peg it down Sheepe street, but before he could do so the small man was at my side, peering up at him.

"Reasonable?" I looked at him. What's reasonable? "Reasonable Blackman?"

Rufus made a grunting noise.

"Aye." He nodded slowly. "His Majesty thinks you're dead, you know!"

I looked to Zita. She pointed into the kitchen. "Let's make our way in here. I'm sure we all need something warm to drink."

"Indeed, Zita. My hands are stiff from the cold," said the guest.

"We can't have that." Zita pushed open the door.

"Why did he call you a reasonable black man?" I whispered to Rufus.

"Because that is my name," he whispered back.

"What?"

"Sit," hissed Zita.

Hildy had the kettle on the fire, and she looked nervous. Had this man come to put the witches in prison for their marriage, perhaps? My eyes were flickering between the four of them, trying to divine the truth.

We all sat down around the table. "Forgive me, I am not familiar: you are?" The messenger cocked his head at me.

"I'm Maude." He waited for more of an explanation. "I'm a new wisewoman who resides here."

"Oh, I understand! I expect you will be a part of this summons too."

I looked at Hildy. She avoided my eye. What was the summons to? A trial? Had we been accused of maleficence?

The messenger got out a parchment. I'd never seen such an adorned piece of paper. Gold lettering curled its way up the side of the parchment, and red and blue ink had been used to write what I could only presume was our death sentences.

"He'll be expecting you for the full twelve days of course." He paused, looking at Rufus. "He'll want to know you're well, Reasonable."

"He needn't know about this, Thomas," Rufus muttered.

Thomas shook his head. "It'll mean my neck if I keep it from him! Surely he'll only be pleased, Reasonable."

"What if he takes *my* neck for my deceit?"

The messenger shook his head disbelievingly. "No, that's nonsense! I'll tell him you're coming with the witches."

"Don't," Rufus said. His voice sharp and very deep. "I'll come. Don't tell him, but I'll come. If I don't show up, you can inform him."

The man took a moment, but then nodded. "You better show," he said threateningly.

"I will." Rufus hung his head, annoyed.

"Is this all clear, goodwomen?" The man looked to Hildy and Zita, who were perusing the summons.

"Just like last Yule." Hildy nodded. "We are honoured and cannot wait to return to the King's service."

The man nodded, smiled and then did up his cloak.

"I'll see myself out and we'll be met again at Yuletide! Make sure you show up, Reasonable, or I'll dob you in."

Rufus grunted.

"Hookey," Thomas said again.

"Hookey," replied everyone but me, and the infernal messenger left.

I stared at the three of them.

"I want the cake," I demanded. "And some sort of strong drink."

"I told you I had my stories, Maude." Rufus retrieved the wrapped-up, severely misshapen cake from his coat and Zita passed me a cup of wine.

"Have you all known each other all this time?" I asked.

"We go to Court most years for the twelve days of Yuletide; we entertain, tell them all ghost stories and read their stars. We met Rufus there."

"Why didn't you tell me you get to go to Court?"

"I didn't want it to fuel your lust for ascension." Zita gave me a tight smile. I returned it with a blank stare. Rude. But she wasn't wrong. I was already envisioning some elegant and dramatic return to favour with my family, even after all this time. I turned my head to the fairy.

"So we may finally confirm that you are no fairy."

"Hush. He is a fairy, that much is true," Zita chided me.

"A fairy of Court? Reasonable Blackman?"

"I had enjoyed leaving that name behind," he said pointedly.

"I won't call you by it," I said quickly. "But you will tell me more. You are from Court? In the King's service?"

He grunted. "I was excused in order to be married, but" – he crossed his legs – "it didn't go to plan."

"What happened?"

"What happened to your marriage?" he retorted quickly.

"It went to shit." I shrugged.

"Ditto."

"What did you do at Court?"

"I was just a lowly servant, Maude, don't get too excited."

"Why would the King think you're dead?"

"It was the only means I had of leaving my marriage."

"Like me." He nodded. I opened my mouth to ask more questions.

"I'm going to bed."

"No!" I grabbed him by the elbow. "Stay. Tell me why you don't want to return to Court? Will you be in trouble?"

"We shall see, won't we?" He shook me free and went upstairs. I turned to the witches.

"Why not tell me the truth about where he came from? Why not tell me you were acquainted? It seems a pointless lie."

"In deference to our friend, dear Rufus. He did not want his past to follow him here. He will be grieving greatly that he must return to his life at Court."

Poor Rufus. I bit my lip.

"Am I to come to Court with you all as well?" I couldn't help myself.

Zita looked at Hildy. Hildy spoke with her hands. Yes.

CHAPTER TWENTY-ONE

The next month was not as enlightening as I'd hoped. Rufus was hardly talking to anyone. Zita, whilst being less of an old nag, didn't tell me any stories of Court or my mother, despite my asking — a lot.

"You'll find out all about Court when you get there," was her response, every single time.

I hardly even saw Hildy: the whole village came down with hard-hitting sniffles. I was dispensing and treating townspeople from dawn until dusk and we were run off our feet right up until the day we left.

They had curled my hair with a hot rod. My. Hair. So that it was even curlier than my natural hair. I had asked to retrieve my old wardrobe from beneath the floors, but was quickly reminded that I was not attending Court as a courtier. I was attending Court as a witch. So, I was dressed in a black dress, and my pockets were filled with trinkets I could charm. I clinked and chinked as I walked, but I felt beautiful in my own way as Rufus helped me up into the carriage. Hildy and Zita looked stunning: witchly but stunning. Zita's hair was netted back like a true courtier's and Hildy was in a pale blue dress, not unlike the one I had soiled in the forest. Her cheeks were bright pink and she flustered as she sat down opposite me in the carriage and clapped her hands together.

"I love this time of year!" she said delightedly, handing me a tub of sweet chestnuts she had picked that morning. "Carriage snack?" I took a few, and they bled all over my fingers. I was glad I was wearing black. Zita sat next to her wife and took her hand contentedly.

"Rufus? Hurry!" He was lingering at the carriage step.

"Be with me!" I demanded. Reluctantly, he stepped up and sat next to me, crossing his arms.

"Chestnut, Rufus?"

He shook his head curtly.

"To Hampton Court!" squeaked Hildy. Her enthusiasm was catching. I couldn't wipe the smile off my face.

We were breaking up the ride into two days, staying the night in an inn so we could be well rested when we arrived at Hampton Court. I had been excited about the trip to London, and the first leg was pleasant enough, eating carriage snacks and playing card games and winding up the cat. But in the inn that night and on the second day of travel I fell into a quiet, internal panic.

"Neither of you has said a word in over an hour," said Zita, looking across at the fairy and me.

"Hildy and I are bored." We were both staring at the carriage floor. "You look like you're both being carted off to the Tower."

"Mayhap we are," Rufus whispered.

I picked my cat up and held him close to me.

"Codswallop," Zita snapped. "Both of you are being dramatic."

"I know a lot of people at Court, Zita! What're they going to do when they see me there?" I had thought about it before, of course, but the closer we got to London the more terrifying it seemed.

"No one is going to accuse you for your little faux death, if that's what you mean. Your parents will be shocked, but I thought you'd enjoy that. I thought you'd find it fun."

"Hmmm." I grunted. "It could be fun," I conceded. "But what about Beckett?" I had become everything he had accused me of. This was what made me feel sick. He had said that a witch is what I was, and now it *was* what I was. I was a witch. What if his words had been prophecy? *He suckles at your teat.* I was cradling Jimmy like a baby, stroking his black tummy. I should have put him down. I didn't.

"Trust me, all will be well." Zita turned to Hildy, who had a more sympathetic look on her face. "Look at us, Hildy, bringing the dead to Henry's Court."

"We've resurrected only the truly worthy," Hildy added.

I tried to smile.

The smell outside the carriage changed: a dirty, sooty fog wafted into the carriage and I began to worry I might be sick with nerves.

"When we get there, Maude, stay close. It will be busy," Zita instructed.

My tummy turned over and over.

The carriage slowed in the London traffic. Rufus reached for something in his pocket and pulled out a bright green piece of cloth. He sighed and began wrapping the bright piece of material around his head in a turban.

I watched him. I didn't know if it was appropriate to ask. "Is that what you normally wear at Court, Rufus?" I asked finally.

"Hmm." He nodded.

"Is it from your home?"

"It is a Moor's traditional uniform at Court."

"Moors are from the north of Africa and Spain," I said, recalling something my tutor had once told me.

"Hm," he said again; his bad mood had gone to his bones.

"Is that where you're from?"

"No."

"So why are you wearing it?"

"Because people from Court are dunderheads."

"I see."

"We are close to the gates," said Hildy.

"Are you ready to be a curiosity, Maude?" he asked me.

I put my head out of the window, and the red-bricked beauty rose above me. Not even Rufus's determined scepticism and melancholy could stop me experiencing the awe. I made eye contact with one of the terracotta Roman emperors carved onto the walls. A man in livery stopped the carriage and spoke to the driver, then he appeared at the window.

"Your summons?" he said, his long nose wrinkling in apparent distaste at the newest arrivals.

Piffle. He hadn't been personally invited by the King of England to Court. He only worked for the King. Zita handed him the ornate parchment. He unravelled it and took some time perusing it.

"The Moor hasn't been invited," he said finally.

I looked to Rufus, panicked, but he was calm, bored almost.

"His Majesty will be pleased to see me. I am Reasonable Blackman, his trumpeter."

"I must needs check," the man said dully. "Wait here."

"A trumpeter?" I asked.

Rufus raised an eyebrow at me.

A man, different from the one before, appeared at the carriage. "Aye! That is the trumpeter!"

"You absolutely certain?" the gatekeeper asked.

The man nodded. "Reasonable, isn't it?"

"It is. I've been away, and the King will be curious to see me."

"No doubt! He has been most displeased with his replacement trumpeters; he's gone through several! Let him in."

The gateman sighed and signalled to open the huge wooden doors.

It was everything I had imagined. All the stories my brothers had told me, all the chatter about the fountains, the clothing, the noise, the smell — it was all true.

It felt like we were a boat entering a body of water. A lake of russet, with ripples of blue crimson and gold damask. The light bounced off the water, the bejewelled necklines glinting at me. The carriage moved with the current to the left hand side of the Court. Now that I looked closer I could determine who were servants and who weren't. I knew that the grooms and pages were in the bright red; they bustled around with trunks and packages. The higher-ranking officials, like the one approaching the carriage just now, were in a dark red: this would be a yeoman.

Zita handed this yeoman the summons.

He nodded genially. "Your rooms will be here, in Base Court. Just get your carriage to pull up next to the doors."

We began to organise ourselves as several pages swarmed the carriage. Someone helped me down. I relished offering him my hand and stepping down like Queen Anne herself. I watched as they bustled with our trunks and began lugging them off to our quarters.

Rufus was still in the carriage, resting his head on the back of the seat, staring up at the ceiling, completely dejected, as if he was about to be hanged.

"Rufus. Would you stay close in these crowds?" I asked, knowing his instincts to protect me would get him moving. Slowly he slunk his body up and out of the carriage. He stood beside me.

"Just this way," said another small boy in the royal red.

As its name foretold, the Base Court was the basest, the nearest to the exit. But our lodging was the closest to the gates to the next courtyard, which must mean that we were the very highest of the Base Court.

"Those are the Anne Boleyn gates," Hildy said. "He made them for her when they got married. We'll take you through them later." She smiled and squeezed my hand. Rufus sighed heavily.

"You're really killing my mood, Ruf," I said crossly.

The page unlocked a door and let us into our lodgings.

"It's primitive, as always, but it will do," said Zita, directing the pages to put the trunk down at the end of the bed.

It wasn't primitive. Not really.

The bed had four posts like back at Shirburn. I had sorely missed my bed curtains. I liked feeling cocooned while I slept.

The walls were dark wooden panels, and we had a tapestry and a fireplace. Verily, the tapestry didn't have gold thread, and it depicted a simple agricultural scene with a single lonely sheep, but it was regal, in a homely way. It was probably the King's personal sheep. And no, the mantel was not adorned with intricate engravings, but it was lovely, and the fire was already lit for our arrival, which meant the King was expecting us: the King of England was expecting me.

"We'll sleep in this room. You'll be through there."

"This isn't my bed?" I asked, disappointed.

"Nay." Zita opened the door to the next room.

It was smaller than the first — undoubtably the children's room. The bed was short and there was absolutely no room for Rufus, but it still had curtains and a fireplace. No sheep tapestry, but I didn't need a stupid sheep watching me as I slept.

"Where will you sleep, Rufus?" I asked, jumping onto my mattress. Zounds, it was soft.

"If you don't mind, I might just go here in front of the fire. Or perhaps in front of Zita and Hildy's fire."

I slid off the bed. "You won't get a room?"

"I was not invited."

"What about where you slept before? Before you ran away?"

"I slept in the kitchens."

"You did?"

He shrugged. "I was offered rooms eventually, but I had made a good spot, right behind the big fireplace, and the cooks woke me up with the smell of fresh bread and they let me eat the offcuts. It was nice." He shrugged again. Defensive. He itched at his turban.

"How long were you in the King's company?"

"A very long time."

Zita walked in. "Oh you have a view into the clock tower court!" she exclaimed, going over to the window.

I gasped and followed her over. "It's almost as though I am higher status than you, Zita!"

"Maude. I know you're excited, but you're sounding like your mother. Remember who you are."

Her words physically pushed me back onto the bed. I became very quiet. "I was just playing."

She turned from the window to me. "I know you enjoy taunting me but I also know you've waited longer and with more longing than most to get to Court. I want you to understand that you are in for a nasty surprise."

Rufus, in a fit of annoyance, and apparent fit of itchiness, threw his turban on the floor. He scratched his head furiously. Zita walked softly over to him and reached up to touch his shoulder, and he stilled as if she had cast a spell over him.

"If His Majesty is angry, we will run with you," she whispered.

Rufus bent his head, resting his forehead on top of Zita's head.

I had not understood the stress he had been under.

We sat there for a few moments, Zita stroking Rufus's shoulder, Court whirling around outside.

Hildy entered the room.

"Sommers is here," she said.

"William?" Rufus asked, finally lifting his head off Zita.

"Reasonable?" A male voice came from the other room.

Rufus's mood changed instantly. "Sommers?"

He squeezed past Hildy and we followed him out into the front room.

The two men embraced.

I couldn't see the visitor's face but he was wearing bright blue stockings and an elaborate green tunic with a hood.

"I have missed you, Reasonable!" He was saying the phrase repeatedly, not letting go of Rufus. "I have missed you, Reasonable! I have missed you, Reasonable!" Rufus gently disentangled himself and I saw this William Sommers. "Everyone thinks you dead. Including I, until a moment ago when I heard your voice."

"I am alive, Will. It was a misunderstanding," Rufus assured his friend.

William Sommers had such bright blue eyes they looked ethereal — as if he were not entirely of this Earth. I wondered if he was an actual fairy.

"You must be the new witch, Maude." His gaze was penetrating.

"I am."

"This is William Sommers," explained Rufus, "the King's fool."

William gave a very, very low bow.

I returned the gesture. I had heard of the King's jester. A natural fool, they called him. Half his mind in Heaven. Closer to the gods. And Henry liked him that way.

"What exactly are your powers, Maude?"

"I am a reader of people, and a charmer," I explained.

"You read people's fortunes or emotions?" he asked seriously.

"Emotions, I suppose, or their situations. I give advice ..." I trailed off.

"I see," he said, smoothing down his green pleated skirts. "And what sort of charms do you provide?"

"Whatever the patron might need. If he is unlucky in love, I might give him a ... a chalice that gives him confidence with his fancy."

"What sorts of charms do you use? What talismans?"

"Show him," Zita interjected.

I delved my hand into my pocket and showed him the bunch of trinkets. An old brooch, a spoon, a feather, a bit of wool. He approached me carefully and looked into my hand.

"What is this?" he asked.

"That's a bit of cloth."

"From what?"

"I think it is from an old dress."

"Your dress?"

"Yes," I said, though I had no idea.

"Do you have a witch's mark?" he asked suddenly. "Zita's is on her hand and Hildy's is deep in her ears. We cannot see Hildy's, but the gods can. That is why she cannot hear. Do you have a witch's mark?" he repeated.

"I do."

He waited, then pressed. "Where is it? Will you show it to me?"

I looked to Rufus. Be brave, Maude.

"I have one all over the front of my body." I gestured vaguely.

"Draw an outline." William wasn't being aggressive, or even rude. He just seemed very curious.

The witches were watching me intently, neither surprised nor judgemental.

I outlined my mark, tracing from the tops of my thighs, into the weird way it squiggled over my hips and up over to the bottom of my belly.

"Right over your privates," he whispered, in awe. "No wonder you are good at giving advice on loveless marriages. You should find clothes that let you show it off for the evenings."

"I would be naked," I said quickly.

"I suppose you would." William nodded. "The King will like it very much."

I looked to Hildy this time, wondering if she was catching what he was saying.

Either she hadn't read his lips or she was entirely unbothered, for she nodded kindly and smiled at me.

"Sommers, we have a small issue with Maude."

"You do?" I asked, surprised. Perhaps their knowing about my mark had changed their minds about me.

"Her mother and father are courtiers here, as is her

estranged husband." I gaped at her. So we just tell people my deep dark secrets now, do we? "She is presumed dead by most."

"I see," said Sommers, thinking. "Do her kin believe her dead?"

"Nay, her husband and kin knows it was faked."

"What is the husband's name?"

"Edward Beckett."

His eyes flickered fast as though he was checking a list of courtiers that no one else could see. "He is here." Bile rose to my mouth. "Will he make trouble if he sees her?"

"He might," Zita said.

"I'll see what I can do." What on Earth could he do about that?

"Thank you, William — and what is on the cards for this evening? The usual Christmas Eve?" asked Zita.

"The usual Christmas Eve. No big feast. Everyone is still fasting. But the King wants scary stories told by scary people in the evening. I have, of course, recommended you, Hildy."

Hildy nodded.

"And the rest of the twelve days?"

"Would you like to know everything that is planned or just the exciting things?" he asked seriously. His mood bounced from playful to deadly serious: it was disconcerting.

"The exciting things," Zita said.

"Would you like to know what I am doing, or what Court is doing?"

"The Court, please."

"The King? The Queen? You? Or the courtiers?"

There was another knock on the door.

"William, are you in there?"

"My keeper is here," he said plainly.

A woman opened the door and moved inside. She was the

sternest, most severe-looking woman I had ever seen. She had a deeply furrowed brow and grey eyes.

"Ah, you've found the witches." She pursed her thin lips. "Has he relayed the schedule?"

"I'm just about to explain the schedule," William said.

"Hurry along, then."

William took a deep breath. "Tonight is our last feast where we fast, then it is expected that members of our community will tell ghost stories to the courtiers. Christmas Day we have the three masses, then the Yuletide feast. Pageantry is then every single night until twelfth night. Special occasions include a play on the second, fourth and fifth nights. An acrobatic performance is on the eighth. As per tradition, on the eighth day of Christmas there is the hunt and then the presentation of gifts to the King.

"I have heard rumours of a large and boisterous game of blind man's bluff is to happen on the tenth day. And then there will be the final large feast on the twelfth day of Christmas.

"You are expected to attend all major feasts, and at all festivities. You may set up tarot tables or healing booths within the Fountain Court or within the clock tower court; upon invitation you are allowed to enter the King's Gallery and the Queen's Gallery, but right of entry there is not to be assumed."

William nodded his head curtly, then turned on his heel, ready to leave.

"Oh, and Reasonable?" Rufus and William looked at each other. "You should go and join the other musicians."

William's carer hustled him out the door.

I'd barely heard the timetable, still sunk in the moment of revealing my mark. I felt shaky. I had just been stripped naked, it seemed, and had the world see my shame. I don't know why I had just told them all, just like that. William had asked, and I had told. I didn't want to look the witches in the eye. I didn't want to talk about it. Or did I? I was just standing still. Staring at the door.

"Is it why he rejected you?" asked Zita.

"Aye," I said tightly. I felt Hildy's presence at my side. I looked down at her, and she reached out her small hand and put it on my belly.

"No wonder you have so much power, Maude."

"Yes," Zita agreed. "It makes a lot of sense. Why didn't you tell us?"

"I don't tell anyone." I glanced at Rufus, wondering if he would betray me — but he just smiled.

"There have been a lot of secrets in this little family," declared Zita.

Evening fell. I sat on Zita and Hildy's bed.

They were redoing my curls.

In front of me, I watched the flames licking up and around Rufus's body. He was sitting on the hearth, staring into the fire. I made eye contact with the sheep on the tapestry. She was laughing at me.

Ever since William left, I had begun some sort of spiralling crisis. I was rolling down a hill, getting faster and faster, and I couldn't see anything but the spinning of the grass beneath me.

"All will be well," said Hildy, reading my mind as usual. "The King will like you."

"What if I see my brothers? They are undoubtably here. What do I do? What do I do when I see my mother? What happens if the King wants me to charm something for them? I do not know what to do when I am addressed by the Queen of England. What if I lose track of where you are, and I get lost?"

"Maude," said Zita sternly. "Our kin have seen me at Court

most Yuletides and have simply pretended not to know me. You have nothing to fear. Think of it this way, you do not have any brothers. Nor do you have a mother or a father; you have us and the stars looking after you. We are your family."

It was as if someone had jumped out in front of me to stop me rolling: she had stilled me in the middle of ever-escalating motion.

I took a deep sobbing breath. "You are my family."

"We are your family," echoed Hildy, signing it with her hands to confirm.

I looked to Rufus, who touched his heart. "Family," he mouthed.

"We are your only kin." Zita took hold of my chin to look at my hair from the front. "In your past life you were raised to be in Court. You know better than any of us how to behave in front of royalty." She spoke true. I had been trained for this for some time.

"What will they do when they see me?" I asked her.

"Probably panic. What will you do?" She squinted at me.

"I ... won't panic?"

"Exactly. You will take a big deep breath and remember how powerful you are and how nobody can make you small."

"Aye," I breathed.

"You are a powerful charmer," Hildy whispered into my ear.

"You will find family here, Maude, and I do not mean your dead family. William will always be looking out for you, and so will the Queen's fool, Jane. They take care of us here."

"Us?"

"You'll see."

CHAPTER TWENTY-TWO

I have always loved Christmas.

Always.

Even with all my brothers descending on Shirburn like the plague. Even with all the pomp and show. Especially with all the pomp and show.

I loved the feeling of Christmas. I liked the dissolving divide between our world and the next. Something magical crept into our human realm. It didn't even feel like Heaven was falling to Earth. It felt like the fairy realm was creeping in sideways. Our homes taken over by the forest, with all the evergreen leaves entangled into the beams, and all the extra candles littering the corridors. Ghost stories on everyone's tongues, and a frivolity that reminded me of tales about the Fae. Our clothes suddenly and permissibly broke every sumptuary law ever passed. Everyone in deep reds and purples, all trimmed with fur, and all glittering with jewels.

I wore a deep crimson dress for our first night in Court. My hair was out, which was unusual. I would stand out. I wanted to stand out. I think ... I was waiting by the door, ready to leave. The witches fussed with their trinkets and witchy things.

Rufus had retied his turban.

“What will you do, Rufus?” I asked gently. He had not been in the mood to talk.

“I’m just going to present myself to His Majesty and see what happens.”

“I’ll run away with you if you need.” I reminded him. He glanced down at me.

“There is no running away from the King.” Shivers erupted up my arms: had we led Rufus to danger?

“Are you not safe?” I asked. He didn’t reply. My nerves intensified. “How do we get into Court?” I asked, as each entrance was heavily guarded.

“I believe someone will collect us,” Zita said.

Sure enough, the words had only just left her lips when there was a knock at the door. A stern guard nodded his head in greeting.

“I don’t know nothing about the Moor,” he said, surprised by Rufus’s presence.

“I am the new trumpeter,” Rufus grunted.

He looked at him suspiciously. “I’ll have to ask about that.”

We followed him out into the Base Court. The red stone of the palace glowed a golden colour in the dying light. We reached Queen Anne’s gates. I wondered what she might look like: I had heard she was beautiful and that she was with child. I prayed that the baby boy would be born hale.

The gates were guarded by half a dozen armed men.

“These women here are the three witches for the twelve days,” our guide explained. “They are to be let forwards. "This" – he gestured rudely to Rufus – says he is the new trumpeter.”

“He’s not the new trumpeter. He’s the old trumpeter! Where you been?” asked one of the guards.

"I got married," Rufus said shortly. "The King will want to see me." He spoke with such authority the guards hardly shrugged; they just waved us all through.

It was busy in the clock tower court too, but less busy, I noticed. I tried not to wear the smugness on my face, but I couldn't help it. I had been brought up to enjoy social ascension. This is what my parents had raised me for, getting through the gates to higher and higher courts.

The thought of my parents flipped my tummy over. I wasn't sure whether in excitement or fear. I *think* I was excited. I think I wanted them to see me. I wanted them to be confused. I wanted them to panic, embarrass themselves, and then I wanted them to realise I hadn't needed them anyway. I got to Court on my own. Rufus grabbed my shoulder and moved me out of the way of someone presumably important. Everyone seemed to tower over me. Perhaps being important made you several inches taller.

We were walking to the far-left corner of the courtyard where there was a fire in a big pit with people gathered around it.

"Are we to stay outside the whole evening? Does one tell ghost stories outside?" I asked, concerned. A wind was picking up, and it was bitter.

"I should hope not. But we must put ourselves in the right position to get our entry," said Zita, manoeuvring me to face the next gateway. I assumed it led inside the palace itself. "Otherwise, yes, we'll have to set up our stalls here. Near the fire."

Hildy sidled up close to me, whether to get warm or to be kind I couldn't tell.

"Behind you is the King's Gallery," she whispered excitedly. "And opposite, that's the Queen's."

"Have you seen anyone important yet?" I signed, bashing my chest and doing a pompous walk to signal "important".

She looked around. "Ahh. We are about to," she whispered, pointing to the gate. There were people exiting a door on the side of the Queen's presence chambers. Was I more nervous to see my mother or the Queen? I didn't recognise anyone immediately, but the crowd knew what to do. Everyone started pushing towards the ladies-in-waiting. I instinctively began to move with the crowd, but there was a hand on my shoulder. I turned around; Zita was shaking her head, then she gestured behind us. I looked to the opposite end of the courtyard.

There was movement in the King's Gallery.

"I want to be in the King's good graces, not Her Majesty's," she whispered into my ear.

"Why?" I asked.

"She is not in favour." She muttered it so low I only just heard her.

The door opened to the King's Gallery. Zita moved me to face the door. We were too close. We were not important enough. We needed to move away. Even in the bitter wind I began to sweat.

Rufus tried to move back. Zita stopped him with a single finger. "Stay," she signed. Rufus looked down at the witch, tight lipped. Annoyed.

A small corridor made entirely out of stickybeaking, flattering courtiers was made and the witches, Rufus and I were right up the front. Men began moving between the flatterers, and I tried to follow the lead of everyone around me, but no one had fallen into a full bow just yet.

Is he the King? No. Is he my father? No. That looks like my brother! Nay. Is he the King? Is he the King?

No. No. No.

Oh.

Oh yes. I fell instinctively to the floor. Of course. He was obvious. It was obvious. King Henry Tudor. He was everything you'd think a king might be. In full regalia. I had only caught a glimpse of his face, but it was handsome, young almost. His beard was not entirely full, and a friendly orange colour.

I snuck a glance up. His Majesty was taking his time, speaking to people in his human corridor. Rufus was crouched behind me, trying to hide, I presume, and if it hadn't been such a serious situation I would've laughed. Big black fairy cowering behind the tiny white-with-fright witch.

He moved towards us. I lowered my head even further. Oh Christ. I was going to have to address him.

"Good God." It was his voice. The King's. "Reasonable Blackman." I couldn't make out his tone. Was he angry? He sounded more shocked. "Is it you?" I snuck another glance. Rufus was standing.

"Your Majesty." Rufus's voice sounded so different, so ... English. "I'm here to ask your forgiveness." There was silence. Christ. The performance scheduled for the third night of Yuletide was going to be changed to a public execution of a fairy. How horrifically un-festive.

But then I heard a low, deep chuckle. "You fucking cheeky trumpeter!" The King's laughter cut through the cold air. The crowd perceptibly relaxed; some people even laughed, echoing the King despite not having any idea of what was going on. "I've missed you, my brother!"

Brother? I looked up. The two were embracing. The King had a tight grip of Rufus, his hands indenting Rufus's tunic with the effort of his hug.

"I've missed you too, Henry."

I looked sideways to Hildy, and she looked at me, grinning.

"What the fuck?" I mouthed and signed.

I couldn't believe it. Rufus. Our Rufus just Christian-named the King.

"You are back to play with me! You will play for me, Reasonable?"

"It would be an honour."

He pulled Rufus into the corridor of flatterers and indicated he should walk with him. "What happened?" the King asked. Arm. Still. Around. Rufus.

I shook my head as I rose, the King now far enough past that I could stand fully erect.

"She didn't want a blackamoor as a husband, Henry."

"That bitch," I heard him say, now obviously angry. "I tell you, Reasonable, women are betrayers. We shouldn't call us men and women: we should call us men and Judases. All Judases. How came you here?" Henry had stopped to let someone kiss his ring. "Why didn't you come straight back to me?"

"I worried you would be disappointed, Your Majesty, having put so much effort into our match, and so generously paid for the wedding."

"Nonsense," he scoffed. "I, of all people, know what Devils these women can be."

"I told her that to keep her virtue; I would play dead. She is widowed by law. I didn't want to haunt your courts as a ghost."

"You should've divorced her, Rufus! Divorced her and come straight back home. Where have you been staying?"

Rufus glanced back to us. "I have been taken care of by three witches." Rufus smiled at me, and my heart jumped. "They gave me a home and food when I was down on my luck. And, as God would have it, they are your preferred wisewomen at Yuletide."

"They are here?" Henry asked, looking back at us.

"They are."

"Ahhh." He made to turn back. "I remember the Yuletide witches!" I dropped back down to the floor. "The astrologer," he said, letting Zita kiss his hand. "And the healer. My wife will want to hear from you, wisewoman. She is experiencing pains in this pregnancy."

Hildy rose. "It would be an honour to tend to her, Your Majesty."

He grunted.

I was staying low.

"You've taken care of my trumpeter after he was abandoned by the Devil's spawn?"

"We have loved him like one of our own."

Henry nodded, approving. "I will have you in my quarters — you will read the stars for my friends, won't you, witch?" said the King of Fucking England.

My mind was reeling.

"Of course, Your Majesty."

"And Reasonable says there is a third wisewoman?" He looked around, and I made myself raise my head.

"Your Majesty," I said before Zita could introduce me. Time to shine, Maude.

He paused, looking at my face. He looked at every part of me, examining my cheekbones, my hair, my bust, my dress. I allowed him to appraise me. "What is it you do, wisewoman ...?"

"Maude. Wisewoman Maude, Your Majesty. I am a charmer and I read people."

This caught his attention.

"You can read my thoughts?"

"Your feelings, Your Majesty."

"And what do I feel?"

Jesus Christ. Talk about a tricky first day on the job. Prove yourself, Maude.

I looked at him. I appraised his face as he had just appraised mine. He liked it. He liked it a lot. I could feel his body responding to my gaze.

"Do you need to touch me? To connect with my heart?" he asked. "You should touch my face or something?"

What a randy man.

"If I can touch your beard, Your Majesty, I might feel better acquainted with your heart."

"Maude, God save you," whispered Zita. I ignored her.

The King just smiled. "My beard is all yours."

I moved forwards and let my fingers touch His Majesty's beard. It was soft, and I twisted my fingers around it. I could smell his breath: it smelt like wine. I looked into his eyes. He was aroused by me: no doubt about it.

But when I really looked into his eyes, only a few inches from him, I saw a deep sadness.

"You are tired," I whispered. "You need something new."

"Something new?" he whispered back. "What?"

I looked at him. He wanted a new woman. He wanted a new marriage. That's why Zita had said that thing about the Queen. I could see it in his eyes. Desire. For anything but his wife. Even when she was with child. "What new?" he asked again.

I wasn't about to tell him to get a new queen. Another divorce. I reached out for some words, hoping the heavens would find me some. "You need to freshen your life; new faces, new foods. You need Rufus's music," I whispered.

"Who is Rufus?" he asked.

"Forgive me. You need Reasonable's music."

He looked back at the fairy. "I like your new family more than I liked your wife," he told him. "Maude, you will take your family into my gallery. They will practise their spells and tell their ghost stories with me tonight."

CHAPTER TWENTY-THREE

Well, God's spotted toad, that hadn't been very hard, had it? We were passing through yet another gate into the King's Gallery. The next step would be the King's privy chambers themselves. I felt my insatiable lust for ascension rear its head. I bet, given the right circumstances, I could get in there. My hands tingled from the touch of His Majesty's face. I was riding incredibly high.

I kept looking at the witches, wanting to talk to them, to giggle with them — I mean what in God's balls had just happened? But they wouldn't make eye contact with me. Had they known about Rufus's and the King's relationship this whole time? It was unfathomable to me that Rufus, the man who had been sleeping mere steps away from me for the last few months, made free with the first name of the King of Bollocking England.

We entered the gallery. It was a long dark room: wooden panelling sat up against the deepest red walls, and hanging on the walls themselves were nearly a hundred different painted faces. The kings and queens of England, all staring at me, most of them dead, and consequentially most of them all-knowing. Witnessing this witch, Maude, wade into their King's halls. I liked all the faces, and the jewels that adorned their painted necklines, and I even liked their all-knowing leers, but my favourite part of the gallery was the roof. It had been decked out in Yuletide cheer: perhaps fifty kissing boughs had been hung from the beams, big bunches of mistletoe and other evergreen leaves bunched together in these celebratory orbs, hanging from the Hampton Court sky. It was raining forest.

Zita and Hildy had obviously made it this far before.

"We'll go in that corner over there. Ah yes! Do you see Mrs Goodthatcher is waving at us."

A tiny woman who would rise only to my hips was waving to us. She was adorned in pearls and rubies like a tiny queen.

"Hello, Lady Goodthatcher!"

"Good morrow, Zita; hello, Hildy!" she said, waving us over. "I saved you a table in the good corner."

"You're too kind! This is Maude. She's part of the coven now."

"Merry Christmas, Maude. I'm the Court dwarf. You can call me Goodthatcher."

"Well met, Goodthatcher."

"You'll need a table to set out your trinkets?"

"I probably just need a stool for myself and a stool for my patron," I guessed.

"Nay, don't listen to our apprentice," interrupted Zita. "Get her a table, Goodthatcher, I might get her on the crystal ball."

"Leave it with me." Goodthatcher was off.

I was about to protest, having never used a crystal ball in my life, but more pressing issues were afoot.

I hit Zita playfully on the shoulder.

"Maude!" she protested.

"Have you always known Rufus is as good as His Majesty's

kin?"

Hildy looked up at me; she was setting up her wares on the table. "We did."

"Why didn't you tell me? I've been bossing him around these months, making him sweep the floor!" Zita threw me a dirty look. "Tell me! What is his story?"

"You should ask him, Maude."

"Tell me!" I said, getting annoyed.

"He's old friends with the King. They grew up at Greenwich together as young boys."

My mind reeled. "How?"

"He came over from Spain with the Princess Dowager." Comprehension dawned.

"He was the first Queen's slave?" I asked.

Zita nodded.

"Rufus's dear mother hardly left Aragon's side. She was her favourite. She's still with her now, I believe, in exile."

I opened my mouth, about to unleash.

"No more questions about Rufus, Maude, you can ask him yourself."

"As you say, Aunt Zita," I said, making sure my words were dripping in sarcasm. "What happens to us now?" I demanded.

"Most of the courtiers will go into the Great Hall for the feast."

"I thought Court was fasting?"

"Oh, Maude, how much you have to learn about Court." Zita tittered. Why did she goad me so? "They fast in that they abstain from the heavier meats, and might have fewer courses of sweet things. After eating, the music will start to play, and the games will begin, and everyone will mingle and get drunk and we will read the stars, hand out medicine to invigorate the male sexual organ and you will remedy every courtier's broken heart."

There was a kerfuffle at the door: the flatterers were here. There was Rufus. Somewhere in the middle must've been the King. I still had not seen any of my kin, nor my husband. There was a laugh about the mistletoe, and a hoorah of escalating noise until someone kissed another. Cheers of delight.

I might've laughed too, but I was watching Rufus. He had a trumpet in his hand. He held it limply by his side and was laughing with a smart-looking courtier. He was relaxed and totally at ease. I felt like I was watching another man.

He looked over at our corner and he smiled at me. I gave him a small wave. He grinned.

"Will we not see Rufus anymore?"

Zita put her crystal ball down slap bang in the middle of the newly set table. "You'll see a lot of him tomorrow. The musicians eat and drink with us on Christmas evening."

"Can you do tarot, Maude?"

I turned to look at Zita, incredulous. "Have you taught me tarot, Zita?" I asked indignantly.

"Nay."

"Then nay. I cannot do tarot."

"Very well. You be on the crystal ball."

"You haven't taught me that either."

She sat me down behind the large, sparkling ball. "Use your powers to read people and interpret from that as you wish."

"Verily, I think we are a big band of scamming vagabonds," I muttered, looking into the piece of glass. Firelight flickered in its depths.

The three of us sat in a row. It felt absurd. The hall was still very empty.

I turned to my aunts. "Are we the only people to sit in the King's Gallery?"

"No point being where the King is not!" said a stranger's voice.

"Jane!" said both the witches at once.

The Queen's fool had appeared seemingly out of nowhere. I suppose she must've entered through a secret door, one of those that sink into the panelling and are used by the King to fornicate with people discreetly.

"How are you, wisewomen?" Her voice was slightly distorted, as if she was eating something at the same time as speaking. She also signed for Hildy. I hadn't seen anyone sign for her other than the three of us at home.

"We are very well, Jane. Maude has managed to get us into the King's Gallery with a promptness we haven't managed before."

My body actually shivered with pride.

"Maude!" Jane repeated, and then came down to give me a big hug. She held me so tightly I felt emotional. Good God, had I been that deprived of touch that a firm hug made me spring a leak?

Zita began telling the story of my impression upon His Majesty, and I watched Jane's face as she listened intently. It was different: it was possibly the sweetest face I had ever seen. She was an angel, perhaps. It was also obvious that, like William, half her mind was in the heavens. That was why the Queen liked to have her by her side, said Zita. Because she was connected to God. A vessel for divine wisdom.

"You are connected to a higher power, Maude!" she said to me, beaming.

I bowed my head.

"She certainly is!" I jumped. It was William Sommers. Good God, how many Goddamn secret doors were there in this gallery?

"Hallo, William," said Jane. The two of them embraced.

Goodthatcher reappeared with two servants in tow. Hildy got up to greet them, and then so did Zita, while I sat, crystal ball in hand, watching this strange reunion of all the oddballs in Court. I enjoyed it. Goodthatcher winked at me. I smiled. I liked this crowd. I wished Rufus were here.

I heard the doors of the gallery being heaved open, and a whisk of cold air rushed in.

"Ah. Prepare, everyone," declared Goodthatcher.

I sat up straight and took a deep breath. The sound of the courtiers flooded through before the people did themselves, the cold air absorbed by the laughing and the talking and the music. Then came the bodies, and they filled the gallery in a matter of minutes.

"Are you the witch that read the King?" asked a man.

"Yes, my lord."

He sat down in front of me and looked at me expectantly.

Was I going to look into the crystal ball? Should I? I really should have had crystal ball training. This was absurd.

"What is on your mind, my lord?" I asked.

He sighed, annoyed that I couldn't tell him that for him.

"What's on all of our minds?" he said pointedly.

Fuck.

I tried to throw a sideways glance to Zita, who was reading tarot for a woman with the largest breasts I'd ever seen. It was distracting. She looked at me briefly but was obviously not able to surreptitiously feed me the answer.

"The King and Queen," I guessed.

He rolled his eyes. "Is she actually with child?" he asked under his breath. "I cannot see any sort of shape under her dresses." He rejigged his codpiece, and my skin crawled.

"I am not with Her Majesty, my lord. I cannot read the state of her womb through your eyes."

He scoffed, annoyed. Was everyone at Court this unpleasant?

"Well, is she a witch? Is she one of your kind?"

I faltered. "I'm afraid I can only tell you whether *you* are a witch or not a witch, as it is you who sits before me."

"And?" he asked without any humour.

"Not a witch," I said, hoping Zita was catching some of this amusing but stupid conversation.

"That's something." He took a swig out of a flask and crossed his legs, seeming to be settling into this spot. He gazed absently over the ever-swelling sea of courtiers. Whilst he was distracted, I also scanned the room. Mother had a red dress I know she loved to wear at Court, so I began scanning all the ladies in red.

"Who's the tall black man near the King?" he asked suddenly. A question I could answer.

"He's the King's trumpeter. He's been away for some time."

"I don't like the look of him," he said gruffly. "All these Moors and foreigners swarming in our halls. It's pollution."

I opened my mouth to correct the judgemental cunt, but Zita's hand had flown out and was sitting firmly on my knee. I swallowed and composed myself.

"Any other questions for my beneficent magic?" I asked pointedly.

"Eugh." He looked around as though searching for something, anything a witch could do for him. "I suppose I could do with a charm."

"I feel called to give you a charm."

"Verily, because I just asked you for one."

"I feel called to give you a charm to heighten your sense of deception." He leant forwards, interested by this.

"Yes. Yes." I bit my lip and reached into my pockets, revealing to him a dried-out acorn. He tried to take it.

"Wait! I must charm it first." I began whispering to the acorn. I whispered bad intentions, suggesting that the seed might tempt the courtier to make a fool of himself. Preferably publicly. I handed it to him.

"It's ready. Carry this with you. Trust your instincts."

"What does thou mean?"

"You'll see," I whispered seductively.

He got up slowly and wandered off into the crowd in a daze, armed with an acorn.

I turned immediately to Zita, ready to let rip. She was already holding up a long, pointed finger.

"There will be many like him, Maude. Acquaint yourself with their ways."

And there *were* many: I spoke to over a dozen men and women courtiers, more than half of them disappointed I couldn't reveal the secrets of other people. I had spotted my elder brother's wife, who looked directly at me but seemed not to notice who I was. Her eyes just passed over me and onto the next person. I wondered if my mother's new babe had kept her at home. The possibility disappointed me.

A bell was rung and everyone began wandering into the Great Hall.

"Do we follow them in?"

"Not unless we are called to entertain them during the feast, which we rarely are. We eat out here."

I nodded.

The courtiers drifted away. Music was playing. I tried to listen out for the trumpet: I wanted to hear him play.

The final courtier was swept up into the Great Hall. After a courtesy minute, to give time for stragglers, the yeomen closed the doors. The doors creaked shut, and it sounded as though the gallery was exhaling with relief.

"God blimey," said Hildy, reclining and putting her feet up

onto Zita's lap. "There's an outbreak of a rash in Court, and before Christmas at that! None of this lot can keep it in their codpieces." I watched as Zita carefully removed Hildy's slippers and began rubbing her feet, as she did in their own not-so Great Hall. I looked around: what if the Goddamn King of England saw?

Jane, the fool, was approaching with drinks, several fellows in tow. There was a scuffling of tables drawn over the ground and then both the fools, Goodthatcher, a woman with darker skin than Rufus and a man with a stick who appeared to be blind all sat down around us. I was introduced to them all at once.

"You been treating that rash going around, Hildy?" asked the blind man.

Zita translated his question to her.

"Aye. It is rife! I'll need access to the kitchen gardens tomorrow to make more salve! Is Court more than usually randy?"

"The King is lascivious at the moment for certes," said William, who was already onto his third cup of ale.

"How do you mean?" I asked.

"He's hungry for purse," said Jane, her sweet, sweet face smiling kindly. What a thing to say out of that lovely mouth. "And when he wants to have lots of lovely affairs, he prefers it if his whole Court does the same."

"Takes the edge off the guilt," said someone whose name I hadn't caught.

"He feels no guilt," Sommers said very loudly. "Her Majesty is as much of a ribald as he is. He just loves his Court so much that he feels he cannot have all the pleasures for himself: he likes to watch others partake in the fruit he is enjoying."

I looked around; my heart was still beating fast, and I

could only begin to imagine the punishments we would receive if this slandering was discovered. “Do not worry, dear Maude. This is our time. Our time to drink and our time to say as we please,” said Goodthatcher.

I smiled at her, still uncertain.

As their fast-day feasting went on, and it did go on, for a very long time, we became drunker and merrier and I finally loosened up.

This little squadron of misfits was the most quick-witted bunch I had ever come across. My sides were aching with laughter. It was dark humour. Often about their ailments, or their unseemliness. Terribly self-deprecating. Terribly funny.

The conversation whirled around and around, bouncing between Jane saying very inappropriate and obvious things, William mocking everyone around him, Goodthatcher cracking jokes about her size and even Zita making merry about committing maleficence and kissing women. And then it finally landed on me. Maude.

“So, Maude. What’s your affliction?” asked the blind man, who I still only knew as Blind Man, but whom I liked very much.

“I am a witch,” I said simply, wishing I had something much more amusing to say.

“No one is simply born a witch,” said Goodthatcher gently. “How did you become such?”

I looked to Hildy and Zita, who were watching me kindly, holding each other’s hands.

“I *was* born a witch. I have a very large witch’s mark up most of the front of my body,” I said, spurred on by the wine.

“Oh yes, like the Spanish fool with the mark on her face,” said Jane.

I had never imagined a mark on one's face.

The Great Hall doors opened and a few of the musicians exited. Rufus was trailing behind. I sat up.

"When are you two going to become lovers?" asked a voice from behind me.

I felt like my whole body had been dunked in cold water. I turned behind me to see a very drunk Hildy being scolded by Zita. Her tiny little hands covering her mouth, stifling her giggles.

"What?" I snapped.

"Friends," Rufus said, sitting next to us. Everyone greeted him; everyone knew him well, of course. "Have the witches made you angry?" he asked, noticing my frown.

"They're being strange."

"Stop being strange, witches!" He was in a good mood.

"Was it good to pick up the trumpet again?" I asked.

He sighed, his body relaxed. "Yes. It was like being reunited with a very long-lost friend."

"I can't wait to hear you play."

Hildy snickered.

"You're meant to be fucking deaf, Hildy! How in God's name can you snicker at me, when you're supposed to not be able to hear what I'm saying?"

Hildy only giggled louder. "Zita translates!" she squealed.

I stared daggers at Zita. "Your ruff looks ridiculous," I said spitefully.

"They're really getting on your nerves tonight, aren't they?" He was sitting close to me, his side rubbing up against mine.

I looked up to him. "They're relentless, Rufus."

"The King took a shine to you. You were bold to touch His Majesty's face like that."

"I know." I could hardly stop thinking about the moment.

A guard approached.

"His Majesty is ready for a ghost story. He wants a witch."

I looked around. Hildy hiccoughed and fell off her chair onto the floor.

Zita gasped and tended to her.

"Who's going to go?" I asked hurriedly.

"I'll go, I'll go," said Zita, pulling Hildy onto the chair.

"My mistake," said the guard. "He wanted the witch. 'The one from before'," he said, shrugging.

"Fuck, no." The profanity slipped out of my mouth; I couldn't help it.

Rufus put his hand in the small of my back. "You'll be all right, Maude," he whispered. "I'll come back in with you."

"What do I do?" I asked, as we walked hand in hand to the door.

"Go wild. They love performance. Go full witch."

"But what ghost story do I tell?"

"I would start with your favourite."

The tables were configured like a horseshoe, and I stood in the middle of the hoof, looking up to the King and Queen of England. Directly above me was a halo of candles suspended on an iron rig attached to the roof. The light flickered around me, making holly-shaped shadows as it hit the wreaths on the tables.

I had decided not to scan the room upon entry. My kin would be at these tables. I didn't need to know exactly where as I bumbled through this performance.

I was about to tell the only ghost story I knew. The one about the man with the load of beans.

It was very noisy. I hoped someone might hush the room. Did they want a ghost story or not? I tried not to shuffle my feet. Rufus stood behind the King's table. He held my gaze and signed to me. It's *fine*. I promised myself to only look at the high table; I didn't have the strength to see my mother staring at me right now.

But my eyes slipped, and I looked down the row of the head table. That was Charles fucking Brandon. He was as good-looking as they said. Did Charles want a ghost story? I stared at him, willing him to notice me. But it wasn't happening; he was in deep conversation with the woman next to him. I tried several other courtiers, boring my eyes into them, trying to draw anyone's attention to my willingness to tell ghost stories. Or ghost story, singular. Nothing. The King wasn't even in his chair; he was halfway down the table talking to a very pretty woman adorned in royal jewels. There was no getting him to notice me.

My eyes went to Anne. As soon as my eyes rested upon her, she felt me, and looked up. Our gazes met. She smiled a big, genuine smile. It was so lovely I think my heart stopped. After several moments of stunned immobility, I returned her kindness, and smiled back.

She made a shushing gesture with her hands. Nothing happened. Her bright eyes flashed with something. A realisation, I thought. She stood up, looking around the room, demanding silence with her eyes, but no one noticed the Queen. The Court was not interested in her movements. This was not a realisation, this was a confirmation. I could see it in the way her shoulders came forwards a little, the way her jaw tightened. She was not what she had been.

Something ran past me, making me jump. It was the fool. Sommers to the rescue.

"Henry, stop flirting with everyone else's wife!" he bellowed. My body went cold. The sound was wrenched out of the room as if I had gone deaf. I watched the back of Sommers, standing tall, staring at the King.

His Majesty hadn't immediately turned to his fool. He was still staring at the woman he was wooing. He cupped the lady's chin affectionately and then, very slowly, he turned his head.

"SOMMERS!" he bellowed, his fury rattling through the hanging insignia and making the flags blow like his breath was a strong northerly breeze. Then his face broke into a big grin. "Are you saying it is time for some festive ghost stories?"

The Great Hall broke into cheers.

William turned to me. "They're yours now. Make sure you entertain them."

"Why can't you do this?" I asked, in one last attempt to excuse myself.

He frowned at me. "I cannot tell a lie!" He left.

The King took his seat, and everyone hushed.

"What story will you tell us?" Henry demanded.

"You will see, Your Majesty." I smiled. He made a gesture with his goblet that I assumed meant I could go on.

All right. Here we go. I shook my hair. Loosen up, Maude. Say something. I looked to Rufus, who was nodding, encouraging, then I turned to the crowd.

My mother and father.

He wasn't looking at me, but was rather determinedly glaring at his own crotch. My mother, on the other hand, was looking right at me, her lip quivering. Our eyes fixed onto one another's for the one second I had before I needed to start my story. She was rubbing her belly; it was empty of course, but still she rubbed it as she always did when she was anxious. I knew her dark and dirty secrets now. I wondered if she felt guilt over the abortion of her first babe to this day. I gave her a big smile and she blanched.

I raised my hands high in the air and threw my head back. "I summon the spirits!" I bellowed. Someone gave a little yelp. My father had been startled and was looking at me now. I beamed at him. The colour was drained from his face too. I turned to face the King and Queen of England.

"I summon the spirits to people this story of the ghostly world." I paused, as though listening to something no one else could hear. I paced around the horseshoe. "Ahhhh," I whispered loudly, "the veil between us and the other side is thin tonight." A timely chill whisked into the Great Hall. I saw someone shiver. "Tonight, the ghoulies are calling for the story of ..." I turned around to the circle, holding my arms up, grasping the air for my tale "... The Farmer. The Horse. And his Beans!"

The crowd erupted with cheers.

The story was a simple one. It was about a farmer on his way with a load of beans. I painted the picture well enough. Set the scene. I put it in London, so that the Court would feel close to the tale told. But, of course, something unGodly happens on the road and the horse meets with an accident. I made it gruesome, for the fun of it. After the horse is spooked by a strange noise in the King's wood, a broken tree branch lances the beast in his proud chest. The distraught farmer cannot save him. I assured the crowd that blood was everywhere. I could feel the energy of the room. I had them. The story had them. And I hadn't even got to the scary part. I went on, describing the sad farmer stumbling further down the road with his beans on his back — but then he stops in his tracks. What's that? I asked the Court. It was an apparition of his horse. Ghost horse. Terrifying semi-translucent ghost horse. He tries to shoo the ghost away, chasing it down with a wooden spoon, but the apparition persists. I looked the King in the eye. I registered the fact that he was enjoying it. He was watching me intently.

"Of course he has not yet tried to dispel it in the name o' the Lord!" cried out Henry, interrupting.

"Exactly, Your Majesty!" I exclaim. "This would never happen to the King of England!"

But of course, eventually, after much ghostly harassment, the bean farmer remembers he must dispel the ghost in the name of the Lord. And so he does. The horse turns into a ball of bright light and is replaced by another ghostly apparition: a man.

I changed my voice to imitate the new human ghost.

"Do not be afraid, bean farmer! I do not mean you any harm! I only wondered if I could carry your beans for you?"

The Court roared with laughter, it wasn't particularly funny in my opinion, but I took the joy, relishing the performance and waiting for silence before finishing the tale. The apparition carries the beans across the river, the two talk for a bit, and before you know it, the farmer is at his destination and the beans reappear on his back.

I thanked the spirits for their stories, I allowed myself more dramatic arm waving. Then I bowed and there was applause. I looked at my feet. Jesus, maybe I was made for performance. Maybe I wasn't a witch but some sort of professional ghost story teller. Maybe they would want me here full time. I let out a laugh. I think I liked Court. Applause and performance and thrills.

"God bless you, witch!" said the Queen, her voice ringing out over the applause. I looked up at her and inclined my head. She was so very beautiful. But then she looked away, and in a single moment, a beat, a single inhalation of breath, all the magic I had conjured was gone. Sucked out of the room. The King began talking to a tall man with a longer than fashionable beard. The courtiers to my left and right were up and moving into the space where I stood. My parents had gone. The music began to play again. I was being sucked up into the movement around me. Forgotten.

"You need to come with me," said a guard. He took hold of my arm and pulled me from the Great Hall.

"I can escort myself!" I tried to wriggle free, but he didn't seem to care.

No one was looking at me; all my amusement was over and no one cared where the witch was taken.

The guard escorted me back to Zita and Hildy as though returning a lost child.

I was seething by the time he finally released me. I shook him off violently, then stared at the motley crew.

"Is it always like that?" I demanded.

"You're not a courtier, Maude," said Sommers. "You're a witch."

"I know!" I said defensively. "But I just told them a fucking excellent story, which they all loved, and yet I'm dragged off like a bloody heretic!"

Jane came over and began rubbing my back; she was making hushing noises and, surprisingly, the sound settled me. I took a ragged breath.

"You're going to have to shake off that bad mood, Maude, because you're back on duty in a minute or two." She was right: the Great Hall doors were opening.

"I saw my parents," I grumbled, sitting down.

"Did they say anything?" Zita asked, concerned.

"Nay."

"Then there is nothing to worry about."

"I wasn't really worried, per se, more —"

"You don't need them anymore, Maude, so put them out of your mind." She had spoken so forcefully I didn't know how to reply.

CHAPTER TWENTY-FOUR

Christmas morning. The sun filtered through my bed curtains. In the blurry moments of first waking, I thought I was back in my bed at Shirburn — but these curtains were a deep red, not the green of my old home. I ran my fingers through my hair and, as I untangled my curls, the last year of my life returned to me. I felt relief. Relief and excitement. I was at Court! On Christmas morning!

I could hear the fire crackling outside, and I wondered who had tended to it. I poked my head out of the curtains and saw Rufus's long body sprawled out on the floor, ashes dusting his livery. My heart wrenched.

"Rufus," I whispered. He stirred. I got out of bed and reached down to him. "Rufus." I brushed my hands through his hair.

"Maude?" he said, opening a single eye.

"Come get into bed."

"I'm well."

"The floor is stone. You're not fine." I got him up and he stiffly walked to my mattress. "Do you need to be anywhere this morning?" I asked.

He sat down on the bed. "Not until after they break the fast," he said, still only one eye open.

Gently, I pushed him back and he submitted: I got him under the quilt.

I sat on the end of the bed, over his feet, like a cat. To my abject horror, Jimmy had slept in between the witches last night. A betrayal I would never forget.

"Merry Christmas, Maude."

I turned around: he wasn't sleeping, he was staring at me.

"Merry Christmas, Rufus." I smiled. "You don't want to sleep anymore?"

"It's Christmas morning!" he protested. "I'm too excited to sleep."

I laughed and got under the bedclothes at the other end of the bed, leaning my back against the post. Our legs touched. I wondered if he would move his away. I waited a few moments. He didn't.

"Thank you for keeping the fire burning."

"I couldn't let the Yuletide log burn out on Christmas Day." He grinned. He had a big cheesy grin that he used from time to time, when he was being silly. It made him seem young, as young as me, even though I knew it couldn't be true. I wondered what his actual age was: he must have been at least a decade older than I.

"Where are you from?" I asked.

"A long way away."

"Did you celebrate Christmas in a long way away?"

He shook his head. "Nay. But we celebrated in Spain. Princess Catherine used to give us gifts."

"Do you miss her?"

"I do. Not as much as I miss my mother. But aye, I do miss her. She looked after me well."

"Did you get to say goodbye to her?"

"No. Not to either of them. It was a delicate time in Court. Catherine was kept out of sight and when they took her from Court, they took my mother too."

"How come your mother was kept by Catherine but you weren't?"

"I am Henry's property."

"He loves you, no? The King, I mean. It was ... surprising to see how he greeted you."

"You find me all the more shiny and attractive now, don't you?" He wiggled his eyebrows. Goddamnit, I hated myself for him being a tiny bit right.

"How did you become such good friends?"

"When I was young, my main job was to keep out of the way. I would roam around the palace, stay out of sight. So would he. He was a naughty child. We would play, climb, make mischief together."

"I can hardly fathom it," I muttered. "Do you mind being back here?"

"I was scared to return: he has a bad temper. I promise you, the reason I am in his favour now is only because we caught him in a good mood. If he had had a bad cup of wine a moment before, he might've chosen to hold a grudge. It is unnerving. But I like Hampton Court. It is not where I grew up."

"Have you seen your wife?" I asked.

"No. She was not a woman of Court. Have you seen your husband?"

"Not yet. But I saw my parents."

"What happened?"

"My father stared at his lap, and my mother — she looked afraid."

"It's difficult, Maude."

I made a noise of agreement. “Will I get to spend time with you today?”

“Not today. But tonight, after the feast, we are allowed to celebrate on our own. Unless you’re asked to entertain.”

“Who is ‘we’?”

“The Motley Lot. Jane, Goodthatcher, some of the musicians, Sommers of course. All the witches. It will be festive.”

“I look forward to it.”

“Me too.”

Hildy burst in, holding my cat. Both of us jumped.

“Merry Christmas, love birds!” she said excitedly, flinging open the bed curtains.

“Merry Christmas, Hildy,” I replied, taking my baby betrayer back. Zita followed her in.

“Happy Yuletide, children!” Zita was glowing. “Let’s get ready for the day.”

“Leave them a while, Zita,” said Hildy coyly. Rufus and I shared a quick glance. We weren’t tupping; we didn’t need a while.

I slipped out of bed. “You must promise to not leave me behind today.”

“Well, we will certainly be in eachother’s company for the first three masses.” Zita passed me my dresses.

“Three masses. Jesus!”

“In his name!” said Hildy, fussing over my hair.

“If we are invited to the Chapel Royal, you will like it.”

“Like it? Mass?” I asked incredulously. She nodded. “When do we get to break the fast?”

“Not until after midday. You’ll get drunk very quickly. You will need to be careful.”

“I’m not being careful on Christmas.”

"That's the spirit," said Hildy. I was unsure if she had read my lips correctly.

A lot of the courtiers had to leave Hampton Court on Christmas Day to attend mass outside of the King's palace because Hampton Court's chapel could only take so many. Zita spent the morning tempering my hopes, constantly reminding me we would most likely have to leave the Court too.

"The chances are minuscule, Maude!" she said for the thousandth time.

There was a knock at the door. A knock I recognised: the same melody of knocking that William Sommers had used the day before.

"Where to today, Sommers?" Zita asked promptly.

"You've been summoned to the Chapel Royal." He made a quick bow and left.

I couldn't contain myself.

"You're a bloody sycophant, Maude!" Zita said, helping me thread a few pearls into my hair.

I had noble blood. It was hard to unlearn the delight of social ascension.

We stood at the back of a packed Chapel Royal. Zita had been right. I was an aesthetic person. I liked beauty. I liked it in nature, I liked it in people, in my dresses, in my own face, and I liked it in the Chapel Royal.

The ceiling! The ceiling ... like the night sky. Like Zita's rooms, but far superior. According to the whispers around me, Henry had only just had it finished. It felt like a tapestry, draping down upon us with folds of gilt vaults. My neck hurt from my star-gazing, but I couldn't help examining each glittering celestial sparkle individually. When I finally tore my eyes away from the heavens, I fell in love with the floor. It was chequered black and white and the sound of the courtiers moving over it in their finest clothing was so satisfying: a cheery clinking, accompanied by the swish of expensive materials against the marble. Then the walls were the deepest darkest oak panelling, and if I stuck my head out into the aisle I could see the sparkle of the candles that ran along each row of the pews. We were crammed in but that only made it more exciting. I could feel a sort of ... I don't know ... erotic tension? The courtier standing behind me was alluring. He had floppy hair and bright blue eyes. I could feel him pressing up against my back, and I didn't mind it. I think it was the Christmas spirit. Not that I was used to this sort of Christmas spirit: normally Yuletide reminded me of being young. Of being in my white nightgown running around Shirburn. This Christmas spirit was electric and sinful. I preferred it.

I saw Rufus take his place at the top of the church; he seemed totally relaxed, laughing with the other musicians. Taller than anyone. Darker than everyone. He just stood out. I looked around to see if anyone one else was looking at him. And they were. Quite a lot of women were looking at him.

None of those women had shared a bed with him this morning.

Rufus raised the trumpet to his lips. They had arrived.

The King looked like God himself had come down to celebrate His Son's birth. The Queen also looked beautiful, but she looked tired too. Her clothes were made to accentuate the presumably tiny bump of her belly. She caught my eye upon entry, and she smiled. I liked her, despite the stories.

The little Princess Elizabeth, only two years old, had toddled in with her governess behind her parents. Not particularly maternal in nature, I'd never been taken by a child, but Elizabeth captivated me: she was like a tiny angel, with the most delightful hair I'd ever seen. Curly like mine, but fire red. Brighter than her Papa's.

During the boring proceedings, there was a lot of shuffling of bottoms on seats, children giggling and I saw, on more than one occasion, the glint of a flask and the chink of a not-so-covert chalice. I was entertained the whole time, bouncing between the feeling of the codpiece in my back and watching Rufus in the front. It would be so nice to try tupping again with someone who wasn't a prig, and without covering my mark.

I felt the blue-eyed man's mouth at my ear and my whole body flushed with blood. "Will you carry my beans, witch?" he whispered loudly. A few of his mates laughed. That fapsucking bean story. "But for sooth, you must move aside. I want a better view." He pushed past me. I caught Rufus's eye and put all my energy into singling out the sound of his instrument. I wish everyone else would just shut up. I wanted to hear him play.

The Court spent the better half of the morning swooning in and out of the chapel and the courtyards and the gallery. Despite what Zita had said about breaking the fast at the first feast, there was much drinking and nibbling of festive snacks. Roasted chestnuts. Dried fruits and plums. The air smelt of cinnamon and wine. I spent half my time in pure delight, and the other half being knocked out of my revery. I was shoved around a lot. Physically shoved. I was asked for on-the-spot charms and fortune-telling. And worse than all that, I was asked to carry people's beans at least a dozen more times, once by Thomas Cromwell, which both delighted me and mortified me.

"He's very drunk, Maude. He's normally a very respectable gentleman," Hildy assured me.

By the third mass of the day my Christmas spirit was gone.

Vanished. Zita kept passing me pieces of dried apple, but they made my tummy hurt.

"Eat up, Maude. You'll be dead on your feet."

"Feast is next, isn't it?" I asked as the trumpets began to sound again, the King entering again.

"Feast is for courtiers, Maude," Hildy said, shoving a few warm chestnuts into my hands.

I'd never considered myself to be a stupid person. When you grow up in a noble household, you automatically know yourself to be smarter than anyone else. I mean, I could read, for God's sake — both English and Latin, and I had picked them up quickly too. I had taken to Hildy's hand signalling swiftly, and I knew things about herbs and the properties of plants and I was even learning more about the stars, which was an erudite profession. Not to mention the fact I was fifty per cent sure that I could read people's fucking minds ...

But I really hadn't been using all my faculties when I had imagined we were to attend the Christmas Day royal feast. What had I been expecting? A seat by the King? Because I had told a good ghost story? I suppose I had thought, it was Christmas ... Christmas Day! What? Were we supposed to go without eating? On Yuletide?

I had been staring absentmindedly at some poor courtier's arse this entire time, processing both my own stupidity and the stupidity of this situation, which would be for us a Christmas Day without a Christmas feast.

CHAPTER TWENTY-FIVE

Everyone seemed to enjoy the Christmas feast. Twenty-four courses.

The entertainers were kept close at hand, moving from the King's Gallery to the secret back corridors that led to the kitchens. We were fed offcuts and leftovers. It was tradition for the Court to provide more than enough food to the courtiers, so there was plenty left for the unseen underlings huddling essentially everywhere but under the tables with the dogs. I would've huddled under a table for a slice of the fruitcake at the end, though of course that was the one that was entirely eaten.

What I did eat was the following: a few spoonfuls of plum porridge, some beef broth with plum skins and spices (it was good). I had what I thought was some boar with mustard on top, which turned out to be mostly just mustard, and half an entire swan wing, all to myself.

Rufus caught me nibbling on the bone. I was sitting in the corner in the King's Gallery.

"Didn't want to share, huh?" He smirked.

I handed him the gnawed dry bone with a big smile. He laughed.

"How is your Yuletide going?" I asked.

"Exhausting. As always." He sat next to me, picking up the crystal ball and staring into it. "I feel as though I never left and the apothecary was all a dream."

I touched his knee and gently took the crystal ball out of his hands, rubbing off his fingerprint smudges with my skirts.

"I'm here. It wasn't a dream."

"You know he won't let me leave after this. I am returned property."

"What?"

"I can't come home with you."

My whole body fused still: my bones had all melted into each other, and I was now stone. Forever. What was wrong with me? I had half my mind in the clouds, with all this ridiculous courtly intrigue. I was spending all my time thinking about the dresses, and the palace, and how I looked, and where my parents may or might not be. And all this time we were marching Rufus back to the King. His lost property, returned to him — by us.

I stared at him. I was suddenly furious with Zita and Hildy — how could they not think of this? They were the old. They should've thought of this. Or maybe they had known. Then my anger moved to Rufus and I found my voice. "Why didn't you say something?" I hissed. He looked shocked at the venom in my voice. "I didn't know he wouldn't let you go."

He opened his mouth to speak but someone interrupted him.

"Ready for madness, Maude?" It was William. The whole of the King's Gallery was abuzz with palace business, food being taken to and from servants upon servants upon servants, not to mention all the guards, but William stood out. He was playing Captain Christmas. He had been harassing and frightening people all day, like a poltergeist with a festive edge. He was wearing a different outfit from his regular fool's garb, dressed entirely in green and wearing a horrifying mask that had distorted his nose so it was squished back into his face like he had run into a wall. He was also wearing a wig which looked a lot like my own hair, which was mildly offensive. He would be tired, what with the whole of his day rampaging about, shouting and violently brandishing his great big club.

"Madness?" I managed.

"You haven't seen anything yet," he said, taking off his mask, and now somehow looking more ridiculous in just the wig. Is that what I looked like all the time?

"The sun has already set: the day is old. What more is to come?"

Rufus gave a dark chuckle.

Zita and Hildy came out of the door behind us, giving me a fright; they looked ... dishevelled and bashful.

"Christmas tupping," William said matter-of-factly.

"We're in the spirit," said Zita, just as sternly as she said anything else.

"They're just clearing the last course. The mood is ..." William looked to Rufus. "How would you say the mood is, Reasonable?"

"It's fucked up," said Rufus unblinkingly. "More than usual."

Zita signed a version of the phrase *It's fucked up* to Hildy, who pulled a face and then laid out her tarot.

"We better be ready then."

I sank back in my chair, a little afraid. I wondered if my mother was, as they say, fucked up.

There was very little point in trying to read crystal balls or give actual charms to people as drunk as the courtiers in

Henry Tudor's Court on Christmas Day, 1535. It was like trying to read a three-year-old's palm or give advice to Jimmy the cat.

I was midway through trying to remove a whole adult man off my reading table when Jane, the fool, came to fetch me. She didn't really say anything, she just took my hand and dragged me away.

"Jane, there's a lord on my table — I just need to —"

"He can have a nap," she said, smiling her soothing smile. "The King wants to see you."

I felt the swan and the mustard congealing in my stomach as she walked me into the Great Hall. It was havoc. There were people trying to dance in the middle of the hall, but there were also people throwing up and a small fisticuff happening at the door.

Jane, peacefully and temperately, wove me through the chaos and left me at the steps of the King and Queen.

The King was drunk but not as drunk as his courtiers. The Queen sat still, occasionally sipping her wine, serene as ever, cradling her tummy.

"Wisewoman! Approach me."

I walked towards them and curtseyed. A table stood between us, littered with figs and other fruit.

"Come around so you may look into my eyes."

I looked to Anne, and she nodded softly, giving me permission.

This was a very awkward thing to ask of me. Not just because it was intimate and inappropriate but because of the arrangements of the tables. All feast halls were arranged in the horseshoe shape. There are only two gaps in the horseshoe, and they were both at the door from which I had just come.

I was going to have to go backwards towards the door and come all the way around again to the back. But that is what he had asked, so that is what I was going to have to do. I made to turn.

"Come under the table," His Majesty instructed.

Jesus Christ. That wasn't demeaning at all. The King was challenging me. I felt him watching me, wondering if I would do as he demanded. Which I bloody well was going to.

I moved further down towards a spot where no one was sitting.

"Witch," he yelled. "Come under here." He jabbed a finger in front of him.

I looked at his wife. Her eyes shifted, the focus changed; she had taken herself far away.

I swallowed, smiled again, then got down onto my Goddamn knees, amongst the remnants of the twenty-four-course Christmas meal, and went under the King's table. I looked at the royal knees. He was sitting as only men could, his knees wide apart, as though giving room for a medical marvel of a cock.

He shuffled his seat forwards.

Fuck him.

He wanted me to come right up in between his legs.

"Is everything well down there, witch?"

"Just navigating my way through the fields of porridge slup and crumbies, Your Majesty!" My hands would be filthy. I made eye contact with a greyhound who was doing his floor duties down the other end of the King's table. He couldn't have done this section first? Damn dog.

All right, Maude, just do it. I took a deep breath, shuffled forwards and then squeezed myself up between the King's legs, having to use his thighs to lever myself up. He was deeply amused. His eyes sparkled with some sort of grotesque mischief. He wanted to play.

"You certainly made a mess, didn't you, Your Majesty." I

showed him my mustardy, plummy hands. I went to wipe them on my skirts but he stopped me. He clicked his fingers and a steward appeared with a wet cloth. The King took it and wiped my hands. Like Jesus washing the feet of Mary Magdalen, except ... different.

"This is my wife," he said, looking deep into my eyes. I was still trapped. He hadn't moved his legs. I needed to curtsey. But the King wasn't intending to move. I dipped into a curtsey, again having to use his thighs to balance myself.

"Wisewoman Maude," Anne said gently. Her voice was lovely, soft and comforting. I think she pitied me.

"She reads people, Anne," Henry said, and his voice was pointed, sharp.

"What a gracious gift from God," she replied.

"Only if she uses it beneficently," said the King. His knees were coming inwards; I could feel them against my thighs. "Are you a Devil-worshipping witch?" he asked. If being stuck in the grip of the King's thighs was making my heart thump, it was nothing to the way it raced when he asked this question. I lost my ability to speak. "Calm down, calm down," he cooed. "We are not in the papacy's pocket anymore. But you are a beneficent witch, no?"

I regathered my wits. "Verily. My blessings are from God, not Lucifer."

"Some witches have been cursed, though, wouldn't you say?"

What was this? He wanted me to say yes. So I did. "Of course. There is always evil that lurks. I myself met a malfecient practiser of magic in my own town." I hadn't thought of Reggie in a while. Strange he would come to me now, in this situation.

"May God's angels strike her down," Henry muttered, almost seductively.

"Amen," I replied.

"Will you read my wife, Maude?" He was full of intent.

"It would be an honour, Your Majesty."

"She needs to touch you, Anne," he snapped.

I had walked into a very complicated, very awkward, personal argument and I was being used as a weapon. He shuffled his chair and I was finally free. I stepped out of his leggy prison and looked at his wife.

"You will read my thoughts, Goodwoman Maude?" she asked me.

"Your emotions, your feelings."

Her lips had tightened. Her eyes were intelligent. She knew what her husband was doing, even if I didn't.

"No doubt you will feel my festive spirit and my gratitude for my unborn babe." The King coughed. "You may hold my hand," she conceded, giving me the tips of her gloved fingers. I took hold of them and felt her reluctance, her suspicion of her husband.

I held the hand gently to me and looked into her eyes. She held my gaze, but I could tell it was an effort for her: each moment passing she fought not to look away.

She was sad. That much was obvious. You didn't need to be a witch to see her grief. She was scared as well. I rubbed my thumb over the back of her hand, and she took a quick, frightened breath. My eyes shut and I saw something, or knew something, a flash of truth known only to the Queen. Something was wrong with her babe.

She had miscarried before. She knew what it was like. She knew the signs. I saw her fear and I think she saw mine. I tried to search beyond her fear, for something else. Something I could tell Henry. Something that wouldn't hurt her. Or hurt me.

I grasped her hands more firmly, and, to my surprise, she held my hand tighter too.

I was holding hands with the Queen of England. I felt her power. She was masterful, this woman. Perceiver of emotions, an empath, not unlike me. I wondered if she was a witch. Her pupils dilated drastically.

I let go of her hands and my connection was broken.

"Well?" said the King impatiently.

I shook my head, trying to compose myself. "Your Majesty was right. I feel your Christmas cheer, and the deep love for the baby you hold in your stomach."

"You didn't feel anything else?" Henry snapped. Angry.

I searched my mind for something he might want to hear. "It was complicated, what I felt." Just say something very ambiguous, Maude. "Changes are brewing for both of you."

"Hm," said Henry, only half contented.

"A baby boy will bring many changes to our lives, won't he, Henry?" Anne said, her eyes watery.

Henry didn't say a thing.

"I think I will go to inspect the festivities," she finished.

I was standing between their thrones. It was almost more awkward than being trapped against his crotch.

"Do what you want," he said, waving her away.

She stood and I made room for her, and her lady's maids followed as she walked through the hall. The candlelight sparkled against her beaded dress and bejewelled crown.

I hadn't been excused so I remained standing slightly behind his throne.

He made a beckoning gesture with his hand and I returned to his side.

"I know there is something you're not telling me. You saw something else. I want you as my confidante, witch. I see a great talent in you. I am never wrong about these sorts of things." I smiled and bowed my head. "I will summon you tonight and we will discuss what you saw further. You can leave for now." I bowed my head and left the hall — the long way around.

Sinking into the crowds and blending back in, I found Hildy as quickly as I could. She was sitting in the far corner of the gallery, near a fireplace. The light flickered on her pale skin and glinted off the many glass vials of remedies she had displayed on a small table. She looked like she was at a market selling her wares, only she was still very, very drunk. An important-looking man was writing something down for her to see; she read it and nodded, handed him a vial, exchanged coin and then, under the watchful eye of the courtier, destroyed the man's written confession of his malady in the fire.

"Hildy." I waved. There were several courtiers, mostly couples, I noticed, waiting for her services, but she left her table and came to me.

"If one more person draws me a picture of a phallus, I swear ... Maude? What's afoot?"

It was very had to covertly tell Hildy things, sign language seemed more obvious than English.

"Come here," she said and we left through a tiny door into a small corridor.

"I just had to do a reading for the Queen," I said and signed.

She nodded vigorously.

I checked around me to make sure the secret hall was empty. "Something is wrong with the baby," I signed.

Hildy seemed to sober up. "You saw this?"

"I did."

"In your witch's eye?" I nodded again. "Your powers are strengthening, Maude."

"Hildy!" I moaned, desperate for her to understand the gravity of the situation.

"She has miscarried many times before, Maude. It does not surprise me that she is losing this babe."

"Henry will not abide it. He will leave her after this."

"Do you know that?" she asked.

"I think I see it."

CHAPTER TWENTY-SIX

We weren't exactly given leave, but as the festivities rolled on it became more and more obvious that no one would notice if we withdrew. Finally. The Christmas celebration for us. The strangelings. The Wild Ones. The Motley Lot.

We were in the fools' quarters. They shared a large drawing room with thick, rich tapestries, a huge fireplace and an abundance of furniture. Leading off from the drawing room they each had bedrooms and their own privies. They were taken care of as though they had the Tudor name.

I sat on the floor by the hearth, wrapped up in a blanket, I could finally breathe. It was well past midnight and the King hadn't called for me. I think he must've forgotten or got distracted. Aye. I was nothing to him. I was easily forgotten. He had forgotten me. I was half relieved. Half disappointed. My gaze was stuck on the flames; I was unable to look away from the spitting and flicking as it lapped up a new log Goodthatcher had just thrown on.

"Art thou well?" Hildy had to touch me to break the bind between eye and flame.

I blinked several times. She handed me a drink.

"It's been a big day."

"Did you see your mother?" It was Zita. She sat down on the floor next to me, which was a surprise move. Zita was a chair person. The floors were for rats and dust, I had heard her say.

"Only at the feast. Did you?"

"We had a cordial talk."

I squinted, suspicious. She chuckled. "Nay. Thou art right; it wasn't cordial."

"But you did talk?"

"Hmm." She took a big sip of her drink, so did Hildy, and I followed to complete the pattern. There was laughing around us — a card game had ensued, a drinking card game.

"We should join in," Zita said. She got off the floor.

"What did she say?" I asked, reaching out for her hand. She helped me up and Hildy started brushing me down.

"She said you looked like a witch."

"Oh," I said, not sure how to feel. "Well, I am a witch."

"Aye, you are!" yelled Jane, very loudly and excitedly.

I laughed. So did the others. They made room for me at the card table, and I finished my drink.

"Where's Rufus?" I asked William, who had finally taken off his wig and mask. He seemed to know what was happening in the Court at all times.

"He is with the King," he said. "Do the two of you tup?" he asked.

Hildy and Zita started giggling, which made Jane giggle and start coughing, which made Goodthatcher get up on a stool and start smacking her back, and all the while William was staring at me across the table.

"No," I said, once the noise had died down.

"But is that the arrangement you're trying to make?"

"He's technically still married," I said.

"You're still married too." It wasn't a question.

The door opened. It was Rufus.

"His Majesty wants you to join him in his quarters, Maude. I've been sent to fetch you."

I shook my head. I liked it here. "Will he notice if I don't come?"

"Aye," he said.

I felt my head spin with the wine and fear. "Art thou sure? Why don't you stay here with us? He might think you got lost. Or he might forget he sent you in the first place? We can play cards together." I was frantic, getting up and fetching him a glass of wine, trying to force it into his hands.

Rufus was shaking his head. Everyone was watching us. Off the back of the last conversation, who wouldn't? I eyed Jane, who I didn't trust to keep her mouth shut.

"This isn't Zita summoning you downstairs to sweep the shoppe, Maude. This is the King of England." Rufus's voice was very stern. "You can't just say no."

I couldn't say no?

"You're not being taken to your execution, Maude. It is an honour. I thought thou wouldst be pleased."

"I've taken the pearls out of my hair," I protested weakly.

"He will not notice," said William.

"Where is His Highness?" asked Hildy. She also looked stern.

"He's in his privy chambers." I'll be Goddamned: it had taken me two days. "I don't think he would be upset if the two of you came as well, with your cards and crystals — the other men have been asking for you."

"Oh yes, please come. Please." The two of them looked so at ease lounging in each other's arms, but I needed them.

"We were so comfortable, Maude," Zita said, but she was getting up, readying herself to go.

"We'll be right behind you. I need to fetch some things," said Hildy, who was already in her nightclothes.

"I'll send a guard to get you both." Rufus said, taking my hand and leading me to the door.

CHAPTER TWENTY-SEVEN

We kept holding hands even after we had left the room. There was a long silence as we walked through Hampton Court's corridors. Rufus knew this castle. We didn't touch a courtyard and I hardly saw a soul, but even deep in the belly of the palace, in the candlelit tunnels, I could feel the stone reverberating with festive drunkenness. The loud laughs of courtiers who had never had to control their volume were creeping through the cracks in the cold stone and filling the silent space between me and Rufus.

He stopped. I thought perhaps we had arrived.

"Maude. I'm not trying to protect you. I don't want to treat you like a child." He paused.

"Good ...?" I said, uncertain.

"But I just want to warn you that the King — he's more licentious than I have ever seen him."

"Right ...?"

"I'm just here to play the trumpet, and you've been called for your wisdom, but we are all at the whims of his desires. And he has a lot of desires at the moment."

"What're you saying?" He rolled out his neck. He was tired.

I squeezed his hand. "Are you well?" He squeezed my hand back.

"Just prepare your eyes for a lot of ... Adam and Eve."

I frowned. "Naked people tupping one another?"

"Exactly."

"You should've just said that." I let out a controlled breath. "I can handle that."

He smiled back. "I know you can."

We kept walking.

"Wait." I stopped, suddenly panicked.

"Your mother isn't in there as far as I can tell," he said, reading my mind. "But I don't know what your father or brothers or husband look like, so there is a chance."

Oh Christ.

We started ascending a spiral stone staircase. At the top was a single door guarded by one man.

"Is that who he wanted?" The guard in livery looked down his nose at me.

"I'm a witch," I said loudly before Rufus could defend me. The guard shrugged and opened the door, lazily. "And you should watch out for the clap, because I see it in your future," I whispered as we passed. I heard him take a breath just as Rufus let out an amused exhalation.

Adam and Eve after the Fall, after the modesty and shame wore off, and they had built themselves a palace and filled it with decadent furniture, invited their friends, stripped off their clothes and told them to lie on their furniture. That Adam and Eve.

The King was clothed. I did not immediately sight the royal member. He was sitting by the window and, though he was not naked, I could see his bare chest through his loose white blouse. He was laughing and drinking, his feet up on a small table. I recognised but couldn't name his friend. He had a woman sitting on his lap; she was clothed too, but her breasts were spilt out, and her skirts were up and around her very nicely shaped thighs.

Rufus gave me a little nudge in the back and we approached the King. In my peripheral vision, I thought I saw actual tupping. I curtsied.

"I've fetched Goodwoman Maude, Your Majesty," said Rufus.

"Very good, Reasonable."

"The men have asked for the healer and the star gazer. May I send a man to fetch them?" Rufus continued.

"Do so. Then make the others play a new song; this one is too sombre."

I stayed low, staring into my skirts.

"Rise, witch."

I rose, composing my face into what I hoped was a mild and unsurprised expression.

"Entertain yourself for a while," he instructed. "I will call for you later."

I bowed again and moved away. How to mingle in a party such as this? I looked to Rufus who had returned to his musicians. He pointed towards the door. Blessed stars, Zita and Hildy were there already.

I hurried to them.

"I don't know what to do. The King doesn't need me yet."

"Stand by us; we will set up our cards and crystal." We found spare chairs and a small sticky wine-stained table. Zita's nose was wrinkled in disgust.

I sat next to them and finally took in the scene.

There was another dwarf, younger than Goodthatcher and dressed only in undergarments, dancing on a table near the back. Men were throwing coin at her as she danced. She winked at me and I smiled. I hoped she got to keep the coin. There was gambling, and card games going on in the far corner. I heard the tinkling of dropped gold and an uproar of delight and disgruntled disappointment as someone undoubtedly won a rather large hand. The musicians were playing in front of the fire; one of the nude ladies had stolen a lute and was playing it very badly. The real lute player looked put off, to say the least.

These were the finest men in Court, bedraggled drunk and swimming in sin.

Zita and Hildy attracted a crowd almost immediately.

We went to work.

Over time, I detected a distinct change in the atmosphere. It was becoming more than drunkenness: it was a room of beasts with permission to do whatever they pleased. I could feel Hildy getting overwhelmed — she couldn't read the lips of the men shouting at her — their language was hard enough to understand with good ears, they spoke so slurred and messy.

"Tell me, when will I bear a son?"

"How many women shall I tup tonight?"

"Which woman shall I choose?" said someone, shoving two actual women in my face. I couldn't see between the legs and bodies that surrounded me. Even Hildy, who was once only a span away from me, was whisked off by the madness. I was plied with drinks. I had a bare-bottomed woman sit on my lap and force me to try a chalice of something that tasted like fire. I was overloaded but trying to remain calm, always aware of the King in the corner of the chamber.

I gave out several dozen blessings for good love-making, yelling them over the noise.

A woman with her breasts in my face very genuinely asked me for a cure for an itching purse, so I sent her to Hildy.

Surely the sun would rise soon.

"How do we know these are going to work?" barked a man wearing two stuffed ferrets, letting them sit around his neck like a gold chain.

"I am a witch, my lord."

"But how do we know?"

Out of the corner of my eye, I saw a man trying to kiss Zita. I felt sick. I looked to Rufus. But his attention had been taken by a woman who was grinding her backside up against him; he looked annoyed. "How do we know?" my client asked again.

"Yeah, prove it to us! Perform a spell!" said a very beautiful woman with very rouged cheeks.

"She'll have a mark," said Thomas fucking Cromwell. That cunt was really out to get me. He sat, seemingly sober, in a chair not far from me. "*Do* you have a mark?" he asked, his voice carrying easily over the noise.

I nodded. "Most witches do, my lord." My head span. "But doesn't my wild hair prove it enough for you?"

"Show it to us." The idea spread through the group of men like fire in hay. It consumed all their minds and now I was sat in the centre of a fortress of lords trying to undress me. I felt the threat of violence. I was about to be ripped apart. I held up my hand.

"I'll show you!" I barked, trying to gain some semblance of control.

A naked woman helped me out of my corset. There was much clapping and hooting as the process progressed.

I tried not to shrink. I felt like I was fading away, but I didn't want to fade away. I didn't want these men to make me fade away.

My corset fell to the floor and I was only in my chemise.

"There it is!"

"It's huge!"

Was this better or worse than my experience with my husband? I pondered the question. I think it was marginally better; at least I wasn't trying to hide.

"I'm keeping my shift on. You can see well enough! It is too cold to be without!"

"How far does it go down there?" asked someone.

"Not to my toes!" I yelled.

"Your beauty exceeds mediocrity," said the working girl who had undressed me. I was unsure whether this was a compliment, but she looked very genuine.

A younger man lunged at me, grabbing the hem of my shift and pulling it over my head. I lashed out. I heard a collective "ahhh" as I struggled with whichever Devil was holding my dress. I felt a hand on my belly, and I kicked out with my foot, making contact with someone's soft parts. I wrenched down my chemise and felt someone grab me from behind, pulling me out of the crowd.

It was Zita, and she pulled me back into a corner of the room. The men followed, but Rufus stood between them and me.

"I shouldn't have brought you." Zita's bright blue eyes were wet with tears.

I put a hand on her shoulder. "I am unharmed, Zita."

She shook her head, apparently furious at herself.

"I am unharmed," I said again.

She took hold of my hand. "I'm so sorry."

I felt someone's eyes on me. I looked to my left and froze.

My husband, Edward Beckett, was looking at me. I blinked slowly, sure it was a vision.

It was not a vision. I looked at his face and read him. He was ... afraid.

It gave me an inch of my power back.

I pointed at him. My nails were long and witchy. I pointed at him and smiled. A big, huge, terrifying smile.

He broke at the knees: I heard them smack on the floor. His kinsmen came to his aid.

The King had been watching the ruckus from the window.

"You will leave my witch alone!" he finally barked at them all. Better late than never, I supposed. "She is invited here to serve me. She is not a plaything for all your whims." He moved towards me, parting the crowd. "Get dressed, or don't, but then come sit with me."

"Yes, Your Majesty."

When I was presentable, I went to the King's chair by the window. Rufus said nothing but would not take his eyes from me, monitoring me for signs of distress. I did not feel distress: I wondered if I was holding it all at bay for one big breakdown when I was finally alone. I could no longer see my husband.

"Merry Christmas," Henry said, smiling and looking me up and down.

"Merry Christmas, Your Majesty." I smiled.

"Do you find my chambers festive? Does it remind you of your Christmas at home?"

I took the liberty of looking around.

"It reminds me of one particular Christmas, Your Majesty." He raised a wily eyebrow, amused. I continued. "When I escaped my governess on Christmas morning before she could wrestle me into dress, and I ran around the halls naked, filled with the Christmas spirit. I was but four or five."

He looked at me curiously. "What witch has a governess?" I felt my body go cold. I didn't say anything. He continued looking at me, genuinely curious.

"How do we know she is a witch?" said the man sat opposite him.

"Did you not just see me being stripped by your kinsmen, sir?" I asked with a bite. "I am marked by the divine."

The King took me by the wrist and bought me closer. "What do you see in my dear friend Lord Seymour?"

He pushed me into the Seymour man's lap. I thought to remind him I wasn't one of his whores but I held my tongue. I might as well be.

Lord Seymour had grey eyes. I picked up his hand with my own and felt how reluctant he was to be held. I stared into his eyes a long time.

"Don't break eye contact, Edward," said Henry, laughing.

Eventually, I felt Edward's body succumb to my gaze. I saw his discomfort at being here. I saw a sadness and a vulnerability that were quite beautiful. I had touched upon something in his heart, his eyes were beginning to water. His wife, I think.

I felt a quake in his chest and he broke the connection.

"My eyes are watering from not blinking!" He laughed, rubbing them.

I got off his knee.

"What did you see, Maude?"

I looked pointedly at Henry, not saying anything.

"Go entertain yourself with a whore, Seymour." The lord looked nervous but did as asked. "Take his seat, Maude." I sat down. "What did you see?"

I felt very uncomfortable telling secrets. It felt like maleficence, but if anyone was going to make me spill the beans, it was going to be the King.

"His heart is broken," I said in an undertone. "His wife."

Henry nodded. "Yes. It is rumoured she is sleeping with Seymour Senior."

"She's sleeping with her husband's father?"

Henry nodded.

"Well, that's what's on his mind. Not much else."

"I had thought as much. I am sorry for the rowdiness of this crowd. Festivities often turns to frivolities which turns to ... savagery, I suppose."

"I am surviving, Your Majesty."

"Yes. I am glad Reasonable rescued you." He hadn't. Zita had. But I let him have it.

"I am always glad of Reasonable."

"What did you see in Her Majesty's eyes?"

I had known this was coming, of course. "She's scared, Your Majesty. She was very guarded."

"Like she's hiding something from me." It wasn't a question.

"Possibly."

"If you had more time with her, would you be able see more deeply into her soul?"

What a fucking question.

"Perhaps."

He stared into his chalice for a long time. He uncrossed his legs and spread them bizarrely far apart again. He indicated I was to get nearer to him. Awkwardly I shuffled my chair. It screeched along the ground.

"I want to enlist your services to be with Anne and her ladies until the twelve days of Christmas are at their end."

"To what end, Your Majesty?"

He beckoned me further in, then grabbed me almost violently and placed me on his knee. Like a child. "It is said that she is one of your kind, Maude." He was whispering, his breath tickling my ear. I looked out into the crowd and immediately made eye contact with Hildy. She had been watching me. "I want you to learn if the rumours are true, if she has any otherworldly ability, any witch-like tendencies."

He touched my cheek, pulling my face in to look at his. I could feel his breath on my lips.

"And if she is?"

"I respect your craft, Maude. But my great kingdom deserves more than a witch at her helm." I nodded. "I know it is not like your kind to betray another of the coven." I thought he was going to threaten me with death. I thought he was going to make me imagine the silver edge of the axe on my neck. "So let me pay you for your faithfulness." He was whispering in my ear again, his lips touching my skin. In spite of myself, I felt shivers erupt up my spine. I looked at Rufus. "What will it cost? I want your loyalty, Maude."

I spoke without thinking. "I want Reasonable," I said quickly. "I want him to leave with us when the twelve days are past."

He loved this exchange. "You know he is married."

"I am married," I whispered back.

He looked at me, sitting back so he could take in my face. "Are you now?"

I nodded. Scared and unsure as to why I had revealed that titbit.

"I am."

"Happily?"

"I have seen him twice since our wedding night." I could see the conversation pleased him. Miserable marriages enjoy company.

"Did he love another? You didn't get an annulment, or a divorce?"

"It was complicated."

"You should have been allowed to divorce." He was almost angry.

I tried to scan the room to see if he was still there.

"Is he here?" He was a gossiping maid. Delighted. He looked around. "You must tell me Maude; I am the King."

"I think my appearance frightened him away, Your Majesty."

"What man of Court has married a witch? You must tell me!"

"I tell you what," I said. He leant in, beaming. "We are to give you gifts on the seventh night, is that correct?"

"You are."

"I will give you his name."

"The perfect present. Gossip."

I laughed. I actually laughed.

He tucked a curl behind my ear. "I will give you Reasonable if you give me a true answer about Anne." I nodded. "I will organise for you to be let into her rooms and be with her ladies."

"Yes, Your Majesty."

"I will be sad to lose Reasonable again." He paused. "What is it you call him? You do not call him by the name I gave him."

I wondered if I was to get in trouble. "I call him Rufus."

"Rufus," he repeated.

"May I ask why His Majesty calls him Reasonable?"

"I am his name giver. I christened him with it when we were mayhap ten or twelve. Reasonable, because he is just that, and Blackman, because he is just that."

CHAPTER TWENTY-EIGHT

I sat on the bed; it was morning, but we had only just got to our rooms.

Hildy had got a damp cloth and was blotting my neck and face.

They were concerned about me ... to say the least.

But I did not want to discuss the nudity. I wanted to discuss the King's request.

"What the fuck is wrong with these people?" Rufus was pacing, visibly upset.

"I am well, Rufus. I am well. We need to talk about what the King wants from me."

"And the King!" said Zita, throwing her hands up in the air. "All over you. I am surprised he didn't take you to his bedchambers!"

"On your first trip to Court!" Hildy tutted.

"I've never seen them all like it." Zita was undressing in a rage. "Oh, but just looking at you standing there, Maude! Totally exposed!"

I was angry now. "Far worse has happened to me, Zita," I

snapped. "I am not a child anymore. I am a witch. I can handle these things."

Her bright blue eyes finally stilled upon my own. "Of course you can," she whispered.

"The King has asked something of me that I fear is more terrible than my naked body."

"What?" said Rufus very quickly.

"He's not asking me to fuck him, Rufus. He wants me to join the Queen's ladies. He wants me to tell him whether Her Majesty is a witch."

There was a pause.

"She almost undoubtedly is," said Hildy.

That wasn't what I had been expecting.

"What?" I signed quickly. "She can't be. How do you know?"

"She is otherworldly, connected to spirits unknown, for cert. You didn't feel it when you were near her?" Hildy asked, surprised.

"She is guarded." I shrugged.

"For a reason," said Zita.

"Jesus Christ! I thought he was just being facetious."

"Just tell him she isn't a witch, Maude. It can't be that hard."

"He is looking for one answer. He wants a divorce."

"Another one?" Rufus asked.

"You cannot out her as a witch. Verily, the King will find another way to divorce her."

"In return for my services, he will let Rufus return with us." I had been nervous to reveal this. I wondered if Rufus would be angry: maybe he didn't want to come home.

"What?" He seemed confused.

"The King asked what I wanted in return for this service." His expression was unreadable. "I said your name. I asked for your freedom from Court ..." Silence. "But I am sure you can stay if you want to. He was not happy about letting you go." He had cocked his head to one side. I couldn't read the expression on his face.

"You should've asked him before you made this arrangement, Maude," Zita said sternly.

"You should've asked the witches." Rufus spoke softly. "I have already taken up their hospitality too long."

"Nonsense," tutted Hildy. "We would welcome you back."

"Forgive me, Rufus. I should have asked what it was you desired. I thought only of myself. It was all I yearned for when he asked me what I wanted." I swallowed, not able to look him in the eye; why would I confess to that? There was an awkward pause.

"You have no choice but to join the Queen's court." Zita was back to the pressing topic at hand. "Stay quiet, out of sight; we will have to play it by ear."

"I fear my mother will be there."

"Oh Christ." She sat heavily on the bed. "We shouldn't have brought her, Hildy. We should've left her at home with the shoppe."

"Do not speak like this, Zita! I am perfectly able to deal with these situations. I am just tired and looking for support! But if all you are going to do is treat me like a child, then I am going to bed."

I left their room and shut my door heavily, then I threw all my dresses onto the floor and quickly tucked myself into my bed. Freezing.

I shook from anger and the cold. I waited for sleep to descend. Surely, I was exhausted.

After a few moments, the door opened. It was Rufus. I watched him as he tried to creep quietly into the room, so tall, so broad, so un-fairy like. The ceilings in this kingdom were at least a foot too low for him.

He looked at me and realised I was awake. We looked at each other for a long while. My shivering exacerbated, from nerves now.

"Are you shaking with anger at the witches?" he asked.

"Nay." I paused. "I am shaking because I am afraid I have upset you and also because it is cold ... I acted selfishly, without considering your feelings."

"You are always very thoughtless."

"I know."

"You think only of yourself."

"I know."

"Do you need another blanket?"

"There are no m-more," I chattered.

"Are you clothed under there?" I shook my head. "Where are your nightclothes?"

"In the other room."

"Do you want me to fetch them?"

"No."

"You are too stubborn," he muttered.

The shivering was uncontrollable now. Rufus pursed his lips, took an audible breath in and then out. Then he took off his shoes, walked behind me and lay on top of the covers. He put his arms around my body and rested his chin over my head.

He was so, so warm. I shuffled closer into him.

"Is this better?"

I turned my body to face him. "Aye."

He looked at me with those unreadable eyes.

"I'm sorry for not asking you what you wanted. I will endeavour to never be so unthinking ever again." He raised a sceptical eyebrow. I was no longer tired. “I thought it would please you.”

“It pleases me to have a choice. Do not worry yourself about it.” He brushed his nose against my own. “Just like you English to be bargaining for this poor black man’s future.”

My stomach flipped over. His expression was playful and he was winding me up, but I felt nearly nauseated by the truth he had told.

“Forgive me,” I whispered, and again he brushed his nose against my own.

There was silence for some time, then I gathered my courage. “I would hear some of your stories from where you’re from, if you ever wanted to share them?”

“I have no memories of my homeland. My first is of the boat that brought us o’er.”

“What was it like?”

“It will ruin your sleep.”

“If you wanted to tell the story, I would sacrifice my sleep.”

“Well, let me see. What are the highlights?” His face was an inch from mine. “I recall my kinsmen got so sick they looked like white men. I remember sitting in my own vomit. I remember the rocking. I had to shit into my clothes, and my mother had to do the same. I remember my friends dying and being taken up on deck. I remember hearing the splashes of the sea, and wondering if those splashes were the splashes of bodies. And then we were in Spain.”

I didn’t move my face away from his, but I wanted to. I think he was relishing my discomfort. I wanted to squirm, to retreat. But I also wanted to touch his cheeks and hold his head to my breast.

“Sounds shite,” I muttered.

“Verily, it was shite,” he concluded. He moved his head

forwards. He kissed my forehead gently. I wanted to return the gesture, but I couldn't find the courage.

Jane, the Queen's fool, retrieved me at about midday. She wore a pearl-adorned gable, and the triangular frame around her perfectly round face looked almost comical.

"I will take care of you," she said kindly, linking arms with me.

"Thank you, Jane."

"The Queen won't like you because she'll think you're a spy."

"I know."

"You are a spy." It wasn't a question.

"Do you think I should just say silent, out of sight?"

She nodded dramatically, her gable bouncing up and down precariously. "Yes," she said, very excited that I knew what to do. "That's an excellent idea."

The Court was still quiet, people resting their weary heads. The day itself was a delight. The air was cool, but the sun shone generously down upon me. Not even the glorious weather could rile this Court of slugabeds.

We crossed the clock tower court and went into the Queen's Gallery.

Oh God. I stopped, my mind choosing now of all the times to start processing what was unfolding. Zounds, this was the day I'd dreamt of. The day I'd sat in waiting for during my first eighteen years. The day I became one of the women. In waiting. Jane gently coaxed me forwards.

The guard opened the door into a drawing room.

It was smaller than the room King Henry had been entertaining in last night, but it was similarly furnished and the floors and walls were covered in tapestries. It was homey and pleasant. Perfect for a day such as today.

The Queen's ladies decorated the room, much like the women strewn over the King's rooms the previous night, but these ones glittered with jewels and there was not a breast in sight.

I saw my mother immediately, sitting in the corner of the far room, hidden in shadow. She had moved violently when I entered. I wondered what had happened to my newest brother. If he was alive, and well? He would be with a wet nurse, I supposed.

And then, of course, I saw the Queen. She sat on a stool, glittering in candlelight. She was stitching.

"Thank you, Jane," she said without looking up.

Jane curtsied. "You're welcome, Anne." I looked around, deeply surprised she had used the Queen's first name. No one else had flinched.

Everyone but the Queen and my mother was watching me.

"This is wisewoman Maude," said the Queen, still finishing off a stitch. "She is a fortune-teller and a witch. She will be here to entertain us throughout the festive period. A gift from my husband." I dipped into a deep curtsey. "Maude, you will entertain yourself, and remain quiet unless I, or any of my ladies, request your services."

"Yes, Your Majesty."

"What do you think of her, Jane?" Anne asked. I looked up from my curtsey. Jane was standing by Her Majesty's side.

"I think she is a spy." Goddamn it, Jane.

"I think so too," said Anne, not perturbed. "But I do not think she wants to be one."

I stared at them both. Neither seemed angry or upset at me.

"You do not need to pretend you are anything but a spy,

Maude." She smiled. "Jane is connected to the heavens; she knows all." I didn't say anything. "I am sorry my husband has put you in this position. I can imagine it was not what you intended to do over your festive season." Was this a big old trick? What the fuck was I meant to say? "You do not need to say anything for now." I exhaled. "Can you stitch?" I nodded. "Good. Join us. Lady Mary?" Christ. My mother stood.

"Your Majesty?"

"Fetch Maude all that she needs. Maude, you may sit over there." She pointed to a spare stool.

I went and sat. I stared into my lap.

"Here." Hands appeared in front of my face. It is peculiar how well you know your kins' hands. I recognised the length of her fingers, the lightly freckled skin, the rings. I looked up. My mother was handing me needles, thread and cloth.

"Thank you." Our hands brushed as I gathered my things. She didn't look me in the eye.

It took me mere moments to remember how much I hated stitching. God, I was bad.

It was silent, except for the sporadic tinkle of me dropping my poxed needle.

I had, yet again, made a rose with far too big thorns for the size of its petals. I sighed.

"Were you in the King's chambers last night, Maude?"

I jumped. It had been so quiet for so long. A few titters and whispers, but no one had spoken out loud.

"She was," said Jane loudly.

"I was, Your Majesty," I repeated.

All ten of the women's eyes were on me.

"What was it like?"

I looked into Anne's eyes from across the room. She

cradled her stomach. Henry hadn't told me not to tell her. He told me to spy. It would probably only gain her trust to be honest about the situation.

"It was Dionysian, Your Majesty." Twitters and shaking of the heads. Anne remained still.

"How many whores were there?"

"Surely over a dozen, Your Majesty."

"Any women of the Court?" The air in the room changed: it was harder to breathe. Or perhaps it was entirely unbreathable air. Either way, no one dared take a breath.

I looked around the room, seeing if I recognised anyone's face.

Yes. She had been there. The woman looked the worse for wear, and her eyes boggled at me, begging me not to betray her.

"Were you harmed?" Anne asked before I could reply. She must've seen my eyes linger; she knew who I had seen. The air became breathable again. I was touched by this question.

"There was a trying moment, Your Majesty, but I was left physically unharmed."

"I hope none of the men violated you." There were several gasps. I hoped one of them might be from my mother.

"They did not."

"Did the King seem to be entertaining anyone in particular?"

"In all truth, Your Majesty, the only person I saw him with was Lord Seymour." To my surprise, the air was poison again.

"Edward Seymour?"

"Yes, Your Majesty."

"Did you hear anything of what they discussed?"

"His Majesty wanted me to read Lord Seymour."

"What did you see in him?"

"Your Majesty, I hope you won't mind if I keep that to

myself. It was personal business. I hope you understand: I would not ever betray a reading from you, and I wish to show that by example, by not betraying Lord Seymour."

Anne nodded. "I respect that. What happened after the reading? Did they discuss anything further?"

"He sent him away, Your Majesty."

"What a shame, I would love to have heard what he said. Perhaps you can enlighten us, Lady Seymour?"

I turned to see the small woman in the corner.

"I do not know my brother's business, Your Majesty," she whispered.

"Of course you don't!" Vehement anger. That relationship was not a happy one. "Thank you, Maude. You may sit here." She pointed to the chair where my mother sat, by her side. "Mary, swap seats with Maude."

My mother looked horrified. She didn't move. She just stared up at Anne. The Queen looked at her for a long time, cocking her head, as though trying to understand this bizarre reaction.

"Mary," she said again.

My mother got up and staggered over to my stool. My heart in my throat, I sat by the Queen's seat.

"You're her favourite today," said Jane, too loudly.

There was a knock on the door and a guard came through.

"Your Majesty, it is time for the jousting tournament."

"At what time does my husband ride?"

"Soon, I would think, Your Majesty. He is eager to get his joust in hand."

"He will undoubtably want to impress you, Lady Seymour. Wear the necklace he gave you last night." Jane Seymour did not look up from her feet. "Unfortunately, I am unwell. This babe exhausts me." She smiled around at all of us. "You will all have to attend without me." Slowly, the women began collecting themselves. I was unsure what to do. "You stay with me, Maude," said Anne quietly. In my mind's eye, I witnessed all her composure and all her kindness leaving the room with her ladies, leaving me with a monster. A monster, with child. I had dealt with my mother's pregnant mood swings all my life and they were genuinely something to fear.

Mary left last. She turned to look at me. And she made eye contact for the first time. I felt guilty. Which felt unfair.

The door shut and there was a long silence. Lady Jane was still there too.

"Is Lady Mary your mother?"

I stared at the door, unable to move my eyes from it. I was frozen in this time and this place, forever. My body was immovable. My mind fixated on what she had just said. How could she know? She turned to her fool.

"Jane, I want you to enjoy the joust too. You are to leave."

"Aye, Your Majesty!" Jane left, content and at ease.

Still staring at the door through which Jane had just left, I tried to take a breath. I felt a hand on my shoulder.

"I'm sorry to surprise or upset you."

The touch removed me from my reverie. I got off my stool and fell into a curtsey at her feet, my skirts pooling around me.

"How could you know that, Your Majesty?" I managed.

"I've never seen Mary behave in that way. Something about the way she looked at you ... I just knew."

"Will you reveal this to the Court?"

"Not if you do not want me to."

I nodded, extremely grateful. "I am indebted to you, Your Majesty."

"What did you read in my eyes last night?"

I looked up at her again. I was hit with a cart of lethargy. I felt tired. "Your Majesty. I don't want to tell you."

"If you truly are a witch, nothing you can say will be news to me."

I looked at her for a long time. I think she knew what I saw. "I saw sadness, Your Majesty."

"We are all sad in some way or another."

"I saw fear."

"Everyone fears, Maude. Are you a fraud? Or a seer?"

"I saw fear over the life of your child."

"Over Elizabeth?"

"No." Her hands went to her stomach. "Are you bleeding? Is something amiss with the babe?"

Oh God, the silence went on forever.

"I do bleed," she whispered. "But I bled in my pregnancy with Elizabeth."

"But this is more," I said.

"Yes."

"My kinswoman Hildy is a healer. Known for her work with unborn babes. She is also discreet." A moment's pause.

"Will you fetch her?"

"Of course." I rose.

"Not right now," she said quickly. "What did Henry send you here for?"

I stared at the delicate necklace around her neck, a pearl necklace with the gold letter *B* at her throat.

"I am scared, Your Majesty. I don't want to be punished for disloyalty."

"Nor do I, Maude," she said pointedly.

"He did not send me here to question your loyalty to him."

"He didn't?" She seemed genuinely surprised. "Then why?"

"Will you tell him I betrayed him?"

"You will not betray him. You will still spy on me; I will just know why."

I ran my hands over my bodice, over my mark.

"He wonders if you are like me."

"A witch?"

"Yes, Your Majesty."

"Huh." She sat back in her chair and stared into nothingness. I let her sit in her thoughts and tried to harness control over my breath. "What do you think so far, Maude?"

"I think you are a woman of power and intuition, Your Majesty."

"Does that make me a witch?"

"Only if it gets in a man's way."

She managed a laugh. "How did you know that you are a witch?"

"The world deemed me a witch because I have a mark on my belly. A large witch's mark."

"And your practice? Does it feel true to you?"

"It didn't at first. But as I recognise my powers, they grow. I am a witch because I am sensitive, because I can feel people's feelings and emotions through my touch and through my eyes. I am powerful and intuitive."

"You saw my bleeding," she whispered.

"I did."

She rubbed her forehead. "How?"

"I just ... I felt it." I shrugged.

We both looked at each other for a long while.

"How did you know that Mary was my mother?" I asked quietly.

"I felt it," she whispered.

CHAPTER TWENTY-NINE

Her Majesty sent for Hildy and as we waited I made the Queen a charm out of her bodice. I laid hands on it and spoke good words to her babe.

I cooed to him and let him know that he was safe. I reminded the baby it was not time to come out yet, but that he should make himself as comfortable as possible in his mother's belly. I whispered it in Latin. I whispered it in broken French. I whispered it through my gentle touch. Anne sat in her throne, eyes shut, whispering her own prayers as I went through the process.

"Your Majesty?" Hildy was there.

"She is deaf, Your Majesty. She will read your lips."

"I see," Anne said, beckoning Hildy forwards. "You must leave," she said to the guard at the door. He gave it a moment's pause, and then left. "He's a spy like you, Maude," said Anne teasingly.

Hildy threw me a look. "What can I do for you, Your Majesty?"

"I have brought you here as my confidante. My physician

is, like Maude, like my guards, like most everyone at Court, a spy." Again, she threw me a wicked smile. "I need you to be on my side. The mother's side." Anne was speaking clearly, but not condescendingly. Hildy had understood.

"I am always on the mother's side, Your Majesty." Hildy's voice was true, deep and filled with conviction. My stomach turned over, first with the power of her words but then with fear. We were meddling in dangerous affairs. We were putting our very lives in peril by going behind the King's back. "How can I serve you?" Hildy asked.

"Do you not know through your witch's sense?"

"Are you bleeding?"

"Maude told you."

Hildy inclined her head.

"How old is the babe, Your Majesty?"

"It has been over three full moons since my last regular bleed."

Hildy nodded. "May I touch your belly, Your Majesty?"

"You may. Maude has just blessed my bodice and belly with her work, so make sure you don't disturb her magic."

I felt a deep love for her as she spoke those words. She was so earnest, so respectful of my power, so desperate to save her baby.

"I would examine you somewhere with a bed. Somewhere more private?"

Anne nodded and got up, taking us into the next rooms. Again, I felt the nerves. I was suddenly this woman's carer, her baby's Earthly guardian. I was filled with a fierce need to protect and I stared at the guard on her sleeping-chamber door with a vehement glare. Don't fucking spy on this woman. She is an angel, I said through my squinted glare. He looked confused at my reaction, and a little bit scared. He was also dismissed. These were secret things we did. Secret, dangerous things.

Hildy got out her tinctures and herbs and laid them at the end of the Queen's bed. She closed the curtains and asked Anne to get undressed. The Queen did not fear nudity. I helped her undo her corset, and she placed her charmed bodice with deliberate care on the bed, then handed me the rest of her skirts to drape over a chair on the other side of the room. She returned to her mattress and, lying down, she gestured for me to pass her the charmed corset.

"Best to keep this near, I think," she whispered. I was now glaring at Hildy. Take care of this woman, Hildy, I tried to say into her mind.

"Why don't you tell Her Majesty stories as I investigate what is going on?" suggested Hildy.

"Of course. What story would you like to hear, Your Majesty?" I sat cross-legged up by her head, and she turned to me.

"Your story." Hildy was focusing on Anne's belly and could not hear what we were talking about. "How is your mother here, and why is she pretending that you are not her own?"

"You will keep it a secret?"

"Will you keep my secrets?"

"Yes," I said, my hands now unpleasantly moist with sweat. I believed my words. I did not want to betray this woman to the King. But my conviction meant my very life was in peril. I was not ignorant to Henry's ways. I was no fool. I knew his power. I knew what he could do if he sensed I had changed allegiances.

"Then I will keep your story a secret. And we will always be connected to one another through the safekeeping of each other's stories."

I smiled at her. I liked the idea we would always be connected.

"Agreed."

"What is your name?"

"Lady Magdalen Beckett, formally of my father's name, Shaftsberry."

"You're the one that died of Spanish flu."

"Aye. I am deceased."

"Why?" I saw Anne wince a bit as Hildy touched her belly.

"May I show you something, Your Majesty?"

"You may."

I lay down next to her, pulled my skirts up around my own belly, and tried to show her my mark.

"Your witch's mark."

"It's very big. My husband, Edward Beckett, he thought it was a sign of witchcraft, though then I was but a virtuous maid — he thought I would bewitch his cock."

"Edward Beckett," she repeated, thinking. "He is at Court. Have you seen him?"

"I have."

"What happened?"

"I bewitched his cock."

She laughed but then cringed and looked down at Hildy.

"You're hurting her, Hildy," I snapped.

Hildy had not been watching us, so she had not noticed I had spoken. I tapped her shoulder.

"Be careful!" I said clearly.

"You are getting cramping?" Hildy asked, ignoring me.

"I am, but nothing like the labour I had with Elizabeth."

"No quickening as of yet?"

"Nay. But Elizabeth was late to her quickening." Her whole body was taut.

"Here." Hildy made her drink something, and her body relaxed.

"Has your belly grown much in this past month?"

"It has grown." She was defensive.

"Much?"

"Not as much as with Elizabeth."

It was not good news. I could feel it seeping off Hildy's body: a smell of foreboding.

"I think you should spend as much of your time lying as flat as you can, Your Majesty."

"No. Not lying in. Not yet. I have half a year to go."

"No, we will not call this lying in," Hildy said reassuringly. "It's just some precautionary bed-rest. To not over-excite your babe."

Anne nodded slowly.

The door banged open.

I jumped off the bed. Hildy hadn't heard it but she had seen Anne's face turn ghostly white then red with rage.

"How dare you enter my rooms unannounced!" The Queen's voice was very loud and very low, like a man's.

Hildy made sure Anne was covered, then, unhurried, she turned. I was on the floor by the left of her bed. Away from the intruder.

"Anne." It was the Duke of Norfolk. The Queen's uncle. "What is wrong? Who is this?"

"She is a midwife! Checking on my babe! Why have you barged into my rooms?"

"The King has fallen off his horse."

Anne sat up, abruptly. Hildy held her back. I was still on the floor on the other side of the bed; I wasn't even sure he had seen me.

"Is he ...?"

"He is alive. But he is unconscious."

"Uncle!" Anne wailed. Hildy was rubbing her back slowly. I couldn't move.

"I thought you should know."

He looked at Hildy with the utmost contempt and turned on his heel to leave.

"Get me dressed. I must go to my husband," she shouted at Hildy.

"Is that for the best, Your Majesty?" I asked.

"Get her dressed, Maude." Hildy gave me a warning look.

We did so and then left her to a guard to take her to her husband, the King.

"You shouldn't have let her go. This sort of thing could distress her child," I signed to Hildy, as the door banged shut.

"I think the baby is already gone, Maude."

The King was not badly harmed.

But he had been two whole hours on his back, blacked out, and the festive spirit had soured.

Later that night I returned with Hildy to the Queen's chambers: the King had woken, and his physician had declared him out of danger.

"Now she is going to get to look after him," the Queen spat as Hildy tried to get her to lie on her back.

"Why don't you get her in here, to look after you?" I suggested.

She liked that idea. A guard was sent to fetch Lady Jane Seymour.

I sat with Anne and Jane Seymour for three days straight, returning to my quarters in the evening for sleep and being summoned early the next day. Her other ladies had been in attendance too, my mother included, but none were summoned as much as Jane Seymour and me.

On the morning of the fourth day, the King called on me. I was taken through the secret corridor that linked the Queen's room and the King's. It felt very intimate sneaking through the halls that were designed for husband and wife.

The King was also in bed. Perhaps I really had died of Spanish flu, and this was some sort of bizarre afterlife in which I swanned between royal bedchambers.

Several men were surrounding the King. I had a moment of panic, thinking perhaps they were giving him his last rites, and this was the end and maybe he was asking me to tell his wife that he was dying. No. No, Maude. Hold your shit together. I sat in my curtsey. They were talking about money — taxes or something. This was not the last rites. He was just working from bed. He sounded well enough: his voice still rang with that all-powerful tone. He asked them to leave.

"Who is she, Your Majesty?" asked a slimy voice.

"She's one of the witches brought in for the festive season," Henry said with a clear tone of finality.

"I don't know if it is a good idea, with your head still —"

"We are not about to fuck," he said clearly.

"Of course not, Your Majesty." I heard the door close. "We're not, are we?" he asked. I looked up at him. He was sporting a little grin. I hated myself for liking him a tiny bit.

"I don't believe so, Your Majesty," I replied.

"Good, then we can get straight to business. How is Anne?"

"I think it is good for her to rest."

"Is the babe dying?"

I was shocked. I was shocked because he didn't seem shocked. I was shocked because the question rolled off his tongue so easily.

"We cannot know, Your Majesty. Do you expect it to die?"

"She is barren," he said directly.

"But ... Elizabeth."

"Her final child. Do you not see it? With your witch's eye?"

Of course I saw it. Hildy had told me. I bowed my head.

"Are you feeling better, Your Majesty?" I asked.

"I am mourning the Yuletide spirit, which seems to have fallen from the same horse I fell from, but whilst I survived, it died."

"I am sure you can resurrect her." I was a metre away from the King's bed.

"Do you have any understanding of Anne's supernatural powers?"

I took two deep breaths. "I am not sure if it is because she is lying in, sir, but I have not been able to detect any intuition or witchly ways." This annoyed him. He tutted and looked away from me. "There is still time for me to watch her, Your Majesty." I was suddenly scared he was going to ask me to stop spying. I liked being by this woman's side.

"How much longer must she lie in?"

"I believe one more day fully on her back."

"Very well." He sighed. "You can have the rest of the day off. My counsel hath told me it is a pleasant day outside, though they insist I don't enjoy it. Go enjoy what is left of the festivities."

"Thank you, Your Majesty."

"Be back with her as soon as she is walking around and on her feet."

"Yes, Your Majesty."

He smiled at me. "Are you loyally mine? She hasn't got you under her spell?"

"I am yours, Your Majesty."

"She has great powers, Maude, I am sure of it. I was unable

to think of anything but her when she first bewitched me — it would not surprise me if you felt the same."

"I am a witch, Your Majesty, and I have charms of my own to ward off her magic — if she had any," I added quickly.

"I am glad. Now go. Enjoy your youth."

"Your Majesty." I bowed, and left via the usual exit, not the corridor that wound back to Anne's room.

CHAPTER THIRTY

I went to try to find Zita.

She wasn't in any of the major courtyards, despite the lovely, surprisingly warm weather, and she wasn't in the gallery. I found William Sommers in the clock tower court juggling; he was a picture of the Court fool.

"Sommers!" I called.

"Do not interrupt me, witch! I have never been able to go for this long!"

"That's what she said!" yelled a witty soul from the crowd.

"It's my job to crack the bawdy jokes, sir!"

"Have you seen Zita?" I asked again, trying to make eye contact between the flying multicoloured balls.

"She is reading the Duke of Norfolk's stars. She only just left."

I sighed. "And Rufus?"

"Haven't seen your desired today!"

I didn't even bother fighting him. I left to return to my room. Maybe I could sneak back into Anne's chambers but that would confirm that I was under her spell.

I sat myself down in front of the fire, which was still

crackling loudly like someone had recently attended to it. I was under her spell. A warm sunbeam came through the window and lay across my face; it felt heavenly. I did need the day off. It had been the biggest week of my life. I lay down in the beam of light, the fire warming my left side, the sun warming my right.

"Maude?"

I startled. Rufus's head had appeared outside the curtains of my bed.

"Why aren't you working, Ruf?" I asked from the flat of my back.

"The King gave me the day off," he explained.

"The King gave me the day off too," I said suspiciously.

He looked nonplussed and swung his legs over the edge of the bed. "Forgive me for borrowing your bed — do you want to rest?"

"I want to be in the sun," I said, moving my face so it followed the sunbeam.

"Shall we go for a walk?"

We rugged up and went outside.

Hampton Court is in the middle of nowhere. Though it doesn't take long to get the boat down to the middle of London, there are only forests and farmland around the huge redbrick monstrosity. Thankfully Rufus knew the area well: there was the Hare Warren, Middle Park and Bushy Park, the King's deer-hunting forests. But we needn't worry about that, the King was inside today. It was just us.

"Where are we going?" We were walking the path alongside the Thames. "Did you grow up on this land?"

He shook his head. "No, no, Maude." He actually laughed. "I have only spent a few years here. It's brand new."

"Oh, I'm sorry!" I said indignantly. "I don't keep up to date with the King's castles."

"I grew up in Greenwich mostly," he explained. "Down here." Rufus indicated a well-worn path into the forest. I pulled my cape closer around me and followed.

I had spent a lot of time with Rufus in the apothecary. We had been alone a lot. But this time felt a little different. I didn't know what to say. My mouth was dry. Rufus wasn't saying anything and I wasn't saying anything. Perhaps it was all the hinting and suggestions made by the Motley Lot. They had pulled unspoken thoughts from the safety of our minds and made things awkward. Or perhaps it was the situation I had got him in with the King. And now the Queen. I had put our futures at stake.

"These woods are beautiful," I managed. He nodded. They were beautiful. It was filled with pines, all still thick with their needles, and some still frosted with old snow from a few days before. It was enchanting and festive. I saw a few more courtiers enjoying the walk deeper into the forest, they were holding hands. Was this some sort of Lovers' Forest? Had he brought me here to seduce me?

"You're very comfortable with silence," I said. He didn't reply. "Stop it, Rufus!" I moaned, and he started chuckling. "It makes me feel uncomfortable walking in the quiet."

"What do you want to talk about then?" he asked, smiling.

I thought about it. There was actually a lot to discuss, but I was tired of all the courtly intrigues.

"I'm sorry for making you broom the apothecary when you really hated brooming," I said finally.

Again he took a few moments to reply. "I forgive you."

"Did I remind you of your mother?"

"You are as demanding as my mother, aye. But you were nowhere near as scary."

"I'm scary!" I protested.

"You haven't met my mother."

"I'm scary," I repeated, defensively. "Do you think you will see her again? Maybe you can ask the King or someone in Court where she's gone?"

He nodded. "I could."

"What is her name?"

"Her Spanish name is Catalina."

"Why did His Majesty give you the day off?" I asked as we broke out into a clearing. The sun shone fully on my face again.

Rufus glanced down at me quickly, grinning.

"He likes us as a couple."

My tummy flipped.

"Zita and Hildy do too." I was surprised I could get my lips to say such a thing.

"And the fools."

"And Goodthatcher," I added. He was chuckling. I loved the way he laughed.

"Matchmaking is for the simple-minded," I declared, wondering what he would say to that.

"Matchmaking two married people is for the damned."

We laughed, but I felt a little disappointed. I kicked a fallen pinecone.

"Do you like playing your trumpet again?"

"Very much."

"I wish I could hear you play without the noise of Court, or the racket of the other musicians."

"Damn those other players! Interrupting my music!" Again, we laughed.

"Maybe you can play for me alone one day."

"I would love to, Maude."

I reached out my hand and let them brush past the pine leaves. They tickled my palms.

"The woods remind me of you, Maude," he said after a while.

I cringed. I had tried hard not to think about that day, what had he seen as I tore through the woods, grieving, taken by madness, stripping myself of clothes, yelling.

"This pine is like a tent!" My voice was high-pitched. I led him under the alcove of the Christmas tree's curtains. He was frowning at me. I circled the tree, resting my palm on her bark as I went, and he watched me go around and around. "Is it because of Watlington Wood?" I asked reluctantly.

"Aye," he said, to my dismay. He must've read the sadness on my face because he shook his head and stopped me in my circling. The pine was letting in tiny flickers of sun, little needles of light dancing off our skin.

"When I found you in between the trees ..." he paused, looking around, as though the words he wanted were hidden in the canopy of the tree "... I'd never seen anything, anyone look the way you did."

"I was mad," I whispered.

He shook his head, and again he looked to the skies. "You were undone. It was like watching a caged animal free itself. It was like witnessing a lion from my homelands escaping from her cage, and I witnessed you as everything you were meant to be. And I feared you. And I couldn't look away. Because it was just — power — ricocheting of the trees, a bright light, burning off old bindings."

I knew what he said was true, because my body erupted in shivers, and tears flooded my eyes, and I felt the power he spoke of ripple down my spine and pour out of my skin. I had never felt so seen.

"I thought I had lost everything," I said. My voice was clear.

"I thought I was being stripped of everything that made me." I wiped my face with the back of my hand, inexplicable trembling in my fingers. "But I had just been deprived of my masks: I had been left with only myself."

He took hold of my forearm, his thumb rubbing against my skin. He was so much taller than me.

"That was what I saw." His eyes were intense, his brow furrowed with a desperate sort of look, of pain almost.

"What are we doing here, Rufus?" I asked.

"I was hoping we might kiss."

The words, like a rope, tied themselves around us and brought us close to one another. Our bodies were pressed against one another, my back up against the trunk.

I could feel him against me. Were we going to do it, there under the pine leaves?

"The witches think we are going to become lovers." He spoke seriously.

"I hate to prove them right," I whispered.

He raised an eyebrow. "Please don't let your stubbornness ruin this moment."

He put his hand on my chin and tilted my heads towards him.

"Let's just not tell them," I breathed.

"Agreed." He kissed me softly, starting with the edges of my lips, moving towards the centre, and then tugging at my bottom lip with his teeth. I let out an involuntary gasp. He withdrew to check on me.

"You must keep going," I instructed.

"You must sweep the floors, Rufus; you must keep kissing me, Rufus ..." he whispered, moving to my ears now. "Always telling me what to do."

"I think you like doing as I say," I managed.

"Verily, I do." His breath on my ear did something unGodly. "But I am going to take over now. Yes?"

I managed a nod.

Rufus was adept. The way he moved my skirts and manoeuvred my corset was like a dance, a very practised dance.

"Fairies are experienced lovers?" I asked breathlessly, now standing in only my shift.

"I'm a fairy who grew up in Court, Maude," he said, kissing my collarbones. "What do you expect from me?"

I smiled; his expertise was thrilling.

I thought perhaps he'd hesitate to take off my shift. He knew what lay beneath this dress. Maybe he'd like to turn me around and take me from behind — I knew people did that. But instead, he draped his own cloak around my nakedness and then dropped to his knees, his hands tracing my mark, in awe, not unlike my bewitched husband had done back in the brothel, but I had not bewitched Rufus. He was doing this of his own accord.

Then he began to use his tongue, and my husband had not done that ...

CHAPTER THIRTY-ONE

It was the night before gift giving. We were sitting quietly, listening to Lady Seymour reading, the mood certainly more upbeat. The Queen was up and walking, the King was up and walking and tomorrow was the gift-giving day. A little bit of Christmas cheer had returned to Hampton Court. It had certainly returned to my heart. I didn't even care that Seymour had a voice to put rabid dogs to sleep.

"What have you got the King as a gift?" It was my mother's voice, but I assumed she must've been talking to someone near me. Not to me: she hadn't spoken a single word to me since I first saw her.

"Magdalen," she hissed. I felt as though all my insides dropped a foot towards Hell. I turned to her. Horrified.

"My name is Maude," I replied.

She looked very concerned.

"What have you got the King as a gift?" she repeated. I stared at her. "I only ask because I am worried you have forgotten you must give the King a gift, and it will be very bad for you if you have forgotten."

"I have already organised my present for the King. He is

very excited about receiving it." I was trying to keep my voice measured. I wondered if she cared for my wellbeing, or if she cared that I might embarrass myself.

"Tupping doesn't count," she hissed.

"I'm not fucking him!" I threw her a dirty, dirty look. Thirteen-year-old Maude would've applauded its venom.

"Oh, please. Why on Earth are you here then if you're not tupping him?"

"She's here to spy on me, Mary." Anne had been listening; now that I looked around, I realised everyone had been listening. "Everyone knows she's a spy. Don't mix up her crimes." Anne looked at her seriously.

"My apologies, Your Majesty," Mary mumbled.

"You will leave her alone."

"Yes, Your Majesty."

"What gift have you got for His Majesty this year, Anne?" asked Jane, the fool, who was massaging the Queen's feet.

"He's so hard to buy for," she lamented, throwing her head back. "I've spoiled him in years past."

"It is hard to beat the Pyrenean boar spears," said Lady Agnes.

"Yes, that was a very good present. Still, I have him some jewels this year and a very nice saddle. He will undoubtably like them."

"I have him a saddle!" said Lady Seymour.

Anne's face changed into a smooth, beautiful smile. "Well, I imagine you'll have to find him something else!"

Jane looked panicked. "May I be excused?" she asked, her breath shallow.

"No!" Anne said brightly.

Zounds. That was cold. There was a long awkward silence.

"Maude, your skin looks refreshed, and there is brightness about you."

"Thank you, Your Majesty."

"You will entertain us with your sordid affair, and spare no details."

"My affair, Your Majesty?"

"So, you do sleep with the King!" My mother had stood.

"Mary! Go find Lady Seymour a gift to give the King. In fact, I have an idea: go fetch an old shirt, and embroider it with the King's initials. Do it in the gallery."

"But —"

"You are getting very rude and disrespectful in your old age, Lady Shaftsberry."

My mother's nostrils flared like a horse's, and I saw her jaw clamp down hard. She left the room. The door shut.

"That fixes Seymour's problem and now Maude can speak freely about whatever she got up to yesterday." How could she possibly know? "It was with the trumpeter, wasn't it?"

The fool was wiggling each of Anne's toes individually. "Did you tell her, Jane?" I asked. The ladies tittered as they realised I really had been with the trumpeter.

"I didn't tell anybody nothing," said Jane.

"Jane is incapable of being untrue. I am simply perceptive," said the Queen.

I smiled. "I don't know how it happened." I felt the energy of quickly boiling water in my chest, as if I were about to burst.

"Your Majesty, must we hear about the bodily juices exchanged between a common witch and a Moor? It is disgusting and not in the Christmas spirit!" It was Elizabeth Boleyn. The Queen's mother.

The boiling water went ice cold in an impossibly fast moment. I felt the front of my ribs concave and unstick from the front of my bodice. Then I felt tears: good God no. Not the tears. Anne was looking daggers at her mother but there seemed to be some agreement in the group.

"Your Majesty, I must be excused," I managed.

"You all must." She added, "You must all retire." I went for the door. "But you will wait a moment, Maude." Very, very reluctantly I sat myself down. I felt the other ladies leaving around me.

"Come to me, witch." The door closed, and I moved to her chair; I bent down next to it and looked up at her.

Jane was massaging her left hand now. Her other hand remained gloved. It was always gloved.

"Mothers!" she said exasperatedly. I managed a small laugh. "We have to have them! But that doesn't mean we have to like them."

Why was she so kind to me?

She presented her right hand to Jane, who ungloved it. Six fingers. Everyone knew, of course, but it surprised me nonetheless. I was not scared of it. I was not disgusted.

She placed her hand on top of my own, and I gave in to the tears I had been holding back.

There was a long moment: the deformed Queen of England, the marked witch, and Jane the fool. Sitting together in silence, a new coven.

"Was it good?" she said after a long moment.

I managed a smile. "Very." My tummy did a loop at the very thought of it.

"I miss fucking," she said wistfully. Jane managed a giggle. "You must have lots of it, Maude, to make up for my dry, dull pregnancy."

"If you insist, Your Majesty."

She grinned. "Where did you do it?"

"It was not Godly, Your Majesty."

"Even better."

"It was in the forests, under a pine tree."

"How sordid." She was fiddling with her necklace. "Were you standing up?" I nodded. "That's my favourite way."

"Weren't you cold?" Jane asked suddenly.

"Only after," I admitted.

"But then he gave you his cloak?" asked the Queen.

"He did."

"Did he see your witch's mark?"

"He did."

"Was he kind about it?" Anne was very intent on this question, and I wondered if the King had not been kind about her extra finger.

"He kissed it, and traced it with his fingers, and he licked —"

"Stop!" said Anne, hardly being able to bear it. "Oh I miss it all. The wooing, the dance, the play, the cock!"

I laughed hard. I loved this woman. I could've listened to her talk for hours. She was so free, so unhindered.

"They say your courtship with His Majesty was one of the most arousing the Court's ever seen," I dared.

She touched my head, and her finger wound around one of my curls. "It was arousing," she admitted, but she looked somewhat sad. "Will you see the trumpeter tonight?"

"I hope so."

"You must! Come back with more stories for this poor sexless Queen."

"Yes, Your Majesty."

"I will see you in the morning." I rose. "For gift giving."

"I look forward to it, Your Majesty." I moved to the door, an unstoppable grin plastered over my face.

. . .

I returned to my rooms. I was basically skipping. My love for Anne, my love for Rufus, the Court glittering with the evening light: it was all too good.

Zita and Hildy were in bed early, drinking tea and being sweet.

"How was your evening, Maude?" asked Zita, inviting me to sit on the bed.

"It was ..." I didn't have the words. The worst? The best? Magic? Full of witches? With the Queen of England?

"How is the Queen?"

"She seems in much better spirits." I took a sip from Zita's mug of tea.

"You are in very good spirits too," said Hildy, pinching my side friendlily.

"I like the Queen a lot; I like her company." I shrugged. "Where's Rufus?" I tried so hard to make the sentence seem normal, but my voice went high at the mention of his name, and it felt awkward on my tongue.

They knew.

How did they know?

Did they know?

Surely not.

"He's in your room," they said together.

"Very well," I said. I shouldn't leave right away. I took a few beats. "I'm going to go to bed."

"Oh my God, it happened!" squealed Hildy loudly.

"I told you it would happen at Court!" said Zita. "You owe me coin, Hildy!"

"Shhh!" I span around, getting tangled in the blanket, staring at them violently from the end of their bed.

"Was it just a kiss? Or did you tup?" asked Zita, genuinely curious.

"Be quiet!" I saw the witches' eyes move from me to my bedroom door.

I turned slowly to see Rufus leaning against the wall. He had no top on, his smooth, lean, fairy body was just out there for everyone to see.

"We tupped," he said casually, with the tiniest of smiles.

"We're so happy! Was it good?" asked Zita.

"I'm not telling you!" I exclaimed, outraged. "You're my aunt!"

"It was very good," Rufus said.

I turned to him again — my heart was in my mouth — he was looking at me.

"Of course it was good. Where did it happen?" asked Hildy.

"It's not your business!" I was trying to be angry, but I was smiling.

"It's about to happen next door." He grabbed me around my waist and lifted me off the ground.

"Rufus!"

The witches were giggling. I didn't know if I was aroused, embarrassed, or angry.

"I hope you both sleep deeply," he said, smiling widely, before shutting the door behind me and putting me down.

I opened the door and poked my head around. "We're not going to do it," I assured them.

They were whispering together.

"Doesn't bother us, Maude," said Zita brightly, and they giggled again.

"Good night." I shut the door and turned around; Rufus pushed me up against the door and it made a loud thud. His mouth was on mine before I could protest, and as the minutes went by, and his hands wandered, I decided I didn't give a fuck what the witches heard, or did, or thought. I only cared about Rufus.

A door banged open and an ice-cold breeze whipped over my body.

I was completely disoriented. I had no idea where I was. I was sitting up in bed. Rufus was asleep by my side; from what I could tell, he was naked. Standing at the foot of my bed was my mother. My mother was in our rooms. But I wasn't at Shirburn. No. I was at Court. I could hear Hildy and Zita talking urgently in the other room.

"The Queen is in labour," my mother declared. I jumped out of bed. I was naked. My mark was there, visible for all of us to see in this moment. I saw my mother glance at it, then at the still-fast-asleep Rufus.

Hildy burst in the room. "Quickly, Maude. Get changed. We must hurry."

My insides were shivering, like my heart and stomach were cold.

I put on my clothes and cloak.

"Hurry!" whispered my mother.

"We're coming, Mary," Hildy said, incredibly sternly.

Boots on, carrying Hildy's wares, we three witches and my mother ran across the courtyards. The rain glittered in the moonlight. And I was scared.

Hildy practically shouldered the door down while Zita barked furiously at a guard not letting us through. We could hear her screams from the gallery. She was in pain.

"Maude!" she called for me, her hands outstretched, her veins protruding.

I went to her side and began stroking her hair; she was soaked through with sweat.

"Your Majesty, this is wisewoman Zita," explained Hildy. "She is going to ask you questions."

Zita began firing off questions, but Anne only half managed to answer them.

Her normal midwife wasn't at Court, of course — everyone was at home for Christmas, and the Queen was still in the early days of her pregnancy. No one had been expecting this. Zita suggested calling the physician, but Anne begged us not to.

"He will kill me! The King will kill me!" she wailed. "You have to make it stop!" she kept saying. "You have to make her stay inside."

The babe was a "her" now.

Hildy started brewing her teas and tisanes. I sat by the Queen's head and received the mugs of this and that, getting her to swallow slowly. Most of it went down her face and onto her nightdress. She was bleeding very, very heavily. I prayed to God she wouldn't die.

The teas seemed to ease the pain, but only for a moment. In the early hours Her Majesty was writhing in agony again. She was trying to put herself upside down. Putting her legs against the wall and hanging halfway off the bed.

"If I lose this child, I will lose my life!" she cried. I tried to turn her upright.

In a moment of stillness, when the Queen had screamed herself into exhaustion and she fell into a brief sleep, the three of us convened.

"How has the King not heard her screams? He is only a corridor away."

"I don't think he is in the chambers tonight. A guard said he is in a further wing." Zita looked at me with intention.

Another one of his Bacchanalian parties perhaps; Jane was in the other room, so he wasn't bedding Seymour.

"She is close to passing the babe." Hildy looked over her shoulder to make sure the Queen couldn't hear, as if Anne didn't already know.

"We should get rid of the remnants before the King sees it," Zita said firmly.

"Art thou sure? What will the King surmise has happened? That it was a phantom pregnancy?" I wrung my hands.

"I know not, but he shouldn't see the foetus," Zita said, determined.

"How do we get rid of it?" My voice shook.

"The fire?" Hildy signed. Christ.

I looked to Anne in her feverish sleep; my mother sat by her side and stroked her hair. I joined her.

"This is what happened to your youngest sibling," my mother whispered.

My stomach dropped. "I had thought he was with a wet nurse."

She shook her head. "With God."

"I am sorry, Mother." I thought of my curse. What if I had done this.

"I blamed your spiteful words for some time, but I know 'tis my own fault. I was greedy. I took too many babies for myself."

I didn't know what to say.

"You died, and then she died, not a week later."

"I am not dead," I reminded her.

"She was a girl. When I thought perhaps she'd live, I thought to call her Maude."

I shut my eyes, just when I thought we were having a moment and she says that ... "I am not dead, Mama," I said again.

I felt Anne stir beneath me; she had begun a new round of whimpering and moaning.

Hildy came to check her, speaking sweet words as she looked between her legs.

Lady Jane Seymour entered the room. "Someone needs to tell the King," she said meekly.

"Get out!" I snapped at her. I hated her so much in that moment. She was going to use this, wasn't she? She was going to tell the King. I was yelling at her to leave, but if she left surely she would betray Anne. "Wait! Lady Seymour." She looked at me, fear in her eyes. "I am sorry for my outburst. You are right. I will find His Majesty."

She looked as though she might protest, but she hadn't the guts. She nodded.

"How long until the child is born?" I signed to Hildy.

"Soon."

"I will take my time, but I will bear him the bad news," I said, low-voiced, to the witches. "It is better that I tell him, not Jane fucking Seymour."

A guard took me to a part of the castle I had not seen before.

I could hear the party. I felt sick to my stomach.

The yeoman opened a door for me.

It was a small hall. There were tables set up with food and wine, much like they had had at the gathering I had attended. The guard guided me to the far corner of the hall, where I saw His Majesty. Again, he was with the Seymour boy.

"Witch!" he said delightedly, then he saw my face. "What is wrong? Do you have news of the Queen? Has she conjured some sort of demon?" He was serious. Very drunk but very serious.

"I have news of your wife, Your Majesty."

"What of her?" I came close to him; he grabbed my wrist. I

couldn't really prolong this conversation. There was only one thing to say.

"She has lost her child, Your Majesty."

His breath quickened. "She has lost my child?"

"Yes, Your Majesty."

He grabbed me by the shoulders and shook me. "Did she bewitch it?"

"No, Your Majesty, it is a normal miscarriage."

He shook me harder. "Take me to her."

"Are you sure, Your Majesty? It is just screaming, and blood and women." I didn't think he would want to see her. I had made a mistake.

"Take. Me. To. Her."

"Very well, Your Majesty." I led the way.

"I am not surprised this has happened. She is barren. Cursed. A witch!" He roared the same things over and over again as we walked closer and closer to her quarters. The news would spread around the Court within minutes. I couldn't hear her screams anymore. I worried she had died.

Just as Hildy had done, the King shouldered open the door.

It was perfectly timed. If the Devil had timed it.

Hildy held the baby. A stream of moonlight illuminated her where she held both placenta and the three-month-grown child.

It had arms, legs and a head, but it was unrecognisable as a baby. Its middle was twisted, and its head malformed. It was equal amounts heartbreaking and terrifying.

The king came close to Hildy and stared at it.

"It is six months too early, Your Majesty. This is what babes look like at three months." Hildy's voice was strong.

"It is a demon," he said in a loud whisper. "I have never seen anything so foul."

He walked over to Anne, who was lying splayed-legged in her own blood, face white, blank. No expression. He grabbed her wrist. "You cursed my child. You are Satan's witch."

Something shuddered through me. I felt myself speaking, loudly. "She is not, Your Majesty!"

The King stared at me, eyes still not able to focus because of the wine.

"I promise you, Your Majesty, she is no witch, she is not evil. I have spent time with her, and through my own witchly eye I can see her, Your Majesty — I can see that she is not what you say! I swear it."

He glared at me.

"I swear it to you!" I said, voice raised now.

"Well, if it wasn't Boleyn who cursed my son, then it was that healer witch!" He turned his face to Hildy.

"No!" both Zita and I cried.

"Take the healer away!" he demanded.

Hildy jumped violently, not having heard the guards coming from behind. They grabbed her and held tightly, even as Zita did her best to detach them from her wife.

"Your Majesty, no! Hildy was only trying to help! She was only trying to help!"

I'd never properly understood just how frail and slight Zita was: she bounced off a guard's shoulder and crumpled to the ground. I watched as she tried to grab hold of his ankle, but all it took was a mild jerk of his leg and she had been shaken free. Hildy looked at me, just before the door closed.

"Anne," she mouthed.

"Throw the other two out of the palace. They have brought evil within our halls."

I only just heard him, because upon Hildy's instruction, I had turned to Anne.

She was unconscious.

"Your Majesty," I said, my voice deep. "Your wife needs our help, otherwise she will die."

Zita got off the floor. "She needs Hildy, Your Majesty!" she wailed.

The King looked at Zita with disgust. "That woman cursed my baby." He looked at his wife. "She will die?" I saw the thought. He wondered if it would all be easier if he let her die. He thought that thought, even if it was just for a moment. But then a semblance of humanity returned to his eyes.

"Fix her, Maude," he spat. "Take that one out of here." He pointed to Zita.

The King left, posting four different guards in the room as he did. I tried to close the bed curtains to give her privacy, but they wouldn't let me. They thought I'd curse her more, perhaps.

This woman was cursed to the hilt.

I stared at Her Majesty.

You will kill another of your kind. Reggie's words came to me so clearly, I thought someone in the room had spoken them. Hildy was going to die because of this. Anne too, maybe. It was my fault. This was my fault. It was prophecy.

I did what I could for the Queen, giving her the herbs and tinctures I had been taught might help with blood loss and shock, but it would be a waiting game. I might've been too late. As I mopped her head and monitored her, I tried to think. I needed to find Rufus. He would know what to do for Hildy. He might even be able to petition the King.

Anne stirred. I had got a little water in her eye. I dabbed at it gently.

"Your Majesty?" I whispered, not even daring to hope.

"Mary?" she mumbled, eyes flickering. Was she calling for my mother? We hardly looked alike.

Her eyes opened, and she turned towards me. I let out a measured exhalation. Thank Christ.

She was staring at me, trying to figure out who I was. “The witch,” she whispered. “My baby.”

I gave her valerian to relieve her of the memories. She would survive the night.

“Is she alive?” asked the burliest of the guards.

“She will survive the night.”

“Then you must leave her. Come.” He approached as though to grab me.

“I will come on my own.”

CHAPTER THIRTY-TWO

They took me to my rooms.

I was to stay there and go nowhere else until the King had decided what to do with me.

They locked me in. I ran to the door in the back as soon as their footsteps softened into the distance, but it was locked too.

"Maude."

"Fuck!" Rufus was still in bed. Of course he was; it could only be a few hours past midnight. Still, how could he have slept through all of it? How could he have been dreaming peacefully whilst I went through Hell?

"What's happened, Maude?"

"What do you think happened, Rufus?" I yelled. I wanted to crumple up and cry. I wanted to tell Rufus that all was lost, and that there was nothing to be done. The only way of holding back my tears was to stay angry, and the only person who could soak up the rage was Rufus. "Why weren't you there?"

"The Queen?" He was up and getting dressed.

"She has lost her babe, and they are blaming Hildy for it!"

"Jesus fucking Christ."

"There's no point getting dressed! The have locked us in!"

"Maude," he whispered.

"Don't whisper! This isn't a time for whispering! This is a time for yelling! They've taken Hildy to a dungeon, or to the Tower of London or something! Reggie said! He prophesied that I would kill another of my kind! This is it! I've killed Hildy!"

"Nay, Maude, nay." he hushed. "Reggie can't predict the weather when the storm clouds are right above him."

"He was right! The prophecy is coming true!"

"Explain to me exactly what happened."

"STOP WHISPERING, RUFUS!"

"Why did they take her?" he asked, volume normal.

"Because they think she cursed the baby. But no one cursed anyone: it was born half a year too early. That's what they look like! Hildy won't be able to hear anything, she won't be able to hear what they tell her, she won't be able to defend herself..."

Rufus held up a finger. "You sound like Zita," he said sternly.

"So?"

"Don't underestimate Hildy. She is not a child who needs mothering. She will be able to look after herself for the time being." His voice was so firm, I was momentarily stunned into silence. "What happened to Zita?"

"They threw her out of Court."

"And the Queen?"

"She will survive the night."

"Does the King think she is a witch?"

"I swore to the King she wasn't a witch and that is why they took Hildy. He said if it wasn't Anne who had cursed the child, then it must be the healer, a known witch. It was my fault. I saved Anne and betrayed Hildy. We must do something."

"You are exhausted. Your mind needs rest first."

"Zita will be distraught. She will be freezing! She is out there, with no money. With nothing." I harnessed what was left of my anger. "You have to break down the door, Rufus!"

"Do others know of the miscarriage?" he asked.

"The King was loud about it as he came to her chambers, and there were many guards and ladies present."

"And were you known to be with the Queen, were you witnessed with her?"

"Lady Jane and my mother saw us there."

He nodded. "Jane, William, Goodthatcher and the like will know. We must put our hopes in them. For now, you must try to sleep."

"We *wait*? Wait to see if Sommers or the wizened blind man will be our accomplice?"

"Do not underestimate them." He was cross. I felt immediately guilty.

With some force, he took my hand and put me into bed. I lay there, silently crying. I had never felt so hopeless.

"I can't sleep."

"Give yourself more time," he whispered back.

There was a long, drawn-out silence. He was awake; I could feel it. I rolled into him, hoping his touch would take away the images of Hildy burning at the stake.

"Catherine of Aragon died yesterday," he mumbled. My eyes opened. He was staring at the canopy of the bed.

"She died?" I asked. "How do you know? Does the King know?"

"I would doubt it. I heard it from the organist, Fayrfax. He had gone to visit her, in secret. He returned late last night with the news."

"Will he tell the King?"

"Not if he wants to keep his head."

"Why would he visit her if Henry disapproves?"

"The Court loved her, Maude. You have no idea. She was adored. I am sure he is not the only one to sneak away to dote on her."

"Then why didn't you go see her? You could be reunited with your mother!"

"I am a slave, Maude. A trumpeter, at the very best."

"Robert Fayrfax was allowed to go, and he was just an organist."

"Fayrfax is the organist at the abbey and the first doctor of music at Cambridge!" He glared at me. "I would not be privy to the whereabouts of the Princess Dowager, let alone be granted an audience with her ... still I mourn her." His voice cracked.

"What of your mother?" I asked hesitantly. "Did Fayrfax say?"

"I do not know what will happen to her." He wiped away his tears. But then his lips quivered again. "Mayhap I am the one who is cursed, Maude. Mayhap you are cursed because you are near me. Mayhap my wife could see the dark magic that seeped from my skin, and that is why she left."

I sat upright. "No." I didn't know what else to say. "You are only good," I added stupidly. "Fuck your wife," I concluded. He smiled weakly at me. "Rufus. You are not cursed. This is my fault. My business."

There was a click of the lock. I flinched with fear, but the door didn't open. Rufus swung his long legs off the bed and went to look.

"It appears we are indebted to one Jane the fool."

. . .

We were going to try to get out of the servants' gate to find Zita. We were both hooded, and, please God, unrecognisable. Rufus promised me that leaving wouldn't be the issue: it would be getting back in that would prove the challenge.

And he was right, the gate had a guard standing by it, but he was wandering up and down the wall, leaving his post and walking a hundred or so steps and then turning around again. We crouched behind a statue, waiting for an opportune moment. When he was halfway up his trodden path, we walked quickly to the gate and Rufus shook it.

It was locked.

We were fucked.

"Oi," said the guard, doing an awkward shuffle to get back to his post. "Where are you two trying to go?"

"We want to leave," said Rufus.

"God, you're as black as this night, aren't you? Don't get many Moors around here."

"We are from the late Lady Catherine of Aragon's household. We came here to give word of her death." Rufus's voice was sure.

The guard's face fell. "The Queen?" His face paled at the mistake. "I mean, the Princess Dowager? She's dead?" He looked upset.

"We have been sent to the river; we need a boat to London. There are people in town the King wants to inform before he breaks the news in the morn."

He was completely dumbfounded. "Dead?" he whispered again.

Rufus put a hand on his shoulder; the poor man was beginning to weep. "Mourn in secret," he muttered.

The guard swallowed, and without saying anything he opened the door and let us out.

We took the path around to the front of the palace in silence. Now what were we to do ... search the forests in a dark, foggy winter night to see if Zita had camped under a tree? Walk for miles until we reached the nearest village to see if she had taken refuge there? Catch a boat to London to see if she had done the same, and if she had, then what? Search the whole of London? And even if we did find Zita ... we would, what? Storm the castle, kill the guards, take Hildy and then live safely back at the apothecary, free from any harassment, despite the fact that the King knew where we lived? Fuck.

I let this disastrous plot play out in my mind and then I grabbed hold of Rufus's arm.

"What're we doing?" I asked him. "There are too many places she might be. This is useless."

He shook his head, pulling me further down to the riverbank. We reached the docks with the boats. The smell of rotting fish filled my nostrils.

Rufus began looking into each of the barges — did he think Zita had just picked a boat to hide in? It didn't seem like her.

He wrapped on a bigger boat's hull.

"John!" he hissed. He knocked again. A man poked his head out of the small cabin.

"Damn your blood!" grumbled the old man. His grey pointy beard was at a distinct angle from sleeping on it. "Reasonable?" he mumbled rubbing his eyes. "What in God's name?" he began.

"John, we got a problem."

"I should bloody hope so." His boat rocked as he stepped off. He threw a look to me.

"It's nearly your time to rise, John: don't be dramatic," Rufus said.

John chuckled. "Hardly. I get up with the sun these days! I got another four hours, easy!"

"We are in search of a woman thrown out of the palace," I said, cutting through this wasteful chatter.

"Who're you?"

"Maude," I replied.

He shrugged. "I 'ave seen someone: was taking a piss when I saw a small lady, blonde hair."

"That's her," Rufus said. "Thank God for your bad bladder, John."

"I'm glad my leaky cock is good for something, but I will say, she weren't in a good way, wailing and screaming."

"We need to find her, Rufus," I said desperately.

"A few men got angry at her racket and she must've moved away because I didn't hear her for too long. Don't think I heard her come past my boat. That all I got." John shrugged. "How's your missus, Reasonable?" he asked, more relaxed. "We've missed you at our dice games."

I tuned out as Rufus began explaining his situation. I looked up at the moon and let myself have a few indulgent tears. It was a full moon. That would mean something to Zita.

"Ah well, she wasn't worth your trouble if she didn't want to fuck —"

"The screaming banshee went into Hare Warren!" called a man from a few boats down.

God bless these sleepless boatsmen.

"Let's go, Rufus!" I grabbed his arm and marched off in the direction the man was pointing.

"You owe me a game of dice, Reasonable!" John called after us.

The fog was thicker in the woods. Rufus had stolen a torch

off one of the last boats, and I was grateful. We went a little slower so as not to trip, but we had only walked five minutes or so when we found her. In ordinary circumstances the sight would've been beautiful. In the middle of the clearing there was an ornate stone statue, a statue of an angel. The figure stood, half in flight, her wings spread and her white tunic folding beautifully in the soft moonlight. At her feet was another woman, not stone but flesh. She was on her knees, singing. I wouldn't call it singing, it was wailing. It was haunting. I ran to her.

"Zita!" I called. She turned, shocked, scrambled to her feet and ran into my arms. My knees buckled and we fell into a heap on the floor.

"We're here, Zita. We're here." After some long, drawn-out sobs, she found her words.

"Did you get thrown out too, fairy?" she asked.

Rufus sat down next to us. "No. We left to find you," he explained.

She rested her head on my chest, her small body folded in between my legs, and she looked at Rufus like a small upset child looks at her father while being cradled in her mother's arms. It felt so wrong.

"Hildy?" she managed.

"We don't know," Rufus said.

She didn't continue crying, but her body seemed to get smaller still, crumpling in on itself, as if it didn't want to exist.

"She won't be able to hear," she whispered into my chest.

"What should we do, Zita?" I asked, desperate for our usual dynamics of aunt and niece to be returned, but she didn't appear to hear me.

"What should we do?" An absent echo. She was hardly present.

Zita wasn't going to be able to help us.

A strong, chilled breeze whipped around us.

"*You will kill another of your kind*," I whispered.

I had thought it meant Hildy. I was going to kill Hildy.

But it didn't mean Hildy.

A witch for a witch.

A trade.

CHAPTER THIRTY-THREE

"I need to get back in," I said to Rufus.

"I will be able to get back in," he whispered, "but you won't be allowed entry."

"No, it needs to be me," I whispered.

He bit his lip. "I can get back in and ask the King to see you?"

I couldn't think of a better idea. "Very well."

"If I promise John I'll play a game of dice with him, he will let you both stay on his boat."

"Why's this John like you so much?" We got to our feet, though nearly all of Zita's weight was upon me.

"Because I have notorious bad luck when it comes to dice." He didn't elaborate. We walked back down to the boat.

"We're going to get her. We're going to get her," I repeated, arm around Zita's shoulder as I helped her aboard.

We sat in the corner of the small cabin and we waited, for how long, I couldn't be sure. We both slept a bit. John's crude voice was in my dreams, but I didn't wake until he shoved me.

"You'll want to see this."

"Is Rufus back?"

"What's this name you keep calling him?"

"Is Reasonable back?" I snapped.

"No. He ain't. But something is happening."

All my tummy did was flip and turn these days.

I rested the still-sleeping Zita on the seat and followed John out. It was fully morning now, and a fleet of small boats was arriving at the gate.

"Who are they?" I asked.

"Couldn't tell you yet."

Witch burners. People employed by the King to burn witches. Witch hunters, from the continent. Witch sniffers, people who had a nose for magic and could smell it out.

"They're Spanish," he said, noticing the flags.

They were; they were so close now I could hear them chattering in their lyrical language.

The boatsmen helped them dock and then they started alighting. Everyone was in black.

Oh.

"She's dead," I said.

"Who?" John replied.

"Catherine of Aragon."

It was her household. Or what was left of them. And that man — I pointed at a sharply dressed man, with jet black hair. "That's the ambassador," I whispered. "And that ..." It was her, surely it was her. There were no other black people in the company.

"And that?" asked John, taking a puff of his pipe.

"I think that's Reasonable's mother."

"Well, I'll be damned."

"I have changed plans," I said to John quickly. "Rufus will play two whole games of dice with you if you take care of Zita, perhaps feed her a bit if she wakes."

"Two games?"

"Yes."

"What if she makes a racket again?"

"Tell her that Maude and Rufus are fixing everything."

"If she makes a racket, he has to play three games."

"Deal."

I shook his worn hands and moved towards the group of disembarked Spaniards.

The woman was standing near the back; she was just a servant, after all.

Guards were approaching, and words were being exchanged. The men at the bank of the river were helping tie the boats up and there was enough hubbub for me to get close without too much attention on me.

I pulled my hood over my head and sidled up beside her. "Excuse me, goodwoman?"

She was bending over, picking up a trunk. "Aye?" she said, wary.

"Is your son named Reasonable?"

Nothing betrayed her. She looked blankly at me. "It's not his born name," she said finally. "But some call him that."

"I am his ..." I searched "... friend. There is trouble for me and him in Court."

"What sort?"

"What sort of friend?" I asked, heart thumping, an idiot.

"What sort of trouble?" Oh.

"It is a long story. I need to enter the Court with you."

"Is my boy well?"

"Yes. He is well."

"He is at Court?"

"He is."

"How can I trust you? What if you are a vagabond or a thief?"

"Your Spanish name is Catalina." She raised her chin at

me, still unsure. "And Rufus hates to sweep the floors," I tried. "I mistakenly made him sweep on several occasions, to his deep displeasure."

She looked at me again with new eyes. "Are you my daughter-in-law?"

"No, I'm not his wife."

She was suspicious about that. "I will get to see him?"

"I will make sure of it."

"Then stand by me as we enter. Keep your head down."

I did so. "You are here without Lady Catherine?" I confirmed.

"She has passed."

"I'm sorry for your loss," I whispered.

"She was my captor. She took me from my home."

We began to move closer to the gates.

I looked at Catalina; her words were cold but her eyes mourned: sad, sad eyes. But then again, perhaps she always looked like this. Perhaps this grief was for her homeland, for Rufus.

It was no problem gaining entry. The ambassador had brought so many people with him that I just slipped in with the group. None of the Spanish even noticed me. The problem would be getting through to where the King was — I was not sure how far the Spanish servants would be allowed to go.

Base Court was fine. Then we were passed to the clock tower court. Easy. Now for the King's Gallery. I got myself ready to peel off if we were not allowed entry, but the ambassador took every single one of us to the King's Gallery. He even directed me and Catalina to stand in front of him. He looked me straight in the eye and told me in Spanish to stand before him. I was astounded, but I did as I was told and became part of the human chain mail around his precious personage.

We entered the gallery.

We were made to wait. There was shuffling and whispering in Spanish. Catalina stayed quiet. I followed her lead.

I heard a rustling from the passages that led to His Majesty's rooms.

I had only known the King a handful of days, but I already knew how to read his heavy footfall. He was angry. Confused. Irritated. I could hear it in the way his shoes landed on the stone.

I looked around, realising what was about to happen. I was at the front of a pack of Spaniards. I, the witch who had helped birth the King of England's "cursed" baby. I was meant to be imprisoned in my own rooms, accused of the Devil's work. I was definitely, definitely, not meant to be at the front of a group of Spaniards who were about to announce the death of the King of England's first wife.

The door banged open, and the King, followed by his closest counsel, flew out into the room. I dropped to the floor in a deep curtsey and my dramatic gesture frightened most of the other servants into doing the same.

"What in God's name are you doing here?" he bellowed. "What does SHE want?"

It seemed strange to me that he couldn't gather what had happened. I suppose he had got little to no sleep last night, his mind preoccupied with the loss of his child. But this was Lady Catherine's court, all in black. I wondered if he would cry upon hearing the news. I retreated further back into my hood.

"Your Majesty," said the ambassador, standing amongst his company. "Bad tidings. "Your" – I heard him swallow – "your sister-in-law, the Lady Dowager Catherine of Aragon, has been taken by God."

There was a silence, interrupted by the noise of the ambassador swallowing.

"Thank you, ambassador, for giving me this news." The King took a large breath; I wanted to look at his face. His deep exhalation was released suddenly, in an erratic, alarming laugh.

"God be praised that we are free from all suspicion of war!" he said loudly, obviously addressing his counsel. He continued to chuckle, and there were other sighs of relief from the English. "I am sorry for your loss, ambassador," the King continued, still sounding jolly. "We will of course conduct proceedings to mourn the Princess Dowager." I heard him move away and there was much chattering between the English. There was mention of the French, the war, the pope, all the words infused with excited energy.

I was dumbfounded. I looked to my right at Catalina. I caught the moment a tear hit the floor. She was weeping.

"Get the Spanish rooms," he demanded to the guards.

"Your Majesty," said a bodiless voice, "there is no space at Court: Yuletide fills us to the brim."

"Ask people to leave then!"

"Aye, Your Majesty."

"And get them food and wine."

"Of course, Your Majesty."

"Take your company to the Great Hall," he instructed the ambassador. We made to move, but the King stopped us.

"Wait, what of a will?"

"She left everything to her servants and to your daughter, Your Majesty." There was a tight pause.

"Quite right." Another pause. "Anything for me?" he added, like a child. This man was astonishing.

"A letter, Your Majesty." The ambassador leant over me, handing the King the parchment.

"Were you going to keep this from me?" he snapped, snatching it.

"No, Your Majesty."

"Go to the hall."

We all rose, and I turned inwards, planning to follow them. But this was my chance. Two forces were battling out within my insides — my body was moving away from the King, but my mind was trying to convince my legs to stop, stay, this is your chance.

"Catalina." I reached for her hand. "The rooms closest to the inner gates in the Base Court. I will meet you there before evening."

She didn't say anything in reply.

I managed to still myself. The rest of the dowager's small court moved past me.

"Your Majesty?"

The King was hugging the Duke of Norfolk. Delighted. Smiling bigger than I had seen him in a long time. He turned to me. I dropped my hood.

His eyes widened.

"Guards," he barked.

"Your Majesty. I beg of you, I need a moment with you, I have much to say that you will want to hear."

"How did you get out of your rooms? Why were you with the Spanish?" He tilted his head in amazement. "Good God, you are of another realm."

I bowed low again. "Your Majesty, you need to hear what I have to tell you."

"You think anything you have to say is of more importance than the death of my sister-in-law. I'm grieving!" he said loudly, half laughing again. I wondered if he might actually be very sad.

"Your Majesty. I have seen things."

Norfolk spoke. "You do not need the wild ramblings of a witch girl, Henry."

"You need my words too, Norfolk," I said quickly.

He slapped me across the face. I had heard about this man's reputation, but I hadn't been expecting a slap. I looked up at the King, my face stinging. Norfolk had been sporting a large and sharp ring. Why backhand me? Why not use the palm? My eyes watered, but I did not take my hand to my face. "Your Majesty. This is a day of good news. I have more to give you," I tried. He liked me, he had from the start. Something about my insolence perhaps.

"Send her to my chambers," he said to a guard. "I will meet you there in time. Do not leave her unaccompanied."

I exhaled slowly. Someone grabbed me by the arm, and I was taken to the King's chambers. For the second time in a week.

I stood in the audience chamber, staring at the guard who was assigned to keep watch. He feared me, giving me furtive looks. Other people were there too, with gifts for the King. Yuletide presents that had turned to get well presents after the King's accident, that had then miraculously transformed into mourning presents. The chamber was abuzz with the news from the most eventful Court Christmas in their time. Thankfully, word of Anne's miscarriage was not on anyone's lips. I tried to focus on Hildy, sitting in her eternal silence, in the dark. I hoped I was not too late. I moved my weight from one foot to the other, trying to stay focused, stay awake. This was for Hildy. For the child who lost her mother, who loved my aunt, who was so gentle and so kind and loved me like a daughter, or a sister. Hildy who respected me and my powers — The door banged open, and I jumped.

It was Norfolk. "The King is not receiving any visitors until after today's feast." There was a grumbling of impatient flatterers. I tried to make eye contact with the duke: did that mean me? He caught my eye and sauntered over. He had a droopy face, like it was melting.

"You think you are an exception, don't you, witch?"

"I have the greatest gift to give the King. Better than all these saddles and shirts. One he should not wait for."

Norfolk sat down in the King's throne. Bold. But he hadn't yet excused me. The room emptied, but I did not move. He watched me, thinking.

"You want to make a bargain for the return of your coven mate?"

"Yes. A witch for a witch," I said, my mouth dry.

His eyebrow rose.

The door opened, and my mother, Jane the fool, her guardian, and the Queen walked in.

She was alive. She was still pale, and my mother held her up. But she was alive. I fought the impulse to tell her to lie down. Why tell her to lie down when your intention is to see her burn? At the thought, I searched for my mother's gaze. I wanted to be young again, a child, without any responsibility. She wouldn't look at me.

"Norfolk," the Queen said, voice stronger than she looked. "You ..." She was pointing her finger at him.

The King and his company entered. He was wearing an entirely yellow outfit, with a big white feather in his cap. He was the picture of joy. He stopped at the strange spectacle and Norfolk slunk out of the King's chair.

Anne continued. "What happened last night, happened because of you, uncle. The way you told me about my husband's fall. It shocked me into labour. You intended to shock me."

Norfolk rolled his eyes.

The King held up his hand, calling for silence. "You haven't heard," he said to his wife, walking over to his throne.

"Heard what?" she whispered, as though all her energy was suddenly gone.

"The Princess Dowager is dead." He sat and crossed his legs contentedly.

Anne's mouth parted. She let out the same relieved laugh as the King had a moment before.

"Then I am the one true Queen." It was only then I realised that the old Queen's death could be detrimental to my cause. This could re-ignite everything. I looked to Henry.

"You were always the true Queen," he said, his expression unreadable.

"Your Majesty. You should rest," I said to the Queen, intentionally resurrecting the memory of the night.

The King turned his head to me. "You are the strangest, boldest little thing I have ever come across." He wasn't upset.

"Queen Anne," I said, ignoring him. "You shouldn't be standing up."

Anne's once bright eyes looked into me, like I looked into her. Then she nodded. "I will want a yellow dress, and I want wine and food brought to me, to my bed. I intend to celebrate the death of the false Queen," she said clearly. "Finally, I am safe." She said those words directly to me. Then she turned and left.

Henry sighed heavily, fingering the white feather in his hat. "She spoils my good mood," he said absentmindedly.

I swayed on the spot, my exhaustion getting the better of me.

"Let's deal with you before you keel over, or worse, annoy me," said the King. "Your lover begged me to see you on my way to these chambers. I told him you were, in fact, awaiting me here."

"That would have been confusing for him."

"He was puzzled," he confirmed, giving me a small smile.

He swivelled on his chair so that his legs draped over the armrest. A servant offered him wine and he took it. He took a deep sip. "It has been a strange few days."

"The strangest," I agreed.

"You speak out of turn," said Norfolk.

"I wish to speak to the King alone," I clarified.

"Do you know in what company you are in?" said Norfolk.

"I am very aware of it, my lord," I said.

Henry liked it when I was audacious.

"You will all leave me; I will give the witch a moment." Everyone present made noises of disapproval but Henry didn't respond, and slowly the lords left the room. All the servants stayed. It's funny how, at the end of the day, the servants are privy to all.

The air stilled.

"Sit." He gestured to the floor by his feet. Fine. I put myself onto the floor and looked up at him. "To remind you of your place, which you frequently forget."

"Verily, I do need reminding, Your Majesty." He wanted me to play, but I did not want to play. This was the very worst thing I had ever done in my life.

"What do you have to say to me that is so important?"

"I lied to you."

"You want me to return your witch sister to you so you will say anything to me. Why should I believe what you are about to tell me?"

"I do want you to return her to me. I want a witch for a witch."

"My wife? You are calling Anne a witch now? You were so determined to keep her safe yesterday."

"Today you get two gifts from God," I said, rising onto my knees, as though bent in prayer in front of him. "One gift is the death of Aragon: a clearing of an old, seemingly neverending threat. But I give you a gift too, from God. Because Aragon's death doesn't make space for Anne: that is not the divine plan." He was looking at me intently now, his air of jest gone. "Anne is one of my kind. I knew it very quickly. She knew things about me that no one knows, just by looking at me. She told me who my mother was, one of the greatest secrets that I keep. Anne's baby, while born early, was not just an unformed child. Something was wrong with him. His body was twisted. I cannot explain it without the supernatural. Hildy is a healer, known only to make things better. But Anne, your wife —" I was crying and my nose was running, but I didn't do anything about it. "I wanted to save Anne because she is one of my kind. But it is not worth it to me, if Hildy must take her place, when Hildy is beneficent and Anne is maleficent. The Queen is a witch. You felt her spell when you fell for her. I felt it too. I wanted to protect her, love her, care for her. But she burns whatever is in her path: her womb is burnt because of the magic she has used to bewitch you. She will never bear you a living son, only half-formed demons." I was speaking so steadily, with such ease: it was disgusting how easy the words came to me. "She has England bewitched; I can confirm it. She needs to be discarded, to make room for the new."

"Who is the new?" he asked. I took a deep breath, I let my eyes look up as though God himself was about to give me this answer, even though Henry reeked of her perfume, and his jewels adorned her pretty little neck.

"Seymour," I whispered.

He actually gasped. "Jane?"

No, her brother ... good God.

"Jane," I said to him.

"Everything that has happened? It is to make room for Jane?"

"It is a divine clearing of the way."

"It gives you great pain to tell me this?"

"Yes."

"Why?"

"Because I like your wife very much."

"Because she has bewitched you ..." he muttered.

I exhaled and closed my eyes.

He believed.

"I thought perhaps she would die." He was almost talking to himself. "Maybe she still will."

I wanted to leave, but I needed him to give me Hildy.

"Will you release Hildy?"

Norfolk entered. "I think you have given her long enough, Your Majesty."

"Fetch her deaf kin. She has done no wrong."

I exhaled.

"Thank you, Your Majesty."

"And I suppose you still want my trumpeter?"

"I ask for a lot, don't I?"

He nodded, but he was not upset. "I want him here for the funeral procession for Aragon. Then you can have him."

I fell into a deep curtsey. "It's Beckett, Your Majesty." I said into my skirts.

"What's that?"

"Edward Beckett, Your Majesty. My husband. I owed you his name." I looked up.

He looked amused. "Ahh, I know the man. A whiffle-waffle. You have done well to avoid him."

I smiled my thanks. He gestured towards the door, excusing me.

"What will you do with the Queen, Your Majesty?"

"Tis none of your concern, witch."

CHAPTER THIRTY-FOUR

I returned, with an escort, to my rooms. Rufus was there.

"What happened?" he asked abruptly. I was relieved of my guard. I thought perhaps Rufus might be angry, but he scooped me up and held me to him, my feet dangling off the floor. He kissed my ears and hair and I cried into his body. He put me down as I really began to wail.

"What has happened? Have they taken her to the Tower?" He was so worried.

"Nay, nay, Hildy is to be returned to us."

"You did it?" His voice broke.

"I got into the palace with your mother."

"What?"

"Your mother is here."

"What?"

"I told her to come to us."

"What?"

"Rufus. Listen. All of Aragon's people are in Court. Bringing the news of her passing. I'm surprised you did not see them! Your mother is here. She will find us soon enough."

"My mother?" He spoke loudly; he was clearly having trouble comprehending it.

"Do not raise your voice to a lady." Catalina poked her head around the door.

"*Mama*." Rufus's whole body relaxed when he saw her. They embraced, and Catalina reached up to stroke his head. "Lady Aragon?" he asked, still being cradled by her.

"She didn't want to be here any longer." She released her boy and shut the door behind her.

"Are you free, Mama?" Rufus asked. Light shone through the windows. I moved gingerly to the spot on the floor where it fell and sat in the chequered patch of sun, held my knees and shut my eyes. Jimmy nuzzled against me, but even his soft purrs did nothing to soothe my soul.

"I am free, it said so in her will. She gave me some coin too."

I listened to them talking to one another. He spoke to her so respectfully, so solemnly, but I could tell that Rufus was joyous. "And Maude has got Hildy back. All is well. All is well." I could feel the contentedness in his voice, but the only light I felt was the actual warmth of the sun, and even that wasn't enough to stop the hairs on my skin from standing up.

"We need to fetch Zita," I said, eyes still shut.

"Where is she?"

"With John. You owe him two, perhaps three games of dice."

Rufus laughed again, a manic, relieved outburst.

"When will we get Hildy back?"

"I don't —"

A shadow flickered across my closed eyes. I opened them; people were out by the window.

There was a firm knock on the door. Rufus opened it.

"The witches are to leave the Court, immediately," said the guard. They shoved Hildy into the room. "Pack your things."

Hildy ran to me on the floor; she cocooned me in her arms and I did not hold myself together. I bawled. I cried and I cried in her arms and she cooed to me, whispering sweet things to my ear.

"You did well, sweeting."

It took me some minutes before I got my breath.

"Are you well?" I signed as she took a moment to look at me.

"Yes. Hungry and tired but I am well."

My lips quivered. "I thought we'd lost you."

"You saved me."

I didn't want to explain to her how I'd managed it.

"Where is Zita?"

"In a boat."

She squinted at me. I tried to sign it. She nodded, not understanding but not asking for clarification.

"Rufus." My voice was rough. "He says he will let you go, but he wants you here to ... celebrate Catherine's death."

"As he wishes."

"I will stay until then too," said Catalina.

"I have packed your things," Rufus said, gesturing to the trunks.

"Will you come back to us, Ruf?" I asked.

He kissed me, then he lifted me off the floor again and I held him around his neck.

"Verily, I will. But let's not say goodbye now. I will come with you to find Zita. John will want his game of dice."

"Three," I reminded him, trying to smile. He jingled his pocket and I heard a few coins. "If you want to stay with your mother, you don't have to return to me."

"I want to be with you."

He tucked my hair behind my ears and put me down. I nodded, choosing to believe him. He took my trunk and we followed Hildy out of the door.

Jimmy meowed mournfully on the way to the Thames but none of the rest of us spoke.

"John?" Rufus called.

"About time! You owe me a dozen throws by now! It's been havoc. I had to tie her to the boat!"

I jumped aboard the boat. Sure enough, he had tied Zita's hands to the side of the boat.

"Maude!" she gasped, her voice hoarse.

"I've got her, I've got her."

I felt Hildy board the boat and she appeared behind me. I untied Zita's hands and I left the two of them alone.

Rufus helped me back on land, and John was already getting his dice table ready at the front of the boat. He was grinning a big toothless grin.

"Go home, Maude. You're safe now. I will return to you soon," he promised.

CHAPTER THIRTY-FIVE

Rufus and Catalina came to the apothecary several weeks after Yuletide.

He had no news of Queen Anne, only that she seemed well again, and that she smiled during the funerary processions. People hadn't liked that. They said it was disrespectful. But she was smiling because she thought she was safe.

I began to think I was safe too. Safe from having the Queen's blood on my hands, safe from having my kin taken from me. We had even dug out my dresses and jewels with the intention to sell them and find a space that would fit this family of five. If the Shaftsberrys hadn't retrieved them by now, they were hardly going to risk the King's witches' wrath after the happenings over Christmas.

The light was lingering later and later now, and I liked the longer days. I sat in my room, looking through my box of charms, trying to find something appropriate to give to a farmer whose sheep were dropping like they had the plague, listening to Rufus and Jimmy playing in the corner of the room. We had fashioned him a little bell on a string, and it was the best thing that had happened in all of Jimmy's nine lives.

My cat loved Rufus. Sometimes I thought he might like the fae more than he liked his mama. I couldn't blame him. I think I might even like Rufus more than I liked my cat ...

I stood up from my stool and a bunch of lavender got caught in my hair. I untangled myself, and, as I did, I looked out the window.

Zita was talking to Reggie. Reggie, of all people! I moved closer to the window and pressed my face against the pane. Something deep in my gut knew what they were talking about. I saw it in the gleeful way he stood, leaning back, cock first. I saw it in the way Zita stood, keeping her distance.

"Something bad has happened," I said to Rufus. The jingling of the bell stopped. I looked down at him and Jimmy on the floor. Both cat and fairy looking up at me. Neither saying anything.

I heard the apothecary door close, and I moved to the top of the staircase, looking down to Zita. She stood still. Lips pursed.

"Maude," she said curtly. "The Queen is to be beheaded."

I shut my eyes. "For witchcraft?" I asked.

"Not specifically."

"What could she be accused of?"

"It's a motley accusation: a little bit of adultery, a little bit of incest, a sprinkling of conspiracy and a strong insinuation of witchcraft."

My heart broke for Anne. I thought of her on her bed, covered in blood. I involuntarily pictured her without a head.

"This is because of me," I said.

"Come down," she demanded. I obeyed. "Why do you think this is your fault?" She indicated that we were to walk in the garden.

"Reggie's prophecy. That's what he came to gloat about, no?"

"What prophecy?" she asked, harvesting snap peas.

"He said," I whispered, "that I would kill another of my kind."

She stopped still. Then turned to me. "Oh Maude." She embraced me.

"Just as it was predicted. It's happening," I muttered into her shoulder.

She released me. "They pit us against each other, Maude." She continued, "When you live under the boot of men, the boot of this world, this kingdom called England, they will make you betray one another, they will make you hate one another, they will make you kill one another. It's easier that way. They don't need to wipe us out if we wipe out one another." She resumed picking the peas. "Reggie didn't need to be a prophet to know something like this would unfold."

I tried to speak, but she raised her finger. "This is not your fault. This was in the stars. Immovable and certain. What matters is, you saved my Hildy: that *was* your doing." She looked intently at me.

"Was Reggie here to gloat about it?"

She nodded.

"He's still practising, isn't he?"

She nodded again. "We cannot fix the many problems of this world, Maude. We must simply do our sacred work."

"Is her death to be public?" I wanted to be with her. To see her.

"You cannot stop this, Maude."

"I know. I just want to be there."

It was just me and Zita. We spoke little. I had asked to go alone but Zita was determined to be with me. London was crazed; people were everywhere. To my horror, it felt joyous — spring flowers had popped up in every dirty crack of every street, and children ran wild and excited. We were told by many on the streets that the date and time for the wondrous event had changed: tomorrow they said. The false Queen dies tomorrow. I had thought for a small, ignorant and hopeful minute she had been spared, but it was a distraction. To keep her away from the crowds. Away from potential pity. We spent a silent night at an inn. I wondered if there was anything to be done. If these few extra hours were given to me to do something. But I could think of nothing. There was nothing to be done.

The next morning, I woke up in a sweat. We got word it was to happen at Tower Green. People thronged the streets, but Zita had a way of manoeuvring through them like oil through water. I held onto her.

She got us about a hundred feet from the black scaffolding. We were there with divine timing. As we found our spot, the crowd hushed. Anne was already there and she had taken a breath, and with that breath she had sucked all the noise from the air.

"Good Christian people," she called.

My whole body erupted in bumps, as if she had cast a spell.

"I am come hither to die, for according to the law, and by the law I am judged to die, and therefore I will speak nothing against it." Her gaze danced across the crowd, and then they lighted upon me. "I am come hither to accuse no man, nor woman, nor to speak anything of that whereof I am accused and condemned to die, but I pray God save the King and send him long to reign over you, for a gentler nor a more merciful prince was there never: and to me he was ever a good, a gentle and sovereign lord. And if any person will meddle of my cause, I require them to judge the best. And thus I take my leave of the world and of you all, and I heartily desire you all to pray for me. O Lord have mercy on me, to God I commend my soul."

I watched my mother, Frances and Elizabeth come forwards and remove her hat and cloak.

I found my lips winding their way around a spell of some sort, just as they had with Reggie, an unknowable, unforeseen string of words being whispered by my own mouth to ensure that she felt no pain.

She knelt. And as she knelt, something rippled through the thousands of spectators, and we all knelt too.

I whispered,

"*Two Angels that came from the west,*
one brought fire and the other brought frost."

The man raised his sword as I spoke.

"*In frost. Out fire.*
Leave with ease.
Peace transpire."

She hardly noticed the stroke that came down. Her head rolled loudly in the silence.

I repeated my spell, again and again, in case that rolling head still felt pain. In case her body was left with agony. Leave with ease. Peace transpire. I felt a hand on my shoulder; I stopped chanting; I turned to look to the owner of the hand; and saw I no one there.

ACKNOWLEDGMENTS

As always, I am indebted to my editor Kate - thank you for never once trying to explain to me how speech tags work, but just relentlessly fixing them every time anyone in my novels speak. To Linda, my publishing consultant, thank you for holding me and supporting me during the scariest part of being an author. To Lena, my cover designer - thank you for understanding my stories and translating them into picture.

To my husband and favourite author, James Winestock, thank you for believing in Maude even when I felt totally and utterly over her.

And, as always, thank you to the community of creatives who accompany me on my journey. Thank you for seeing me.

ABOUT THE AUTHOR

Amie McNee is an author, speaker and creative coach. Amie studied medieval history at university, focussing specifically on sex culture, sex work and pornography. Alongside her historical fiction, Amie has written several much loved books all of which discuss the realities and magic of leading a creative life.

Amie is known for speaking, teaching and coaching artists all over the world and helping them to achieve their creative dreams. She has been called to create supportive, empowered communities for writers and artists. This is a big, beautiful but oftentimes hard journey, and creatives don't need to do it without support.

You can find Amie on Instagram, Pinterest and your podcast app.

Made in the USA
Monee, IL
21 January 2025

10294791R10215